I0822468

CRYING IS FOR WOMEN

CRYING IS FOR WOMEN

A Song of Trains, Farangis, & Freedoms

A Novel

ZAFARUL AZAM

Paperback ISBN: 979-8-9869013-9-8
eBook ISBN: 979-8-9869013-7-4

This is a work of fiction. Names, characters, places, and incidents are the products of the author's imagination or are used fictitiously. Any resemblance to actual events, locales, or persons, living or dead, is entirely coincidental.

This work is based upon real and fictional events. Events, dialogue and characters were created for the purposes of fictionalization.

To my grandfather, the stationmaster of 1930s Indian Railways,
whose train stories made this novel possible,

and

To my parents, who made me viable,

and

To my wife, whose constant support and encouragement
made this project a reality.

ACKNOWLEDGMENTS

Thank you so much for picking up this hardback copy of my book, Crying is for Women.

I never thought that a small writing project that began as a short story of a man born at the turn of the 20th century would turn into a full length historical fiction piece. But, here it is, and I would love to hear your thoughts about it.

This novel would not have been possible without the sincere efforts of my Beta Readers, Editors, Critics, Family Members and Friends.

Cover design was done by Chris Berge of Berge Designs. Manuscript Assessment by Gary Smailes of BubbleCow and the first three rounds of Editing by Dr. Vonda and Dr. Jeff from FirstEditing.

I am deeply appreciative of them for their efforts.

Among all the editors and critics, Ummehaany Azam, Erum Sultan of mybookshelf.com.pk, Ghazala Aslam, Humera Sultan of Ferozsons Ltd., and Nuzaira Azam of The Global Beat Foundation, elevated the manuscript from its not-ready-for-primetime state to an elegantly finished novel. It would have been impossible to publish the work without their rigorous oversight and endless hours of poring over the manuscript.

I owe them all a debt of gratitude.

-Zafarul Azam

NOTES

A few notes on the content and any liberties I took from standard writing practices are listed below.

The year under each chapter heading doesn't necessarily indicate that all of the chapter is set in that year.

A character's name used in dialogs may be different from their name in non-dialog text, depending on the relationship between the speakers. One example is Zeena, Zeenat and Zeena Bai. Her name is Zeenat, but known as Zeena Bai in the Nautch house. Raja called her Zeena, others addressed her as Zeenat. She is also referred to as Zeenat in later text.

I have used italicized text to indicate the thoughts of the major characters which is not common in fiction, and for foreign words which is standard.

The use of footnotes is not seen in fiction, but for the reader's convenience, I use footnotes for foreign word meanings and some background notes or explanations.

CONTENTS

PROLOGUE
Pre-1920

THE GOOD RAJA
1830s

Thick monsoons clouds had brought torrential rains all night and by the crack of dawn they had moved on, giving the early morning sun a peek of what lay below.

Heera, the homeless hermit, was out as usual, collecting water chestnuts by the river. Heavy rains had sunk the leaves and brought the corms up to the surface. He loved the free aquatic vegetable.

As he walked over a group of rocks, lying just below the surface of the gently flowing Ganges, he noticed a hand extending out of the water. It was moving back and forth with the river current, as if trying to attract someone's attention.

***

Taimur Babar always wanted to be a stonemason. He was born into a very poor Muslim family in the north central Indian town of Meerut. His mother affectionately called him Raja, prince.

On his only childhood trip to anywhere, he had visited the Lal Qila-Red Fort in Delhi, the capital of India. Its towering red walls, made of red sandstone drawn from local quarries, impressed him. His mother told him stories of how these ramparts had withstood trebuchet fusillades of the largest boulders, cannon bombardments of the biggest cannonballs, and innumerable efforts to undermine it. He listened to her stories of the Fort and its past, but he was more interested in the present, fascinated by the stonemasons, who worked huge shapeless red boulders into perfectly sized blocks to build and repair the crumbling sections of the wall.

The masons were still working to repair a small section of the wall damaged in the last war. Watching the stonemasons cut and shape those boulders, he aspired to be like them, and that was all he wanted to do for the rest of his life.

Raja's work life started in his early teens. He was put to work when his father died. Bansilal, a local money-lender and his father's former employer, gave him a job delivering documents from one business to another for a few *paisas*[1] a day. Precocious and under the strict guidance of his mother, he worked diligently to keep his father's boss happy. What he didn't know was that in addition to the papers in the sack he was to deliver, there were also bags of opium that his boss sold surreptitiously.

One day, on the way to deliver some documents, a gang of street boys with batons and homemade knives surrounded him. They demanded to know what was in the bag. He told them it has some worthless papers that he was delivering for Bansilal, the *bania.*[2] They tried to snatch the courier bag off his shoulder and in the struggle, a few papers and a couple of opium bags fell to the ground. Confused seeing the extra items in the satchel, he wondered how they got there. And then he understood.

The boys were trying their best to take the bag from around his neck. While keeping a tight grip on the bag, he was weighing the consequences of losing the papers. As the struggle continued without a clear winner, the entire gang fell on him, beating him with their sticks and batons. Raja was screaming *bachao*[3] *bachao*, while taking a terrible beating. He held on to the courier bag as if his life depended on it. He had figured the

---

[1] Lowest denomination coin in India.
[2] Hindu money lender.
[3] Help, help.

documents were just a smoke screen, the little bags were the real commodity he was delivering, but losing any of the items in the bag would bring him an even worse beating from Bansilal and a loss of his job. Passers-by who saw the young teen being beaten up by a bunch of older boys came to his rescue. The rascals took off, but not before one of them slashed his arm and left him bleeding. Raja quickly gathered up the papers and the bags and made his way back to report the incident to the owner.

Bansilal saw the open bag and without a word slapped him hard across his face and started cursing him for opening the bag. Raja showed him his injuries and told him the story of how he had fought off the gang to save the precious documents from falling into the wrong hands. Bansilal was unimpressed, for Raja had failed to deliver goods that had already been paid for. After accounting for everything in the bag, the *bania* calmed down. He told Raja that if this happened again, he would not have a job to come back to.

"I should stop being so generous lest I go bankrupt," Bansilal said as he threw a few coins, the daily wage, at Raja and walked away. Raja was expecting something extra for bravely protecting the opium. None was forthcoming. Laughing loudly when asked for a reward, he said, "Remember, no one gets rich giving away their money. I am just a poor *bania*."

Although very upset with him, Raja remembered to thank Bansilal and walked out with the *bania* taunting him about expecting a reward for 'doing his job'. Sore from the beating, he walked with a limp and an unappeasable wrath for his employer. He could have been killed while unknowingly committing an illegal act for the miser. His rage knew no bounds as he thought about how close he had come to getting maimed for life, or worse.

He wanted revenge.

Instead of going home, he kept walking until he found two of the gang members hanging around a food shop trying to get free food. Raja went over to the shop and bought some food. He told the boys he bought it for them so that they can be friends. The boys, thinking him to be an imbecile, took the food and walked away.

A few days later, after another delivery, he saw the smaller of the two boys sitting idly on a side street. He went over and asked if he was hungry. He knew street urchins were always hungry, even when they were not. They walked to the food shop, and he bought some *samosas*[4] to eat together. As they sat down to eat on the side of the road, the other, much bigger boy, appeared from nowhere and joined them. There was just enough food for two, but seeing the size of this interloper, Raja divided his purchase into three parts.

Enjoying the unexpected lunch, the short one asked him, "Hey boy, why are you doing this?" Raja told him his name and said that he preferred they call him by it.

The short one said, "I am Bholu, and he is Juddoo the wrestler. We can be friends, really good friends, if you keep buying us food like this." Juddoo laughed and slapped Bholu on the back in agreement. Raja, not wanting to spend too much time with them, gave them his leftover food. Satisfied that the two idiot brutes were now workable putty in his hands, he left.

After the day of his beating, he had kept an eye on everything Bansilal did at work. He would follow Bansilal home, to learn everything about his wealthy employer who couldn't spare a *phooti kauri*[5] as a reward for him. Raja started working long hours at the shop, demanding no extra pay. He had Bholu do early morning reconnaissance and Juddoo evening scouting on Bansilal's activities, in exchange for free meals, until he had a complete picture of Bansilal's day.

He learned that once a month on Thursdays; the *bania* rode to the banks of the River Ganges very early in the morning. Once

---

[4] Popular North Indian fried or baked pastry with a savory filling.

[5] One eighth of a Paisa.

there, he would first perform *ashnaan*[6] to cleanse his body and soul in the holy river. He would then climb up a small, rocky hill that led to a spot on a rock jutting out over the rocky riverbed. This rock was believed to have been a prayer spot for Lord Krishna.[7] Bansilal would sit there and pray for another week of great profits, for his son Harilal to become business savvy like him, for his daughter Tara Devi to find a suitable boy, for his departed parents, and above all, for a very long life like Lord Shiva's.[8] After his prayers, he would ride back to Meerut and open his shop for business.

Raja, at his mother's insistence, would also start his day with prayers, but only for Bansilal's death. He had become an angry man.

***

The body Heera found was retrieved from the river bed. It was Bansilal, who had died from a fall onto the rocks below the cliff. His foot must have slipped in the rain, but no one knew for sure. The local *Muhtasib*,[9] after some investigations, didn't suspect foul play and, with Harilal's agreement closed the case as accidental death.

Raja was at Bansilal's cremation crying louder than everyone there, but in his heart, he relished that he had been avenged.

A week after that, Bholu and Juddoo died from drinking excessive amounts of *thurra*,[10] which was later determined to have been toxic due to contamination, or a flaw, in the distillation process. The *Muhtasib* arrested the owner of the *Daru-ghar*[11] for

---

6 A soul cleansing bath in Hindu traditions.

7 The most widely revered and most popular of all Hindu Deities.

8 Hindu God of long life.

9 An overseer of law and safety, a Mughal legacy position, renamed as police inspector after 1857.

10 Illegal alcohol fermented and distilled from molasses, a by-product of sugarcane.

11 Bar mostly selling cheap illegal alcohol.

selling illegal alcohol but later released him due to a lack of evidence. The case was closed by the *Muhtasib*, who had received a gift of some fine *Farangi*[12] whisky from an anonymous friend of the barkeep as a recognition for his 'selfless services' to the town. Some wondered if it was a bribe.

Raja mourned them and was the only one crying at Juddoo's cremation and Bholu's burial. He had developed a fondness for the two, but didn't enjoy paying for their food all the time. Their deaths relieved him from that burden.

He kept his job at the shop, now delivering documents for Harilal, who saw Raja as the only real hard worker his father had. He had always taken Raja's constant presence and extra work without asking for more money as a sign of his goodness: The good Raja.

Raja helped young Harilal come up to speed on his father's businesses, who increasingly felt obligated to young Raja's selflessness. As Harilal gained more confidence in running his business, he gave Raja a bigger role and with it, bigger rewards.

Raja still had a strong yearning to become a stonemason but would suppress it, thinking of all he had achieved with Harilal's support, who also paid him exceptionally well for being there when he needed an advisor and a friend. He was comfortable in his role and started thinking about building a small house for his mother and serving Harilal for the rest of his life.

[12] European. Origin from the crusade era Arabian name for Franks or Franj.

SCHOOL GIRLS
1840

The monsoon season started like any other in South Asia. The arrival of the first rains washed away fears of a drought, bringing smiles to the faces of farmers, big and small. For city dwellers, monsoons were an unwelcome guest. It brought muck in the streets, a stop to any bullock cart and other traffic, overflowing sewerage drains, and general inconveniences they could do without.

Wanting to remind people of its destructive power, the monsoon decided to hang around a little longer. The rivers reached flood levels and the mighty Ganges overflowed, its banks flooding vast areas of northern India, including the town of Meerut. One rainy night, the thatch and adobe hovel which Raja had built for his mother was carried away by the floods, taking his mother along with it. Raja was now alone with only Harilal there to help him get through this difficult time in his life.

Feeling for Raja's losses, Harilal gave him a small room to live in at the back of his house. Seeing this and other acts of kindness by Harilal and his family, Raja was often hit by serious bouts of remorse and depression about Bansilal's death. He considered going to Harilal to acknowledge his role in his father's death and ask for forgiveness, but self-preservation and better judgment prevailed. Instead, he resolved to be completely loyal to

Harilal.

Harilal's only sister, the 15-year-old Tara Devi, attended afternoon classes at a girls-only school. At the start of a new school year, the Scottish Principal of the school, to increase enrollment, started matriculating boys into the previously girls-only afternoon classes. They could continue to attend the afternoon classes with the boys. However, in keeping up with the local culture, and not wanting to lose any female students, he gave the girls' parents a choice of sending their daughters to girls-only morning classes, which he had recently started. All the girls moved to the safety of girls-only classes.

Walking alone to school a few blocks away at midday had not been a problem for Tara. However, the deserted streets of the early morning were not considered safe for a girl walking alone. Harilal, following his father's tradition of starting work very early in the morning, asked Raja to accompany Tara to school on his way to work. Raja had always thought of Tara as the little sister. He had spoken with her many times and regarded her as no different from Harilal or his mother. Pleased that Harilal had trusted him with her safety, he agreed to chaperone her to school every day.

Raja had seen a young man walking his sister to school, always a few steps behind. While accompanying Tara to school, he also stayed a few steps behind her, like the other fellow, and keeping a lookout for street hooligans or dogs that may threaten his ward.

At nineteen, he was a well-built, good-looking man with an income and a home to come back to. A few times while passing through the streets of Muslim parts of Meerut, he had a flower or two thrown at him by unseen admirers, but he paid no attention to them.

One morning, as they left the house, he noticed Tara's bag to be unusually heavy. She was constantly shifting it from one shoulder to the other. He offered to carry the heavy bag for her. She smiled and kept walking. A little further down, still seeing her struggle with the weight of the bag, he reached up to her and tugged at the leather strap.

She pushed his hand away playfully and said, "You think you are strong enough to carry my load?"

Without thinking, he said, "Sure sister, that's what I am here for."

Her expression changed. She looked at him and started walking faster.

Worried, he asked, "Are you offended?" By this time, they were a few yards from the school.

Tara stopped, turned around, and asked him, "What do you think of me?"

Her question puzzled him, so he asked, "Did I say something wrong?"

She kept quiet.

He could sense she was upset, and wanting to clarify, he said, "I think of you as someone who could have been my little sister. But I am just a servant to your family, and a Muslim, and you come from a wealthy Hindu family. I can never think of myself as an equal to you, let alone your older brother." He paused, expecting an answer. None came, so he continued, "However, I try to do the things for you that I would have done for my sister."

She glared at him without responding, so he asked again, "Why are you upset? Did I offend you in some way?"

"Yes," she said as she turned around and disappeared into the school compound while he stood there, confused and shocked at what had just happened.

The next morning, as he waited for her outside the house, she stuck her head out of the door and told him. "Go on to your job. I don't need you to follow me to school. I am smart and strong enough to protect myself."

"Okay, although I don't think it is safe for you to walk alone. Let me inform Lal Bhai that you don't want me to escort you. Maybe he will take you to school each morning."

She started walking. He followed her. She stopped at the big iron gate of the school and faced him.

"You think you are too good for me? Isn't that what you really think?" asked Tara, a dark-complexioned, short, chubby girl with pimple marks all over her face.

"You don't like me?" She stepped closer to him.

Raja, never having had more than a few words with a female, felt disoriented in this uncharted territory. His sharp mind was of no help in trying to rescue him from this anomaly.

He still didn't understand why Tara was acting this way and could only say, "I like you, Tara Devi. What makes you think of all this? I always think of you as a little sister I never had."

Hearing this, she exploded, "Yeah, that's the way you men reject girls like me by calling them sisters. You are all alike, you and all of them."

She moved towards him and screamed, "Leave me alone! Don't touch me, you Muslim animal, you are all alike wanting to dishonor us Hindu girls." She pushed him hard, but herself fell to the ground.

A school teacher and a few students gathered around them. The big school *Chowkidar*[13] jumped in and slapped Raja hard. Others joined the *Chowkidar* in this melee, trying to hit him, but succeeding only in hurling insults at him and at Muslims. The *Chowkidar* was threatening to kill him for touching a *nari*[14] with his *malich*[15] hands. Raja finally freed himself from the big *Chowkidar*'s grip and took off. He ran and ran until the last of the men chasing him had given up hope of catching him.

He wandered around for a little while and then sat by a small stream, trying to untangle what had happened. Finally, he decided to go to the shop to speak with Harilal to clear any

---

[13] Guard, gate keeper.

[14] Unmarried, young Hindu girl.

[15] Dirty, unsanitary.

misunderstanding. When he arrived, he saw there were a few people gathered in front of the shop, including the father of a good friend of Tara's. He had seen him dropping his daughter off at school. Seeing Raja, the angry father charged at him with a big *lathi*.[16]

"There's the *malich* who has been trying to seduce my daughter for weeks now, trying to lure her into the forest with sweets and trinkets."

He swung his *lathi*, which Raja stopped with one hand. Grabbing the middle of the *lathi* with his other hand, he wrested it away from the angry man. Then, continuing the same motion, Raja landed the *lathi* behind the man's knees so hard that they buckled and he fell flat on the ground, a well-executed *lathi* fighter's trick he had learned from Bholu and Juddoo.

Seeing his expertise with the *lathi*, the other men backed off. He saw Harilal standing behind them, his eyes red, like he had been crying. He came forward toward Raja, unafraid of getting hit.

"Why Raja, why? Why did you do these things? My father gave you your first job when you lost your father and had no income. I treated you like my brother and trusted you with everything. I trusted you to protect my sister from others, and you tried to dishonor her."

Raja wanted to say it was all just fabrication and false accusations. But he was confused, confused about what had made Tara so hostile. He had no inkling of what the other father was talking about. He had never spoken a word to that other girl, let alone offer her sweets or trinkets. Did Tara spur her on to falsely accuse him of all this?

Above all, he was hurt and disappointed with Harilal, who had already judged him to be guilty without giving him a chance to respond to the charges.

Harilal approached him, tears flowing. Raja could see a knife in his right hand, held low against his body. He let the *lathi*

---

[16] A long thick metal capped bamboo cane, used for protection.

drop from his hand as Harilal got close. With one swift motion, Harilal plunged the knife into him. Raja winced with pain as the blade cut into his organs. Falling back, he heard himself say, "Lal Bhai, you are mistaken. I have done nothing, not to Tara or her friend. It is all a lie."

He saw Harilal standing over him, who let out a long, full-throated, guttural cry of pain and dropped the blade. Everything went dark for Raja when his head hit the hard, dry ground.

UPWARDLY MOBILE

1850

Nearing age 30, Raja was working as a day laborer, doing odd jobs at the East India Company Army Cantonment. His jobs never lasted more than a few weeks, as he had developed a taste for Nautch House girls and all things opium. Every payday, he would indulge in his favorite pastime with his junkie street buddies at the local house of ill repute, late into the night. Money kept opium drinks and *thurra* flowing, and the girls dancing. After his money ran out, he would find himself on the street, or worse, in a ditch.

Invariably, the next day he would be fired from his job for showing up intoxicated or not showing up at all. After a few days of no work and no food, he would be back to his senses, promising himself, and anyone who would listen, that he would never indulge in these vices again.

Fortunately for him, the Meerut Cantonment was being continually expanded, which meant he would always find a job even with his poor work history. The power and landmass of the East India Company was growing by leaps and bounds. It needed an ever-expanding cantonment to accommodate the growing number of sepoys[17] in the army. The need for more and more soldiers was causing a general labor shortage in this mostly agrarian society.

---

[17] Anglicized version of Sipahee. Native soldier.

His desire to be a stonemason was always present, but he never acted upon it. During one of his drug-free stints, he met a stonemason at the cantonment. He was able to convince the mason of his resolve to become a master stonemason. The mason promised to teach him the basics of cutting, chiseling, and polishing stone, and building basic structures. Raja was a quick study and learned this craft well.

During this period, he kept away from the Nautch girls and opium, thus keeping his laborer job for an extended period. Besides, he had seen the stonemason's daughter and wanted to marry her. Not particularly interested in the girl, but marrying her would give him unrestricted access to the old man's tools, but also help in eventually replace him at the cantonment job.

The mason, always worried about his daughter's lack of suitable marriage prospects, had noticed Raja's interest in his daughter. He was fooled into believing that Raja had given up all his vices and was now a changed man.

Raja and the mason's daughter were married on Eid-ul-Fitr, the feast at the end of Ramazan. Raja was happy to get access to his father-in-law's tools, and the mason was glad to have found a groom for his daughter. He had high hopes for Raja and his daughter. The newlyweds were given a back room under a huge *Peepal*[18] tree that provided shade over a small courtyard with a back door. Using the back door, Raja was free to come and go as he pleased without disturbing his in-laws.

His wife gave birth to a son the next year. Raja named him Zaheer Babar, after the first emperor and the founder of the Mughal dynasty in India. By this time, he had reverted to his old ways of long, late-night sessions on paydays at the Nautch House with his street buddies and opium. But now he had a place to return and was smart enough to leave on his own two feet, though intoxicated out of his mind. He would still lose his job for not showing up, or showing up with a sapping hangover, as before.

[18] Species of fig, native to the Indian subcontinent.

Marriage and fatherhood had not changed him.

His father-in-law would remind him of all the promises he made and the assurances he had given before his marriage, to no avail. When sober, Raja, worried about being kicked out of the house, would agree with him and ask for forgiveness, promising to try harder to fight his impulses. Not having any other options, the stonemason, for the sake of his daughter, would help him get his job back by speaking to their common employers, the *Gora*[19] *Sahibs.*

***

The third global plague pandemic reached India in the early months of 1855, taking a devastating toll on the poor population of northern India. Meerut was not spared; a quarter of its native population succumbed to the deadly Bubonic plague. Raja's wife and in-laws fell victim to this scourge after spending their life savings on religious charms, remedies, and unproven cures for the disease.

Raja and Zaheer survived.

East India Company's empire was bigger than ever and the cantonment expansion work still had to continue. With a quarter of men, women, and children from the town and its vicinities dead and buried or cremated, Raja's job prospects became robust, and things looked up and up. He was now the sole owner of his father-in-law's property, the almost depleted cash box with his wife's and her mother's leftover jewelry, and above all, the precious stonemason tools. Despite Raja's limited competency, having a fully outfitted master-mason's toolbox meant he was now a craftsman to be valued.

One fine day, he got a haircut and a shower at the local barbershop, put on his father-in-law's clean clothes and mason's cap, and presented himself at the cantonment gate to apply for the mason's job. He was sent in to see a Colonel John Finnis, commandant of the 11th Native Infantry, who was also leading the

---

[19] European (literal. White/Caucasian).

cantonment expansion project.

Colonel Finnis was about 50 years old, a father of seven children, the youngest four living with him and his wife in Meerut. Most of the British staff of the East India Company treated the natives as sub-human pack and draft animals with adaptable bodies and limbs to perform complex tasks. Raja found this *Gora Sahib* different from the others; he was more tolerant than the others he had the misfortune of coming across at the Cantonment. The Englishman knew his hands were tied, so the company offered Raja a permanent job with a better pay. Raja had achieved his childhood dream.

He was now the stonemason, a job he had always aspired to.

Colonel Finnis, aware of Raja's habits from his work history, moved his payday from Thursdays to Saturdays so that he can "relax and take care of his health and welfare" on Sundays-his day off.

Relax and take care of his health, he did, by being back in business at the Nautch House. His treatment at the house was like nothing before. Now he was a man to be taken seriously. A man of standing, with some impressive resources at his disposal. He was treated with respect. The off-duty girls babysat little Zaheer upstairs, while the working ones entertained him downstairs. He had Sundays off to erase the lingering effects of his boisterous payday evenings.

The next two years were bliss. Raja selected the Nautch House's prettiest girl, the fair-skinned, doe-eyed, slender Kashmiri beauty Zeena Bai, as his exclusive host and consort. He could visit her anytime or send an *ekka*[20] to fetch her to his house on short notice. The senior madam at the house was paid good money for Zeena's undivided companionship. As a further favor to the madam, Raja started introducing some of the younger *Gora Sahibs* looking for "safe female company" to the Nautch House girls. He

---

[20] A small one horse, two wheeled covered cart for two or three people.

soon became the madam's favorite customer.

Zeena Bai started taking care of little Zaheer during the day while Raja worked in the cantonment. She developed a fondness for the boy. She also loved the way Raja spent money on her for food and gifts.

Raja had everything; a job he loved, money, companionship, and a child. Over time, he gave up drug use to build a good life for his son. He wanted to excel at work, putting in long hours to make sure that things went as planned. He was soon supervising a large team of masons and laborers. His reputation and standing at the cantonment grew swiftly. Colonel Finnis, impressed by his improved work ethic and developing knowledge, started taking him on inspection tours of new cantonments under construction elsewhere in India. In this pre-railway era, the inspection trips would sometimes last for months at a time. While he toured, Zeena would stay at his home and take care of Zaheer. This mutually beneficial monogamous relationship, in time, evolved into genuine affection for each other.

When new girls were brought to the Nautch House, it was the custom of the elder ladies of the house to teach them reading, writing skills, religion, art, and poetry. This was done to prepare them to converse intelligently with customers. Sons from landowning families, high position holders and administrators at the Mughal court were all customers of Nautch Houses all over India.

Zeena Bai was proficient in these skills. She started teaching Zaheer the basics of reading and writing at a very young age. Zaheer became very attached to her, and would miss her when Raja was home, and she back at the Nautch House. To rectify this situation, Raja made another big payment, in the form of a piece of land, to the madam. He was invited to help put down the foundation for a much-improved Nautch House on his donated land. After the foundation was laid, Raja picked up Zeena Bai and brought her to his home, this time for good, to an anxiously waiting Zaheer.

Colonel Finnis noticed Raja's skills at fixing minor problems quickly. He would call him up to his house to help with repairs or other minor tasks at home. Raja would sometimes bring Zaheer with him. The Colonel's wife would let her young children, both girls, play with Zaheer while his father worked. Sometimes, Finnis would ask Raja to join them when the family was having tea in their lawns, a taboo for European employees of the East India Company. Raja would sit on the grass enjoying their hospitality while The *Gora Sahibs* sat on lawn chairs. Colonel Finnis knew mixing with natives was forbidden by the company, and if he were a junior officer, he would have been severely reprimanded. But he was no junior officer; he knew how to walk that fine line between breaking company rules and keeping natives happy, and thus loyal to him.

Raja also introduced Zeena Bai, as his wife Zeenat, to the Colonel and his family. Finnis knew of her Nautch House background, but kept it to himself. He would let Raja bring her to his house on Muslim holidays or when Zaheer tagged along with Raja. She would help Mrs. Finnis with household chores.

An employer who treated him as a human, who valued him more than any other employee.

Life couldn't have been better for Raja.

THE COW AND THE PIG
1856-57

Henry Hardinge, the British governor general to India, introduced the use of the new P53 Enfield rifles in place of the older Baker rifles to modernize the East India Company's (EIC) army equipment. The P53 was the same rifle being used by regular British soldiers all over the world. It employed a percussion lock mechanism for firing, a much more reliable firing arrangement than the Baker Rifles' flintlock firing system.

Unlike the older Baker rifle cartridges, the paper bag cartridges for the new rifle were greased to keep the gunpowder dry in humid conditions, and improve the ball speed in the barrel upon firing.

The gun loading action remained the same, requiring the soldier to bite off the top of the cartridge and pour the gunpowder and the ball from the cartridge into the barrel.

East India Company started replacing the older rifles with the new P53s in 1856. It was a great rifle, but soon a rumor started that the grease used was beef tallow and pig fat.

Cows are venerated in the Hindu traditions. Harming or killing them is considered sacrilegious. As the rumor spread, Hindu soldiers refused to touch the cartridges. Muslim soldiers also started refusing to handle the cartridges, since Islam prohibits the consumption of pig fat or meat.

The East India Company completely misjudged the depth of anger and resentment among native soldiers about the use of the new cartridges. Its leadership in England issued a general order to force the issue and make the soldiers follow the orders.

Colonel George Carmichael-Smyth, commander of the 3rd Bengal Cavalry, a native regiment at Meerut Cantonment was well-known as an arrogant, headstrong career soldier with a very low opinion of the native soldier. He read the orders from London and was ready to teach any troublemakers a lesson.

On 9th May, he called for a 6 am general practice drill with the new cartridges to enforce the order. 85 Muslim and Hindu sepoys humbly refused to practice with the cartridges. Refusal to act to a direct command, however respectful, was insubordination and a breach of discipline. He dismissed the conforming soldiers and left the transgressors standing in 100+ degree blazing heat while he wrote his orders for their punishment. After having a leisurely lunch and a quick nap, he came out at 3pm and called the rest of his regiment for a short drill. After the drill, he read out his orders.

The 85 were formally charged with insubordination and stripped of their uniforms right there in the hot tropical sun. They were then shackled before being led off to start a ten-year sentence. After the sentencing, rumors of the rank and file being at the brink of a revolt spread like wildfire among the sepoys and their families.

That evening, Raja went to the Nautch House to see what people were talking about, after the severe punishment meted out to the 85. There he overheard an inebriated native soldier talk of a plan to kill the *Farangis* when they attended Sunday church services the following day.

Raja rushed to Colonel Finis' house where he was having supper with his family, outdoors on the veranda. Two native servants were fanning them with very large hand-fans. He told the Colonel what he had heard at the Nautch House and that he felt it was something real, in light of the events of the morning.

"So kind of you, Raja, for bringing this news to me. It is certainly alarming that things have escalated this quickly."

"Colonel Sahib, I understand the Nawab of Rampur is camped on the left bank of Ganges, on a hunt with his family and a very large contingent of servants and bearers. It is not safe for your family members here. As a precaution, may I suggest that I, along with a few of your soldiers, accompany Mrs. Finnis and the children to safety across the Ganges with Nawab Sahib of Rampur?"

The Nawab was known as a friend of the British and a protector of their interests in Northern India. After giving it some thought, the Colonel told his wife, Sarah, to get ready for an overnight journey out of Meerut. To keep the children calm, they told them it was a pre-planned surprise camping trip at the invitation of the Nawab of Rampur. Colonel Finnis asked two of his British soldiers and four native soldiers to accompany his family to the right bank with Raja. After transferring his family's security to the Nawab, they were all to return posthaste to the cantonment before sunrise.

The small caravan left at around nine pm, crossing the Ganges at a small town called Mahmudabad. The native men walked with the four horse-drawn carts carrying the family members, the British soldiers, and the female house staff.

After helping the family and the house staff cross the river and placing them in the Nawab's protection, Raja and the six soldiers started the journey back in one cart. They left the other three horse-carts with the family for transportation to Rampur with the Nawab and his entourage.

On the return journey, Raja and the four native soldiers rode in the horse-drawn cart. The European soldiers seemed upset at having to share the cart with five "smelly natives," but the Colonel's orders were very clear. He expected the European soldiers to share the cart with the natives for a quick return. Raja had noticed one of the native soldiers looking at him with disgust. He had tried to speak to him while they were walking to the river, but each time, the soldier would walk away from him without saying anything. Raja tried to reason with him, but to no avail. He kept an eye on him for the rest of the journey, in case things got messy.

It was early morning when they got back to the cantonment. The soldiers retired to their barracks, while Raja stopped by the Colonel's home. As expected, the Colonel was eager to hear how things went. Since everything had gone as planned, he didn't have many questions about the trip. But Raja voiced his concern about the one unhappy soldier. Colonel Finnis called a staff member over and asked him to bring the man over to his office. He then asked Raja to walk with him to his cantonment office, as he had something for Raja there.

Sunday, 10th May, 1857, was an exceptionally hot day in Meerut. Church services in the summers in India were held in the evening to avoid having to sit in the sweltering heat. The evening services had been further delayed by an hour to let the temperature cool down a bit.

At around 6 pm, some native soldiers started abusing and harassing British soldiers out and about in town on leave. This was the start of what came to be known as the Sepoy[21] revolt, or the First War of Indian Independence.

As the word of the attacks on white soldiers and junior officers reached Colonel Finnis, he rushed to where his 11th Native Infantry soldiers had gathered. He spent the next hour listening to their grievances and calming them down by showing concern and reasoning with them. He promised that, as long as he was alive, his 11th Infantry would never have to use those cartridges. A bold statement considering the clear directions from the high command to the contrary.

Having placated his soldiers, he dismissed them to their

---

[21] Native soldier.

barracks and proceeded to the side where soldiers from Colonel Carmichael-Smyth's 3rd Bengal cavalry had gathered to protest the punishment of their compatriots. He didn't have a chance. As he got close to the gathering, he was shot off his horse. Colonel John Finnis[22] fell and died on the spot when two soldiers bayonetted him while he lay injured on the ground.

He was the first British officer killed in the uprising, which became an orgy of plundering and killing for days, followed by years of planned, revengeful butchery of natives and their families.

---

22 First British officer killed in the 1857 sepoy revolt/uprising.

PREAMBLE TO A DISASTER

May 1857

Raja, after being away for more than a day and a half, showed up at home just before noon. Zeena hadn't expected him to be back until late afternoon. She had just put Zaheer down for a nap. He was restless in the sweltering temperatures on his low, small bed. She was sitting by him, trying to keep him cool with a handmade fan.

Raja looked quite agitated, and sat down on his *charpoy*[23], motioning her to sit with him. "Listen to me carefully," he said. "Things may get unruly today. While I will be safe in the cantonment with Finnis Sahib, I am worried about your and Peeru's safety at home."

They called his son Peeru, for the simple reason that his only friend, the neighbor's five-year-old kid, was named Meeru and he wanted to be like Meeru.

"I have to get back to Finnis Sahib, but I came to give you some instructions on how we are going to get through this chaos. There may even be violence of some sort against our *Gora Sahibs.* Yesterday, I heard a drunk soldier talk about killing some officers at church tonight."

This frightened Zeena. He saw fear in her eyes, so he put

---

[23] A bed made with a wooden frame strung with light rope.

his arm around her. "Don't worry, the *Gora Sahib*s are all prepared for this, and not all the *sipahees*[24] will riot. Only some hotheads will try to get the others riled up, like that Mangal Pandey[25] from Barrackpore. He was trying to get other *sipahees* to join him in open revolt against Company *Sarkar*.[26] But you know the result, no one stood up with him. He was arrested and hanged for treason."

Raja was trying very hard to keep calm while burdening Zeena with news from the outside. "If something similar happens at the cantonment, they will arrest and hang the leaders, and that will be the end of that. *Insha-Allah*."[27]

Hearing Raja's poised reasoning, Zeena calmed down a bit. Drying her eyes with her *dupatta*,[28] she got up.

"You have been gone for a day and must be tired and hungry. I have prepared your favorite dish for you. Let me go get it."

He grabbed her hand and pulled her back down. "Finnis Sahib is expecting me back. He is worried about you and Peeru being alone in town. He let me come to discuss steps to stay safe until things return to normal. Keep the food in the *nemat-khana*.[29] We will have dinner together this evening after I am back."

He got up and went to the corner furthest away from the door and removed a small box from under a plank in the floor. The box contained a few gold coins, company-issued money, and some Mughal cash. There was also a curious-looking ring formed from a gold wire that had been wound around someone's finger until it took the shape of a rudimentary ring. The last item in the box was a thin stack of papers in English with official-looking stamps. He then fished out a similar note from his pocket and

---

[24] Plural of Sipahee, native soldier.
[25] A sepoy turned freedom fighter hanged for treason in early 1857.
[26] An honorific.
[27] Allah willing.
[28] A large cotton scarf/stole used as head covering by Muslim women.
[29] A free standing closet with fine mesh screens around it, used for keeping food items, before refrigerators.

handed it to her.

"Protect this as if your life depends on it," he said seriously.

"What is this paper?" She asked.

"You don't need to know what it says, but Finnis Sahib wrote it and then stamped it in my presence. He told me to keep it safe. I am giving it to you. In case something happens to me, this will be your salvation." Saying this, a foreboding sense enveloped him and he desperately wanted her to understand what he was telling her. The gravity of the situation did not escape her; she started crying again.

"If we are separated, and you don't hear from me, take it to the *chaoonee*.[30] Bring Peeru with you. Insist on talking to the commandant there. If they give you any trouble, you can show them one of these papers. They are proof that I have been a selfless servant of the company for years, and that you are my wife." They were not married, and he had shown no desire to marry her before. She stopped crying and looked puzzled.

"But…?"

"I know we are not married, but in my heart and the eyes of Allah and our Rasool, we are."

Zeena gasped, trying to control her tears. Tears rolling down her cheeks.

"Peeru's presence with you will be a proof of it for the *Gora Sahib* who reads it. You will have custody of Peeru to raise him as a God-fearing, respectable man. I want him to get an education, which I was never afforded." Seeing her eyes welling like a dam ready to burst, he leaned forward, kissing her eyes and her forehead, and held her tight.

"I swear you are my love, and next time we meet, I will bring a Mulla to make this official." Holding back his tears, he picked up the ring and kissed her right hand, and placed it on the only finger it would fit on, her pinkie. "This was my mother's

---

30 Cantonment.

wedding ring made by my father for her."

He desperately wanted to believe what he said next. "We will be fine. If anything happens here, we will move to another town, maybe Srinagar, your hometown. We will present these papers to the Company Resident of the Raja of Kashmir. He will help us. We can start life afresh there and live happily ever after."

Hearing this, Zeena started crying again, "Allah will protect you and Peeru, and *Insha-Allah* we will be together. I know you will take care of him like his birth mother would have. May Allah place her in heaven."

"One other thing, if things get worse in town, keep your doors locked and don't light the lamp at night. Stay in the back of the house and don't answer the door. Always keep the money and paper hidden on your person. Never let Peeru out of your sight, as he will be your gateway to a good life if I am not there. Keep the papers safe. The two together will convince *Gora Sahib*s of my loyalty to them, and the reality of our relationship."

He returned the box under the plank. "I will put the chain up on the front door and put the big lock on it. You can always leave from the back door if need be."

He turned to the sleeping Peeru, leaned over and kissed him lightly on his head and cheek. Saying a long prayer under his breath, he blew it gently on his face, as is customary in Muslim tradition. His eyes brimming with tears, he shook his head again and again, desperately wanting to shake off the feelings of utter helplessness.

He wanted to wake himself up from this nightmare. Zeena was behind him with her hands on his shoulder, clutching his shirt, not wanting to let him go. He turned around and held her quietly. She had never seen him this emotional.

He trusted Zeena to take care of Peeru if he was killed in the rioting, but he was also wary of her background from the Nautch House. She had never spoken about her past and had always changed the subject when it came up, telling him that it hurts too much to think about her painful existence before she met him, and that she would kill herself if she had to go back. Raja never pressed her about it and would never bring it up again.

While she had been the kindest and nicest to him and Peeru, no one could predict what her behavior would be in such a situation. If he was gone, she may find Peeru to be a burden and decide to do something about it. Now that he was facing death, he had to make sure that his child would not perish and the only way he saw for his survival was through Zeena adopting him as her child. Raja was providing her with all the resources to do that and live a comfortable life.

He was still worried that she could drop Peeru off at an orphanage - or worse, and move on with her life as a wealthy woman. No one at the cantonment, except the Finnis family, knew that Raja had a child. So, as another precaution, he had requested Colonel Finnis to tell his wife to check on Peeru and Zeena from time to time if he was killed in the uprising especially since he knew that many native soldiers hated him for his support and loyalty to his *Gora Sahibs*. Colonel Finnis told him to not worry about that, as he would not let any harm come to him and his family. But to assuage Raja's worries, he would let his wife and other members of his staff know about Zeena and Peeru, and to look after them if something happened to him and Raja.

He then dropped this heavily veiled warning dressed up as good news on Zeena. "I asked Colonel Finnis to look after you and Peeru if I die. He said he will tell his wife and all his staff members to look after you and Peeru if something was to happen to both him and me."

Zeena's voice broke as she said, "I will pray for your safety until you return. *Insha-Allah*, nothing is going to happen to you. As long as I am alive, I will gouge out any eye that is raised at my child."

Raja felt these words in his heart and cursed himself for having doubts about her. He gave Peeru a last kiss and embraced

Zeena, not wanting to let go. His heart was broken, and there was nothing he could do. He felt that an unescapable countdown to his death had already begun.

And then, as if his name had been called, he left the room, leaving a completely distraught Zeena gaping unbelievably at the now-empty space where Raja had just stood. She sobbed; her heart sank as she heard the front door chain rattling against the door, and then the finality of the big padlock being engaged.

CARNAGE BEGINS

May 1857

An eerie feeling engulfed Zeena. A feeling of a permanent loss, like when someone near and dear has died, something an 80-year-old would be all too familiar with in their advanced age.

She felt distraught. "I will never see him again. It is my fate that will keep me from finding stability in my life. Love and stability were all that I wanted from life. Raja was the first person who really loved me and brought a semblance of stability to my life."

Zeena loved him more than anything and would have taken care of him without asking for anything in return. She wanted to grow old with him, though she knew the reality of her existence and help raise his son to be a God-fearing, educated man as her own child.

She sat at the same spot where he had left her for what seemed like an eternity, worrying, thinking, praying until she was brought out of her stupor to reality by Peeru's loud cry of Mama.

She fed him some left over goat's milk, but he was still hungry, so she took out some of the food and lovingly fed him with a little spoon the Colonel's wife had given him on one of his visits. Peeru kept trying to grab the spoon from her, wanting to eat by himself, saying "myself, myself" until the food was done. She gave him the spoon to play with while she took the wooden plate to the kitchen to wash it. She washed the plate carefully, still thinking of what the day may bring, still hopeful that Raja will be back by the evening and she will serve him the food on the plate.

"I will never let him leave. I will go everywhere with him." She said to herself.

Peeru was now more active after having eaten. He wanted to go out and collect some berries from the field. He wanted to go next door to play with Meeru and his little sister. She picked him up on her side and brought him back into their room.

"I need to tell you something. We will leave on a trip to meet some friends tomorrow. We may have to start tonight because it will be a long journey. You should take another nap."

"Is Baba coming with us?" He asked, looking around with confusion showing on his face.

"Where is Baba?"

Zeena wondered if Peeru already knew that she was not his mother and is that why he is always looking for his father, or is it that his self-preservation instincts lead him to only consider a male his protector. She couldn't decide and shook her head.

"Don't worry, he will join us later. He has gone to get some of those big, sweet mangoes that you like best. We will go on our own to *nanee's*[31] house first."

Peeru called the head madam of Nautch House *nanee.* Zeena had left her courtesan life for a monogamous relationship with Raja and had never wanted to go back. The cunning head madam would stop by from time to time, ostensibly to see her little Peeru, but actually to ask for money and to judge if Zeena was ready to return. She wanted Zeena and Raja to break up, so she could have Zeena back as a source of income at the house. Her motivations were quite transparent to Zeena, who despised her but would never show it. She always acted respectfully towards her and always sent her away with money and fruits.

From time to time, Zeena would go to the front of the house and look through the sole window into Baker's Street, the

---

[31] Maternal grandmother.

primary thoroughfare of Meerut, to observe what was going on outside. She was waiting for Raja to return, praying for his protection from the storm brewing outside.

Zeena heard the *Muazzin*[32] call for *Maghrib*[33] prayers. Spreading her *Jai-Namaz*[34] on the floor facing in the general direction of Mecca, she was ready for her prayers. Hearing loud noises and commotion outside, she took the stairs up to the roof to see what was going on. What she saw, she didn't believe she would ever see. Raja's words were taking shape right in front of her eyes.

The carnage had begun.

She saw some native soldiers beating up a *gora* soldier right in the middle of Baker's street, while others watched and some egged him on. It was Jeremy, a casual visitor to the Nautch House, who came mostly for the drinks, but also sometimes for the dance shows. He had learned a few of Mir Taqi Mir's[35] Urdu verses, which he would recite to impress people, although his knowledge of the language was next to non-existent. At the Nautch House, he would shout out some of these verses at the dancers to get their attention as he got increasingly plastered. Not getting their attention would lead to him making passes and groping the dancers. Knowing very well that he was a stingy customer who would never have a penny for them, the showgirls would reject his advances and even slap his hands away if he got too aggressive. Things would then escalate quickly with him getting further upset at the rejection by "these nigger witches" and additional disorder and commotion would ensue. The Nautch House hoods wouldn't dare touch him, as he was a *Gora Sahib*, albeit a low-grade one. It would take a while to get the situation under control, usually with another *gora* soldier or junior officer intervening and coaxing Jeremy back to the barracks.

---

[32] Prayer caller at a mosque.

[33] Fourth of the five prayers of the day at sunset for Muslims.

[34] Small Prayer rug.

[35] 18th century Urdu poet.

Seeing Jeremy getting beaten up, Zeena thought Jeremy's drunken behavior may have gotten worse this time and things had spilled outside. Then a short native soldier went up to him and cut him down with his service issue sword.

This is no Nautch House brawl gone badly.

Allah help us.

Remembering what Raja had told her, she rushed downstairs. She needed to get her plan into action. Since Raja's departure, she had been thinking about all the possible calamities that could befall her. She needed to get ready if they came to her home. She emptied the contents of the box into a small bag and then stuffed some other basic needs stuff into it.

On second thought, she left some cash and a couple of papers in the box. If they come here looking for him, not finding anyone home, they would ransack the house and would definitely find the box hidden under the old plank in the corner. With money and papers still in it, they will think that Raja hadn't told "the Nautch house whore" about the money he hid in his house and would not come after her. She cut small pieces from the bottom of the old worn-out window curtains. She then sewed small pockets with these patches on the inside of her tunic, as well as inside Peeru's little shirt that was lying nearby. Inside out, the clothes looked like they had been patched up. Then, placing a little bit of cash in each, she sewed the openings shut.

She took Colonel Finnis' letters and rolled them tightly until they looked like small sticks. Then she dripped melted wax from a candle, one drop at a time, all over the little cylinders until they were ensconced in wax and safe from moisture. She then slid these down the middle of her chest and used a couple of jute strings to hold them in place above her waist.

To safeguard the gold coins, she inserted them one by one into the belt sleeve of her petticoat and then packed some food to take along. She was now ready to leave at a moment's notice.

She sat on her *Jai-Namaz* praying, waiting, hoping the storm raging outside would die down. Peeru, disappointed at not being able to go out and play, was dozing off on Raja's bed. Zeena started praying for Raja's security, and safe return home, dreaming of better times ahead. She was tired and may have dozed off when she felt a very sharp pain in her upper back. It felt as if someone had stabbed her.

"Did someone stab me? There is no one here." She heard herself saying.

"What does it feel like when stabbed?" she had asked Raja after hearing of the time he was stabbed by Harilal. Raja described to her in excruciating detail what it felt when he was stabbed. He had learned somewhere to let his body go limp before the actual stabbing to minimize organ damage. He said that had saved his life that day. Hearing his theory, she had smiled and said something to the effect of, easier said than done.

Remembering his lesson, she let her body go limp. She didn't move. No sound, no pain. She touched the sore spot for any sign of blood under her blouse. Nothing. She turned around. There was no one. The pain was gone. It must have been her imagination, and then she knew what it was.

"I felt the weapon as it entered his body."

Realizing what it meant, she let out a long scream and fell into a *sajda*[36] crying uncontrollably at the top of her lungs, letting out all her pain and sorrow.

Woken up by his mama's cries, Peeru jumped out of the bed and came running to her. She was prostrated on her *Jai-Namaz*, crying. He had never seen her crying. Instinctively, he put his little hands on her back and started crying himself. Feeling his hand, she sat up and pulled him into her arms, now trying to control her sobbing and comforting him at the same time. This made him wail even louder. She sat there crying, holding little Peeru like she never wanted to let go, until they fell asleep on the prayer rug.

---

36 Prostration.

A DARK NIGHT

May 1857

It was much later when Zeena woke up; she thought it must be time for Isha.[37] Peeru was sprawled next to her on the floor with his little hands wrapped around her. She could hear sporadic sounds of rifle report coming from the direction of the cantonment. She went upstairs to see what was going on.

Baker's street was now vacant, but she could see two buildings of the cantonment ablaze. The rebellion was in full swing. Some native soldiers and citizens had surrounded the buildings, raising slogans and shouting obscenities. Jeremy's mutilated body was lying a few yards from her front door. Stray dogs would sniff at the carcass and move on, thinking it too much work to tear it for food. She could not bear to watch the gory scene, and scared for her own and Peeru's life, rushed back downstairs.

She hurried around the room collecting things for her journey, then she woke Peeru up and washed his face quickly with some water sitting in a cup next to him.

"We are going to *nanee's* house," and gave him a small plum to eat.

She put on her full-length *burqa*. Exiting through the back door of the house, she put a padlock on the chain at the top of the

---

[37] Last of the five prayers of the day for Muslims.

door and started walking, Peeru still enjoying the ripe plum. Not wanting to be seen on the main road, she stayed in back alleys. The Nautch House was on the other side of the cantonment. She took the longer but safer path behind the cantonment.

As she passed the cantonment, she saw some people emerge from an alley, three women in *burqas* with a toddler, hurriedly walking close behind two men.

The alley was a back exit from the residential section of the cantonment, reserved for the English. It was mostly used by the servants to come and go. Zeena had been scared walking alone in the dark, deserted alleys. She walked up to the group and asked the tall man leading the lot if she could walk with them.

"Where are you going? We are on the way to Mahmudabad. We all live there." He replied in a hurried but compassionate tone. She knew the village. It was at one of the river crossings on the Ganges. Hearing of their destination, she changed her plan.

"Can I come with you? I have to go to Rampur. My husband works there for the Nawab of Rampur. I am trying to get away from what is happening here."

The man didn't respond. He was looking over his shoulder towards the cantonment.

She asked again, "Can I come with you? My child is afraid of the dark, and we may not find the way, so please let us walk with you. We will not bother you or ask you for anything. Allah, our protector, will bless you and reward you for your kindness towards us."

"Okay, but you will have to walk fast, make no noise, and keep that child quiet. There may be robbers out there. We have nothing of value, but they kill without reason." Then he added, "You can walk with the other women, but don't talk to them. They are all scared."

She slowed down for the other women to catch up to her. Soon, walking at a brisk pace, they cleared the cantonment limits.

The night was pitch dark. The tall man knew his way. Peeru saw the outline of another child holding his mother's hand. He thought it was his friend Meeru and started calling, "Meeru, Meeru." When the child didn't respond, Peeru started crying. Zeena picked him up and consoled him while trying to keep up with others. He kept looking at the other kid, calling him again and again, to get his attention. The woman with the other child, also worried about the noise, brought her child and started walking next to Zeena.

Zeena was relieved, and said, "Salaam sister, I am Zeenat. Thank you for coming over. I didn't know how to get him to stop making so much noise. I am so afraid."

"*Waleykum As Salaam* Zeenat. I am Safia, and that man is my husband." The woman whispered.

"Everybody quiet!" came an admonishment from the front.

Peeru got down from Zeena and grabbed his newfound friend's hand, and started walking, moving their hands back and forth like a swing. Seeing the silhouette of two little boys walking hand in hand in the dark night, without a care in the world, the tension eased somewhat. Little did they, or anyone, know what awaits them.

After walking for about half an hour, they came up to a narrow road, crossing their path. An old man was sitting by the road holding a lantern with a dying flame. The leader signaled everyone to stop. They all stopped and quietly sat down on the ground. He cautiously proceeded ahead to get information from the old man. After a brief discussion, he came back and said that the man was just resting there on his way to Meerut, uninformed of what had happened.

While they were discussing this, Zeena saw three men come out of bushes ahead on their right. Zeena saw no reason to get upset or worried, but other members of the group started behaving like mice caught in a mousetrap. She heard Safia whisper,

"*Allah rahem karey.*"[38]

It was a group of native soldiers. They snatched the lantern from the old man and surrounded the group. They pushed Safia and another woman to the ground. Zeena, already holding Peeru's hand, pulled him into her side so he could not see what was happening. With her other hand, she reached for the other child and pulled him to her as well. She didn't know what was going to happen, but whatever it was, she didn't want them seeing it. She tightened her grip on them and held them with their faces buried at her sides. Another woman still standing and, seeing Zeena holding the child, started to move towards her. The sepoy nearest to her stopped her with his outstretched sword.

"Who are you and where do you think you are going?" he roared.

The woman stayed quiet. The sepoy came closer and put his sword on her shoulder. "If you don't answer, I will kill you right here."

"Who are you?" He asked again, now raising his sword.

"*Yeh hum hain*,"[39] she said meekly; there was a hint of an English accent in her Urdu delivery. The sepoy noticed it too. He pulled off the top of her *burqa*, exposing a Caucasian face in the dim light of the lantern.

He growled, "*Haramzadi*[40], you came to rule us? Huh? I will show you who rules here."

Before anyone could say a word, his sword had pierced her neck. She let out a loud, blood-curdling scream and fell to the ground, blood gushing out of the large wound. Zeena tightened her grip around the two children, not wanting them to see what she was seeing.

The other sepoys, their swords drawn ready to kill, moved closer and ripped off the *burqa* tops of the three women sitting on

---

38 Allah help us.

39 Urdu phrase meaning "It is I."

40 Bastard.

the ground. A look of disappointment flashed on their faces, as they were expecting more British women in *burqas*.

"Who are all of you and why did you hide this devil woman amongst you?" One of the sepoy shouted as the flickering lantern ran out of oil and sputtered before the flame died. It was now pitch dark again.

Before anyone could answer, Zeena, still holding the two boys tightly against her, quickly made up a story that they were traveling to Mahmudabad, their hometown.

"Along the way, we saw this woman in a *burqa* lying by the side of the road, unconscious, lost in the wilderness. We didn't know she was a *gori*[41]. It was too dark with no moonlight. The men not wanting to leave a woman all alone, carried her on a makeshift stretcher they made of their *lathis* and some branches from a dead tree. After she regained consciousness, she wouldn't speak or answer any question."

Safia was listening intently to Zeena's story. One of the sepoys asked her where she was coming from. She repeated Zeena's story and added that she worked for Zeena as a nanny for her two boys. He asked her who Zeena was. Safia, now less scared, gave them the name of a native soldier who was one of the 85 men who had refused to follow the command and was now in jail. She said Zeena was his wife and mother of his two children.

Hearing the name of the respected sepoy, his attitude changed. The rebel who had just killed the woman approached Zeena. "Sister, we are on the way to Meerut. By the early morning, we will have freed your husband from those bastard *goras* and their native stooges. I will tell him the story of how I met his two boys. Please forgive me for ripping off your *burqa*. I hope I didn't offend you in any other way."

"*Sipahees*, how will just the three of you free my husband? Aren't you bringing others to help free him? I hear the jail has four layers of walls before anyone can get to the cells where they are

[41] Caucasian female.

keeping him. You will need a lot more men and ammunition than you three and your swords to break the jail open."

"Don't worry sister, over a hundred men are coming behind us on this road. They will be here soon, and will be glad to meet our hero's two sons."

He searched in his pocket and took out a couple of fruits. "Your boys must be hungry? I have some fruits we can offer you for the little freedom fighter *sipahees.*"

She almost smiled at their gullibility, and took the fruits from him.

"I would have liked to stay here and personally pass on a message he had given me for every *Jawan*[42] I come across on this road. But I am going back to my village because my mother-in-law, the mother of my great *mujahid*[43] husband, my *Khala*,[44] is suffering from an ailment. I need to hurry to take care of her and tell her that her son is fine."

She paused and waited for the other two to step closer to her, now eager to hear the message for them. "He said to tell you all that he is ready to die one thousand times to liberate our motherland from these *Farangi* devils, and to not cry for him if he lays down his life for the cause. You should all fight to that end too, and be ready to die for these little boys and all our children and future generations."

"Freedom for India or death."

The sepoys got very animated hearing the message and together shouted *Allah O Akbar*[45] and gave the two boys a British style military salute.

Still terrified, but keeping her wits about her, Zeena took leave of the sepoys and joined the rest of the group, waiting for her to continue their journey.

---

42 Soldier.

43 A person involved in a Jihad.

44 Maternal Aunt.

45 Allah is great.

AN ISLAND OF RESPITE

May 1857

It was still dark, and the tall man led the group energetically through the heavily wooded terrain. To speed up their progress, the men had the two boys jump on their backs. They also had to stop a few times to console Safia, who was crying for her murdered *memsahib*. They reached the outskirts of Mahmudabad before the crack of dawn and made it straight to Safia's house. It was a small one-room straw and mud-brick hut with a courtyard surrounded by a high adobe walls.

There was a bare *charpoy* bed with no covering on it. Zeena spread her *burqa* on it and asked the men to put the sleeping boys on it.

As the men were leaving for the town, Zeena addressed the tall one, "Bhai, please sit down and eat these fruits before you go. I can never pay you back for your kindness and for what you have done for my son and me. You acted like a brother to me when you met me, a powerless woman wandering around, not knowing where she was going. I have no words to thank you and Safia for bringing us to your house and providing shelter for us when we had no one to turn to. I will always pray for you. May Allah reward you."

The tall man nodded his head in a gesture of thanks and said, "Sister, we owe our lives to you. Your presence of mind saved us from probable death."

After they had left, Safia brought two cups of water and a container of *suttoo*[46] powder. She gave one cup to Zeena, who took it with gratitude, letting her mix the powder in with the water. She had eaten nothing for almost a day.

"You don't know this, but this is not my son," Safia said to Zeena in a hushed tone.

"I figured he is a *gora* child."

"Yes, I am their *Ayah*.[47] My husband is a *Sais*[48] by profession. We are all Captain Peter Sahib's servants. When we heard they had killed him at the parade ground last evening, we begged the *memsahib*[49] to leave with us so she can hide in our home until things got better. She was reluctant about leaving her home, thinking the *gora* soldiers with the loyal native *Sipahees* will easily overpower the troublemakers. May Allah forgive her soul. She was a kind lady."

"Later on, we saw a suspicious-looking sipahee walking around in the residential section of the cantonment, near their home. We suspected he was checking out the area. Worried that he would be back with more to cause trouble in our area, I helped the boy and the *memsahib* change into *desi*[50] clothes and put a *burqa* on her. Things got worse when some native *sipahees* broke into our home. We hid our *memsahib* and the boy in a large trunk used for storing grains, telling the rogues that she had taken her child to Simla[51] for the summer. Luckily, they believed us and only took away a basket of ripe mangoes and guavas from the table. They moved to the next house where they found Captain Willis' *memsahib* and her two children hiding in their basement. They were both killed on the spot, along with their four *desi* servants who

---

[46] Powdered ground cereal, usually taken mixed in water for quick energy.
[47] Nanny.
[48] Stableman, horse trainer.
[49] European Lady.
[50] Indian native.
[51] Hill station which later became the summer capital for the Raj.

tried to protect their masters. Their house was set on fire."

"Seeing this, our *memsahib* decided to leave with us. We left from the back door and took the back way out of the cantonment where we met you. Captain Peter Sahib had told her that if anything happens to him, she should find her way to Rampur. When you met us, we were on the way to Rampur to ask the Nawab for his protection."

"What is the child's name?"

"I don't know, but everyone calls him Bumpy, because when he was young, he was always running into things."

There was a knock on the door. It was the *Sais* looking quite elated. "The Nawab Sahib's camp is near here with a huge entourage of family and friends on his annual hunt. He has opened up his camp for those escaping from Meerut Cantonment."

"How about the native rebel *Sipahees*? Did you see any?" Zeena asked the *Sais*.

"I saw many native *Sipahees*, but they are all here accompanying their *Gora Sahibs*, all loyal company soldiers. I spoke with two who accompanied their junior Sahibs for protection from Meerut. They are terrified of how bad things maybe for their families living there. The mutineers are in control of almost all the buildings in the *chaoonee*. Only a few of the loyal *Sipahees* and officers are left barricaded in the remaining buildings. Most of the others have fled. About 50 have been killed, including Colonel Finnis, Captain Willis and Captain Peter sahib."

Hearing of Colonel Finnis' death, Zeena's heart missed a heartbeat, but she managed to keep her self-control. Knowing where their loyalties lay, she decided to come clean with them.

"You know, I was also not completely truthful to you. I didn't know what side you were on. My husband is the head mason at the *chaoonee*. He was supervising the construction at the new barracks and the training ground stadium."

"Are you Raja's wife?" The *Sais* asked.

"Yes."

"I used to see him sometimes at Colonel Sahib's house. He is a good man. Is this your son?"

"Yes, his son, Zaheer Babar. We call him Peeru." She didn't know how she could have let that out. Safia picked up on it. "He is your son too!" Safia interjected. "I hope I will soon have a son like your son. We have been married for a year and *Sais ji* wants to have four sons and four daughters, so we can have a big family when we are old."

"*Insha-Allah*, you will. You both are the kindest people I have met. Allah helps those who are kind to other humans." She was relieved that the discussion had moved on from Peeru's parentage, and to move it further along she asked, "*Sais ji*, did you find out what time the boatman starts his river crossing service?"

"Yes. He starts right after *Fajr*, but today, since all going to the left bank and none coming back, he sets only sail when there is a customer. We can go anytime, but it's safe to stay here for as long as you want."

"I think we should start soon. We need to bring Bumpy to the camp before anyone finds out."

"Let Peeru and Bumpy sleep a while, and you take some rest too. When they are up, we can feed them and go across the river. Safia and I will come with you. Since Colonel Finnis' *memsahib* is the only one left who knows Bumpy, we will leave him with her. I know she is already there at the camp with her children. They came last night. The boatman said he ferried her with her three children, her servants, two *gora* officers, four company *sipahees*, and one other man, last night. Nawab of Rampur had sent his men to the dock to receive her. He didn't know who the one *desi* was, but he went back to Meerut with the company men."

Zeena knew Raja had accompanied Mrs. Finnis and her children, to the river crossing. She couldn't stop thinking of Raja, where he could be, what he might have faced, hoping he had gotten away from the rioters. Maybe he had returned home and not finding them there, looked for them at the Nautch House. She missed him so much. Her body ached, not from the arduous trip, but from wanting to be with him.

She was upset at Raja for leaving them. "Why did you have to go to Finnis Sahib? You had already delivered his memsahib and the children to safety. It was time for you to think of your family and your safety. You should have listened to my pleas."

"What am I thinking? He is a man of his word. He would never turn on his word, and he had to go back. Allah, please bring him back to me. This time, I will never let him go. Please, please, Allah!"

THE NAWAB
May 1857

As they crossed the river to the left bank, Zeena saw the company carts waiting to carry them to the Nawab's camp. They got on the two carts and started towards the encampment. Bumpy had cried constantly, searching for his mother since he had woken up. Nothing could bring peace to him as he looked closely at every woman in a *burqa* on the boat, hoping to find his mother.

When they reached the camp, Bumpy saw Mrs. Finnis' children playing. He stopped crying and started waving and calling them. The Finnis children ran over and hugged him and they all started talking loudly. Peeru woke up from the noise. The Finnis children recognized him too and took them both to where they were playing.

There were chicken, lambs, and a small dog in the play area. Pretty soon, it looked like any other backyard of a home with kids playing, laughing, and throwing a ball at each other. Before Peeru went to play with the other kids. Zeena remembered to take off his outside shirt, the shirt with the money sewn in, for safekeeping.

Zeena and Safia waited outside the Mrs. Finnis' tent until they were called in. Zeena saw a distraught woman, whom she could hardly recognize as Mrs. Finnis. She must have been weeping a long time, her face white, like freshly sprouted cotton, drained of blood and life. Seeing Zeena, she got up and came over to her, wrapped her arms around her and let out a loud cry of sorrow. Zeena was completely taken aback by her behavior. Memsahibs never sat with natives, let alone embrace them. She had met Mrs. Finnis many times before and had always found her to be kind, but very formal. Zeena had kept her emotions in check while in the company of others. Hearing Mrs. Finnis crying loudly, she couldn't control herself anymore and broke down. All the servants in the camp were staring at the two and wondering about Zeena and the *memsahib*.

After a few minutes, Mrs. Finnis separated from Zeena and, still holding her hand, moved to her chair. As she sat down, Zeena sat on the floor at her feet, holding her hand with both hands, kissing it, her tears flowing freely.

Zeena composed herself and addressed Mrs. Finnis for the first time. "Thank you, respected Mrs. Finnis. Colonel Finnis has been nothing but the most benevolent and gracious employer to my husband. I cannot find words to express my sorrow for you and your children for this irreplaceable loss. Please accept my sincere condolences on his passing. Since the time I met you and your family, you have always been most kind to us and there was nothing more I could have asked for. Today I see you in this condition and I ask myself, what I can do here and now for you? I see the Nawab Sahib has put his resources at your disposal for your protection and care, but please let me know if there is anything I can do." Zeena was crying again.

"My dear Zeenat, I also don't have any words to thank you and your dear husband, who is more than an employee to us. We could all have died yesterday with my husband, had it not been for Raja informing John about the plan and then escorting me and my family to safety. I would have been happy staying in Meerut and dying there with my husband, but the thought of protecting my young children made my decision to leave Meerut very easy. Please stay with me until we can locate Raja and things get back to normal. That is what I wish for you and your smart little boy."

Zeena kissed her hand and held it there, now crying uncontrollably, wondering if he would ever come back to her. She also had tears of joy mixed in for the relief that Mrs. Finnis had offered her. A servant brought water for Mrs. Finnis, which she took and gestured to bring another glass for Zeena.

A male servant knocked on the makeshift door to ask her if the Nawab could have a few minutes with her. She nodded yes to him, and with a hand gesture dismissed all in the tent to leave. As Zeena got up to leave with all the others, Mrs. Finnis tightened her grip on her hand, signaling her to stay.

Another servant brought in a chair and a small table and placed it next to Mrs. Finnis. There was a low gong outside the door, Zeena got up ready to greet the Nawab with a formal deep bow while Mrs. Finnis stayed seated.

Nawab Sayyid Muhammad Yusef Ali Khan *Bahadur*[52] of Rampur entered the tent, followed by a female servant dressed in black from top to bottom, carrying a basket of fruits and a tall jug of *sherbet*.[53] He motioned her to place them on the table and leave. He nodded at Zeena, who was still bowing in the traditional Mughal fashion. She got back up and quietly took her place at the feet of Mrs. Finnis. He was a very tall, clean-shaven, handsome man of about forty with a traditional Rampur handlebar mustache. He was dressed in a plain black Bengali silk *Angarkha*,[54] a black cap, and black *Saleem-Shahi*[55] shoes. Cognizant of European traditions of dressing in black at bereavements, he was attempting to show his support for her grief.

He took a seat next to Mrs. Finnis, his thoughtful face reflecting sorrow.

He sat quietly with his head down, letting the gloomy air in

---

52 Nawab of Rampur 1855-1865.

53 A red sweet fruit-based summer drink of Turkish origins.

54 Traditional outer garment.

55 Traditional slip-on shoes worn by men of higher standing.

the room persist. Mrs. Finnis, having composed herself, addressed him, "Your Excellency Nawab Sahib *Bahadur*, I am most grateful for your kindness in sheltering us at this time of great danger to me and my children. You have been a constant friend and supporter of the company for a long time before you ascended the throne of the great state of Rampur. We are fortunate to call you a partner in helping India develop into a modern industrial nation."

"Thank you, Mrs. Sarah Finnis. Please forgive me for my intrusion in your private quarters in your moment of sorrow. I am here to show my deepest heartfelt sadness at the loss of your brave gentleman husband and my friend Colonel John Finnis. May he rest in peace. He was a man of most honorable character, in words and actions. A soldier at heart, he was respected, admired, and above all, loved by his soldiers, European and natives. We will all miss him."

Mrs. Finnis nodding her head slowly as he continued, "Please believe me when I say, without hyperbole, he was an irreplaceable friend for the state of Rampur, and we all mourn in his passing with you."

There was quiet in the room for a few minutes with everyone thinking about their losses, their uncertain futures, and where it will all will lead to. Then the Nawab clapped his hands lightly, the Mughal way of calling for servants. The black-clad female servant entered the room with a few fine crystal glasses. She poured the *sherbet* into two cups and offered the first one to Mrs. Finnis and the next to the Nawab. Mrs. Finnis took a couple of short sips and nodded her head in thanks.

The Nawab Sahib followed suit and took a small sip of the cool red drink, then clearing his throat, he continued, "Mrs. Sarah Finnis, I am here to invite you to stay at the Royal Guest House, built by my great grandfather and founder of the state of Rampur, as my personal guest. You can stay there as long as you like with your children, your servants, and any friends in need of shelter from these unfortunate events threatening peace, stability, and prosperity in India."

He had learned the company line very well indeed.

She replied, "Your Excellency Nawab Sahib *Bahadur*, I will always be in your debt for your thoughtfulness and generous offer to shelter me, my children, and members of my staff at the Royal Guest House. I accept your kind invitation with gratitude and respect from myself and my children."

The Nawab acknowledged with a nod and said, "Preparations are underway for all of us in the hunting party to leave early tomorrow morning." He pointed to the girl who had been serving them since their arrival and continued, "My *kaneez*[56] here will be at your service to coordinate with my *wazir*[57] to get you ready for the journey tomorrow."

"Your Highness Nawab Sahib, words fail me to express my gratitude for your kindness and care you have shown for us. I have nothing here to pack. We left at short notice when the news of trouble came. One of my husband's most loyal cantonment workers, Raja the stonemason, had brought news of an uprising in the cantonment planned for the next day and had suggested to Colonel Sahib to send us here for safety. You were most kind to accept our presence at this encampment without hesitation."

Then, putting her hand on Zeena's shoulder, she said, "This is Zeenat, the stonemason Raja's wife. She arrived this morning with her child and a British toddler whose life she saved. They walked all night on back roads to get here."

The Nawab was now looking at Zeena, nodding his head lightly. "Where is he now, your husband?" He asked her directly.

"*Aalijah*[58] Janab Nawab Sayyid Yusef Ali Khan Sahib

---

[56] Female servant.

[57] Minister.

[58] High Exalted.

Bahadur of Rampur, *Aadaab arz hai.*[59] My *sartaj*[60] and my master Raja Taimur Babar, was with Colonel John Finnis all morning yesterday, he came to see me just before Zuhr.[61] He was in a great haste and wanted to warn me of the danger lurking in the city. After giving me instructions to follow in the event of further escalation, he returned to help Colonel John Finnis without having lunch. That was the last I saw him. I don't know what happened to him. May Allah have mercy on him and protect him from any harm."

She had a lot of poise and etiquette for a woman of her class and the Nawab found her performance strangely charming.

"*Ameen*," he said under his breath, then continued, "He must be a great man to put his life on the line for others. I will ask my *wazir* of security to locate him and safely get him out of Meerut."

Seeing the Nawab getting up, Mrs. Finnis and Zeena followed suit. Zeena bowed down to her knees, glad that the Nawab Sahib will send men to rescue her beloved. She wanted to believe that he was alive.

"I ask for your leave now, but please let my *kaneez* know if there is anything you need to make your stay more comfortable, while we figure out a way to bring back Colonel Sahib's remains so they can be interred properly with full military honors." He left the tent leaving behind his black-clad *kaneez*.

Mrs. Finnis turned to Zeena, "My dear Zeenat," she said, "I have also asked the junior officers who escaped from the cantonment last night to send out word to the loyal natives to locate Raja and to let him know you and your son are here safe with me and that you are eager to hear of his safety. I am sure we will hear from him soon." Then she added, "As you would say, *Insha-Allah*."

---

59 Salutations.

60 Term for a dear husband (Literal. Crown of my head).

61 Midday prayer time.

"*Insha-Allah*" repeated Zeena, but she was feeling her heart sinking faster than a stone dropped in a pool of water.

***

They left for Rampur very early the next morning. The Nawab's caravan was a moving spectacle. A vanguard of about 20-25 brightly clad, well-armed *sipahees* led the march on foot, with several drummers following behind them. They were there to drum out orders from the Nawab to his men in the caravan. The Nawab of Rampur rode in a colorful *howdah*[62] firmly fitted on the back of the biggest elephant, with his favorite wife and his heir. Protecting the rear and flanks of the Nawab's transport were 20 *sipahees* on horsebacks. Behind these personal guards of the Nawab came the displaced European families and their servants in horse-drawn carts that had brought Mrs. Finnis and her group the previous morning. A few mounted junior English officers on East India Company horses escorted the European family group, comprising Mrs. Finnis and her companions and servants and another escaping family. Other freshly escaped loyal company sepoys were marching behind this group. The rest of the caravan followed, which included the Nawab's many *wazirs*, their families, and servants with cows, goats, load-bearing donkeys, bullock carts, and implements for hunting. The rear of the caravan was protected by another 30 well-armed mounted soldiers who could move around the caravan quickly in case of trouble.

An impressive sight for the onlooker and well-wishers of the mighty Nawab, but a warning, in the form of a mighty castle moving through, to his detractors and those who may dare to lay a claim on his holdings or hope to extract some undeserved gains from him.

Sitting with Peeru in Mrs. Finnis' horse drawn carriage in this fabulous spectacle of a hunting caravan on the march, the only thing on Zeena's mind was when and how will she find Raja, or will she spend the rest of her life searching for him.

---

[62] A canopy seat for riding an elephant.

She started praying, "O Allah, please help me find Raja. Please help all these soldiers who are looking for him. I cannot live without him. Please, please don't make Peeru grow up without his father."

HUMAYUN

1920-1964

IN THE TIGER'S DEN
1920

Humayun Babar, thirteen, was fascinated with trains that passed by a few blocks from his home. From early in his life, whenever he felt the rumble of a passing train, he would run up to the rooftop to watch it barreling to some place fascinating. There was something captivating about the lumbering giant locomotive that mesmerized him. He would stay there long after it had disappeared into the horizon. He never had the good fortune of being carried away on the friendly giant to that exotic land.

Walking back from his *Khala's* home, he would sit by the railway tracks to watch the trains pass, a scene that always stopped him dead in his tracks. The locomotive struggled to pull a series of carriages loaded with goods and people, people always looked so happy to be on the train. He would wave to them, wishing he was also on the train, happy like them, going to some place far away. The train would soon be gone, and he would be dragged back to reality. And thus, the cycle of his unhappy, wretched existence continued unabated.

He entered Baker's Street, his head down, walking slowly, oblivious to his surroundings as if nothing mattered except the train he had just seen passing by, full of all those lucky people. As always, he was imagining being on it looking out the window, leaving his unhappy world behind.

The street was full of activity, and a cacophony of sounds and smells filled the air. Everyone was in a hurry to get somewhere, well, almost everyone, except for the hangers-on. They stand on street corners passing their time, usually in a group of three or four, watching the world go by. He never understood why one would hang around on a street corner for hours, aimlessly wasting time as if there was nothing more important than being a voyeur of events on the street corner.

There was the occasional fishmonger, carrying unprocessed fresh river fish in enormous baskets that kept him off balance with their weight. His burden would be reduced as he sold off his inventory, but summer was not a good time to sell fish in India. The heat played havoc on the raw fish with nothing to keep them from going bad. It was a common belief in these parts of India that consuming fish in months without letter 'r' in their names could cause the diner to come down with a stomach ailment, so only a few people bought fish in summer. Not a good season to be a fishmonger.

Unlike the fishmonger, *behishtees*[63] loved summer, for it was their peak business season. They were the town water carriers, delivering water to home in large *mushucks,* or water bags made from cleaned out whole goat or lamb skin with the four legs and other openings sewn up. Only the neck was left open to fill or empty it. A strong, puncture-proof bag for carrying water.

There were cows, sacred cows, roaming around, holding up rickshaws, *ekkas*, bullock carts, and other traffic. No one could raise a finger at them, lest they become the cause 0f the next communal riot. Fearless monkeys sat on rooftops and high ledges, watching and waiting for an opportunity to pinch a banana or other food item from the hands of its preoccupied owner.

A *behishtee* with a full *mushuck*, acting as if he owned the road, bumped him hard. Using the weight of the water as an excuse, he yelled at Humayun for coming in his way.

---

63 Water Carriers (literal: destined for heaven).

Homes on both sides hanging over the street were old, with patches of peeling, chalky whitewash and cracked adobe and plaster, displaying a lack of resources of the owners, for this was a middle and lower-middle class, mostly Muslim, part of Meerut. The area still carried scars from the 1857 Indian sepoy mutiny.

Some homes had a basket hanging next to their door or from an upper story for their usual daily purchases. Pre-approved peddlers working on informal credit plans would fill the basket with vegetables, fruit, or meat, followed by a hard knock on the customer's door to let them know their basket was now full. Any delay by the customer in picking up the merchandise would invite the attention from the rooftop monkeys and an emptied basket.

Humayun lived with two half-siblings, a stepmother, and fading memories of his mother in these lanes. His domineering father, *Pir Sahib*,[64] a *munshi*[65] to the court of the state of Safpahar, was usually gone for months at a time. His family carried on as if nothing mattered with the father absent most of their lives. He was a distant father-king of the household, who, when present, would pass judgments on things that did not necessarily need any verdict from him, things like the boys' life plans, the girl's marriage prospects, the family's excessive food spending, and most often, their afterlife prospects and how to improve them

Abba says, by strictly adhering to His prescribed religious path.

It was common knowledge that his father was a great *Pir*[66] in Safpahar, and a good portion of his income came from his disciples. The very wealthy feudal Nawab of Safpahar was his most devoted follower. He had also heard that his father in his youth was a minor hustler who had figured out how to be a real *naukar*[67] to the *Gora Sahibs*. That was how he had laid the foundation for his very comfortable and prosperous life. He didn't believe everything

---

[64] Sir, Mister.

[65] An accountant.

[66] Religious spiritual guide.

[67] Servant.

he heard from people, and certainly not the vile stories about his father.

As Humayun turned the corner to his home's back street, he caught sight of his father's fully saddled, but tired horse next to his fancy rickshaw parked amongst some cows and goats. Whatever was occupying his mind was lost at the sight of that brightly painted human-powered machinery adorned with Allah's commandments and random verses from God and man.

Having a mode of personal transport was considered a great luxury and a status symbol, two personal modes of transportation elevated you to the top. The horse was used for long distance journeys while the rickshaw was used for the Pir Sahib's visits around town, mostly to the homes of his wealthy *mureeds.*[68] All others would visit him and wait outside his house, sometimes for hours, until he was ready to meet them and to listen to their woes. The two modes of transportation always followed him, to be at his beck and call.

As Humayun got closer to the back door of his compound, he could see a line already forming outside the side entrance.

There were mothers with ailing children, young men with something on their minds, and old men and women who could barely stand even with the help of their canes. The very elderly were there with their sons and daughters, while others, accompanied only by the hope that Pir Sahib may have a blessing, a *dua*,[69] a solution for what troubles them. Some, too frail to stand, had already given up and were sitting on the bare ground. A few crying with pain, while others quietly bore physical and mental anguish under the blazing tropical sun. He saw a few mothers with their daughters of marriageable age likely there for help from the Pir Sahib in finding a suitable match.

His first instinct was to turn around and leave, go back to his *Khala's* house and try to lie low for a few days until Pir Sahib

---

[68] Followers or disciples.

[69] Prayers.

had left. He didn't want to face the grilling from his father about what he had done to improve his hereafter and why, after living in the comfort of a home with three free meals a day, he had not improved his grades in school, or found work. He knew his father would be extra caustic this time, as his older brother was returning after graduating with a BA degree from Oxford University.

Or was it Oxford College? I wonder what life is like in Vilayat.[70]

"How could you be so careless and inconsiderate of your parents by not trying to make something of yourself?" His father would ask him at first glance.

Shershah, his half-brother, who was about ten years older, was the child everyone wanted their children to be like. He loved his brother but was sick of hearing about Shershah wherever he went.

Aren't you proud of your brother?

When is he coming back?

What does he like to eat?

Has Pir Sahib picked a bride for him?

What an intelligent and hardworking student! His education expenses were all paid for with a scholarship from Company Bahadur.[71]

Would a Vilayati school accept you if Pir Sahib pulled some strings?

His *Khala* was the only one who would ask him about him, his day, if he had he eaten yet. She would mend holes in his clothing, set up a bath, and help him clean up, giving him a coconut oil head massage to make him smarter, and putting kohl in his eyes to improve his eyesight. She would tell stories about his mother, how much she loved him, and how she cared for him before she passed.

His mother died when he was seven. Shershah was Pir Sahib's first child, whose mother had succumbed to a serious infection after childbirth. Pir Sahib married Humayun's mother within months of his first wife's death. She was the only mother

---

[70] Britain in Urdu.

[71] Deferential term to the East India Company.

Shershah had known, and she cared for him as her own for 17 years before she, too, passed away.

After her death, a middle-aged lady stayed with them for months to take care of them. Her name was Zeenat Khatoon, a respectable lady of substance and wealth. She had raised their father after his parents were killed in the 1857 mutiny. His grandfather, a lay stonemason, wanted Peeru to be educated when he grew up, so he had hired Zeenat Begum to teach Peeru to read and write very early in his childhood. After the parents were killed, she took him under her care and raised him as her own. She did not have any children of her own. As he was growing up, she made sure that the orphan never felt the effects of the deep chasm left by the premature death of his parents. Peeru grew up to Pir Sahib.

Zeenat Begum tried to keep Shershah and Humayun happy by doing everything for them herself, making homemade sweets, putting them to bed with bedtime stories. She instilled a love of reading in him and his brother. He wished she had stayed longer than the two years or so that she had.

A wave of consciousness hit him, bringing him back into reality as he felt the hair at his nape stand, warning him of danger ahead and to be careful, a sensation he had previously experienced.

He didn't want to face his father, not now, not with Shershah coming back. Pir Sahib's presence in town meant the imminent arrival of Shershah.

Abba must be here to welcome Shershah. I must leave.

As he began to retrace his steps to the only caring and loving house in the world where he could hide for a few days from his father when someone called his name.

Hearing that shrill, nasally voice, he froze and slowly closed his eyes, wishing he was far away from here. He wished he had not entered the back street. He wished he had taken a longer bath at his *Khala's*.

He wished… he wished...

ME AND MY BROTHER

1920

Humayun's tainted and hardened view of life and existence resulted from a very tough childhood after his mother's passing. He had lost his innocence early on, thanks to a tough father, a cruel stepmother, and circumstances. His life was all about day-to-day survival. He didn't expect anyone to offer a helping hand if he tripped and fell, but when it all became unbearable, he would make his way to his aunt's house. He tried very hard not to bring his sorrows to her and make her cry. That was the only temporary shelter left for him.

Her husband, a lowly clerk in a local office, after returning from work would take him to the mosque for Asr[72] prayers. After *Namaz,*[73] he would make sure to drop Humayun off at his father's house, letting his stepmother know, in no uncertain terms and cruel words, what he thought of her parenting skills for letting the child wander off to other people's homes to eat their food and bother them. The stepmother would withhold the scraps that had been set aside for his dinner as punishment for the berating she took from "that nasty ogre of a man."

***

"Hello?" He heard the voice again. Even though it had

---

[72] Late afternoon prayers. 3rd of 5 daily prayers for Muslims.

[73] Prayers.

been a few years, he still recognized the shrill nasally voice of Shershah.

"Where you off to, brother?"

"You didn't come to the station to receive me."

Humayun turned around slowly, looked up, and shrunk in his worn-out slippers. Shershah was standing on the balcony with his hands stretched wide on the old, rusted metal railing. He had an unfamiliar look on his face.

Is that the look of long-lost friends meeting again?

A glint of love in his eyes, or just contempt disguised as pity for a lost soul which happened to belong to his half-brother?

Shershah had grown up from the last time Humayun saw him waving from a Calcutta-bound train a few years back. He seemed to have changed in so many ways that Humayun could not count. He had changed his appearance, possibly to make himself look less Indian, by dressing up in a starched white shirt and dark pants.

Bhai wearing pantaloons? Queen Victoria, or is it King George, must have put a spell on him while he was there. He looks like a Vilayati now.

Humayun's confusion about the sovereign of the United Kingdom echoed his poor knowledge of current affairs and history, or geography, or math, and other subjects. Unlike Shershah, he was a hopeless under-performer in class.

What would have Abba[74] *thought of Bhai dressing up in Farangi attire?*

He is still dressed in that foreign garb, which must mean Abba has approved his new look and his short Farangi beard.

To Humayun, it really didn't matter how Shershah was dressed or how he had changed. What mattered most to him was to quickly find a way out of the position he was finding himself in.

He quickly recovered from his daze and found words.

"*Salaam* Bhai, I didn't know you were arriving today. I was coming back from *Khala's* and saw Abba's horse and knew he was

---

[74] Father.

here to receive you. I turned to go to the flower shop, for some garlands for you." He lied.

Shershah liked his response and replied, "*Waleykum As Salaam*, Humayun. I am so glad to see you. I missed you so much while I was there. I was actually lonely without you. I didn't miss the others though, only you."

He jumped down from the balcony to the boundary wall to the ground. This was their quick exit path when trying to avoid having to face Pir Sahib and his snap judgment machine, holding *Halaqas*[75] in the drawing-room downstairs.

This was news to him, joyful news. His brother cared so much for him, more than anyone else. He didn't believe his ears, and acted like he didn't hear what Shershah had said.

"What did you say, *Bhai*?"[76]

Shershah, now standing right next to him, repeated the sentence. Humayun's heart was filled with pride and joy at hearing this message again. It was as if spring had suddenly descended, lifting all the surrounding darkness and kicking off the start of a permanently happy life. Growing up, he had always cherished Shershah, trying to follow in his path, but his love was never reciprocated. These few words erased all the bitter memories of trying to make Shershah happy and proud of him. This was absolutely the first time Shershah had expressed such warm brotherly feelings for him, and he was over the moon.

He was already planning long talks with Shershah about everything and nothing, like he imagined brothers do. With tears in his eyes, he stepped forward with his arms outstretched to hug him. All he got in his outstretched arms was a whiff of air from Shershah, who had quickly moved back and offered a sweaty, limp hand to shake.

"Men don't hug," Shershah said seriously, "it's what women do. Men shake hands with their heads held high and a

---

[75] Religious education and discussion sessions.

[76] Brother.

straight face. Smiling is a sign of weakness, Humayun. Keep a straight face even when you are happiest in your life, as you are now seeing me. Remember this - men don't show emotions, crying is for women!"

Men don't show emotions. Crying is for women.

"I don't want to soil my Savile Row tailored shirt with whatever excrements you are carrying around on your ugly loose *desi* excuse for clothing. If you want to move up in this world, get some better clothing, Western clothing. Britain will be greater and greater for the rest of this century. I wouldn't be surprised if they ended up ruling all of Asia. So, you need to be prepared for it, otherwise, you will get nowhere, like all the other worms that live in this town."

Humayun was taken aback. He did not know what hit him and felt whip-lashed by the talk of brotherly love and then the sudden turn to such nasty caustic comments.

Which one are you, Bhai? You must have learned this in Vilayat. You were not like this before.

I liked you better when you were always trying to ignore me.

Shershah continued, "I picked up a pair of pants and a shirt for you from the Army-Navy store in Calcutta before I got on the train to come home. Once you get a decent job, you can pay me back."

Wiping the sweat from Shershah's clammy handshake on his side, Humayun turned towards the backyard, which had two giant mango trees towering over it.

***

It was a few days later when Shershah was showing him his *Vilayati* BA degree that Humayun learned he had also completed several courses on human psychology and became an active member of a club for Indian students and businessmen to develop their social skills, The East & West India Club. The club and its leadership, mostly former stockholders and retired officers from the old East India Company, did all they could to protect and maintain the status quo of the colony. They did this by endeavoring to Anglicize its Indian members and mentoring them for successful careers in government or business when they returned home. The club thrived on supplying white, and later, native Indians, to the venerated Indian Civil Service.

Indian students from resourceful families studying in England were encouraged to become student members of the club. It was promoted to them as the place to learn "how to make friends, influence people and win arguments." The Indian students had come up with an Urdu-English hybrid nickname, derived from the club's stated goals -How to Make Friends, influence people, and Win arguments. So, The East & West India Club became the "HumFew[77] Club", and the members, the HumFewers. The nickname meaning (Us Few), also pointed to the exclusiveness of its membership.

---

[77] Hum means we, but also used for I in Indian provinces of UP & Bihar.

UNDER THE MANGO TREES
1920

As they stepped into the large backyard on the way to join their father's gathering, Shershah looked up at the mango trees loaded with mangoes in all stages of ripening. He had forgotten how full a mango tree gets around this time. The fruit-laden trees were spreading their sweet, inviting aroma in the air. A few parrots were flying around looking for the juiciest fruits on the trees to quench their thirst. At a loss for words, Shershah just shook his head in admiration and said, "Let's go. He is waiting for us."

Malka Roshan Ara and Ayaz Babar, their younger half-siblings, still in their school uniforms, were running around playing with other children in the cool, oversized shade of the mango trees. A youthful *Ayah* was keeping a watchful eye on the kids while the *Chowkidar* nearby was keeping his eyes on the *Ayah* with keen interest.

Roshan Ara, seeing Humayun, ran up to him and gave him a big, excited hug. Her hands were dripping with the juice from a big, half-eaten golden mango that left orange and yellow blotches on his shirt after the hug, but he didn't mind. She was his little sister.

"Bhaiya, please eat this, it is so good, I want you to try it. It is soooo sweet." He couldn't resist her and took a big bite of the mango. It was indeed very sweet and juicy, and the juice rolled down the sides of his mouth.

He wiped his mouth with his sleeve and returned the remaining portion to her. "I have never tasted a sweeter mango in my entire life, Roshan Ara. It is so good! But my little sister is so much sweeter than the sweetest mango in the whole wide world. You better eat it before I change my mind and eat it all."

"What about me? Don't I get a bite too?" said Shershah, not used to being left out of anything.

Roshan Ara looked at him with disdain and said, "The mango is too juicy and will spoil your shirt," and walked away. Shershah let out a loud, embarrassed laugh as he watched her run back to her brother.

Unlike Roshan Ara, Humayun could not walk away from Shershah. There was no escape, now that Shershah had caught him trying to sneak away to avoid facing Pir Sahib. Reluctantly, he followed Shershah into the drawing room. Pir Sahib was surrounded, as usual, by several followers and *mureeds*. He seemed to be in a trance listening to one of them, a Masjid *Imam*[78] from Mahmudabad, reciting Arabic verses from the Quran. His recitation style was more Indian than Arabic-the language of the book.

As the recitation ended, Pir Sahib raised his head and saw his two sons standing side by side. He motioned them to sit down, which Shershah obediently followed by dropping down to sit where he was. Humayun didn't move. Pir Sahib, not one to be disobeyed, stared hard at Humayun, expecting full compliance.

"*Aadab* [79]Abba, I didn't know you had arrived. I hope you had a comfortable journey. It has been almost five months since you visited."

"Shut up and sit down. Can't you see we are in the middle of a *Quranic dars*?[80] How can you be so disrespectful of our holy

---

[78] A Mosque leader and care taker, who also leads all the prayers.

[79] Salutations.

[80] Study/ lesson.

book and its teachings?"

"Abba, I waited to speak until after the respected Imam Sahib had finished his sweet and heart-rending recitation. I never forget what you teach us. I learned from you to not speak or interrupt when someone is reciting the Holy Quran. May Allah punish me if I bring disrespect to the recitation of our beloved Quran Sharif." Before Pir Sahib could say anything, he added, "I had not seen you after you arrived today, and our Rasool Allah commands us to greet elders and youngsters with *Salaam* when you come across them. I was just following his commandments, which you have so lovingly taught me."

Humayun was no lawyer in training, but his defense was incontestable. Pir Sahib could not counter it without losing his standing in the eyes of the faithful, watching this father-son interaction with interest.

Reeling from Humayun's disobedience, Pir Sahib found himself in a tricky situation. By further reprimanding Humayun, he would be seen as minimizing the Prophet's message, considered as blasphemy by some. Thinking he would deal with this disobedience later, he turned to the Imam and said, "*Masha-Allah*,[81] see what good Muslims my youngsters are. They will even stand up to their father to follow the commandments of Allah and Rasool."

He then turned to Humayun and said, "*Waleykum As Salaam*. Now sit and listen for more lessons to remember and follow."

The gaggle of followers broke into shouts of *Subhan Allah*, *Masha-Allah*, and *Allah O Akbar* in praise of this precocious teenager.

Humayun quietly joined his seated brother, with no signs of this small, ephemeral victory on his face. He knew his father a lot better than anyone in the room.

Pir Sahib cleared his catarrhal sinus with a loud air-sucking throat-clearing cough to call his audience back to attention. All the

---

[81] What Allah has willed.

small conversations that had started after Humayun's performance came to a quick halt. Pir Sahib waited another minute before turning to Imam Sahib and asked him to carry on with the rest of the plan for the gathering. The Imam called a young man by the name of Qutlugh Mirza to come closer. A well-dressed young man with a confident look on his face got up from the back of the room and came over by Pir Sahib and the Imam.

"*Masha-Allah*, Imam Sahib. Is this young man the lucky groom of your daughter?" Pir Sahib, saying *Mubarak*, *Mubarak*, extended his right hand towards him. Qutlugh Mirza clasped it with both hands, dropped to his knees, and kissed the extended hand with reverence. Pir Sahib was starting to say something but decided not to, as Qutlugh Mirza had gotten back up on his feet quickly and was now towering over him and the Imam.

As everyone looked on, Qutlugh Mirza put his hand in his side pocket and fished out a small red and gold brocade pouch. He offered it to Pir Sahib with both hands, his head lowered respectfully. At this, the Imam interjected, "Pir Sahib, Qutlugh Mirza's father passed away last winter, he is the oldest son, with his mother, two younger brothers, and three unmarried sisters to take care of." Pir Sahib, ignoring the comment, took the bag and pocketed it quickly.

He wanted to move on when Qutlugh Mirza spoke for the first time. "Pir Sahib, thank you very much for your kind referral of Imam Sahib's daughter to my mother. My father had never discussed this proposal with either my mother, myself, or any of his siblings before he left us for his eternal abode, the afterlife, where we shall all have to go one day and face our creator to share with Him a tally of all our good deeds, as well as getting a reckoning for all our sins. May Allah protect us all from sins, large and small." His head was still lowered, but his eyes were fixed on Pir Sahib's face.

Qutlugh Mirza continued, "Despite this, there was no reason to doubt your word, Pir Sahib, the word of such a religious scholar. The respected Imam Sahib, his daughter, my mother, and I are all here to thank you in person for your kind help with arranging for my wedding. I don't want to take too much more of your time, but my mother, who is sitting amongst the women in the next room and listening to your teachings, requests you to do a special prayer for me to have a male child and preferably more. She wouldn't be in such a hurry to have grandchildren if Imam Sahib's daughter's childbearing years weren't ending soon. At age 23, she doesn't have much time left to bear many children."

Having already received the *Nazrana*,[82] Pir Sahib was bored out of his mind and wanted this to end. He immediately raised both hands in prayers and started praying for a long, happy married life and many male children for the couple. After finishing the brief prayers, Pir Sahib dismissed the group and retired to his private dining room with the Imam Sahib and others, including Shershah.

As an after-thought, he turned to Humayun and told him to join them.

Humayun knew he would hear from Pir Sahib about what happened earlier, possibly with a thrashing in the name of disobedience to elders, but for now, he was looking forward to joining his father for lunch; he couldn't remember the last time having a meal with Pir Sahib.

---

[82] Monetary offering.

A SHADOW IN THE DARK
1920

As Humayun walked behind the others to the dining area, he had a litany of worries and feelings pounding around in his head. He also felt bad for the poor girl being blamed for being too old to bear children.

Qutlugh Mirza, with his innuendos, was very unfair to her. It is Allah's will that he is married to her, and only He will decide how many children she will bear for him. May Allah forgive him for not putting his trust in Him.

He stepped out to wash his hands, as his father would call him out for it. It was common practice to build toilets and bathrooms away from the main living areas, as outhouses, still within the outer boundary walls of the house, usually across a courtyard. There was a small, mud-brick structure at the end of the courtyard, which housed the family toilet, bathroom, and a general wash area, all built in a row inside the small shack with a straw roof. Closer to the main house, there was also a guest toilet at the edge of the courtyard. A group of men stood waiting to use the guest facilities. Seeing the crowd, he walked to the family bathroom.

The outer door leading to the shack was open. Coming into the area from the bright sun, he couldn't make out if there was someone in the facility. The doors to each of the three areas were open. As he waited a few seconds to let his eyes get accustomed to the dark, he thought he saw a shadow and heard a low sob. He saw the outlines of a woman leaning against the wall on his right. She hadn't seen him. As his eyes adjusted to the darkness, he saw a pretty woman, a bride, as evidenced by the heavy jewelry and the makeup she was wearing.

Imam Sahib's daughter, Qutlugh Mirza's bride!

She heard his footsteps and looked startled. Her eyes were red, and the kohl from her eyes was running down her cheeks. With an embarrassed look on her face, she started cleaning her eyes and face with a yellow embroidered silk handkerchief.

He pointed to the washroom and said, "*Salaam Bibi*,[83] please go ahead. Your family must be waiting for you. I will wait."

Without a reply, she walked into the washroom and closed the door behind her, emerging a few minutes later. Her face had been washed, and new kohl and makeup had been applied to cover the signs of anguish. She was now looking more like a new bride.

He gave her the yellow handkerchief she had dropped when she had gone into the bathroom. As he was going in, she said to him, "Wait, what is your name?"

"Humayun Babar. Pir Sahib, who arranged your marriage with Qutlugh Mirza, is my father. "

"Humayun, like the son of Babar, the first Mughal Emperor?"

Humayun nodded to her.

"I had gotten some dust into my eyes, and I came here to wash it out. Thank you for letting me use the washroom first."

"I know the reason for your tears. I was in that room," he said almost flatly, then continued, "I was sorry to hear them dishonor you like that in front of everyone. We are all prisoners of a depraved social system. But don't worry, I won't tell anyone."

She nodded her head and quickly stepped out.

As he walked back to the dining area, he thought about her

---

[83] A term for addressing a young woman, e.g. Miss.

and his father's connection to arranging her marriage.

Was it just for money, or returning a favor to the Imam?

Qutlugh Mirza said that his father had not told anyone, not even his brothers, about agreeing to this marriage before he died.

Did Abba lie? He always teaches us to be truthful. He wouldn't lie for a few coins. Was there another motivation?

'Wallahu Aalam bis Sawaab.[84]

He was seeing cracks in the God-fearing parts of his father's suit of religious armor.

He thought of Zeenat.

She never told us where she lived, or whether Abba visited her like any other son.

She raised Abba after his parents were killed by a mob. It must've been a mob of Indians, as there aren't that many Farangis to form a mob. If my grandparents were killed by an Indian mob, whose side were they on?

Who was she? Like Abba, she also never talked about herself. She was old, but didn't seem much older than him.

How did she know my grandparents? She was rich. She said she didn't have anyone but him. Is Abba going to inherit her wealth?

Maybe she is living in Safpahar, to be near him, even though he has never mentions her.

I wonder where she is now.

Unable to answer any of his own questions at the moment, he hurried to get to the dining area before the food ran out. People were sitting in rows on large *chandnis*[85] spread all around, food was served on silver plates on large *dastar-khwans*[86] spread in front of them. They were all eating, chatting and drinking cool *surahi*[87] water or red *sherbet* in traditional silver bowls.

He sat down next to his brother, who was sweating profusely in the elevated temperature and complaining about the

---

84 Allah knows the facts, Allah knows best.

85 Very large decorated cotton sheets, spread on the ground for people to sit on. Usually quite plush for comfort.

86 Center mats for serving food to a group of people.

87 Earthen water vessel with a narrow top for easy pouring.

spicy dishes and how he was not fond of them.

Having heard Shershah earlier talk of his disgust for Indians, he was now seeing his intolerance for Indian foods.

"Bhai, you have turned into an Anglo-Indian. I will never go to England, I will do whatever I have to, in India."

"Sour grapes?" asked Shershah with a sarcastic smile.

AN ODE TO INDIAN RAILWAYS
1922

Humayun had passed his middle school exams with barely enough marks to get second division in the final examinations. People getting second division marks were usually told to find a clerk position some place, usually a dead-end job with no opportunity for advancement, a low salary, and long hours with no raises for years, leading to an impoverished life with barely enough to feed the family and nowhere to go in emergencies.

These jobs had been created by the British to keep the bulk of otherwise unemployable adult men working, since unemployed men, under foreign rule, start dreaming of a better life in an independent country ruled by one of their own, which can cause problems for the masters. Pir Sahib had a clerk position lined up for him even before he passed his middle school exam, but Humayun had other ideas.

"What do you do all day, Humayun? Why don't you find a job?" Shershah asked Humayun the day after his middle school exams. He was visiting his wife, Sakina Begum, who was at her parents' home, expecting a baby any day.

After returning from England, Shershah had been made an Assistant Commissioner in Balrajpur district in eastern UP[88]

[88] Upper Provinces. (Renamed Uttar Pradesh after independence in 1947).

province. The highest position natives could aspire to in the *Raj*[89] in those days.

Pir Sahib, always eyeing opportunities to rub shoulders with Indian elites, sent a marriage proposal for Shershah to Sakina Begum, a niece of the Nawab of Rampur. The Nawab Sahib loved having prominent government officials in his pocket and having an Assistant Commissioner marry his niece would really work well for him. He accepted the proposal without hesitation.

After the wedding, Shershah spent his holidays at the royal guest house of Rampur state on the Nawab Sahib's open invitation. While there, he would make a trip to the home where he was born and raised, but not for more than a day or two. He didn't want to be reminded of his childhood in that unhappy house. Pir Sahib would pay him a visit in Balrajpur once a year, where he would catch up with him on family affairs, and the state of their farms and other plans.

The past was never brought up or discussed. Shershah had tried to get Pir Sahib to tell him about his childhood, but each time his questions had been snubbed by Pir Sahib with a curt, "Let's stick to now and the future. Leave dormant what is buried in the past."

***

Shershah and Pir Sahib were both in town. They had already finished a long meeting during which no one was allowed to disturb them. The topic was Shershah's new venture, a sugar mill. Sugarcane was the abundant cash crop of Balrajpur district, providing livelihood to thousands of farmers and farm workers. Using his Indian Civil Service connections, Shershah had gotten a permit to set up a sugar mill in town.

He was an employee of the British government. To avoid any appearance of a conflict of interest, he had brought in his uneducated, worthless brother-in-law to be the chief at the mill.

The sugar mill, the only one in the district, prospered even

---

[89] Government (Urdu), specifically for the British rule over the India.

with the idiot brother-in-law running it. Shershah felt the business could be much better if he brought in a challenger to his dull brother-in-law, and naturally, the only person he could think of was Humayun. He came up with a plan to bring Humayun to Balrajpur. With this, he would kill two birds with one stone; improve the mill's profitability and get his lazy brother out of his comfort zone of home.

Together, they called Humayun to the room where they had locked themselves up for most of the afternoon. The hair on Humayun's nape was telling him something was up and so he took a few minutes to think about what they were going to unload on him.

Could it be about putting me to work somewhere as a clerk?

He entered the room. Shershah smiled and pointed to a *dewan* for him to sit down.

Must be something he really wants. He is smiling and wants me to sit down. That has never happened. He must want something really badly.

He kept standing, and before they could say anything, he announced with a fake smile, "*Aadab* Abba and Bhai, I am so happy to see you both here at the same time. I miss the times we all used to be here, together, a big, happy family. I had been waiting for weeks to share my good news with you; I have found a job as an apprentice to the signalman at the Meerut rail station. The pay isn't that good, but the signalman will train me for the job, and if I do well, I will soon be the signalman, as he is retiring in a year."

Pir Sahib and Shershah seemed uninterested in what he had to say, but he continued, "Railway is the new way to travel. It will change the way we travel, and I want to help bring the change to our great country. The Railway offers a faster, safer, more comfortable method of travel for all Indians, rich or poor, as we Indians travel across this magnificent land of ours from the Khyber Pass to the Burmese border."

Ignoring most of what Humayun was saying, Shershah

started his pitch. "Humayun, listen to me. I have found a job for you that's much better than being a scum to another scum. It is in Balrajpur. You will be the head of accounts at a sugar mill, the only one in the region. They will pay you a monthly salary equal to six months what you will get shining the rails at some stupid railway station." He intentionally held back the sugar mill ownership information.

"But Bhai, you know I love Meerut, and I don't want to leave Roshan Ara and Ayaz."

"Would your train-counting job pay you enough to get a place to live? Now that you have passed middle school, Abba thinks you should find a job and get married. Do you think you will be able to afford a home and feed your wife polishing rails and counting trains?"

So they want to ship me off to some dead end village in the middle of nowhere crushing sugarcane at the sugar mill which I know he owns."

That' is not happening.

Shershah continued, "The sugar mill will provide you ample income to save some money for a house when you are married and have children. It is a simple decision that's best for you."

"I don't want to leave Meerut," Humayun said resolutely.

"You will have to find a place to stay, on the day you get your first paycheck." Pir Sahib said getting upset.

"But Abba, this house has many rooms. I can even sleep in the empty room next to the servant's quarters and pay you rent for that."

Pir Sahib didn't like his answer and growled, "Don't be an idiot. It's not about collecting rent. This is about making a man out of you. Listen to this highly educated Assistant Commissioner rather than talking nonsense about the railways and how you are going to help them. They have thousands of people, much smarter and certainly a lot more educated than you, who can do a much better job than you ever will. They don't need help from a person who has just barely passed middle school. The only way you are going to get anywhere in this world is by following the advice of your kind-hearted brother, who has put his job and reputation on the line, helping you find a job at the sugar mill. You know he can lose his job if someone finds out that such a prominent official of the Raj has put in a personal recommendation to get employment for his middle-school-pass brother."

I want nothing to do with a job at a sugar mill far from home.

I will do whatever it takes to find work at the Railway station. It is my goal in life. There I can work to help make those happy travelers happier.

A railway job will give me a chance to travel for free and maybe somewhere, some day, I will meet Zeenat Begum. She holds the keys to Abba's childhood and upbringing. Since he never tells me anything, she is the only one who can answer my questions about him and my grandparents and their lives.

"Abba, I am not being ungrateful, but I want to stay here in Meerut. I can support myself with this job, not shining rails, but as an apprentice to a signalman who controls all the train traffic at Meerut."

Pir Sahib was unimpressed and furious, but before he could say any more. Shershah tried to close the discussion by saying, "Humayun, the position I found for you will not wait for you, as your dream of this railway career fizzles out. You can think about it."

When Humayun stayed quiet, Shershah asked, "When do you start your new job?"

Humayun could only come up a "Soon."

Shershah turned to Pir Sahib, "Abba, can I ask you to be so kind to this upstart to give him a year to get his footing, polishing rails and counting trains, before you throw him out of your house?"

No response from Pir Sahib usually meant he would rather not waste any more time. The deal was done.

"I will never forget your kindness, Bhai," Humayun mouthed to Shershah as he left the room.

The problem was that he didn't know a signalman who was retiring or, for that matter, any signalman, and he definitely didn't have a job. On the bright side, Shershah had gotten him a year to get it done.

HELLO WORLD!
1922

After tricking his father and Shershah into believing that he had a job at the Meerut station, Humayun was worried about how he would be able to back up his claim.

A day later, he was surprised to see Shershah still in Meerut. Shershah took him aside. "So when are you starting your rail polishing job?"

"Bhai, it's not rail polishing. I will be an apprentice under the signalman of Meerut station."

"What is the name of this signalman?"

What does it matter to you?

Are you fishing to trap me?

Does he know?

He must know!

"Bhai, I didn't ask his name. He is the signalman."

"No, there are two signalmen at Meerut station. I spoke with the stationmaster. They don't have any openings for an apprentice."

I need to come up with a plan quickly before I am shipped off to Balrajpur. Time to come clean. Allah save me, so here goes.

"Bhai, I am so thankful to you for getting me off the hook from Abba yesterday. You know how I love this town and don't want to be away from my siblings. Since you have already figured out that I don't have a job here, I can tell you I will visit the nearby stations to see if I can find a job there. There must be a job available. All the young men had been recruited for the war against our Turkish brothers, and many of them had never returned. The *Gora Sahibs* are always sending town criers with drums through Baker's Street and other markets, calling for men to apply for labor and other work in the cantonment. I have even seen some looking for men to work on new railway lines being laid to smaller towns around New Delhi."

"So, are you going to apply for day labor work? It's tough work all day in the sun with not much of an earning?"

"Bhai, please don't tell Abba. I will find something at the station soon. I am sure of it."

"Why don't you come to Balrajpur with me? Stay at my house, meet the manager of the mill, see what the job is all about, and if you don't like it, you can come back."

I need to hold my ground. One slip and I will be in Balrajpur working day and night at the sugar mill. I don't want to even think of that.

"Bhai, I hate saying no to you, but I want to work for the railway, to learn about it and become successful at it. Please, if you can help me, I will always be in your debt. By the way, there has been no occasion to wear the pants and shirt you brought me from Calcutta. I am afraid they may not fit anymore. But don't worry, I will still pay for it from my first salary."

Shershah playfully ruffled his hair. "You can wear the pants and shirt for your interview with the stationmaster at noon tomorrow. Since you were so interested in the railways, I have gotten you an interview with the stationmaster. I saw him this morning; he is a decent man from a village near Balrajpur. Very respectful after I told him who I was. His brother is a matric-pass like you and looking for a job, just like you. He doesn't want to leave his hometown, also, just like you! So, I am thinking I will have him work at the sugar mill, in the position you rejected."

"And…?" Humayun cried out.

"So, I told the stationmaster about you and your interest in working for the Railways. He wants to meet you tomorrow. He will have you start in an apprentice position at the station, different tasks on different days depending on where he needs help. The pay will be very low, like a coolie's salary, but he will try to find something better for you later on. But keep all this to yourself, forever. So, go see him, work on whatever he tells you to do, and learn everything you can, and I am sure you will be fine."

"Bhai, is this true? You are not putting me on, are you?"

"No, have you ever seen me joke?"

"Oh yes, I remember the last time I saw you being a prankster. NEVER!" Humayun was euphoric. "I don't know what to say." He tried to hug his brother and got the same response as before. A whiff of air and a limp, sweaty hand extended for a handshake. Humayun didn't feel bad this time. He took Shershah's hand and started kissing it.

Shershah withdrew his hand quickly. "You remember what I told you?"

"I know, I know, men don't hug; it's what women do. Men shake hands with their heads held high and a straight face. Smiling shows weakness, keep a straight face even when happy. Men don't show emotions, only women do." He rapidly recited Shershah's lessons for success from before.

"Very good. I thought you never paid attention to what I said."

"Bhai, now you know I do. Always!"

"I have to leave in an hour, to see Sakina in Rampur and then leave for Balrajpur tomorrow. Come with me; I'll buy you some cholay snacks and sweets from the tuck shop for you to bring to *Khala* to give her the good news. She will be so happy. And be sure to tell her, I arranged it all for you."

As Shershah started walking, Humayun grabbed him from the back and hugged him hard. Shershah didn't resist the hug this time and reached back with his hand and ruffled his hair again.

***

Being an apprentice to the stationmaster was hard work, long shifts seven days a week, but he paid attention to everything, quickly absorbing the details of the work he was assigned while learning other functions of running a busy main line railway station. He read every book that he could get his hands on about railways, books on engines and electrical currents, and how things work. He found a book about radios and the telegraph and learned that, too. The stationmaster had noticed his work and when the third signalman quit his job to go back to his village; he had no reservations about having Humayun move into that position. Within a year of Shershah's recommendation, Humayun was the junior signalman at Meerut station.

He never let up on the unrelenting pace of his self-education, something he learned from Qaisar *Mian*[90], who he met right after he started the apprenticeship.

Qaisar Mian, a railway guard,[91] was a thoughtful, well-read, older man, who happened to be transsexual.

Transsexuals lived in an Indian society which didn't know how to deal with someone who was different from the accepted norms, so they were looked down upon, ridiculed and, lot of times, subjected to undeserved gratuitous violence just for being different. They tried to hide their reality behind several curtains and keeping low profiles in life.

Qaisar Mian followed a similar pattern of existence. For keeping a low profile, a guard's position on a goods train was perfect for him. There was no passenger contact, and long journeys across India with little human contact. He could hide in his caboose from the world for extended periods of time, with no one missing him. Not that there was anyone who would.

He didn't have a family except two younger brothers. They

---

90 Alternate for Sahib, usually to address youngsters. Also a surname.

91 Person with overall responsibility for a train, they are usually housed in the end caboose or brake van.

were both killed in the Great War, strangers in a foreign land they didn't know, fighting for a cause they didn't believe in, and then buried in places with names they couldn't pronounce.

Above all, he enjoyed the more laid-back schedules of goods trains.

Qaisar Mian developed an empathy for this bright boy with a sad face and a fervent work ethic. Every so often, his train would stop at Meerut, loading and unloading cargo. Goods trains were known as a guard's palace. They ran at his pleasure, and never moved until he had given an all-clear signal, regardless of what the ground signals showed.

Qaisar Mian always had plenty of time for Humayun. He would buy tea and biscuits from the platform shops, and they would talk. Besides teaching him about the business of managing and running trains, he also taught him the basics of human relations and the art of dealing with people, which Humayun found fascinating.

"A person's mother tongue is very dear to them. Try to use their language when dealing with them. If you can't learn the language, learn a few words to break the ice and start a conversation."

Qaisar Mian never wanted any other job, having refused many offers for promotion. He would say, "Love what you do, otherwise, find something else."

On one of his stops, he told Humayun about an open competitive examination that the railway authorities would be conducting to recruit talent for management trainees. It would be a grueling, day-long written affair. A face-to-face interview would then be arranged for the best candidates before a final decision was made on their applications. Qaisar Mian was always impressed at how much Humayun had learned since starting his apprentice's job. He suggested to Humayun to appear for the exam.

"They require all applicants to have passed matric. I only have a middle school certificate. I don't qualify."

Each time Qaisar Mian passed through, he would bring more information about the examinations and even found an old book about the history of railways for.

"Humayun, you would not have any problems passing the exams, and it will change your life."

Humayun was unconvinced. "It would, but I don't want to make a mockery of myself by applying and getting rejected for a reason I already know."

One day, Qaisar Mian came running out of his train as it came to a halt. Humayun was sitting in the signal room, studying the control levers and their connections to the rails. He threw a sheet of paper at Humayun. The paper was a newly added addendum to the examination requirements. The board had lowered the requirements to middle school graduates with first division marks.

"Humayun, someone up there is watching out for you. Don't throw away this opportunity that Allah has bestowed upon you. You owe it to yourself to take the exams. You will not regret it."

***

It was an arduous examination, but Humayun thought he did fine. The results were supposed to come by mail in a month. When two months passed, and he didn't hear from the board, he thought he had failed.

Qaisar Mian wouldn't hear of such gloomy conjecture and promised to go to the headquarters on his next trip to Lucknow and find out why he hasn't received his results.

Another month had passed when Qaisar Mian showed up with a big grin and a letter addressed to "Mr. Humayun Babar, Signalman, Meerut Railway Station."

Humayun was to go to Lucknow and see a Mr. Richard of the Staff and Establishment department. He took the earliest train.

Mr. Richard seemed glad to see him. "We have been looking for you for a while, and had given up. Your contact information had been lost by a clerk. If it hadn't been for your friend, Guard Qaisar Mian, you would have never heard from us."

Not only had he passed the exam, but he also aggregated high marks, placing him among the top twenty candidates.

After a formal interview, and given his second division qualification, Mr. Richard could only offer him a sub-stationmaster position, and that on a trial basis at a small station near Meerut. He must prove himself in the following 12 months, working under a veteran stationmaster.

Richard asked, "Mr. Babar, will you accept this offer?"

Accept? Are we joking here?

Would Majnu have accepted Laila[92] *as his wife?*

This is my dream job. I would take a coolie job if that came with this one-year trial period to a stationmaster position.

He slapped himself hard to make sure he wasn't dreaming. The report of the blow and the accompanying sharp pain announced he wasn't. After giving the pain a quick second to subside and with Mr. Richard watching on in amusement, he accepted.

---

[92] Laila-Majnu a tragic tale of lovers.

JAFAR THE SEAGULL
1925

His train stopped at Bareilly station. It was one of the bigger railway junctions on the network. Humayun was to switch trains here for his return home. There was a six-hour wait. The station was spread over acres of land with three platforms to accommodate multiple trains passing through. He had never been to Bareilly and, with time to spare; he decided to explore the station.

There were people, lots of them, milling around. Passengers getting off trains, while others waited to board. Then there were the relatives, a lot more than the actual passengers, who came to receive or bid farewell to the passengers, a common sight at stations. Most travelers had tiffin carriers full of prepared foods and earthen or brass water vessels for their journey. Many had live chickens in small coops, or a goat or two. There were coolies in red shirts and red turbans, carrying bags for passengers, some balancing four or more pieces stacked high on their heads with the turbans cushioning the heavy load. It was pandemonium all around. No one could afford to miss their train. Missing a train meant a wait of at least a day or more.

Besides the crowds of people, there were the seagulls. They were everywhere, and they were fearless, snatching food wherever they can get it and making a loud noise, almost drowning out guards' and train's whistles.

Humayun remembered Qaisar Mian telling him about the seagull of Bareilly. It was said that when an Indian politician died; he became a seagull and came to the Bareilly station, to keep creating trouble for people like they did in their past life. Perhaps that was why the government did not take measures to eradicate the seagulls from Bareilly station. If they were chased away, what will the future politicians do after passing? Where will they all go to keep busy?

Coolies, with two, three, or four pieces of luggage on their heads, hurriedly picked their way through all the multi-colored patterns drawn all over the platforms, of droppings of the freshest variety to weeks old, by these gulls. Passenger following close behind their coolies, trying to get to their bogies quickly.

Humayun noticed a man dressed in crisp white clothes from top to bottom, carefully picking his way through gull droppings to his compartment. There were people with large pieces of luggage, all trying to enter the same carriage at the same time, holding up others trying to get on.

A big seagull with black spots on its back and neck was also watching this all-white clad passenger from the top of a high perch. Finding this unacceptable, it took off and after a couple of somersaults in the air, dived straight at the man and dropped a large load on his shoulder just before he was to enter the train. Seeing the black and green blotch on his shirt sleeve, the disgusted man lost focus and stepped right into a mound of previously dropped gull poop at the edge of the platform. Cursing the seagulls, the man disappeared into his bogie.

Humayun was intrigued by the behavior of this seagull, who was now back on top of the carriage, nodding his head and making a sound resembling that of a man laughing his heart out.

It must be true about these seagulls being politicians. They haven't lost their meanness even after death.

Shaking his head in disgust, he wished he had his father's

12-bore shotgun to blow this gull off his perch. He walked to the waiting room at the end of the very large railway station building, reserved for travelers with Inter or third-class tickets.

It was a sizeable room with windows at the front open to the platform and to the trains pulling in and out of the station. It looked like it had not been cared for since the time it was built. Most of the furniture comprised wicker chairs. They were spread around the room in groups of four, each with a small table.

Humayun found a clean chair to sit on. He pulled the straps of his bag around his neck and sat down, clutching it tightly for fear of theft. He didn't own any luggage, so when he told Shershah about his upcoming interview in Lucknow, Shershah lent him his lucky English leather travel bag for good luck on his trip. Humayun was terrified of losing it. The chair was quite comfortable, but he was restless. He couldn't wait to get home and tell everyone about his new job. He tried to take a nap, but sleep was not something his body needed. The platform looked deserted, so he came out to further explore.

A lone sweeper was sweeping parts of the platform with a reed broom, a never-ending task for one man, given the size of the station. Humayun asked him if there was a newsstand at the station. The sweeper told him to go outside the station to find one next door.

To leave the station, he had to use an overhead bridge to cross four sets of railway tracks. The newsstand was basically a man sitting on the edge of the road who rented out his only copy of a week-old newspaper for an hour. He would read it aloud for a little extra at the renter's request. Humayun gave him some money and sat next to him on the curb, scanning the worn-out paper. As a courtesy, the newsman made some tea for him to sip while reading the paper. The tea tasted strange, but its warmth relaxed him.

On the way back, he had to cross the overhead bridge again. As he reached the middle of the bridge, he heard someone say something. No one was around, except a big seagull sitting in the middle of the narrow bridge, a few feet away. It appeared to be the same gull he wanted to shoot down off that high perch. It had a sort of small black crown on its head, a first for seagulls.

It is different from the other seagulls. Wonder, wonder. King of the seagulls?

It was looking at Humayun as intently as Humayun was looking at it. The difference was his uneasiness. Humayun shared a mutual distrust with animals of every kind. He didn't feel threatened, just uneasy. He didn't like the way the seagull was examining him.

Live and let live, so get out of here and I won't bother you.

His first thought was to turn and walk away, but then he charged towards the avian with hands flailing, making loud noises, trying to scare it away. The seagull didn't move. Humayun stopped within a few feet of his nemesis, feeling silly.

"Why did you stop?" He heard that same voice. "Are you afraid I will bite you?" The seagull was still.

Afraid, me? Of a stupid bird?

"You know, fear is not a bad thing," he heard. "It saves you from the ruins of failure. If there was no fear, men would jump off mountaintops unaided. You don't seem that stupid. The one who conquers fear can use it to achieve great heights. There are risks involved with each step, risks which put fear into the hearts of men. A good leader can overcome fear and take calculated risks. This is the difference between a common man and a leader."

It was all very surreal to Humayun.

"Is this really what is happening?" he mumbled, worried that someone watching him from the platforms might think him mad, speaking to himself.

"I am here in front of you. What can be more real than this? I can prove it if you still don't believe me."

"Do the somersault you did earlier."

The seagull took off and did a flying somersault,

"Do you believe me now, or should I drop a load on you to make you believe?"

The seagull was now sitting on the bridge railing.

"No, no, I believe you." He quickly replied in a loud voice, then looked around sheepishly to see if anyone had heard him speaking to a seagull.

I don't believe this is happening. Was there something in that tea?

Humayun sat down on the floor against the railing on the other side, so he couldn't be seen from below.

"Okay, so I believe you are real, and all this is happening to me, but tell me how you came to be a seagull and who posted you to Bareilly railway station." He tried to make a joke about politicians becoming seagulls.

"You seem like an upstanding fellow. It doesn't become you making fun of the dead, but there is some truth to what you have heard."

"Have you heard of Syed Mir Jafar Ali Khan *Bahadur*? I used to be a man of power and influence. I was the Nawab of Bengal. Have you heard the name Syed Mir Jafar Ali Khan?"

"You are Mir Jafar, the traitor. I mean, you were?"

"Watch your tongue. I was no traitor. I didn't betray my people or my country. These are all lies spread by the Mughals because they were weak and despondent. I wanted to liberate Bengal from their clutches to make it an independent state. Siraj,[93] the boy Nawab, was a gay blaspheme, who was not fit to lead the Islamic revival in the state of Bengal, so I ended his rule with prejudice. But then that conniving bastard Clive[94] betrayed me. He is that pathetic old featherless creature sitting under the Union Jack."

Humayun craned his neck to look over the railing but didn't see anything, while the seagull continued, "Ever since his arrival here, Clive has been the main target of all of us. He is

---

93 Nawab Sirajud Daulah – The last Ruler of Bengal under the Mughals.

94 Major-General Robert Clive - First Governor of the Bengal Presidency.

constantly being picked on, literally, and losing his coat of feathers from our assaults. He can't die and will stay here for the rest of the time getting flagellated by anyone who wants to stick it to the *Farangi* rulers, or is just having a bad day and needs a place to blow off steam. Clive's punishment will continue until India gains Independence and maybe then he will be allowed to die."

Humayun was finding the seagull's narrative fascinating. "Who else is here biding their time?"

"Well, you can also see Mir Sadiq of Mysore here. He was the real traitor. A cold-blooded murderer of a national hero. He did it for wealth and fame; he got neither and will forever be remembered as the man who built the bridge for the British hegemony over India. No one likes him because he is the one who poops the most."

"Then there is the other English pimp, Hastings, and many, many more. You will end up missing your train if I start on all those others. But I'll tell you about someone else who is here, who will be one of the biggest forces in the Indian Independence struggle."

"Will be? How can a seagull be a force in Indian independence?" Humayun asked with a smirk.

"No, silly, it's a man awaiting his connecting train in the upper class waiting room. He is a lawyer returning from a meeting of the All India Postal Staff Union. He has been nominated as one of the candidates for president. The elections are in a few months. He has been told that he is seen by some of its members as too much of a *desi-angrez*,[95] and his chances of winning the election are bleak. He may be a little upset about that. Very smart and a persistent bugger, he doesn't give up. By hook or by crook, he will be elected president of this union next year, and that will be a minor achievement compared to what he is destined for. His name is Mohammad Ali Jinnah."

"Should I go meet him?"

---

95 An Indian who tries too hard to act like westerners.

"What kind of question is that? Never ask a seagull a dumb question or you may get some poop dumped on you, too. Our droppings are reserved for the dumb and on those working against Indian independence, like that man in white, earlier." Saying, "Now run off and do whatever you have to do," Jafar flew away.

He walked back to the station building. It was still a few hours to go before his train arrived. He saw a weak, featherless skeleton of a seagull sitting on the crossbar of the flagpole. It was barely alive.

This must be that deceitful devil Clive, he deserves everything he is getting and more. I should go and kick him in his still-puffy chest.

Humayun was completely mystified by everything that had happened. Some seagulls were still flying over the almost vacant station, but Jafar was not amongst them. He decided to test Jafar's information and made his way to the upper class waiting room to see if this Jinnah was there. It was empty, with no sign of anyone.

Fooled me again. That rascal Jafar, he must be laughing somewhere at me for falling for another one of his lies.

The chairs here look a lot more comfortable than the lower class waiting room. If someone wants to check my ticket, I am an employee of the East Indian Railways. I can relax here.

A TRYST WITH GREATNESS
1925

Humayun found a reclining chair and glided onto its hard-yet-comfortable surface.

I must have been hallucinations caused by the tainted tea. I must go back to the newspaperman and give him a piece of my mind for serving contaminated tea.

Maybe later, too tired now.

Sitting in the comfortable chair and thinking of the bizarre events of the day, he dozed off. A sound of the bathroom door opening woke him up. A tall Englishman in a black suit and top hat came out, drying his hands with a small white hand towel. The bag he was carrying looked very similar to Shershah's bag. Without paying him any attention, the tall Englishman moved to a chair at the far end of the room, checked the time on his pocket watch, and started reviewing some files.

Humayun fell back into his afternoon siesta. The next time he woke up, three native men were standing around the tall Englishman and speaking with him in low tones. Humayun's ears perked up when he heard a mention of the All India Postal Staff Union. He got up and hoping to pick up more; he passed close to them on the way to the bathroom. They were talking about some elections at the union.

Hmm. He is not an Englishman, but a light-complexioned Indian dressed in an English suit like Bhai. A Desi-Angrez!

He washed his face and walked out straight to Jinnah, who was still discussing something with the men. Their conversation came to a sudden halt when Humayun said, "*Salaam*, Sir, are you Jinnah Sahib?"

The man with a serious face and piercing eyes looked up at him and nodded. "Do I know you?" in English.

You would have recognized me if you knew me.

"No, sir. I am Humayun, junior signalman at Meerut railway station. An acquaintance of mine told me you are passing through here, so I stopped by to say my *Salaam* to you."

"How did he know I was passing through?"

"Sir, he is a smart fellow and knows most things happening at this station."

"What is his name? Does he work at the station?"

He will think I am a mad man if I tell him a seagull named Mir Jafar, who dumps on traitors and dumb people, told me.

"He is Jafar, Sir, retired, and spends a lot of time at this station watching trains and people come and go."

"Where is he? I want to speak with him. What did he tell you about me?"

I don't think you would want to talk to him if you apprize your sanity.

"No sir, he left the station when I came here. He told me you are a Muslim who had gone to England for higher education and is back now to serve his people. My older brother Shershah is also a *Vilayat-palat* Indian, now back serving his country."

"Humayun, what is your full name? You say you work in Meerut, so what are you doing here at Bareilly station?

Is he getting upset at me for barging in on him like this? Does he think I am spying on him or something? He doesn't seem like a nice person. No wonder people don't want to vote for him.

"Humayun Babar, Sir. I am on the way back to Meerut after meeting Mr. Richard at the Railway Board."

"Who is this fellow? This Richard, what did he want from you?"

"Sir, there was a railway board examination that I took two months ago. I didn't get the results, instead they sent me a letter to go to Lucknow and meet Mr. Richard on some personnel matter."

"What was his full name, this Mr. Richard's?"

"I forgot to ask his full name, Sir. I am shy. This was the first *Gora Sahib* I have ever spoken to in my life."

"Forgot? Shy? They are people like you. Living in the dark for centuries has made their skin lighter. Anyway, what did this Mr. Richard want from you?"

Lord, get me out of this before he pulls my insides out.

"Sir, he informed me I have passed the exam, and he offered me a temporary job."

"Very Good. What does your father do?"

He is asking about my father now. Should I be worried?

"Sir, he is a *munshi* for the Nawab of Safpahar."

"What is his full name? Something Babar too?"

Oh my God, what have I gotten myself into? He is a lawyer and questioning me like I am a criminal. I shouldn't have listened to that seagull. Damn you, Mir Jafar!

"Yes Sir, He is Zaheer Babar, Sir."

Humayun had gotten increasingly flustered by Jinnah's questions, standing there like an accused in front of a judge. During the questioning, he had dropped his bag on the floor. Jinnah had gone back to reviewing his papers. Humayun wanted to get away, but thought of something Jafar had said.

I shouldn't tell him what Jafar told me about him. He will not like it and will skin me alive here.

But I should tell him, so he can mend his ways. Sometimes small things can make a big difference. After telling him what I think, I may not come alive out of this waiting room, but for the sake of Indian independence, this will be a small price to pay.

So here goes. Hope he is a reasonable man…

"Sir, if I may be so bold."

"Yes, what is it?" Jinnah replied without looking up.

"Sir, Jafar also told me that some people think you dress and act too much like *Gora Sahibs.*"

Jinnah slowly raised his head, his eyes squinted, his face showing distaste. Humayun could sense his wrath, but continued. "Sir, these perceptions are mostly from what they have heard. I believe their opinions can be changed by presenting them with something different, something better. Maybe if you go to their meetings in Indian attire, they may reconsider."

Jinnah said nothing, but his eyes were fixed on Humayun, who could not find a hole deep enough to jump into.

He quickly added, "No disrespect to you or your clothes, Sir."

I was trying to be helpful. Now he is going to kill me.

One of Jinnah's companions stepped forward and started berating Humayun. "Who the hell do you think you are? Barging in like this and trying to waste Jinnah Sahib's time with some nonsense and disrespecting him. Get out of here, you idiot." He started beating and pushing Humayun towards the door. The other two joined in the commotion.

Jinnah got up from his chair and, in an irritated tone, said to the men, "Wait. Hold on. What do you people think you are doing? This is the first smart idea I have heard all day today, and you three are abusing him. You should be ashamed of yourselves." The three backed away, their heads lowered. "Humayun, come here." His face was now calm as he extended his hand towards him. "I am glad you stopped by here. Congratulations on passing your exams."

Humayun, nodding his head vigorously, took Jinnah's dry and firm hand and started shaking it energetically while the other three looked on wide-eyed, feeling stupid. A sharp engine whistle and a high-pitched metal-on-metal scraping noise announced the arrival of a train.

"This is my train," Jinnah said, and headed to the door. One of the men picked up the bag and followed him out of the waiting room. From the door, Humayun watched them step into a second-class carriage.

Hmm, second class, even Vilayat-palat Desis can't ride first class. They are for the exclusive use of real Gora Sahibs.

As the train started to move, Humayun turned and came back to pick up his bag. He noticed the name tag on the bag with something written on it. Shershah would never write his name at a visible location. He was too cautious to let strangers know his name without formal introductions.

He instantly guessed what had happened.

He felt the wrath of Shershah coming down on him as he came running out of the waiting room; the train was picking up speed and had cleared the platform and there was no way he could get on it even if he ran as fast as he could. He stopped, turned around, and started running in the opposite direction. Near the end of the platform, he had seen a door marked: SIGNAL ROOM - STAY OUT

There was no one in the room. The signalman must have stepped out for a few minutes after setting the signal down for the train to leave. Humayun saw the very tall levers installed on the floor and knew exactly what to do, as there were only two levers that were set to the down position. He quickly reset the two levers. Almost immediately, he heard a faint double whistle followed by another one: the locomotive's brakes were being applied in an emergency.

Humayun smiled and started running on the tracks towards the train, which was now slowing down. He had raised the outer signal, instructing the driver to halt. The guard would have to walk back and investigate the reason for the emergency stop signal. Humayun passed the guard, who was now walking on the tracks towards the station and suspiciously looking at him. He climbed into Jinnah's carriage and found him sitting on a window seat, deep in thought, paying no attention to what was going on around him.

"Sir, I am sorry."

I am not.

Jinnah looked somewhat irritated. "You again? I thought you were going to Meerut."

"Sir, our bags got exchanged. I believe this is yours."

Jinnah looked puzzled. He looked at the name tag, nodded his head, and then looked crossly at the man who had picked up his bag in the waiting room. He reached under his seat and pulled out Humayun's bag.

"Did you stop the train for this?" Jinnah said, handing it to Humayun after taking a quick glance in the bag.

"No, Sir. Not for that, I stopped the train for your bag. My sack contains a few clothes, nothing important. Your bag is important. You are an important man, and you need your bag to carry on the work you are doing. Luckily, there was no one in the signal room and I was able to signal the engineman to stop the train."

"Young man, I don't know what to say, other than thank you for a second time. I don't know what I would have done without these papers. Your quick thinking has saved me many restless days and sleepless nights. Thank you so much."

He got up and reached into his pocket and took out some money and tried to give it to Humayun.

"Sir, I didn't do this for money. Allah has given me plenty for my needs."

Jinnah fished out a visiting card from his coat pocket and wrote something on the back.

"Take this. It is my visiting card. I wrote my address in Delhi on the back. Call on me when you are in Delhi. I look forward to seeing you."

"Sir, I have bothered you enough. You are a busy man. I don't want to take any more of your precious time."

The engine let out another sharp whistle, and the train

started to move.

"Humayun, I insist. Stop by my office in Delhi the next time you are there. I will be in Delhi all next month."

"Now go."

Humayun nodded his head and ran to the door, ready to jump out when Jinnah called him, "The next time you see your Mr. Richard in Lucknow, tell him they need to do something about these damn seagulls defecating everywhere and making life difficult for passengers."

Humayun suppressed his smile at the thought and jumped out of the moving train.

A MOST INCONVENIENT ARRANGEMENT
1925

Humayun was working as a junior signalman when one day Pir Sahib, on a surprise visit to Meerut, called him to his room. As he entered, he saw Shershah was there too. He instantly recognized the setting. Another life-changing decision was going to be thrust upon him. The hair on his nape had not warned him about this, but as usual, he was ready to face whatever was thrown at him.

"*Aadab* Abba and Bhai, I am sorry I have been very busy at the station. You see, my stationmaster, who Bhai knows personally, is not well, and so I have been also taking care of his work while he recuperates at home. He told me to tell you that his mother prays for your success each time she is on her *Jai-Namaz*. You helped her son realize his wish of working and staying in Balrajpur, like me wanting to stay in Meerut. I was going —"

"All right, all right, we know all that," Pir Sahib cut him off. "Shershah tells me you are doing well at your job. Even though you didn't listen to me about following him to Balrajpur for a job that would be so much better than this junior signalman job, seeing your good progress at the station, I am willing to forgive you for such disobedience."

Oh my God. Not another one of those jobs you wanted to send me away to. So what do I have to do to receive your forgiveness?

"Now is the time for you to show me you can stand on

your own two feet. I have found a suitable girl for you. A beautiful, pious, mature but reverent girl from a religious family. She will take excellent care of you, day and night, and free you of day-to-day chores so that you can concentrate more on your work. She is the daughter of Imam of Mahmudabad, who you already know. A very mature girl, *Masha-Allah*, her name is Nasreen. Very difficult to find maturity in girls these days. With your responsible nature, you two will be a perfect fit for each other."

Humayun knew the Imam had several children. He had briefly met his oldest daughter, who was married to Qutlugh Mirza, a few years back.

Regardless of the girl's background and suitability, I am not interested in getting married. I don't want to get bogged down with additional responsibilities and all the complications of a married life.

But he kept quiet.

"I have invited the Imam Sahib of Mahmudabad to come on Friday to complete the arrangements for your *Nikah*."[96]

I don't want to think about getting married until I am thirty or more. Abba was forty before he got married the first time. Delaying getting married helped him become successful.

Humayun refused to even consider getting married.

Pir Sahib got very upset and told him to get out of the house. Humayun looked towards Shershah and found him looking down at the floor.

No help coming from Bhai this time.

He left the room cursing his life. In times of turmoil, there was only one place where he would go - his *Khala's* place. He told her what had transpired and how his father was pressuring him to marry one of Imam Sahib's daughters.

"*Khala*, I don't want to get married."

She listened to him quietly, as he ranted about his father and how he wants him to get married at a very young age. When she detected a break in his outburst, she brought him some food

96 Islamic betrothal pact.

and *sherbet.* He was upset, and hungry, too.

She watched him eat and complain more about his father.

"You know, it may not be bad for you to get married and have someone to care for you," she said softly after he had finished eating. "I haven't told you this, but I won't be around too long. There are lumps on my body that are growing and I am getting weaker. A good wife will take care of you and be a partner in your goals. You can build a life with her, have children while you are young so that they are adults by the time you retire and need help."

Hearing of Khala's ailments, Humayun forgot why he was there. "*Khala,* that will not happen. I will take you to Delhi Army Hospital, where the best doctors will treat you. You cannot die! You can't. I won't let you."

"Don't be silly. We all have to die when the time comes. When we are old, we need help. Some are lucky to have grown children to help them in old age. Others, childless like me, don't." She sighed.

"*Khala*, please don't say that. I am your child, and I will take care of you, no matter what."

Then he thought of something and he said, "Okay, I will get married to this girl, if that is what you want me to do. But her only task will be to take care of you when I am not around. We will both take care of you when I am home."

She pulled his head towards her and gently kissed his forehead, twice, tears flowing. "Allah bless you, my child. I know you are my only child, and I love you more than anyone." She looked at him solemnly.

"I want to see you as a groom before I die. Now go back to Bhai Pir Sahib, apologize, and tell him you will marry this girl."

"*Khala*, don't be in such a hurry to die. I will need your help in raising my children to be good people and in finding matches for them." Humayun tried to break the gloom in the heavy air. His aunt smiled sadly and kissed his right hand. "I will wait for you to bring me good news."

***

Humayun was married to Nasreen in a simple ceremony in Mahmudabad. His *Khala*, happy and proud, gave Humayun a gold bangle that her mother had given her at her wedding. Humayun was thrilled that he had a gift for his wife on their wedding day.

By the time they got back to Meerut, it was late. He would see his bride for the first time on their wedding night.

Roshan Ara, with *Khala's* help, had decorated the bridal chamber. It was set up with fresh linens and decorated with a profusion of flowers. She had even managed to find some ice, a rare commodity in town, to cool down the traditional red *sherbet* for their first night together.

As Humayun stepped into the room, he saw his bride sitting in the middle of the bed, dressed in traditional red, covered from head to toe under an embroidered veil. He sat down next to her and took her right hand, admiring it and her slender fingers, adorned with intricate *mehndi*[97] designs. He kissed it lightly before slipping on his grandmother's gold bangle on her slim wrist. Without raising her head, she glanced at the bangle and brought her hand up to her eyebrows in a traditional *Aadab*.

He gently removed the huge veil from over her, and with his right hand under her chin, lifted her head. She had tears in her eyes, and a yellow embroidered silk handkerchief in her hand to dry them. He still couldn't see her full face.

"Was I forced upon you?" She asked softly. "I can't understand why you would marry a widow ten years older than yourself."

He recognized the voice as she removed the handkerchief, exposing her face. She looked directly at him with her beautiful, gray, sad eyes.

It was her. The bride he had found crying in the shadows,

---

[97] Henna.

the day Shershah returned from England.

This must be a nightmare. I have always had a history of bad dreams since childhood. It cannot be anything but. They come and go. I must wake up.

***

In the northern Upper Province city of Ayodhya lies a religious site claimed by both Muslims and Hindus. The mosque on the site, Babri Masjid, was purported to have been built on the orders of the first Mughal Emperor of India, Zaheeruddin Babar, on an open piece of land for the Muslims inhabitants of the area.

The ground below the Masjid was claimed to be Lord Krishna's birth. Hindu Mahasabha, a sectarian political party formed in 1906 to protect the rights of Hindus in India, launched a campaign in 1920 for the destruction of the mosque and construction of a temple dedicated to Lord Krishna. The party asked Hindus from all over India to be in Ayodhya on Lord Krishna's birthday that year, to help bring down the Mosque and raise a temple.

Babri Masjid administrators and Muslims from Ayodhya launched an appeal to Indian Muslims for help. A campaign was started by the Khilafat Movement,[98] to bring as many Muslims as possible on the day to help protect the Masjid.

Qutlugh Mirza, an active member of the organization, heeded the call from Ayodhya. In the ensuing riots around the Mosque, he was critically injured defending the main building. The Mahasabha crowd was repulsed, and they withdrew to plan another attack.

By this time Viscount Frederic Thesiger, Viceroy of India, had had enough with the violence and loss of lives in Ayodhya. Expecting more bloodshed and upheavals, he issued a 24-hour ultimatum to all outsiders - Hindus and Muslims, to leave Ayodhya or face long prison sentences. He also deployed the army to drive out or arrest insurgents and bring peace to the city.

---

[98] A failed Indian Muslim Movement in support of preserving the Ottoman Caliphate after their defeat in World War I.

Qutlugh Mirza couldn't leave Ayodhya in his condition and died a week later. Nasreen had only been married for a few months.

Blamed for bringing bad luck to the family, she was immediately sent back to her parents' home, never to return.

***

He pinched himself.

It's not a bad dream!

My God, what has Abba done to me?

This time he has tricked his own son into marrying the Imam's much older, widowed daughter. What does the Imam of Mahmudabad know that my father keeps duping men to keep him happy?

Humayun was angry at himself for not anticipating something like this from his father, and for not asking questions about her before agreeing to marry her. The more he thought about it, the more upset he got.

I have been tricked, but it's no one's fault. I should have been more diligent. We would have known the truth if I had asked Khala to go meet the girl. So stupid of me. It's all because of my inattention.

Others will always try to take advantage of me, and I should have been on guard. I can never let that happen again. Ever!

He wanted to leave the room and tell the Imam to take his daughter back. Nasreen could sense his inner turmoil, but stayed still, awaiting his verdict. Just when he thought his head was going to explode, suddenly it became clear what he needed to do.

Now that it's done, I can't let this become a punishment for her. The poor thing didn't have a say in this marriage either.

After all, she was a widow. This is probably the best thing that could have happened to her.

O Allah, please forgive me for this lie which I am about to tell. I can't let her feel that she was not my choice, my only choice!

He moved closer to her. "I have loved you from the day I first saw you on that hot summer day, leaning against that bare wall in the dark, drying your eyes with this beautiful yellow handkerchief."

"My grandmother's bangle looks perfect on your slender wrists? Do you like it?"

She nodded.

"This is the last time you will cry until I am around. I will love you more than anyone else and do everything to make you forget the miseries of your past life. You will never be forced to do something against your wishes."

"I promise."

Nasreen started weeping quietly as she nodded and put her head on his shoulder.

A MAGICAL PLACE
1926

Humayun's trial year as a sub-stationmaster began in earnest. Already familiar with all aspects of running a station from his time as a signalman, he jumped headfirst into his new position. The stationmaster, a tired, older man known for his sharp temper, was counting the days to his retirement.

Humayun discovered the stationmaster was suffering from a terminal ailment that he had kept hidden. His secret was safe with Humayun, who took on additional duties to help him out. The disease got progressively worse until one day he told Humayun of his decision to retire early.

He wrote a glowing letter to the Railway Board in praise of Humayun's capabilities. Humayun was promoted to full stationmaster as he turned 20, an unheard of achievement for a native Indian.

Having realized his dream of running a railway station at a very young age, he was a happy man until Nasreen started having severe headaches and tiredness. Humayun was worried about her health and, upon his *Khala's* suggestion, he took her to her parents' home for a few weeks of relaxation.

A few weeks later, when he visited her, it seemed she had gained some weight and looked relaxed. She was smiling. "I have some good news for you. *Hakeem*[99] Sahib thinks I am on the family way. But he advises complete bed-rest until the child is born."

Before he could say anything, she continued, "I can't leave you there by yourself with no one to cook and care for you."

Humayun was jubilant at hearing this. He hugged and kissed her. Having a child was his only other wish. He couldn't believe nature was so good to him.

"Nasreen, you stay here and rest until our little baby is born. I can deal with anything now that Allah has granted our wish. There is nothing more I want from Him. I can spend the rest of my life as a stationmaster, taking care of you and my baby. I have you and my job and soon, our child. What else could I want? I am the happiest, most fortunate man in India."

"The least I can do is to cook and clean until you are back home with the baby, and then I can cook and clean for the three of us."

First the stationmaster's job and now this. Oh Allah, I know not how to express my gratitude for all Your blessings.

Nasreen was smiling at his euphoric behavior as he talked about the baby. She had never seen him so happy, not even when he was promoted to station master.

***

It was not to be. Nasreen had a miscarriage. She lost not one, but two babies, twins, barely surviving the ordeal.

The next few years were dark and gloomy for them. They struggled with grief, not finding solace anywhere. In search of relief, Humayun immersed himself further into his work, Nasreen, in her religious texts and scriptures.

Near the end of his second term as stationmaster, he received a notice of transfer to Behramgarh, a small railway station on a minor route in Northern UP province.

He was an outstanding stationmaster. His staff, and others

---

99 An Indian medical practitioner, usually Muslim, who practices traditional medicine based on herbs and minerals.

who knew him, were surprised to hear of this transfer. With his stellar track record, he should have been given a larger station. Initially, he was distraught.

Ya Allah, is this a continuing punishment for an unexplained action or word on my part? First the loss of my babies, now having to move far away from my Meerut. I will lose my job if I resist the transfer.

Rumors were floating among his staff, who didn't want to lose him as their stationmaster. Humayun didn't know the reason for his transfer, but he stopped letting it bother him and started telling everyone that it was Allah's will and that he accepts it without question.

He has chosen this path for me, and there must be a reason He is sending me to Behramgarh.

He started preparing for the handover with a renewed vigor. One day, Qaisar Mian showed up. After some chit-chat, Humayun asked for his opinion on the transfer order.

Qaisar Mian looked surprised, but happy. "Don't worry about Behramgarh being a smaller station. A new place, and a new life there will be very good for you. The move will also help leave behind your sad memories."

"Why do you think so?"

"Believe me, it will be great. Behramgarh is a choice posting for young men like you. It is a small town in the north. I have never been there but have heard great things about the posting. Someone on the railway board must have developed a liking for your work."

"Humayun, my little brother, I will miss seeing you. My trains never travel the route to Behramgarh. We have little to deliver there." He added with sadness in his eyes.

They sat quietly, pondering all this.

And then Qaisar Mian suddenly got up as if he remembered something. He was in a hurry to leave.

"I better go now."

Maybe he doesn't like long goodbyes.

"The engine driver must be getting anxious. Hopefully, our tracks will cross sometime, somewhere. If they don't, remember me when you become the head of the East Indian Railways. I will still be a guard, running the same routes, delivering goods."

Humayun laughed. They hugged. Qaiser Mian blew his guard's whistle, and waving his green flag, hopped on the caboose as it started moving.

I will miss Qaiser Mian's ebullient visits and everything else about this man who, in his own unassuming ways, has taught me so much more than my father, my brother, or anyone else ever did.

He even taught me Punjabi language when I was having trouble dealing with Sikhs and other Punjabis passengers passing through.

I hope he is right about Behramgarh. Nasreen can use a change of scenery. Surely, it can't be all bad.

***

In the foothills of the Himalayas, a stone's throw away from the Nepalese border, sat the inconsequential town of Behramgarh. Its population comprising about equal numbers of Hindus, Muslims, and Buddhists.

A few Catholics also lived there with a tiny Catholic church serving them.

Father Fernando De La Cruz, an aging minister of Goan-Portuguese ancestry, headed the church. Every Sunday morning, services were held for the 20 Christian residents of Behramgarh. Some Hindus, Muslims, and Buddhists would also attend in a show of support for their neighbors, and for the aging Padre's efforts. After the services, he would provide tea and a small lunch for everyone, along with seasonal fruits for the young children. Skeptics attributed the robust weekly attendance to the attraction of free food.

Since building the church over a decade earlier, Father De La Cruz had been successful in converting a grand total of three people: a man, a woman, and their child. To Father De La Cruz, ever the optimist, things were looking up and up at the dawn of

1931. Many people had attended the Christmas mass and feast and he felt he was at the cusp of converting more people, with his weekly sermons of love for all. He believed that, in their hearts, a large segment of the non-Christian attendees had already accepted Christ as their Lord and Savior, without openly renouncing the religion of their forefathers.

Outwardly, this small town had nothing that distinguished it from the thousands of other small north Indian towns. It had a railway station. It was the last station on a single-track branch line. The railway traffic was limited to one passenger train each day. Plans to extend the line into Nepal had been discussed, but because of the topography of the mountainous region, and the high cost of such a venture, the plans had not come to fruition.

The town of Lumbini, one of Buddhism's holiest sites and thus a pilgrimage location for Buddhists, was right across the border from Behramgarh. According to Buddhist traditions, Siddhartha Gautama Buddha was born here around 563 BCE. Each year, large numbers of Buddhist pilgrims from all over India took the train to Behramgarh on their way to Lumbini. They would walk the rest of the way to Lumbini to cleanse their souls and repent for worldly transgressions.

Behramgarh railway station had three paid positions funded by the East Indian Railways. Headed by a stationmaster, it had a ticket collector and a signalman. There were several coolies, appointed by the stationmaster for hauling luggage for passengers.

The ticket collector ran the ticket windows, selling tickets to the passengers, and handling other ticket and cash-related matters.

The signalman's duties included clearing each train for entering or leaving the station, without which a train would not enter or leave it.

The stationmaster handled the overall management of the station. He was solely responsible for protecting unsold tickets, all ticket revenues - cash or otherwise, as well as any cargo to be loaded or unloaded. One more duty of the stationmaster was the safekeeping of lost and found items left behind by travelers passing through.

An occurrence that people found unusual was that Behramgarh stationmasters never stayed there for long. Almost all were transferred elsewhere after a two-year term. This was inexplicably different from other stations, where stationmasters would be posted for years and some would spend their entire career at the same railway station. It was rumored that former Behramgarh stationmasters had found great success in their professional careers, or private businesses ventures. These rumors were so prevalent that there was a long list of young stationmasters yearning for a Behramgarh posting. To accommodate as many candidates as possible, East Indian Railway did not extend a stationmaster's term beyond the minimum of two years. This practice was unofficial and, for obvious reasons, was never instituted in East Indian Railway policies.

Getting a Behramgarh appointment was usually meant that someone high-up had pushed the candidacy.

Father Fernando De La Cruz heard from an acquaintance at the East Indian Railway Office in Delhi that a new stationmaster would arrive soon. He immediately went to see the stationmaster, the son-in-law of Bombay's largest cotton trader, also a Goan-Portuguese Christian.

He had already been given his transfer letter and was in high spirits. He had tired of living in this small village in the middle of nowhere. His father-in-law had pulled some strings to get him this position, and he didn't know why? His wife had gone to her parents' home after a month in "this hellhole in the middle of nowhere," promising to return when he got a new posting elsewhere.

The happy stationmaster confirmed Father Cruz's news and told him the name of the new stationmaster, Humayun Babar, a twenty-four-year-old Muslim from Meerut.

EVERY LITTLE BIT HELPED
1931

Humayun spent the first year in Behramgarh not only learning about the railway station but also about the people who lived in town. He spent most of his time at the station, first reorganizing the flow of passenger and improving wait times for the customers, and then getting the waiting room repainted and cleaned up.

The railway terminal, being the hotspot for travel, made him a star in town. Everyone wanted to meet him when boarding a train, or returning home, or when just hanging out at the station. By the end of his first year, he knew almost all the people in town. He settled in daily routine of work and home life, expecting no changes in his situation for at least a couple of years.

As he was walking home one day, after an unusually hard day, he heard someone call from behind, "Sahib." He turned around and saw a disheveled old man scrutinizing him. He had not previously seen this man who looked like a beggar.

"Go away," Humayun said. "There is no money. Why don't you find a job rather than begging on the streets?"

The man angrily replied, "I didn't come here for your money. If it weren't for your kind wife, I wouldn't even spit on your shadow. She is a kind, caring woman. I always pray for her to have a child, which she so desperately wants. She brings food for the poor every Friday. May Allah keep her and give her a lot more and bless her with a son who can be her support in her old age, a son who will shine like a sun during the day, like a moon at night. A son with the wealth of Qaroon[100] and a big generous heart of Hatim Tai[101] the great."

Why would Nasreen go to distribute the food without telling me? Is she hiding something?

"What do you want?"

"Like I said, I need nothing. You have been called by Hanafi Sarkar."

"I have never heard of him. Who is he? What does he want from me?"

Humayun was getting irritated again.

All these Pir Faqirs[102] are frauds, and she shouldn't be involved with them.

"If he wants to meet me, tell him to come to the station tomorrow."

"Hanafi Sarkar wants nothing from anyone, and you don't deserve his kindness. May Allah give you humility." Saying this, he turned around and disappeared into an alley among the small mud and straw homes lining the street.

Humayun asked a few people, including Father De La Cruz, if they knew a Hanafi Sarkar or the *Faqir*. No one had heard of them.

For the first time, he was distrustful of his wife, and decided to show up at the mosque during food distribution, ostensibly to help distribute the food.

The timing of the Friday prayers clashed with the arrival time of the only daily train. Going to the mosque just to distribute food and not join the prayers could invite snide comments from some of the Muslim community members.

He came up with a plan. During a lull in activities at the

---

100 A mythological king with caves full of jewels and gold.

101 An Arab prince of unlimited wealth, piety and generosity.

102 A panhandler. Sometimes used for a dishonest person.

station, he called his young ticket collector to his office and sat him down in one of the rickety chairs in his office. "You don't know this, but there is a program at East Indian Railways to identify smart employees early, and provide them with hands-on training by an experienced tutor. I have been observing your work. You are a very smart employee, and I have been very happy with your work and put in an application for you to be added to the list of employees for the training program."

Humayun paused to look at the ticket collector's face carefully to tell if the young man was believing his narrative. The arrow had hit the target. The collector's face was lit up, so he continued, "The good news for you is that upper management has approved my recommendation, recognizing you as a smart employee who, with proper training, can soon be promotable to a sub-stationmaster."

"As the stationmaster and an experienced officer of the East Indian Railways, it is now my duty to make sure that you are given proper training to get you ready for the prominent position of the sub-stationmaster. I will personally take the time out from my very busy schedule and train you to handle the very difficult and demanding job of the sub-stationmaster." piety

The ticket collector took the bait hook, line, and sinker. He broke into a shriek of childlike laughter, then he grabbed Humayun's hands and started crying and enthusiastically kissing them, liberally spreading tears and saliva all over them. "Sahib, I can't wait to tell my father about the great news you have brought me. I can never forget this. Our family will always be in your debt, come what may. Even after you have retired, Sahib, you or your family will never have to buy a ticket at my station."

Humayun continued maintaining the same solemnity, "But I must also warn you, this is a serious high-level business. No one should hear a peep from you about this. No one! East Indian Railways will never forgive you if you leak out a word about this. You cannot talk about this even after you are promoted.

Disclosure of this news will cause major problems for East Indian Railways with other employees, all wanting to get the same training and promotion. Any leakage of this, and you can kiss your sub-stationmaster promotion goodbye, as well as losing this job. In addition, you will be placed on the employee blacklist of the Indian Employment Board, which will make you ineligible for any job in any place in India, any British colony, and even in the great land of Britain. It will be worse than death for you."

Terrified, the ticket collector fell to Humayun's feet. "Please, Sahib, I will die before anyone hears of this from me. I am the most loyal employee and servant of East Indian Railways for three years, but never had a better Sahib than you. I would never, ever let you down by sharing this information."

Humayun let him beg and plead for a little while longer before breaking his silence. "Get up, compose yourself. If you want to be an officer, start acting like one. East Indian Railways officers never cry or fall on people's feet. Only women cry. What I just told you have been approved by the highest levels of Indian Railways management, by the *Gora Sahibs.* Now it is all up to you to pass the training program and work extra hard to show my superiors and, of course, me, that I didn't make a mistake by putting you up on the list. Above all, take this information to your grave without ever uttering a word of this meeting and what we discussed. You are not to ask me anything about this until I tell you the next step on the path to your promotion. Now get ready. The train is due in an hour."

Without waiting for a response from the ticket collector, he stepped out of his office. His plan was coming together.

The following Friday, Humayun called the ticket collector to ask him if he was ready to start the training. The collector nodded so hard that it looked as though his head would fall off.

"Your training starts today. You have seen me deal with the passenger train every day. I believe you are a very observant fellow. This will be a test of your observational skills and your first hands-on training session. You have to manage all the situations from the memory of how I handled those events. You can't make a mistake. I know you won't."

"Today you will be in charge of the train duties. I will leave the station so that you don't keep looking over your shoulder to see if I am monitoring you. However, I have arranged for some observers in the incoming and outgoing trains, who will watch your work and report on your performance to me. I will be gone from 15 minutes before the train arrives, to one hour after the train has left. During this period, I will stop at my masjid for prayers, where I will also pray for your success, even though you are a Hindu. It will take me an hour or so to get your performance feedback from my observers. Be good to each passenger, as any of them could be my observer."

The day didn't go well, with multiple passengers boarding without tickets and others losing theirs. The departure had to be delayed when the nervous ticket collector had a sudden case of the runs.

Upon his return, Humayun stayed calm and pointed out the issues in the poor sap's performance. He advised the collector to observe him for the rest of the week to be ready for next Friday.

After the performance review, Humayun opened the lost-and-found room and took out two drinking cups that had been left behind. He gave one to the collector as a consolation award, and promised him the second if things went better the following Friday.

As weeks passed, things improved somewhat, but not much. Each week, Humayun would start by asking the ticket collector to go over what deficiencies he had experienced that day. The poor collector always had a long list of questions about where he felt needed to improve, and so it continued.

Humayun was now a regular at the Masjid on Fridays. After prayers, he would help his wife distribute food. They always ran out of food before running out of needy people waiting in line.

He saw men and women talk to his wife with reverence, as if she were a saint. At home, she would fast every Thursday to save food for the poor on Fridays. Seeing all this, he concluded that she was genuinely concerned for the poor and hungry. During these weekly visits, he saw the acute needs of the poor, and developed a sincere interest in helping his wife provide for their needs. He was very ashamed of himself for not seeing the needs of the poor earlier and having been suspicious of her.

Seeing the stationmaster distributing food on Fridays, people from around town also started bringing their leftovers for the poor for them to distribute. Still, there was never enough food for all the people lining up on Fridays.

On one such Friday, there seemed to be a lot more people than usual in the crowd waiting for food. The amount of food was the same as any other day. It consisted mostly of dried bread, raw radishes, and cucumbers and some corn that a farmer had brought for distribution. They put all the bread in a large earthen vessel that was usually used to store water at home. Humayun wondered where all these extra people had come from and worried that a lot more would go hungry this time.

As they started the food distribution, it began to rain. People wanted to get out of the downpour but, not wanting to miss out on the food, they stood in line getting drenched.

The jute tarp over their makeshift food stall started to leak. Some water got into the vessel containing the bread. Nasreen drained as much water as she could from the vessel and covered the opening with a cardboard piece. The food distribution continued from the covered bread container.

After serving about half of the line, Humayun removed the cardboard to assess how much bread was left in the vessel. It was still half full.

The rainwater must have puffed up the bread.

The vegetables soon ran out, with some people still remaining in the line. So they started doling out a little extra bread in lieu of the depleted vegetable stocks.

It had started to rain harder. The last person in the line seemed to move much slower, so Humayun called him to hurry up before they close up. The man had a cloth wrapped around on his head and face, only exposing his eyes. When he got closer, he asked if he could take all the leftover bread since he had a big family. The husband-wife looked at each other, smiled and said yes in unison. The man pulled out a small, untidy scarf from his side, spread it on the ground, and helped Humayun dump all the remaining bread from the vessel on it. He said a prayer under his breath and sauntered away with the bundle.

Humayun disassembled the stall, getting ready to return home. As he raised the empty bread container from the ground, he heard something rattle in it. He looked into the narrow-necked vessel but saw nothing. He put his hand in it and fished out what felt like a coin wrapped in a piece of paper. As he unwrapped the paper, he discovered it was a gold coin with the face of Queen Victoria on it. Instinctively, he looked around to see if anyone had seen his discovery. No one was out in the rain, except the man. He was on the other side of the road looking back at him with his now uncovered face. He was the same old man who had told him about his wife providing food to the poor on Fridays. The man spun around and disappeared into one of the side streets, just like the first time.

Giving no thought to where the coin came from or the consequences of keeping this small fortune, he accepted it as a gift from God for all their work for the poor. He put the coin in his pocket, happy that they now had enough money for better food for the poor for months.

Walking back to the station, he couldn't stop thinking about the day, the rain, having enough food for all, the gold coin, and the man.

How did the coin get into the bread container? Was that Hanafi Sarkar? Who is Hanafi Sarkar?

HERMIT HANAFI
1932

The training masquerade came to an abrupt end when the ticket collector came down with smallpox. He was very sick, but still wanted to come to work on Fridays to complete his training. Humayun had to put him on leave of absence and prohibited him from leaving home for any reason.

As a result, the situation now demanded Humayun to do the ticket collector's duties besides his own, until a replacement was sent by East Indian Railway.

After finishing up all his work, an exhausted, short-staffed Humayun closed up the station and walked out to get a *Tonga*[103] home. Although he lived a short distance from there, the sun was blazing down mercilessly and the high humidity of the monsoons made walking unbearable. Very few were brave enough to venture out on this exceptionally hot day. The Tonga walas, not expecting any more passengers until the following day, had all left.

Sleepy and tired and not wanting to wait around in the oppressive heat, Humayun started walking.

Where have all the Tongas gone? They couldn't have all left town at the same time.

He heard a horse neigh behind him and saw a Tonga.

---

[103] A two-wheeled one horse carriage with seats facing front and back. A common mode of transportation in the Indian subcontinent.

Humayun quickly jumped into the rear-facing back seat and told the coachman his address. As it picked up speed, the comforting breeze lulled him to sleep.

When his eyes opened, the Tonga was outside of town, traveling on a narrow lane in the middle of wheat fields.

"Where are you going? You left my house way back in town. Why didn't you wake me up if you didn't know where to go?"

The coachman turned his head and said, "Mian, I know where your house is, but we are not going to your house." It was the same mysterious old man who Humayun had come across twice. He was wide awake and feeling almost refreshed for some reason.

He didn't want to miss this chance. "Hanafi Sarkar?"

"No, Mian. I am the dust under my Sarkar's feet, a lowly messenger for his eminence and my lord on earth. You are a lucky man. He is giving you a second chance. All because of your pious wife, her pure heart, and her selfless services to the poor. May Allah bless her and fulfill her wishes. Shame on you for doubting her. You should ask for her forgiveness the next time you see her. Allah will forgive you for this sin."

Humayun, wondering how he knew what he was thinking, had nothing to add. Curious to find out who Hanafi Sarkar was and what business he had with him, he relaxed and let things take their course this time.

The old man gave the horse a gentle tap with his whip, and it broke into a brisk trot. "We'll be there soon. You don't want to keep Hanafi Sarkar waiting."

Soon, the Tonga pulled up in front of a small homestead. "Go ahead. Hanafi Sarkar is waiting for you."

"Can you wait for me to take me back home after I am done? I will give you a paisa for waiting."

"Stop wasting time and go in. Hanafi Sarkar has arranged to bring you here. He would have also arranged for your return."

The old man gave another gentle tap of the whip to his horse and left Humayun behind, wondering what was next.

The day was not as hot anymore. Even with the sun shining brightly and no clouds, the temperature was quite comfortable for late summer. A small, well-tended garden of flowers was on one side of the small mud-brick house. Some chickens were running around in a coop, made from wood pieces and jute fencing. There was no one anywhere within sight of this only house in the middle of a large meadow surrounded by tall trees.

He looked around once more and entered through the wide open front door. The room was fairly large and somewhat dark, with sparse furniture consisting mostly of floor *divans*,[104] a couple of well-worn leather ottomans, two small rattan chairs, and a small table on the side with an earthen water container and two earthen tumblers. There were several shelves on the walls, with copies of the Quran and several other books on religious topics commonly found in Muslim homes. There were other works in Arabic and Farsi were also neatly placed on the shelves.

He saw English-language books on some shelves in one corner of the room, mostly with philosophy in their titles. This could have been the home of any upper class Indian.

Humayun had assumed Hanafi Sarkar to be a *Faqir* like those found all over India who bilked people of their earnings on promises of wealth, a male child, or whatever they desired.

I assumed wrong. Hanafi Sarkar is no Faqir. From all these books and the setup of this place, he appears to be a learned multi-lingual scholar of religion and philosophy.

His adrenalin was slowing down, but he was still busy in his thoughts when someone put a hand on his shoulder. He instantly turned around and saw a neatly dressed, tall, clean-shaven old man. He had piercing bright eyes and a very kind face.

"Hanafi Sarkar?"

---

104 Low back, chair-like floor seating.

"Well done. Mian," the elder replied with a smile. "It took me a long time to finally meet you. Come here and sit. I have much to talk about with you."

"As do I, Hanafi Sarkar. I have also been searching for you."

He pointed Humayun to a chair. "It must have been a long trip. You must be thirsty." He poured some water into a tumbler and placed it in front of Humayun, along with a plate of fruits.

"I have heard so much about you and your virtuous wife, and all the work you two do for the underprivileged and poor. *Masha-Allah*, you are doing well in worldly matters, too. You must come from a good, devout family."

He sat down and continued, "So tell me where you come from, your father, grandfather."

A quietude descended over Humayun. He was feeling at ease in this environment. Normally a very guarded person, he felt he had little to hide about his background. Humayun told Hanafi Sarkar everything about him, what he knew about his father, and his own struggles in life.

Hanafi Sarkar listened to him attentively.

They talked for what seemed like hours about life, its struggles and its rewards, good versus evil, and the value of hard work. It was as if time had stopped for Humayun, who was feeling that he was swimming in a pond of knowledge from which he could imbibe as much knowledge as he wanted.

It felt like a journey of revelations to him.

Towards the end of this enlightening afternoon, Hanafi Sarkar told him he knew how much he and his wife wanted children of their own, but Humayun was too afraid to talk about wanting children lest it bring bad luck for wanting it too much. It was one of his idiosyncratic beliefs that if you want something and you bring up your desire in the open, you could cause it to be never fulfilled. He didn't want to jinx the chances of having a child by bringing up the subject.

He told Hanafi Sarkar that he was prepared to live a life without children.

Hanafi Sarkar smiled at his superstition and said, "Humayun Mian, go home. Pray to Allah daily with a clean heart and ask for children from Him if that is what you want. The leave it all to Him. He is the most merciful and generous."

Humayun couldn't resist saying what he felt. "Doesn't he know what I want? If he was going to give me a child, he would have done so by now."

Hanafi Sarkar replied, "Never give up on Him. Children keep asking their parents for something they feel they want, even after being rejected every time. You haven't even asked him once and expecting Him to know what is in your heart. Yes, He knows what is in your heart, but you have to ask for what you want, sincerely, before He will hear it. He is our only Allah. There are millions and millions of humans who, unlike you, are asking Him every minute and every second of the day. Maybe if you ask Him, your voice can find his ears. It will find His ears, I am sure of it. So go start today and ask Him. You shall soon have glad tidings, your wishes will come true and your life will change."

He thought of something and smiled. "You know there is a saying in English: the squeaky wheel gets the grease. Now go, before it is too late."

"To get back home, follow the path to the right. Someone is waiting for you at the end of the trail. May Allah bless you and your family."

Humayun left the house and followed the narrow path to the right. He walked for what seemed like an hour or more through a forest of tall trees that started right behind Hanafi Sarkar's home. He had crossed a few cross paths, and worried he was lost. The jungle was getting dense as he moved on. He was afraid there may be wild animals.

Have faith, he remembered the hermit saying. Then, remembering a saying of the Prophet, "Trust in Allah, but tie your camel," he picked up a fallen branch for protection, just in case.

The more he walked, the more frustrated he got. Suddenly, it was all behind him, and he found himself standing in a clearing. He saw rail tracks about a hundred yards from where he had emerged. A goods train was stopped in the tracks. Humayun started running towards the caboose to see if he could get a bearing on his location from the guard. The guard turned out to be Qaisar Mian.

"Humayun? What are you doing out here, in the middle of this jungle?"

Humayun was ecstatic seeing Qaisar Mian. "Long story, I will tell you later, but why is your train stopped here in the middle of this jungle?"

"You wouldn't believe this, but for the first time ever, my train contains goods for Behramgarh, so I am heading there. I am not sure what happened, but the boiler pressure suddenly dropped, bringing the train to a halt. We have restarted the boiler and are now waiting for the steam to build up for the engine to start rolling."

Soon, the locomotive let out a whistle. Qaisar Mian waved his green flag, and they were on the way.

For the very first time in his life, Qaisar Mian was headed to Behramgarh while they tried to make sense of the day's events as related by Humayun.

A CHANCE VISIT
1932

The ticket collector replacement never came. Because of his meticulous nature, Humayun would never leave tasks unfinished or done hastily before going home. His work hours were long. He would first finish his work for the day, then pick up the ticket collector's job and lastly translate and transmit each telegram, and all the while keeping the telegraph printer inkwell filled and the telegraph machine oiled and ready for the next urgent telegram.

He would stay at the station for long hours, just in case if something happened, or worse, a senior manager dropped in unannounced from Lucknow, the regional railway headquarters.

One night, it happened.

He had dozed off in his chair trying to solve some lost luggage problems, when he was awoken by a sharp train whistle. No trains were scheduled. He jumped out of his chair and walked out onto the railway platform. He could see a locomotive with a caboose stopped about five hundred yards short of the railway station, waiting for the 'clear' signal to proceed.

Humayun went to the signal room and set the signal to green to let the locomotive move up to the platform. As soon as the locomotive reached the platform, he saw three well-dressed British officers jump out of the caboose. The platform lighting was low, as usual, so he couldn't tell who they were. They were talking to each other like old friends out on a picnic. One of them was holding an open bottle of rum.

Three Vilayati officers at the same time. I am in trouble. They must be here to dismiss me. I don't know what I have done. My clothes are wrinkled, and I am wearing chappals[105] *at work.*

Allah save me from all evil.

He ran up and greeted them, "*Salaam* Sahibs and good evening. I am Humayun Babar, stationmaster at your service, Sirs. Welcome to the Behramgarh railway station. This railway station is operating at its full capacity with only two people, myself and the signalman. You see, our ticket collector fell ill to smallpox and since that time, the signalman and I have been serving our passengers with no hitches. Sirs, if I had known of your visit, I would have been better prepared by having my uniform cleaned and ironed to welcome you. Since you are already here, let me open the waiting room for your comfort. It is one of the cleanest waiting rooms you will find in this railway sector. I can also start a pot of tea, Sirs, if you will give me a minute."

He ran to the waiting room, quickly unlocked the doors, and turned on the lights. It was a large room with a few rattan sofas and chairs spread around, with tables next to them.

He noticed a small piece of luggage beside one sofa, which surprised him since the signalman had mentioned no left luggage when he had cleaned and locked the waiting room earlier that afternoon. He made a mental note to ask him about it and deposited the small suitcase in a storage room at the back. The first British officer, an old man, was entering the room as he locked the storage room door. The other two came into the waiting room as the older officer took the first chair. They followed suit and sat on a sofa next to him.

Is that Mr. Richard? But first, let me find the reason for their unannounced visit.

---

[105] Slippers of any kind, usually without back straps.

"Mr. Humayun Babar, stationmaster of Behramgarh station, please sit down here." He smiled encouragingly at Humayun, tapping a chair next to him.

"No problem, Sir, I can stand." he said energetically, shaking his head from side to side.

"Oh, come on, young man, sit with us. We'll tell you why we are here at this late hour."

Ignoring the bottle of rum in the hands of one officer, Humayun said, "Let me make some tea for you. Sir."

The senior officer pointed again to the open chair and said, "It's well past tea-time for us. Sit, sit."

Humayun eased into the chair, "At your service, Sir"

"I am Sir Jonathon McDonald, MP[106] from East London, Director General, retired, of East Indian Railways." Then he pointed to the shorter of the other two and said, "This is Mr. Daniel Craig, Chief Engineer Maintenance and Operations from Lucknow. And over there, the tall gentleman holding a bottle of the finest rum, and eagerly waiting for someone to get him a glass, is my son Mr. Richard McDonald, Chief Engineer, Staff and Establishment, also from Lucknow."

"Very glad to have your acquaintances, Mr. Daniel, and so happy to see you again, Mr. Richard."

Richard smiling ear to ear, nodded his head and said, "Fancy meeting you here, Mr. Babar. You remembered me."

"Yes Sir, how could I forget you? You were very kind to me, even though my qualifications were sub-par. I have always remained thankful to you for the opportunity."

Turning to Sir Jonathon, Richard continued, "Father, Mr. Babar had only passed middle school when he took the Railway boards exams, but placed in the top 20 candidates from all of India. We were very impressed, and I decided to interview him personally. He was an excellent, self-educated candidate. The interview brought out his high intellect and a well-balanced

106 Member of British Parliament.

personality. After the interview, we offered him a sub-stationmaster position on a trial basis to see if he could handle the work and grow from there."

Sir Jonathon seemed genuinely surprised at hearing this and said, "So great to meet young men like yourself, who are the future of India. You will be running this country very soon." And then quickly added, "Shoulder to shoulder with us, of course. Let's do a toast to your achievements. Do you happen to have some glasses here?"

Toast? I don't have any bread to toast. But let me get the glasses.

Humayun got three small tea glasses from the store.

Sir Jonathon looked at the three glasses and asked, "Would you like to have a glass of rum with us? We can do this since no one here is on duty."

Then on second thought, he quickly added, "I hope I am not offending your religious sensibilities by offering you *sharaab.*[107] You, being a Muslim."

He had never indulged in alcohol.

They are drinking it, so it must be some good quality sharaab. This is as good a time as any for me to try it, plus no one else is here. It should be fine.

Could they be testing me?

I should be careful. I shouldn't drink.

The three of them didn't seem like they were here to check on him or to test him.

The hair on his nape was not signaling anything.

It should be fine. I'll try. Allah will forgive me.

He quickly got up and brought a fourth glass and put it on the table, along with the others.

Sir Jonathon looked at him and laughed out loud, "Good man, jolly good man!" and poured small amounts of rum into each glass, pushing one towards him first, and then offering the other two to the others.

He raised his glass. "A toast to you, Humayun Babar, for

---

[107] Alcohol.

continued success. Never hurts to have a drink with your bosses. Gentlemen." The two officers raised their glasses said cheers in unison.

So that is a toast.

Raising his glass like the others, Humayun followed them, taking a small sip of the dark brown liquid. He felt a warm, bitter stream flow through his body. This was a new sensation. He took another small sip. It felt better the second time.

Karwa,[108] *but not that bad.*

"Sirs, may I ask, how can I be of help?"

He addressed Sir Jonathon but looked at all of them, one after the other.

"We are a small station here, but we take care of every passenger that passes through here. We keep our facilities looked after, our waiting room spic and span and all our equipment running well, following all the maintenance schedules. I have been here for a year, and don't want to take credit, but the passenger traffic has grown from previous years."

Sir Jonathon emptied his glass, then stretched back in his chair. He was old, but looked fit and alert. He said, "I can see that, Mr. Babar. You are running the station very well. I looked through the files for this station before we came here. But that is not the reason for our visit."

Humayun was puzzled but just said, "Sir."

"I am seventy-eight years young, and this is my swan song visit to India, my home and my love."

Swan song? What is that? I'll have to look it up in my dictionary.

Sir Jonathon read his mind and said with a smile. "My last visit to Behramgarh."

"You see, old swans sing a beautiful last song just before they die, and thus the term swan song."

"I was the first British officer posted in Behramgarh back when there wasn't even a train line or a railway station here. I was

---

[108] Bitter.

sent here to build the station and get the tracks laid to complete the line that originates in Gorakhpur. That was a long time ago."

"Oh Sir, so great to know. Welcome back to your home." Humayun was now relaxed.

"So, I told my son and his friend Daniel here, to find us an engine, a caboose, and some bottles of good old East India Company rum so we could go on an inspection tour of my first major project posting, and here we are." He said to Humayun with a wink and a smile.

"I am glad, Sir."

"Behramgarh was my first step to a satisfying career with the East India Railways. It brought me close to the local population here, and I learned a lot about India and the common Indians."

"What a career, Sir. I wish I can have a career half as successful as yours."

"You have started on very solid footing, in Behramgarh. It is a great place to start. Look what it did for me. Keep up the hard work, and I know you will run the Indian Railways soon."

Humayun couldn't help but add, "Shoulder to shoulder with you, Sir. *Insha-Allah.*"

Sir Jonathon nodded and said, "*Insha-Allah,*" before bursting out in a loud clap of laughter joined by Richard and Daniel.

Humayun, trying to follow the ways of the *Gora Sahibs*, joined in with his own style of subdued mirth.

A WILD (K)NIGHT
1932

Sir Jonathon was enjoying his rum. "You know, I was born in India but was sent back to England for my education. I came back after I was old enough to make my own decisions."

"So, you are Indian by birth. Can I be so bold to ask where in India, Sir?"

"Meerut."

"Really, Sir? You were born in Meerut? I was born in Meerut, too. My grandfather and both my parents were also born in Meerut."

"A small world! Isn't it stationmaster Babar? Here we are, an ancient, retired Englishman meeting a young and vibrant Hindustani gentleman and we find we were both born in the same town hundreds of miles away from here. I am glad to meet you. Can I call you Humayun?" Sir Jonathon asked.

"Yes, Sir, I would be honored if you call me by my first name. In fact, Sir, you seem to be about the same age as my father."

"Hmm. Humayun, can I ask you a personal question?"

"Of course, Sir, you can ask me anything you want. I am at your service."

"I was born in 1850. So it seems your father must also have been born just before the Meerut upheaval."

Upheaval? Riots? Mutiny? Revolt?

It was our first War of Independence.

Sir Jonathon continued, "His family must have been affected by it, by the resulting disorder, I mean?"

Disorder? It was a lot more than a disorder.

Hearing the mention of the 1857 uprising, both Richard and Daniel became alert. It was a touchy subject, not usually brought up in mixed gatherings of the English and native Indians. They seemed shocked that Sir Jonathon would bring up the mutiny with a low-level stationmaster. The Raj had expressly forbidden British expats from discussing the sepoy rebellion with natives. At his age and status, Sir Jonathon appeared to think little of disobeying the order.

"I am sorry to tell you, Sir, both my grandparents were killed in the riots. Luckily for my father, a close family friend hid him and saved him from the same fate."

He didn't mention Zeenat.

I should keep her out of this. It just doesn't feel right opening up with strangers.

"Sir, my father was raised by this family friend as their own."

This revelation seemed to have struck a chord with Sir Jonathon; his face seemed to have lost all its blood, his earlier cheerful demeanor vanished. Richard walked over to him, and put his hand on his shoulder, "Father, can I pour some more rum for you?" and poured some into his glass, and then some in Humayun's.

"So sorry to hear this, Humayun. I know what he must have gone through," Sir Jonathon said. Humayun noted the strong emphasis on the "I know" and found it peculiar.

How could he know what it felt like?

Sir Jonathon continued, "Did he develop a hatred for the English for killing his parents?"

"His parents were killed by a mob, Sir. An Indian mob."

Sir Jonathon went quiet. He abruptly got up and disappeared behind the door on the far side wall that had the words "WC" on it.

Humayun was still pondering the sudden exit when Richard cleared his throat and said, "Mr. Babar, my grandfather, Captain Peter McDonald, was killed in the cantonment on the 10th of May, 1857, in Meerut. His Indian servants dressed up my grandmother in a *burqa* and got her and father safely out of the cantonment. They joined a small group of natives trying to escape from Meerut. On the way out of town, they were stopped by rebel soldiers. Upon being discovered, my grandmother was killed there, on the spot. My father was saved by this clever lady in the group, who convinced the attackers that my father was her son, and grasped him against her to hide his face from the attackers."

"Ya Allah, what terror he must have suffered seeing his mother cut down in front of him, a small child. I am so sorry to have brought up my grandparents. I am so sorry, so sorry." Humayun was close to tears now. He got up to shake those feelings.

Richard, also close to tears, came over and put his hand on his shoulder quietly. Humayun was trying very hard to keep his composure.

Men don't show emotions. What will Mr. Richard think?

I can't show emotions. I am a man. I am in control.

"It's not your fault, Humayun. He has fought the image for years. He came back to work in India to bury the memories of those demons, the demons of war, cruelty, and inhumanity. All his life, he has fought them. He did everything he could to erase the picture of his dead mother, but could not banish those memories that have haunted him all his life. My mother tells me he still wakes up in the middle of the night with horrible screams and cold sweat all over his body."

The bathroom door opened, and Sir Jonathon came out, now fully composed.

"Sir, I must beg your pardon for bringing back the sad memories of your parents and the horror. Mr. Richard told me about your parents and how you were saved from death."

"Humayun, many times I have questioned whether it would have been better if I had also been killed. But then I look at my children and grandchildren and I thank my Lord and say a prayer for the lady to whom I owe my life, my happiness, and everything. I was told her name was Zeenat Begum."

Humayun felt a hammer hitting his chest. He started to collapse, but caught the top of a chair to steady himself. Looking down at the cement floor, trying to hide his emotions, he was lost.

It cannot be? How can it be? How many Zeenats were there saving children that day in Meerut? It had to be the lady who took care of us when my mother passed.

"We took refuge with the Nawab of Rampur, along with Colonel Finnis' wife and her three children. The Colonel was also killed with my father in the cantonment. Lucy, their youngest daughter, and I became close friends and kept in touch in England. She told me Zeenat's name and told me she had a son, Peeru, whom I used to play with, at the Nawab's guest house where we were all sheltered during the rest of the upheaval. I don't recall his name. "

Humayun could not believe what he was hearing. He was overcome with emotions that he had never felt, a sense that history had taken him back in time. He could only manage to say, "Sir, my father was Peeru. Zaheer Babar."

Sir Jonathon couldn't contain himself anymore. He grabbed Humayun's by the shoulders and started crying uncontrollably.

"Oh, my lord Almighty. Is this why you brought me to Behramgarh today? Will Behramgarh ever cease to unfurl the layer after layer of the secrets it holds? Is this what I have been searching for all my life?"

"How is your father? Where is he? Where can I see him? I

want to waste no time and go see him. We have an engine and a caboose. We can go anywhere he may be right now. I want to see him so badly."

Humayun had to gather all his composure to give Sir Jonathon the bad news. "Sir, I am so sorry to tell you he passed away last month peacefully."

I need to control myself. Men don't cry.

Crying is for women!

Sir Jonathon let out a cry of desperation, "Why Lord? Why? You brought me so close and then slammed the door shut on me."

He tightened his grip around Humayun, not letting him go from his embrace as if he had just found a long-lost child. Buried in an imaginary father's embrace, Humayun didn't want him to let go, a warm affectionate embrace he had never experienced from his own father.

They were both sobbing and crying like, some would say, women, and it felt so good to let it all out in this under-furnished waiting room at a far-flung station on a peripheral route of the mighty East Indian Railways.

The two other officers looking on in wonderment at what just unfolded before their eyes, the magic of Behramgarh.

LEAVING BEHRAMGARH
1933

Humayun got a telegram from Roshan Ara from Meerut announcing the news of Nasreen giving birth to twins, a boy and a girl. Filled with joy in his heart and a sense of relief, he thanked the Almighty and prayed for his wife and his children's health and safety.

Nasreen had gone to Meerut and was staying at her in-laws' home during her prenatal period. The city had an excellent hospital, and it was close to her parents' home. His step-mother, now traveling around India, free of charge, as the mother of a railway stationmaster, had become very loving and caring to him and his wife. She was leaving no stones unturned to make Nasreen comfortable during her stay in Meerut. She had even invited Nasreen's mother to stay at her home to be with her daughter in the last weeks of her pregnancy.

He took the first train to Meerut.

Humayun suggested naming the girl Malka Gayti Ara after a Mughal princess and asked Nasreen to suggest a name for their son. She decided on Saleem, the birth name of the fourth Mughal Emperor, who was better known as Jahangir.

I am a father now, with a loving wife and my dream job. There is nothing more I can ask Allah for.

***

The struggle for Indian Independence was picking up steam. He had no ill will towards the British, but felt a yearning to help India achieve independence. Now a father of two beautiful children, he started thinking about their future and didn't want them carrying the yoke of slavery on their shoulders, but he didn't know where to start. He had seen Jinnah's name mentioned a few times in connection with the independence movement after he had won the presidency of the All India Postal Staff Union, as predicted by Jafar the seagull.

In many of his recent photographs, he was wearing a *Sherwani*[109] in public meetings.

So he took my advice! I should go see him, he will have some ideas about how I can help the independence movement.

Humayun felt bad about not following up on Jinnah's "I insist" invitation, as there was never a good time and his work kept him in eastern UP, far from Delhi.

Upon his return to Meerut, he found an official letter from Lucknow waiting for him. He had been promoted to be the stationmaster for Lucknow station. The letter gave Humayun a month to hand over the charge to a new stationmaster.

The letter brought back memories of Sir Jonathon and his chance meeting in Behramgarh. He remembered that after the great discovery, Sir Jonathon had said to his son, "Richard, I hope you will be a brother to Humayun. Please be there for him in his moment of need, as his family was there to save me from an early horrible death." Then, turning to Humayun, he had said, "Humayun, I don't know how long I will live, but please be a brother to Richard. If you ever come to England, you will get the chance to meet my wife and my other child, Hazel. I know they will want to meet you after hearing our story."

Humayun had been overwhelmed. He had seen the treatment of common Indians by the English masters in India. Being called a son and a brother by distinguished members of the

[109] A long formal jacket worn mostly by Indian Muslims.

British upper echelon was all but inconceivable to him. He had wondered if His Majesty's *sharaab* had affected them. But over time, he found the feelings expressed on that fateful night had been genuine, and the promises made were kept.

Richard would check up on him from time to time, and always having news of his father from England. Each time, Richard would also not forget to ask if there was anything he could do to help. Humayun never asked for help.

Humayun wanted to see Hanafi Sarkar before he left Behramgarh, but there was no way to contact him. He knew in his heart that Hanafi Sarkar's prayers had played a big part in his life. He felt an inner strength knowing there was someone, a complete stranger, whose prayers were with him. It was as if someone was watching over him and guiding him.

The thought of leaving Behramgarh made him feel as if he were leaving a very close and wonderful friend who had been so good to him and never asked for anything in return.

I will miss this town. Behramgarh has been like, yes, like Qaiser Mian to me.

Today, I feel like how I felt the day he left after I told him of my transfer to Behramgarh. It was as if I was not only losing a friend but also a mentor, a guardian, a sounding board, all combined into someone irreplaceable.

Maybe the future will bring me back to Behramgarh like it brought Qaisar Mian, even if for a few hours.

Or, like Sir Jonathon, I may come back when I am old and retired, for one last swan song trip of my own, to this puzzle of a town.

He was sad, but got to work on making sure that things were all in order. The tickets, lost-and-found items, and other goods were checked and re-checked.

He wanted to get the station cleaned up for the new stationmaster, who would have to send a detailed inspection report to the head office after taking charge.

While cleaning the storeroom, the sweeper found a small piece of luggage. He brought it to Humayun's office. Humayun thought little about it and left for home. Since Nasreen was still back in Meerut, he had a quick dinner of bread and vegetables brought for him by his neighbor. He was getting ready for bed, but something was bothering him, a feeling that he had forgotten something.

Hoping to clear his head, he left the house for a walk and stopped by the empty station. The only light he could see was coming from his office. He unlocked the door, thinking he may have forgotten to turn off the light. Everything was in order; the sweeper had placed the small piece of luggage by the side of his large desk. He picked up the attaché case, which was quite heavy for its size. There was no name tag or writing anywhere else on it. He moved the papers piled up on his desk to one side and placed the case on it. There was no lock, a small jute string was tied where a lock would normally go. He found a pair of scissors to cut the string.

This is the same bag I put in the storage room the night of Sir Jonathon's visit. How could it have been here for so long without anyone noticing it?

Two years? All lost items must be sent to Lucknow, the regional headquarters, within three months of being found.

This would be a black mark in my work file.

How could have I missed it?

I should talk to Mr. Richard. Maybe he can help with this.

That's not a good idea. I can't put him in such a position to do something illegal for me.

He opened the case.

This must be why I felt the foreboding restlessness.

The case contained gold coins wrapped in wax paper in stacks of ten coins each. The stacks were in thick burlap bags. There were a few cotton bags with some precious stones and gold jewelry. The rest was filled with loose burlap packing.

Now he was scared, worried that he had made a mistake by not paying attention to this bag after putting it away in the storeroom.

Someone has misplaced all this gold, but no one has claimed it in two years. It must belong to someone who is a man of wealth, influence, and power.

Why hasn't he come looking for it? Anyone losing such a khazana[110] *would have brought heavens and earth together to find it.*

He opened the lost and found the register; it contained entries going back five years. Most of the items left behind entries were things like caps, scarves, a file of papers, a child's carrying case.

No misplaced suitcases or attaché cases were on the list. Everything was in proper order and all the entries had been followed up and closed properly.

He knew that unclaimed items of value typically ended up being bought by company officers for pennies from the unclaimed goods room in Lucknow.

If I send this attaché case, the contents will end up being split up among the Gora Sahibs.

Humayun came up with a plan to get the lost property to its rightful owner. He removed most of the gold coins from it and made a three-month backdated entry for the attaché case in the register. He then placed it in the lost-and-found area.

This way my books would be closed at Behramgarh. I would already be in Lucknow when this bag arrived there as untraceable property in three months. By that time, I would know if a claim existed for it in Lucknow.

I want to deliver it to the rightful owner, if I don't find him, I will still be able to keep an eye on what happens to the gold in Lucknow.

---

[110] A stockpile of wealth.

THE TWO LIEUTENANTS

1935

Lucknow was a very large station with three sub-stationmasters, as well as many ticket collectors, signalmen, and hundreds of coolies to help run it. Humayun was surprised that the Gora Sahibs had trusted him with such a large operation, but he ran with it. His every move was scrutinized by the watchful eyes of a management board of three British officers. Richard was one of them.

For accommodation, he was given a large house with a proper lawn and servant's quarters that came with servants for housekeeping and cooking. The house needed some revamping and maintenance. The previous stationmaster was an old English widower who kept most of the house locked up, except for a kitchen, a bedroom, and a bathroom for his use.

With the arrival of Humayun and his family, spring had sprung on the old house. Nasreen went to work on restoring the house and cleaning out and replanting the garden. Soon, the house had become the envy of the neighborhood.

Humayun was always very fond of Roshan Ara, but was always too busy to spend any time with her since leaving Meerut. When she had finished her post-secondary schooling, he asked her to move in with them in the big city. She happily accepted his invitation. He enjoyed coming home to see his children playing with her, while Nasreen attended to running the household and attending to her old passion for feeding the poor.

Living in Lucknow as the railway stationmaster was a boon for their social status. Everyone traveled by train. So, people were always coming to him for favors, usually small ones, but sometimes large. He usually obliged. His meticulously kept book of business contacts grew at an unprecedented pace.

Visitors also came on social visits to meet the first native station master of Lucknow station and his philanthropic wife.

Women started noticing his pleasant, marriage-age sister, and soon he was getting marriage proposals for her from good families. Humayun would summarily reject the ones where the candidate was not well educated, which were most of them.

There was one proposal that Humayun really liked. The boy hailed from a respectable Syed[111] family in Lucknow. His schooling had been done at the Colvin Taluqdar School, a school set up in the late 19th century in Lucknow by the British to educate the sons of British administrators and the landed aristocracy or *Taluqdaars.*[112] He had a degree in history from Aligarh Muslim University, the sole institution of higher education for Muslims in India. He had recently been accepted to the Sandhurst Royal Military College, near London, as a trainee officer of the British Army.

The wedding date was fixed for the following year, after Hashim returned from England.

The wedding of Roshan Ara to Second Lieutenant Syed Hashim Pasha was the event of the year in Meerut, the bride's hometown. Guests included relatives and friends, as well as Hashim's *desi* and *gora* military friends. Another graduate of Sandhurst, and his best friend, Second Lieutenant Syed Shahid Hamid, was there too. The celebrations continued for a week in Meerut and then the party moved to the groom's hometown of

---

111 Direct descendants of the Prophet Mohammad.

112 Aristocrats of the Mughal Empire and later, the British Raj.

Lucknow for another week of an outsized *valima*[113] celebrations.

Humayun had invited Richard to both the wedding and *valima* celebrations. Richard was very busy and could only attend the *valima* party.

After the dinner after most people had left, Richard took Humayun aside and told him he was returning to England to be closer to his elderly parents. He also wanted to start something in England after having spent most of his adult life in India.

"My uncle has a large weapons manufacturing business in England and he is getting old and looking for help to reduce his workload. I will work with him to run and grow the business. It looks like war is coming to Europe again soon, so it may not be a bad business to get into. Also, Father asked me if I would like to go into politics, possibly running for his seat when he retires in a few years."

It was no surprise to Humayun that Richard wanted to go back and be near his parents in their old age, and to explore other ventures there. He had also thought about a career change at some point in the future. Railway was his first love, but he felt he had attained the highest level possible for a native employee under British rule. He would have loved to run the railways in an Independent India, but by his estimate, independence was still a decade or more away.

"Congratulations Richard, great news! Sir Jonathon and your mother will be delighted to have you back home. I am so happy for you. I am sure you will do very well in any direction you choose to go."

"Thank you Humayun. I am looking forward to it." Then he continued in the same breath, "Since I will be leaving the Railway Board soon, this is probably the last chance for me to help you with anything related to your employment here. If there is something you need from a career perspective, this is the time to let me know. As always, anything you discuss with me will always

---

113 Traditional celebrations to welcome the bride to her new home.

remain between the two of us. You have done very well on your own, and I am sure, like always, you will do fine, but I thought I should ask, just in case there was something you needed. I promised father I would ask."

This time, Humayun didn't refuse his offer.

"I love working here at the railways and it was my dream job growing up. I could spend a lifetime working at the railways and be satisfied that I did what I loved. However, since you put it as a now-or-never opportunity, I will be honest with you. Would it be possible for me to get a paid leave of absence? I have been thinking about doing something on my own. I could use some time off to explore possibilities."

"Humayun, you are a dynamic young man, and I understand your urge to explore other fields. I made my decision a bit late in my career. I should have done so when I was about your age. Put in an application for a six-month leave and I will approve it. If you ask for a longer period, they will have to bring in someone to run the station and you will be posted somewhere else, if you come back. So put in an application for six months to avoid the possibility of that happening. If after six months you still need more time, you can apply for an extension. This way your position here will still be there if you decide to come back."

While Humayun was still thinking about it, Richard added, "By the way, why don't you come to England for a bit in your time off? Bring Nasreen along. Father will be thrilled to see you two, and you will get to meet Mother and the rest of our family."

WAR AND PEACE
1939

The Second World War came to Indian homes at the same time it did to European homes, but in a different form. The bombs on Indian homes came as news of their husbands' or sons' deaths. India was an economy of single-income multi-family homes, most with extended families, all dependent on the one source of income for subsistence. The death of the sole breadwinner meant a slow march towards destitution for the family.

For a century, Britain had recruited Indian men, initially for use against their own countrymen and brothers, and later on as cannon fodder in its conflicts overseas.

The geographical footprint of the Second World War was large. The British generals were occupied with the dilemma of how to effectively protect the boundaries of the empire where the sun never set, and the recruitment drives for native Indian soldiers were expanded like never before.

The two lieutenants and best friends, Hashim and Shahid, were sent in the opposite directions to defend their master's colonies. While Hashim was sent to the African theater fighting against the Italian and German forces, Shahid was posted to Singapore, trying to help slow down the rapid advance of the formidable Japanese war machine.

Initially, the war raged far away in Europe and South East

Asia, and its effects were only felt by families losing men in those battlefields. Then Burma fell to the Japanese and brought the war to Indian doorsteps.

Humayun was busy helping keep the railways running. It transported crucial shipments of grains from across India to Indian ports to be shipped off to Europe for the fighting men. He wanted to be of more help to the war effort, but didn't know how.

Returning home one day, he saw a few women sitting in a side room knitting woolen items. Nasreen told him they were knitting sweaters for Indian *Jawans* fighting in Europe. They had already shipped the first batch, hoping to send more each week. She told him many other ladies had shown interest in helping knit more sweaters if they were provided woolen yarn.

Humayun knew officials of several wool and woolen products businesses. They all used railways for their shipments across India. Nasreen asked Humayun to approach them for the yarn needed to grow the volunteer effort.

Soon there were bags of woolen yarn sitting at his house and at the station, waiting to become woolen caps, mufflers, and sweaters for the fighting *Jawans*.

The enthusiasm shown by the helping industrialists and businessmen led him to consider other ways of helping the war effort.

He formulated a plan of organizing a flotilla of short trains that would run across the country, stopping at every station to collect warm clothing for fighting men and money for the war effort. He presented his idea to the Railway Board with the assurance that not a penny would be spent out of the Railways' revenues for this. They would come from monies collected by the program.

His plan was well received by the Railway Board and they approved a trial run. Humayun quickly set it up using two trains, each with a locomotive, a goods carriage, and a caboose running the Lahore to Calcutta route. The guards were to act as the fundraiser and entertainer at each stop. Humayun also organized a short training for the guards on how to go about presenting the message to the public at the stops. He instructed the stationmasters on the route to notify people in their towns of the upcoming fundraising events.

The trial run turned out to be an immense success and soon, many more short trains were running across the country, raising money and collecting warm clothing. As the program gained visibility, politicians, movie stars, theater actors, and other well-known personalities joined in. Some traveled on these trains, others met the collection trains at their stations. The movie stars and other celebrities drew vast crowds at each stop. As a result, they raised serious amounts of money for the war, amounts the war office in London could have never imagined from volunteer efforts.

Roshan Ara's husband, Lieutenant Hashim, posted with the 4th Indian Infantry Division in Egypt, had a comparatively easier time chasing Italian and German forces all over northern Africa. His brigade was later moved to help the Free French Army regulars to drive the Germans out of France. As the Germans retreated from Paris, his brigade entered Paris from the southwest with columns of the Free French Army to a raucous welcome from the ecstatic French citizens waving French, British, and American flags and serenading them with "La Marseillaise," the national anthem of France.

On the Eastern front, things didn't go as well. The allies lost Singapore to the advancing Japanese army. The British surrendered Singapore and 80,000 men. Hashim's best friend, Lieutenant Shahid Hamid, managed to escape in a small boat "to fight another day." He found his way to Burma and joined the 48th Indian Infantry Brigade for a last stand against the rapidly advancing columns of the Japanese and some rebel Indian and Burmese men fighting under Japanese command. They had reached the gates of India, his homeland, and the war was now personal for him. He was given the command of a group of about 100 soldiers and promoted to a captain to help stop the Japanese onslaught.

In one of these intense engagements, Captain Shahid Hamid was wounded when his bunker was hit by enemy shells. His eyesight was severely affected and he had to be extracted to Calcutta for treatment and recuperation.

***

At the end of the War, Humayun was recommended for one of the highest civilian awards for his fund-raising work for the war. He was promoted to a position that was equivalent to being an Indian Civil Service officer and posted to the Ministry of Railways in Delhi. His role was much bigger, however, it still involved management of stations and trains running across northern India.

Even with all the accolades and rewards, Humayun was not satisfied. He felt he had done enough for the British government and wanted to do something else, where he could contribute something to his people, to his nation, to India. He needed to find something interesting enough to give up this well-respected, high-paying bureaucratic job before he could take the next step towards his goal.

Hashim returned from the war a month after V-J Day.[114] Roshan Ara came to Delhi to welcome him back. They were staying with Humayun when he received an invitation to a victory party to celebrate the end of the war. Humayun and Nasreen had been invited as guests of the Viceroy Lord Wavell for their outstanding support for the *Jawans*. Humayun invited Hashim and Roshan Ara to join them at the celebrations.

It was a joyous occasion with mountains of foods and beverages, music, and entertainment. There were speeches promising a new day and more prosperity in India. Nehru, the leader of the Indian National Congress, and Jinnah, now the leader

---

[114] Victory over Japan day.

of the Indian Muslim League, were present, along with most of the other Indian political leaders with thoughts of freedom on their minds. They were all planning their next moves towards that goal and were gathered to exchange notes and gauge what the British were thinking. Gandhi, the people's hero of India, preferred to do his thinking with the people and avoided these events.

Humayun saw Jinnah sitting at a table with a few other leaders of the All India Muslim League-the party claiming to represent all Indian Muslims. He had aged a lot more than the elapsed 20 years since Humayun last saw him. He thought of walking up to the table and introducing himself, but decided against it.

Jinnah didn't seem to be enjoying the continuous stream of admirers to his table. He had two tough-looking men keeping intruders under control and moving on.

Humayun had a reserved table for him and his guests. Roshan Ara had never been to such an event. She was with her war hero husband after five years of worry and agony, wishing nothing happen to him and dying several deaths whenever his mail got delayed. Now that he was with her, she never wanted to let him go. Her eyes were constantly on him, examining his face and his hands, looking to absorb everything she could see, anything that may have changed, a wrinkle, a cut, anything. She couldn't believe how lucky she was to be at a gathering of such important people and enjoying and sharing the same foods with all of them. She had picked up some mangoes from a heap of fruits piled high on the serving table and was cutting them into smaller pieces and feeding them one by one to Hashim.

"What about me? Don't I get a bite of these sweet mangoes?" Humayun asked with a grin.

"The mangoes are too juicy and will spoil your shirt," she said, placing another piece into Hashim's open mouth. They both let out a roar of laughter, leaving Hashim and Nasreen clueless about the origin of the comment.

Hashim kept looking at Jinnah, "Bhaiya, see how stylish and dignified Mr. Jinnah looks compared to all the other Indian leaders here, some clad in wrinkled *Dhotis*."[115] Humayun told them about meeting Jinnah at Bareilly station and the story of the switched bags. He left Mir Jafar out of his story but told them about almost falling down after stepping on seagull droppings. They laughed picturing Humayun frantically searching for the signal room with Jinnah's bag while trying to avoid stepping into seagull droppings.

They were enjoying the evening and listening to war stories from Hashim when his friend Shahid, now Major Shahid Hamid, stopped by their table. After a brief exchange of pleasantries, he introduced his wife, Tahira. Shahid told them he stopped by to borrow Hashim to introduce him to some people. Tahira stayed behind while Shahid and Hashim walked away. Humayun noticed that a man from Jinnah's table rose and walked over to them and said something. The three then walked to the back of the room. A few minutes later, Jinnah got up and followed in the same direction.

A war reel started playing a film on a large screen showing footage of the war from different fronts, the amazing victories and the complete destruction of the Axis forces. It ended with scenes of Allied forces entering Paris and Berlin and the Atomic bomb being dropped on Hiroshima.

Hashim had joined them while the film was running. Hashim was star-struck and very animated, having just met the leader of the Indian Muslims. He told them Jinnah thought the British would leave India soon and a Muslim country would be born from it. He was looking for smart young Muslims to help build the new dominion.

---

[115] A light sheet of cloth worn around the waist by men, e.g. a sarong.

A DUTCH PROVERB

1945

Major Shahid who had stayed behind returned to the table. He said, "Bhaiya, Hashim told him about you."

Hashim said, "Yes Bhaiya. I told Mr. Jinnah about the time you met him. He remembers you and appreciated your timely actions. He knows of your fund-raising work for the war and wants to meet you."

Humayun immediately got up. Shahid and Hashim got up with him. As they started walking toward the back of the room where Jinnah was seated, the same man got up again and introduced himself as Khurshid Hasan, private secretary to Jinnah, and asked Shahid and Hashim to wait at his table while Mr. Jinnah met with Mr. Humayun.

Humayun was taken to a small back room, a private office of sorts with a desk and two guest chairs. Khurshid asked him to take a seat and wait for Mr. Jinnah. He left and closed the door behind him.

Humayun sat there, thinking about what he would say to Mr. Jinnah. It had been over half an hour and there was no sign of him.

He is a busy man, could be anything holding him up.

Another half hour and still no sign of him.

Did he forget I am here?

Is he punishing me for not going to Delhi to meet him?

Whatever it was, Humayun would not let this chance go by. Busy in his thoughts, he heard the door open and saw Jinnah standing there looking raptly at him.

"I am sorry for keeping you waiting, Mr. Babar. I hope your wait didn't feel as long as mine."

Humayun got up and said in a defensive tone, "I am so sorry, sir, I beg your pardon. I didn't intend to insult you. You are a busy man, and I was a small-time signalman and didn't want to take any more of your precious time. So, I couldn't bring myself to bother you."

He knew it was his mistake, pure and simple, and before he could say anything more, he heard Jinnah say, "Mr. Babar, please sit down. I thought you were a man with a lot of potential, and seeing what you have done with your life, I was right. But remember, a man's word is his honor and his only standing with others. Here, I jotted this down for you."

He handed a 4X6 card to a speechless Humayun.

The card had a motto handwritten on it:

If your motto would be

"Money lost - nothing lost"
"Courage lost much lost"
"Honour lost most lost"
"Soul lost all lost."

Dutch Proverb

As Humayun looked up sheepishly after reading the note, Jinnah noticed the overwhelmed look in his eyes.

"It's okay. I didn't call you here to browbeat you for something from the past. I wanted to speak with you about the future. Your future and that of a new country."

"As you know, we started a movement for a new homeland for the Muslims of the subcontinent and we shall be successful. I feel we are at the dawn of the greatest event for all Indians, a free nation. We shall soon have our Independent homelands."

"The British, after two centuries of squeezing out the last drops of our blood, have figured out that the time to leave India with dignity is now, before things turn ugly and they are forced to leave after a loss of a lot more lives and their pride."

"We need smart men like you to help lead the cause for independence. Think about it, talk to your family and close friends. Discuss it with your family before you answer. My office is still the same as what was on the card I gave you. You can stop by. Khurshid is always there, and he will set up an appointment for you to see me."

"Sir, I am honored you remembered me. I have thought about how I can help with the movement."

"Your work in helping raise large amounts during the world war was noticed even by Mr. Churchill. In my last meeting with him, he mentioned your work. I thought you would have liked to know."

"Thank you, Sir. How can I help?"

"I would like your help in raising money for a Muslim homeland in India. There are many ongoing efforts, led by some very dedicated individuals to raise funds for this cause. However, I can use someone knowledgeable with fundraising for new ideas of raising funds, as well as help lead and coordinate efforts to reduce waste, and possible abuse."

"Sir, I don't need time to think about it. It will be an honor to help in any way that I can."

Jinnah continued, "Good. There is a meeting of some of the leading donors next week here in Delhi. I would like you to attend the meeting. Khurshid will contact you with the details."

"I certainly will, Thank you. Sir."

"I don't want to hold you up anymore. Your family must be waiting for you. Good night Mr. Babar, and thank you for meeting me." Saying this, he got up and left.

When Humayun returned to his table, Roshan Ara had an impish smile on her face. She said, "Bhaiya, Mr. Jinnah sat there looking at papers for a long time while you were in the room. We were wondering if you had been put in a detention room for not visiting him in Delhi."

They all laughed at the thought of Humayun in Jinnah's lockup.

Humayun still had the unclaimed attaché case full of gold coins he had found in Behramgarh. He never spent any of it on his personal needs.

I have found the best use of the unclaimed wealth. I will anonymously donate the funds to the independence movement.

THE BLACK TRAIN
1948

Firozpur lies on the left bank of the Sutlej River in Punjab. It was home to the largest cantonments in the western parts of the Raj when the British decided to partition[116] India into two independent states, India and Pakistan. It was also one of the largest ammunition and arms depots of the British Army in the subcontinent.

As part of the poorly planned and executed partition[117] of the Indian subcontinent, the armies, navies, currency, and gold in treasury, as well as all war implements and ammunition, were to be divided proportionately between the two states. Even though there were military cantonments in areas that went to Pakistan, most of the modern armaments were kept in areas that became part of the new India.

Firozpur was to remain in India, but the Viceroy assigned all the military hardware stored there to Pakistan. This would make up for more than half of Pakistan's share of the armaments and materiel.

---

[116] Several excellent books have been written about the independence movements and the creation of India and Pakistan by South Asian and British authors, e.g. Jon E. Wilson's India Conquered.

[117] Most of the above mentioned books cover the mishandling of the partition of the subcontinent by Lord Mountbatten. e.g. Stanley Wolpert's 'Shameful Flight', and many others.

***

In the first days of independence, Jawaharlal Nehru, the new Prime Minister of India, set up a Partition Commission to examine and approve all transfers of goods to Pakistan. No transfers were to be made without the written permission of the Commission.

The transfer papers for the Firozpur arms and ammunition, waiting for approval at the Commission headquarters, were pushed down to the bottom of the paper mountain. The bureaucrats and other members of the Commission were busy running a newborn country, they hardly had little time to approve transfer papers.

Pakistan was facing death by starvation in the early days, caused by a lack of resources. Any prospects of receiving its share lay at the mercy of the Commission.

Mahatma Gandhi, the extremely popular, charismatic leader, and a very fair-minded man, was against withholding Pakistan's share of the combined pre-partition resources. He believed the real reason behind the formation of this Commission by Nehru was to deprive Pakistan of its rightful share of the resources. He gave Nehru an ultimatum to disband the Commission and start the transfer to Pakistan immediately.

This was the first public standoff between the two giants of the Indian independence movement. To appease Gandhi, Nehru ordered transfers of agricultural machinery, office furniture, and other lower-priority goods started immediately.

A RSS[118] Hindu fanatic, the militant nationalist Nathuram Godse, upset at Gandhi's demands in favor of Pakistan, shot and killed him when he came out of his house to address a multi-faith prayer meeting.

***

Humayun was still working at the Ministry of Railways and

[118] RSS - Rashtriya Swayamsevak Sangh, a right wing Hindu party, whose members planned and assassinated Mahatama Gandhi in 1948.

trying to decide when to sign the election papers for Pakistan. Having promised Jinnah that he would come to Pakistan, he still hadn't taken steps to declare his formal selection. He brought up the move to Pakistan with Nasreen before she left for her parents' home to take care of an ailing Imam Sahib. She was ambivalent about going to a new land, leaving her aging father, siblings, and all other relatives behind, but promised to think about it once she had a brief respite.

Humayun, a patient man, waited. Everyone expected him to opt for Pakistan, but no one knew why he was taking so long to decide. The Indian members of the Railway Board believed he was up to something and wanted him out. The British members of the board, reminding everyone of his great service to the India, provided cover for him while he pondered.

His secretary would place the election papers at the top of his in-basket every morning. Humayun would move them to the bottom each day. With pressure mounting and a deadline looming from the Railway Board, he applied for a month-long leave to help his wife take care of her ailing father. The leave was happily granted to get him out of the offices, hoping he would never come back. Humayun left his desk as if he would be back the next day.

On hearing of his arrival in Meerut, Roshan Ara joined him from Firozpur, where her husband, now Captain Hashim Pasha, was posted. Hashim had already opted for Pakistan and was awaiting his transfer orders. He also took a week's leave to join his wife for one last vacation with her family in India.

"Bhaiya, would you like to come for a walk with me?" Hashim asked him on the first day of his arrival. As soon as they were out of the house, Hashim brought up the escalating conflict over the northern region of Jammu and Kashmir.

"Pakistan has moved almost all its forces to the Kashmiri border, leaving the rest of the 700-mile-long border with India exposed. If India starts losing in Kashmir, they are bound to start a new front elsewhere. That will be a disaster."

Humayun didn't have such a pessimistic view of the situation. He said, "I don't think there will be a war. We are all old friends and neighbors. We are the same people. There won't be a war for some frozen piece of land in the Himalayas. Once the initial hysteria passes, saner heads will prevail and an agreement will be reached. India and Pakistan will soon become good friends, like France and Germany are now."

"Speaking of agreements," Hashim said, "An agreement was signed earlier this week in Amritsar, by India and Pakistan, to move the Firozpur Cantonment materiel to Pakistan next week. Nehru is only doing this to relieve the tremendous pressure on him exerted by Clement Attlee, the British PM, after Gandhiji's murder."

"They have invited a Pakistani Government official to be on hand in Firozpur to monitor the loading of the train. Since I will shift to Pakistan after my leave, the Pakistan Army has asked me to accompany the train from Firozpur to Lahore. There will be space on the train for my family and our household goods. If you want to send Nasreen *bhabi*[119] and the kids to Pakistan in the safety of an Army train, I can take them with me."

"I don't like this idea."

"Hashim, you should not put your family at risk by placing them on a train loaded with ammunition and all sorts of explosives. Several other trains are planned over the next weeks with military staff and their families. I have information about them in my office and I can get Roshan Ara and the children in one of those."

Humayun changes the subject, asking, "But why is India giving Pakistan all the weapons that would be aimed back at her if the Kashmir conflict escalated?"

"Bhaiya, it's part of the agreement." Hashim replied.

"I want you to go back to Firozpur tomorrow and monitor everything going on there. If they ask, tell them you got bored

---

119 Honorific title for sister in law.

sitting at the in-laws. I will go to Delhi to find something, anything, about this train you speak of."

Hashim said, "It is being called the Black Train by the army rank and file in the cantonment. They are unhappy that Nehru is giving Pakistan all the best armaments that they consider Indian property. I don't know how he has pulled off this agreement politically."

Mr. Nehru is a very charismatic man who has Mr. and Mrs. Mountbatten eating out of the palm of his hand.

I wonder what he is up to. There has got to be more to this Black Train agreement than meets the eye.

"I don't know. Let me find out."

He thought about it as they walked back. The hair on the nape of his neck was warning him of an impending peril.

TEA AND SCONES
1948

Humayun caught everyone by surprise when he showed up at work in Delhi while still on his leave.

He went into the records room and gathered the railway track maps from Firozpur to Lahore and the Firozpur station layouts. He locked himself up in his office went to work on becoming an expert on the materials he had picked up from the records room.

A single-track ran from the cantonment to the Firozpur railway station. This was the only way to enter and exit the cantonment by rail. The quarter-mile tracks passed through some agricultural fields.

After the train is loaded up, there is only one way it will get to Firozpur. This is the track they will use to bring the Black Train to Firozpur. What kind of attack can be mounted on the train on this route?

He traced the tracks from Firozpur Station towards the border. The station had four mainline tracks, two northbound and two southbound, in addition to the one connecting it to the cantonment. Tracing the northbound track towards the border, there was a station on the line before it entered Pakistan, the small village of Hussainiwala. Leaving Hussainiwala, the dual-track crossed River Sutlej. The tracks after the bridge headed downhill towards the Pakistan border, which was a mile or so from the bridge.

He went back to the records room and got the layouts drawings for Hussainiwala railway station. It was laid out like any other small station on the Indian Railways network. After memorizing the location of the signal room, the number, and types of signal deployed at the station, he moved to the detailed track map in and out of the station. The map ended just past the Sutlej Bridge. The edge of the map showed one of the two tracks diverging away from the route to Pakistan.

His first thought was that it was designed this way to go around a small hill or another topographical issue, but there was no way to confirm it. The maps beyond the Sutlej had already been sent to Pakistan since the river was originally marked as the border between the two countries. Mountbatten had later pushed the border back a mile into Pakistan, to bring the Sutlej Barrage waterworks into India as a gift for its farmers.

So once the Black Train leaves Hussainiwala and crosses Sutlej, it is safely in Pakistan. We will have to make sure the tracks from Firozpur to Hussainiwala and to the bridge on Sutlej are secure, a total distance of about eight miles. We can bring a small detachment of Army Jawans to protect the eight-mile route.

I am sure India will object to placing Pakistani army soldiers in Indian Territory, from Firozpur to the border.

He was not feeling any better about his misgivings. But he had some information to go on. He still needed more information on the Black Train.

Pulling up his Rolodex, he started calling people he knew in the upper echelons of the government, mostly Indian. He knew some senior British officers who had stayed behind to keep an eye on the newly formed country under the guise of helping it get on its feet. His query was always the same: any information on this agreement to send most of the armaments from Firozpur to Pakistan on a train. The answers he got towed with the official line–A giant step towards improving relations with Pakistan.

None of his contacts had seen the actual agreement.

Humayun was unsuccessful at finding anything beyond what Hashim had told him.

They really have this thing locked up airtight. It must be very important for them to keep it under wraps.

He stopped by Shershah's home on the way home. Shershah was posted in the Government Secretariat in Delhi, having already signed his election papers to stay in India. He felt his family would be seen as outsiders in Pakistan, and after the euphoria of independence has passed, his children and grandchildren would face discrimination as refugees for years, if not decades.

Shershah and Sakina were having tea in the vast lawns of his government-provided villa.

As soon as he saw Humayun's Morris Minor pulling into the driveway, Shershah got up to meet him.

"Humayun, this is a surprise. Is everything okay? I thought you were all in Meerut."

"*Salaam* Bhai, everything is fine. Something came up, and I had to be back in Delhi. I got back from Meerut yesterday. Hashim, Roshan Ara, and the children were there too. He told me something that worried me and I wanted to speak with you about it, privately."

"Come, let's have some tea first. We can discuss all that bothers you later and, of course, privately as you desire. Sakina just got some freshly baked scones, clotted cream and English strawberry jam from the Army-Navy store. We are lucky she was there when the shipment came in from England. Otherwise, it would have been gone quickly."

Then, with a wink, but no smile, he said, "You know the saying: everything can wait for a good cup of tea."

Humayun nodded reluctantly.

I would have preferred for the tea to have waited.

After tea, he brought the conversation to Indo-Pakistan

politics.

Sakina got up. "Humayun, you have not been to our place for so long. You should stay for dinner, and I don't want to hear a no."

"How can I say no to my only *bhabi*? I will stay for dinner if it is not an inconvenience."

"Not at all." She said and left.

Humayun narrated to Shershah what Hashim had told him and shared his concerns about the train.

"Yes, I am aware of the Firozpur train. It is a straightforward transaction. I don't think anyone is planning to deceive Pakistan. Mountbatten will not let us."

Humayun retorted, "Bhai, Isn't Mountbatten the same man who moved the boundary lines on the award map to give India the critical district of Gurdaspur[120] without which there would be no way for India to move its forces into Kashmir?"

"Well, I don't know if that really happened. I won't argue with you about the past, but he is acting in good faith now to make sure Pakistan gets its fair share of the resources."

"Bhai, I am looking for your help with details of the agreement and the train. When is it supposed to leave, what are its contents, who is assigned to protect it? Anything you can find out will be useful."

"Looks like you have decided for Pakistan."

"No, I haven't, but Hashim has," Humayun replied. "To me, it is a matter of fairness. Even Gandhiji demanded India give Pakistan its fair share quickly without those endless Commission meetings to decide what should and shouldn't go to Pakistan. Hashim was asked by the Pakistan government to accompany the train. They have told him he can bring his family on the train along with his household goods. I have advised him against it. There

---

[120] Mountbatten is believed to have personally altered the boundary line to give Gurdaspur District to India. Stanley Wolpert describes the manipulation in his book, Shameful Flight: The Last Years…..

could be trouble by the RSS who want Pakistan to get nothing."

"Humayun, you are overreacting. I think it should be safe for Roshan Ara and the children. It is a military train. What could be safer than that, for God's sake?"

"I hope I am, Bhai. If I can get more information, it will be easier to decide whether to send my family on the train."

"I will try to find out what I can, but I don't think you need to worry about it. It will happen in a week. The train will safely reach Pakistan without any trouble, and there will be nothing to complain about."

He changed the topic, "You like wine? I have some very good red wine. I'll go ask Sakina to have it out for dinner."

"I am fine, Bhai. Please don't bother."

Humayun was getting a strong impression that the topic was closed. He decided right then and there to take a trip to Firozpur.

A FORK IN THE PATH
1948

Hashim received Humayun at the Firozpur Station as his train came to a stop. Two men carrying the weight of a nation on their shoulders, or at least that was how he was feeling.

Time was not on their side.

They took off for the Hussainiwala Bridge in Hashim's Jeep and crossed the Sutlej by a small bridge intended for motor vehicles. The railway bridge lay about a quarter mile upstream. In the absence of a road, or even a dirt path connecting the two bridges, Hashim drove his Jeep over rocks and bushes, along the riverbank, straight to the point where the ground rose to meet the railway track.

He parked near the right bank entrance to the bridge. It was an awkward climb to get to the tracks. Humayun was worried about being seen near the tracks within a mile of the Pakistani border. They could be mistaken for miscreants trying to blow up the bridge. But they carried on.

As they walked up the tracks, they saw a fork in the tracks. While, the left tracks went straight towards the Pakistani border, a short distance away, visible from their vantage point, the right tracks split off and sloped down a steep hill to the level of the river, ending at the riverbanks into a large mound of dirt. The rotting rail sleepers and the weeds growing between the rails were signs that the tracks had not been used for years, or even decades. Closer inspection of the tracks at the fork showed that traffic on the right tracks could be switched to the left track, and vice versa.

The two sets of movable tracks must be controlled from the Hussainiwala Station signal room.

He explained the mechanism to Hashim and told him how someone could derail the train on either track by locking both tracks to the right-side rails, which went straight down into the mud bank.

"Plan on riding in the engine with the driver," he told Hashim.

"Watch out if the train is put on the right rail coming out of the station. Tell the driver to slow down as it gets on the bridge and then to bring it to a crawl as it reaches this point at the end of the bridge. You will be able to see if the rails have been moved to make the train go right and down into a mud bank below."

"Keep a close eye on the driver and your gun handy, as he could be an agent. Shoot him if he shows any hesitation to your orders at any point after Hussainiwala station. If you have to shoot him, pull the brake lever as hard as you can and keep it there until the train comes to a full stop. The brake lever is the one coming up from the floor on the right of the driver. Your life and Pakistan's future will depend on you stopping the train."

Hashim was stunned at how his laid-back, contemplative brother-in-law had suddenly transformed into a warrior ready to order a kill, as Humayun slowly repeated his instructions, "Keep an eye on the driver and remember, the train needs to be on the left track after the bridge if it is to ever to reach Pakistan."

Hashim nodded, but to Humayun, he looked unsure. Humayun softened his tone. "Don't worry, you will be fine. I will draw it out on paper and explain all this to you when we are back in Firozpur."

"Now let's take a trip around the Hussainiwala station before we head back to Firozpur."

"We have only one chance to get this thing right."

Hashim is a loyal soldier ready to obey orders.

I would have preferred someone stronger. Someone who would challenge and question me at every step of my plan, so that I am forced to account for any and every possibility that could come up.

"I have studied the station layout from the records in Delhi. It looks like any of the hundreds of small stations I have been to. I don't think there should be anything different about it, but we still need to walk through it to make sure."

Hashim finally broke his silence and asked, "What if the stationmaster or someone there questions us?"

"We will be fine, but let me do the talking. Once you are back at the cantonment, load up all your household goods on the Black Train as you were ordered to, and plan to be on the train when it leaves. I will bring Roshan Ara and your children safely to you in Pakistan."

When they got close to the station, Hashim parked the Jeep by the wayside, away from the station. He didn't want the Military Jeep within sight of the railway station. They didn't have to wait for long before a passenger train from Firozpur leisurely rolled into the station. They jumped out of the Jeep and walked calmly into the station.

There were many passengers on the platform, mostly Sikh and Hindu refugees. Most with families, and hauling everything they could in large bags and other luggage. Some were with only the clothes on their backs. All were desperate to get to wherever they were headed.

They must be the refugees coming in from Pakistan, having left their homes for good to settle in a new land, in towns all over India. The disembarking passengers will mostly be Muslim refugees from Punjab and beyond, in similar situations. They will walk the last two miles from here to Pakistan.

I wish there was a better way to exchange the populations. Tens of thousands have been killed on the way to their new home. What a shame for all of us.

The arriving train was full, with hundreds of people sitting on the roofs of the carriages and hanging on in between the bogies. As soon as the train came to a halt, the departing passengers rushed to get on the train while the arriving passengers tried to get off. Lots of pushing, cursing, and berating ensued between the two groups of passengers. Some fights broke out on the platform.

Humayun and Hashim used the cover of the chaos on the platform to walk around the station, noting every detail. They passed a man wearing the stationmaster uniform running towards the fracas. He glanced at them curiously, but kept on. Their clean and ironed civilian clothes made them stand out from the others.

Humayun said, "I had timed our visit to the station, so that we arrived at the same time as the train, but I think he noticed us. So, a change in plan. I will get on the train back to Firozpur. Act like you are here to see me off, then take the Jeep back to the cantonment to see what is happening there with the Black Train."

Hashim replied, "Okay Bhaiya, I will get to Firozpur long before you and will pick you up at the station."

"No, it will be better if you do not show up at the station, just in case someone is watching me on the train. I'll take a Tonga to the Railway Rest House. Come see me there in the evening. Until you leave, take a note of everything happening here. We are also looking for civilian clothed soldiers. They may or may not be part of any plan to sabotage the train, but try to remember the details of anyone suspicious. We will exchange notes at the Rest House."

Hashim was in awe of Humayun, his demeanor, his calmness, and his plan. He wanted to say something, but the overwhelming sense of responsibility and his newfound reverence of Humayun wouldn't let him. He wanted to do well by Humayun and was trying his best to keep up and to perform to the expectations he felt encumbered with. The pressure he felt was like what he had endured on the battlefields of Africa and Europe, but this was something different, something personal.

Humayun got in line to buy his ticket.

"Did you notice the stationmaster standing behind the ticket agent?" Hashim asked Humayun as they left the ticket office window.

"Yes, I was wondering why he is at the ticket office scrutinizing the ticket agent. The agent could be under training, or he was there to check us out after he saw us in the ticket line. I bought a ticket for Amritsar to throw him off."

The guard whistled and waved his green flag. The engine whistled, and the train started to move. Humayun gave Hashim a big hug and whispered, "Let's show them you are here to drop me off. When you leave, keep an eye out for someone watching or following." He ran and got up on the nearest carriage. It was overflowing with people, but not as bad as before.

Back at the Railway Rest House in Firozpur, Humayun was restless and tired. He wanted time to move faster. The train had taken about half an hour to get to Firozpur. The Tonga ride from the station was uneventful. He chatted with Phujja, a Muslim refugee Tonga-walla, trying to make some extra money with his Tonga on his way to Pakistan.

After making notes of the trip in his little notebook, he took a long shower to pass the time. That didn't help. He sat down to re-live the day's events. He heard a knock on the door and looked out. It was dark, but he could see Hashim standing outside.

"Bhaiya, Shahid is outside. He wanted me to make sure no one else was in the room before he comes in."

Shahid Hamid entered the room.

Humayun stepped forward and hugged him.

As they sat down, Shahid said, "I am glad to see you Bhaiya. It has been a long time."

Humayun nodded, "It has, and I am glad you have been assigned to protect the train."

"It's all unofficial. Hashim has updated me on all that happened today. I understand you are anxious about the Black Train, and so are we. Our concern in Pakistan is also for its safety. We had asked India to let us bring some *Jawans* to travel with it, but they have rejected our request, saying they have allowed Hashim to accompany the train."

"What do you think they may be planning?"

Humayun handed Shahid some RSS anti-Pakistan pamphlets and said, "My biggest worry is from these people. They may try to attack or blow it up on the way. But I also don't trust the government; they may try to trick us. Since Hashim will be onboard the train, I may need some men with me here in India in case something happens. Can you arrange for two well-trained, intelligent men who are able to handle multiple weapons? They should only carry counterfeit Indian identification papers in case if they are caught."

"Not a problem. I will have a good guy with me. When do you want us to be here?"

"You mean you and another soldier?"

"Yes, Bhaiya. I am a small man, but these hands are deadly weapons. Hashim knows I won the sharpshooting contest at Sandhurst. I am trained on all modern weaponry." Shahid said with a grin.

"I would rather it not be you. You are too valuable to the country, Major Sahib. Send someone junior to you."

Hashim interjected, "Bhaiya, Shahid is a colonel now."

"Congratulations. Great to hear this. More reason for you to stay back and command the operation from across the border."

Shahid quoted General George Patton, "Do everything you ask of those you command." And then added seriously, "So, please accept my service for something so precious to us."

Humayun smiled, got up and hugged him again, "I hope we will not need to do anything, and the train will cross the border safely, but we will plan for the worst."

"Do you think two men will be sufficient for this mission?" asked Shahid.

"If they are going to attack the train, it will be a few men. A large contingent so close to the border would attract attention. They must know Pakistan has people in border towns reporting back to GHQ."

Satisfied, Shahid said, "I will get a group of commandos across the border ready to jump into India if there is trouble."

"Good. Also, have a couple of locomotives ready to drag the train over the border just in case something happens to the driver of our Black Train." Humayun said.

"Consider it done. Anything else you think we will need?"

"So the train is to leave in three days. I need the men ready and in their position 24 hours a day until it has safely crossed into Pakistan. Have everyone ready as if the train is expected at any moment."

Shahid nodded and Humayun continued, "There is a large forest on the other side of the Hussainiwala station, which would be a good place for you to camp and monitor everything happening in and around the station. From tomorrow morning on, I will hang around the Firozpur station's waiting rooms. If they ask, I am waiting for a train to Amritsar, which runs once every few days."

"Bhaiya, you are such an outstanding leader! You have thought of everything, haven't you? I am so glad we have you on our side."

Humayun thought for a second and said, "We are only as good as what the results will show."

THE NIGHT OF...
1948

It was the night of the day before the Black Train was to leave for Pakistan. Humayun was trying to relax in the second-class waiting room in Firozpur station. Shahid had located a place in the forest by the Hussainiwala station for a camouflaged observation camp and had been camping there for the last two days with another young officer. Hashim had stopped by earlier to tell Humayun that his household goods have all been loaded up earlier that morning. This meant that the Black Train was fully loaded and ready to go.

A final inspection of the train was planned for the next morning by Partition Commission auditors. Hashim had been told to be ready to go after the auditors were done with their work.

Humayun's level of tension and anxiety had not let him sleep for days. He had gotten a few brief naps since meeting Shahid, but woke up each time with nightmares about the Black Train.

There were a few other passengers in the waiting room, some occupying easy chairs trying to sleep like him, others had spread their hold-all[121] beds on the floor and were fast asleep. The level of activity on the platform was almost non-existent except for a few stray dogs searching through garbage piles for food. Passengers with lower-class tickets, restricted from the comforts of

---

[121] Leather lined open sleeping bags for use on any surface.

the waiting room, had spread out their hold-all beds on the platform trying to get some rest. He still had his ticket to Amritsar, allowing him the use of the waiting room.

He was going over all the scenarios in his mind when he heard the familiar screeching sound of a locomotive applying the brakes. But immediately afterwards he heard a guard's whistle, then the engine whistle, and felt the train moving.

Such a quick stop, couldn't be a passenger train, possibly a goods train. But why did it stop?

He immediately got up and walked out onto the platform. It was a goods train picking up speed.

It is a long train. Where is it headed?

He looked towards the engine of the train and noticed it going straight west, leaving behind the mainline northbound track.

Hmm, the Engine has already passed the northern track. It is heading west. Those are the tracks that lead to Hussainiwala.

Are those tanks and Jeeps on it?

It is the Black Train! Oh my God, the fix is in.

They are sending the train a day earlier.

Hashim probably doesn't even know about it.

I need to get on. The guard will probably see me, but I will deal with that if they stop the train.

Humayun started running with the train and jumped on one of the last low bed carriers. It had a Jeep and two tanks on it.

The Jeep was a newer American model. He got into its driver's seat. As the train picked up speed, he got up to look at the two tanks on the carrier. They also looked new.

His mind was racing, trying to deconstruct this change of plan.

Mr. Nehru is being generous to Pakistan. They are sending the train early to reduce any chance of sabotage. I was too harsh on him.

It will be such a pleasant surprise for the Pakistanis when they see the train coast in. Shahid will be glad to see the train speeding by to Pakistan.

Hashim will be disappointed about missing the departure, but happy that the train reached Pakistan safely.

But if they wanted to send the train earlier, why didn't they put him on the train? Or did they? Is he on the train?

The train was taking the last bend before Hussainiwala station and started slowing down. He felt it move to the right tracks before the station.

The right track leads straight down into the mud bank. Oh my goodness, they are going to destroy it, rather than send it to Pakistan.

I need to do something, but what?

The train came to a halt on the right platform. He saw the guard jump on the platform and run into the station.

Humayun jumped off the train too, but on the other side. He started running towards the forest to get Shahid. He didn't have to run far when he saw two men racing towards him, waving their hands at him, or at least that is what he thought. They weren't waving at him; they were pointing back towards the track.

Turning around, he saw another goods train hurtling towards the station from the same direction, from Firozpur.

This one is on the left track. It is going to Pakistan.

They are switching the trains under darkness.

The Black Train was never destined for Pakistan. They loaded all the new equipment from the cantonment on the Black Train, which they always intended on keeping with this sleight-of-hand trick. The other train, a decoy, must be empty or carry some old, unusable, and damaged equipment from other depots.

We have to stop this from happening.

Not knowing what to do, he started running towards the station. He found he was completely out of shape, as the well-conditioned soldiers quickly caught up with him.

"This is a decoy train. It has nothing on it. We have to stop it from going to Pakistan. I need to get to the signal room." He shouted out to Shahid while gasping for more air to breathe.

Shahid handed Humayun a handgun and said, "Use both hands to hold the gun, with the trigger hand cupped at the bottom by the palm of other hand. If you need to, point the gun below the neck and shoot in quick succession."

"Got it." Said Humayun, without really getting it.

"Bhaiya, follow me. I will run ahead and see what I can do to secure the signal room." Then, turning to his companion, he said, "Anwar, Let's go. You go take control of the Black Train. Shoot the driver if he moves the train."

"Shahid, be careful. I saw the guard go in there, and there must be others, too," said Humayun as he started running towards the station, behind them.

Shahid reached the signal room while Humayun was still about a hundred yards behind him. He heard a shot and instinctively ducked, and then stumbled and fell. Two more shots and then nothing. He got up and saw Shahid waving to him from the signal room and started running towards him.

"Bhaiya quick. The decoy train is getting to the bridge."

There were two well-built men with military-style haircuts in civilian clothing lying on the floor in large pools of blood.

"Indian Army *Jawans*; I had to shoot them when one shot at me. The bullet grazed my left arm. One of these guys was the guard who was on the train.

Humayun had no problem identifying the track change levers for the bridge exit. He pulled hard on it as the decoy train engine cleared the bridge. It gave a long, loud whistle before disappearing behind the bridge.

The last scream of a condemned man from the gallows.

Humayun reset the tracks back to the left, with both tracks now leading to Pakistan.

"We need to get our train moving quickly."

They ran to the locomotive. Anwar had the driver, another well-built young man with a military-style haircut, sitting by the tracks with his hands tied behind his back, "Sir, when the shots were fired, he jumped out of the engine to help his friends. I was waiting for him and grabbed him." Anwar said proudly.

Shahid smiled at Anwar, "Well done, Captain Anwar. Do we need him to drive the engine?"

Anwar replied, "No, Sir, I can handle it. I practiced on a similar model on the day we got your message."

"Good man. Start it up. The tracks and signals are already set for a quick passage to Pakistan, but take it slow on the bridge, just in case the decoy's tail is still on the bridge. Now let's deliver this priceless cargo to where it belongs."

Anwar gave Humayun a military style salute and jumped on the locomotive. The train started to move.

Shahid said, "Bhaiya, let's get on the train."

"You go ahead. I have my family to take care of, and some other loose ends to tie up."

"It is dangerous for you to stay in India now. I will get everyone out of India, safe. I promise you. Please get on the train."

"It will be riskier for my family if I go to Pakistan now. You get on the train before you miss it and have to walk a mile to get there."

"Bhaiya, you won't be able to get far walking before they surround the area looking for clues."

Humayun smiled. "Who said anything about walking? There is a Tonga outside the station waiting for me. Phujja will take me to Firozpur from here. He is moving to Pakistan soon. If he comes to you for help, take care of him."

Shahid had noticed a lone Tonga outside the station. He shook his head in admiration and smiled. "I certainly will. Tell him to find me at the Lahore Cantonment."

As he got on the moving train, Shahid shouted out to Humayun, "I will see you soon on the other side, *Insha-Allah.*"

"Bhaiya, you are an authentic hero! Whatever happens from here on, Pakistan will forever be in your debt. *Khuda Hafiz.*"[122]

---

[122] Allah be with you, good bye.

THE TRAIN TO PAKISTAN
1948

Hashim returned to Meerut quite dejected about missing the Black Train, but happy that it had safely reached Pakistan. He and his family members were allocated passage on a train scheduled to leave for Pakistan in a few days.

Humayun wanted Nasreen and the children to go with Hashim. He would join them after completing his transfer paperwork in Delhi. Imam Sahib was still not well, and Nasreen did not want to leave him. After some discussion, it was decided that the twins would travel to Pakistan with Hashim's family. Gayti Ara was excited about traveling with her cousins, but Saleem wanted his parents to come along. He didn't want to go without them. Humayun, too pre-occupied with being identified with the Black Train hijacking, summarily swatted away Saleem's 'childish' arguments, telling him he would be fine once they were in Lahore. Nasreen tried to reason with Humayun about not sending the children, but he didn't budge. They had to go.

A few weeks later, Imam Sahib's condition deteriorated, and he died.

Now Nasreen didn't have a reason to stay in India. Her mother had passed away a few years back. She was ready to move to Pakistan to join her children. She was especially worried about Saleem, who had come down with asthma in Lahore.

The Indian partition, thanks to the ineptness of the Viceregal Administration, had started one of the largest and most violent population exchanges in history. It took over six months for the two governments to bring the savagery under control. Passenger trains carrying refugees from both sides had started running more freely. Presence of army soldiers on stations and trains had helped bring down the violence significantly. Trains were still being derailed and attacked from time to time.

Humayun was still not done with his work in Delhi, and Nasreen was getting more and more anxious about Saleem's health. Every letter from him talked about how he missed her.

Hashim, now a major in the Pakistan Army, had been moved to the border region of Kashmir. Saleem and Gayti Ara were living with Roshan Ara and her two teenage children in Lahore. Nasreen was also worried that the four teenagers may be getting too much for Roshan Ara to handle. The threat of a sealed border loomed large, because of the escalating Kashmir conflict, which would stop all cross-border traffic.

She told Humayun that a good friend was moving to Pakistan with her husband and family soon and she wanted to go with them. Humayun was worried about some reports of attacks and looting on the way. He asked her to wait, as he would be done in a few more weeks with his transfer papers. Nasreen didn't want to wait anymore. She told Humayun she was an old woman of fifty and wanted to spend as much of her remaining time, as possible, with her children. Reluctantly, Humayun agreed to let her go. Soon, she was on the train with her friends and hundreds of other refugees.

The train derailed outside of a small town of Jandiala, about an hour from the border. The attackers had removed a section of the rails just before the train got there. By the time an army train from Amritsar, about 10 miles away, got there, hundreds of men had been butchered and scores of women abducted from the train. Nasreen was among those abducted.

A depressed Humayun, distraught and upset at himself for letting her go alone, fell ill. A deep melancholia set upon him. With no news of her and no signs of hope, he felt helpless, like never.

Having given up all hope of seeing her again, he would sleep for hours during the days and lay awake at night.

As he slept restlessly one night, he felt some movement in the room. The room was dark, but the light filtering from the windows showed Hanafi Sarkar standing at the foot of his bed. Shaking his head at Humayun, he said, "Hopelessness is a curse for humanity. Self-pity doesn't become you. Get up and start acting like the man you are."

There was a peal of laughter from the other side of the room. Humayun turned his head and saw Mir Jafar, the seagull, sitting on the back of a chair.

"If I, Mir Jafar, the most exalted Nawab of Bengal and Bihar, can become a seagull, you can be a Sikh."

Humayun sat up, sweating profusely. There was no one in the room.

Was this a dream?

They are both telling me to take things into my own hands.

He decided to go to Amritsar to look for her.

After hearing of Nasreen's abduction, Shershah didn't want Humayun to suffer all alone in his house, so he had convinced Humayun to come stay with him until some news of Nasreen. He had used all his contacts and sources to get any news of Nasreen. He found out that his friend General S. M. Shrigesh, the corps commander at Amritsar, was leading the derailment investigation. General Shrigesh promised them to track down Nasreen's abductors and bring her back home soon. Upon hearing of Humayun's plan, he asked him to wait a little. Shershah also tried to deter Humayun from traveling to Amritsar. Humayun had made up his mind, and no one was going to stop him. Seeing his determination, Shershah accompanied him to Amritsar.

An army major was waiting for them as they got off the

train at Amritsar. "Sir, my name is Major Arjit Singh. I am very sorry to hear of the calamity that has befallen your family. I have been sent by General Shrigesh to receive you here. He sends you his regrets for not being here in person but will stop by this evening to bring you up to date on the progress of work. He has arranged for your stay at the army rest house for as long as you need to. We are doing everything possible to help find your missing family member."

While driving to the rest house, the major told them that after several raids on different locations in villages around the area of derailment, the army had already recovered more than half of the abducted women, though Nasreen was not amongst them. They arrested the leaders of the attack who, after the application of some seriously enhanced interrogation techniques, had provided leads to where they could find more of the abductees. The army was planning raids on those locations the next morning.

***

Hours turned into days of raids and arrests, followed by more interrogation sessions and still no lead for Nasreen. Humayun wanted to go by himself to the villages to look for Nasreen, but the General rejected that idea, telling him that the tensions were running high in the villages and if they found a Muslim loitering around, they would certainly kill him.

After another week of search and rescue, General Shrigesh informed them that as far as he could ascertain, they had accounted for every man, woman, and child on the train, and everyone found alive from the train was taken to the border and handed over to their Pakistani counterparts. The army had closed the case and handed over the culprits to the civilian authorities.

As far as the case of Nasreen was concerned, he said that he had gotten several reports from those in custody, and confirmed by locals, that an older lady who matched Nasreen's description was seen with some people on a bullock cart moving towards the Pakistani border. He advised Humayun to look for her in refugee camps around Lahore.

Having the doors shut in his face, Humayun had no recourse but to return to Delhi.

Nasreen couldn't have vanished from the face of the earth and would certainly not have gone to Pakistan in a bullock cart. I will go back to Amritsar on my own to search for her, even if it means losing my life. This time no one will know my plans, not even Shershah.

Over the next weeks, he studied the maps of Amritsar and the area around the train derailment site, noting down the names of villages around it, *Gurdwaras*,[123] and their timings. He studied several books on the Sikh religion, its practices, traditions and the way to dress. He grew a beard and learned how to wrap a Sikh-style *paggar.*[124] To learn more about the practices of the Sikh religion and brush up on his Punjabi language skills, he visited many Delhi-area *Gurdwaras*, dressed as a Sikh. He attended their community gatherings to learn their customs and practices. He watched their social interactions in a *daru-ghar* that Sikhs frequented. His last action before taking the train to Amritsar was to sign over the papers of his house and bank account over to Shershah, telling him he was going to Pakistan to search for Nasreen.

Humayun arrived in Amritsar as a mute Sikh refugee from Lahore. He carried a piece of paper with his story written on it.

"One night Muslim rabble-rousers had attacked my village and killed all of my family members in a small village outside Lahore. After hiding under a subfloor for a long time, I tried to escape under the darkness of the night, but was caught by one of the attackers who had fallen asleep by the side of the road. He thrust the barrel of his rifle in my mouth, ready to kill me. My life was saved when the gun failed to fire but burned my tongue badly, permanently affecting my speech."

***

---

[123] A place of assembly and worship for Sikhs.
[124] Traditional Sikh headgear.

In Amritsar, he made his way to the Golden temple, the most sacred *Gurdwara* to the Sikh people. There, he was given food and a small cot to sleep in the vast compound of the temple, along with hundreds of other refugees and homeless. He stayed there for a month gathering information about temples in the derailment area and noting information such as the names of local leaders at each temple and then moved on to a temple nearer to the attack site.

He would spend a few weeks at each temple connecting with locals, showing them his story. To people who he thought believed his story, he would write out questions for them about train attacks in the area. They would tell him stories of looting, murders, and abductions, sometimes with sadness and remorse and other times with pride, telling him it was done to avenge the murders, defilement and maiming of Sikhs like him, from Pakistan. The common thread of the stories was that men, small children, and older women were killed on the spot while women were defiled and abused and then killed or sold off to brothels or landowners.

The train to Pakistan he was interested in came up a few times, the story being the same each time. It was attacked to get revenge for the killing of Sikh refugees and the defiling of their women in Pakistan. A group of about two dozen farm laborers had derailed the train. They killed off as many men and children as they could, and abducted ten or twelve young women before an army train arrived and chased them away. The women were soon recovered by the army and sent to Pakistan.

THE CANTEEN IN JANDIALA
1948

The old man was crying near the altar of the *Gurdwara*, as was his usual. He would come each morning and would pray for a while, always weeping quietly.

I wonder what ails this old man. It appears he may have also lost someone dear to him.

Humayun went and sat with him, with his arm on the old man's shoulder. He sat quietly while the old man finished his prayers, still sobbing.

"I come here every day to ask for forgiveness for my son. Last week he went to the canal for a swim with his best friend. He got out of the water to smoke when something happened. My son, an expert swimmer, drowned. His friend told me he saw an old man in black clothing standing on water in the middle of the canal, push him down and held him under water until he drowned. The friend jumped in to save him, but something or someone held his foot under water. He swears it was like a hand holding him in the water and not letting him go. He couldn't save my son. Please pray for my son." He started crying loudly.

Humayun nodded.

"My son was a sinner. He killed a woman from a train they attacked. He was a good boy who became a reprobate by bad influence and alcohol. They found twelve or thirteen women in the first two bogies whom they tied up and left in their horse carts to carry away after they were done with looting other carriages. As they were ransacking the next carriage, they saw the army train coming and ran."

With his eyes welling again, he continued, "My son told me he had picked up a young woman from the train who he left in his cart before he went back to the train to find money or valuables. When the army came, he got in his cart and got away, but found that someone had switched his woman with an old *mai.*[125] He was so upset at being robbed that he stabbed the woman and threw her by the roadside."

Humayun felt his heart ripped out, but controlled his emotions, patiently listening to the old man, comforting him while he continued with the rest of the story.

"For a few weeks, before he died, he became afraid of the dark, didn't go out at night, couldn't sleep much, and was discombobulated all the time. When I asked him about it, he told me he saw the ghost of the woman he killed. I told him to go to the temple and pray for forgiveness. There are no ghosts, just a sign from God that you need to ask Him for forgiveness for your evil acts."

"But he wouldn't listen to me. He said he saw her at The Canteen in Jandiala when he was there with some friends. They were all having drinks when he felt someone watching him. He looked up and saw the old woman looking down at him from the canteen rooftop. She disappeared as soon as he looked up. He left his drink unfinished and came home with a high fever."

Humayun's ears perked up on hearing about the old woman's ghost at The Canteen in Jandiala. Hopeful of finding some clues there, he made his way to The Canteen.

It was a vast courtyard of what was an abandoned *haveli.*[126]

---

[125] Old woman.

[126] Mansion, mostly in rural area.

A Sikh *jageerdar*[127] had opened a diner and a watering hole for men, which he named The Canteen. The only women there were the cooks or servers who worked under the strict, watchful eyes of a couple of big bouncers.

A bulk of the owner's profits came from covertly sold illicit *daru.* It was a place for itinerant workers, peasants, and other laborers, with its only entrance and exit through a door at the back of the courtyard. The only parts of the house accessible from the courtyard were a kitchen and a washroom. The food was good and cheap, and so the place was packed every night.

Outside, there was always a line of beggars and penniless refugees waiting for handouts from the patrons or leftovers food from the *jageerdar.*

There were no tables or chairs in The Canteen. All the dining was done on *charpoys* spread around the courtyard. Humayun sat on a *charpoy*, observing everything. He had already noted where the kitchen was, how many men and women worked there, and the insolent treatment of the employees and customers by the tough guards. The place was busy with food and drinks being served. He was hungry, but he didn't drink, at least not the alcohol they were serving. Buying a drink was a pre-requisite for the privilege of using a *charpoy*, so had a glass of *thurra* in front of him.

He saw three women emerge from the kitchen. Two of them were young, fresh-faced women in drab saris and tight-fitting short-sleeved blouses. They walked around, taking orders. The third, an older woman with gray hair and wrinkled skin, moved cautiously through the maze of *charpoys* carrying some food and freshly baked *naans*. She was wearing an old but clean jumper and *shalwar*[128] and her head and shoulders were covered with a white *chador.*[129]

---

127 Landowner.

128 Loose cotton pants.

129 A large fabric covering for head and shoulders for women.

With dusk setting in and the absence of any artificial lighting, he couldn't see her facial features. She placed the food in front of two fat middle-aged men sharing a *charpoy*. They made some comment at her which he couldn't hear. She nodded her head without looking at them and moved on. People sitting at the next *charpoys* yelled something at her. She shook her head at them and went back into the kitchen. She reappeared with two kerosene lanterns and placed one in between the two sets of diners. She placed the second lantern near Humayun.

He could see her clearly now. She had aged a lot more than the elapsed months could have aged her. There was sorrow on her face, but she never looked at him.

Thank goodness you are safe! I have searched for you for months, not knowing if you were even alive.

Only Allah and I know how I have missed you, my love.

She spoke in a low, stoic voice without looking at him, "We have some mutton and *daal* and *bhindi bhujiya*[130] with *naan*. What would you like?"

He would have recognized that voice from a mile away, but she was speaking in Punjabi.

Nasreen must have learnt the language to hide her identity, but from whom?

He wanted to get up and take her in his arms, to never let her go, but he checked himself. He let out a noise like a mute trying to say something.

She stopped, then repeated the items one by one, "Mutton?" he shook his head in negative. "*Daal*?" he nodded. "*Bhindi bhujiya*?" Another nod. Nasreen nodded and left. She returned with his *bhindi bhujiya* and *daal* in an earthen saucer, two fresh *naans* in a small basket, and placed the two vessels in front of him, giving the *naans* a light tap. He missed the tap. He was staring at her teary eyes.

Is it the smoky kitchen, the dust in the air or something else causing

130 Stir fried semi wet okra dish.

your eyes to well up? You do recognize me, don't you? Your Humayun, who has given up everything in the search for you, for my love and my life?

He could taste her cooking in the food, his tears falling onto his plate. As he finished the first *naan*, he noticed a piece of paper sticking out from under the second *naan*. He could see some writing on it. Being careful not to draw attention from the ever alert bouncers, he quickly pocketed the wrinkled paper.

Back in his room, he took out the note and carefully unfolded it.

The note read, "My heart was filled with joy seeing you walk into this wretched place, but then the big hole in my heart quickly drained all the joy of seeing you. I knew you would come, but wish you wouldn't have. It is unsafe for you. I don't want anything to happen to you. Please go back to our children, who need you. Believe me, I am fine, truly. I was severely beaten, slashed, and stabbed for being too old, and left for dead by my abductors in a ditch on the roadside. The owner of this place found me half dead by the roadside and brought me to his house and they nursed me back to life. He gave me a job and a place to live."

"If you love me, which I know you do, please don't come back, for my sake, for your sake, and above all, for the children's sake. I don't want to return to that happy life, my old world. I will die there. The people there will not let me live. The shame and the black mark of being abducted and living at someone else's house will forever be stuck to my forehead. I will die before I go there. Please understand and go back. Go back knowing how much I love you and always will. Please try to forgive and forget me, and never tell the children this was what I wanted. Tell them I died."

The message ended.

I can't leave you here, living in poverty in a place so foreign to you! I will protect you against all those people you fear back home. Yes, I will.

Allah, please guide her, give her my message.

TO LEAVE OR NOT TO LEAVE
1948

It had been over a week since Nasreen had handed Humayun the note. He was still trying to decide what to do next. He had been to The Canteen almost every evening. She would serve food to him the same way, like clockwork. A lantern was placed, food ordered, food delivered, water brought, and then she would be gone until the next evening. One day, as she was putting down the food, he held her hand. She looked at him, letting his hand linger, then slowly pulled her hand. One of the guards came over after she had left. He was towering over him, but not angry.

"Not here. You don't touch the girls," he said, shaking his finger at him, his eyes devoid of anger or malice.

"If you want female company, come to the Nautch House with me. The girls there are younger and much prettier than this old hag. She only cooks and serves, nothing more."

Humayun would tip the guards a few pennies each time he was there, and it seemed to have worked. He looked up at him with sadness.

The guard broke out into a loud, hard laughter. "You are in love. You have fallen in love with her? No wonder you come here every day. People are starting to talk about you. Makes sense. She has no one, a great catch for an old mute like you. I can tell her you like her. Do you want me to?" He was genuinely enjoying this distraction from his daily routine.

"You are a mute. How will you talk to her?"

Humayun moved his hand around to mimic writing and made a sound like, "Write, write."

"Smart man, I didn't know you could write. Hope she can read. Okay, come late for dinner tomorrow, and don't leave. I will tell her you want to meet her to write to her in person." He laughed, enjoying his play on words.

"Stay in the compound, otherwise I will lose my job for not keeping customers under control. I would hate losing this job. I have killed men for a lot less."

Humayun, smiling and nodding, took his hands in gratitude while making more sounds of gratitude.

The next evening, he waited for her after everyone had left. After waiting for a while for her to come out, Humayun went into the kitchen. She was sitting on a makeshift stool with her back to the door. He sat down next to her.

He tried every argument he could think of, but she was unconvinced by all his pleading and persuasion. As time passed, he feared she would not change her mind.

They talked for hours. He did most of the talking. She listened attentively, but was unconvinced.

The bouncer came in and told him it was time to go.

This became a routine for Humayun. After everyone left, he would go into the kitchen to talk and to plead with her to come with him. It was to no avail. He had run out of new arguments in his favor on the first day, so he would repeat those in a different order and then sit there quietly until she would say something or try to change the subject to the children, the past, the weather, etc. This went on for a few days until one day, she was not there.

Someone else was sitting on the stool, an older woman, looking straight at him as he entered the kitchen. He had not seen her before. She was much older than Nasreen. She had a kind face, reminding him of his *Khala*. He waited for her to say something.

"Don't be alarmed, Humayun Sahib. I know who you are and why you are here," she said. "I am Jind Kaur. Babaji, my husband, the owner of this place, and I knew about you on the first day you came. Nasreen told us. We were overjoyed that you had come for her. The risk you took to your personal safety shows your character and your love for her. We felt only you can convince her to go back to her life where she belongs with her children. We were hoping and praying, for her sake and the sake of your children, for your success. The reason you could stay late to speak with her was not because of the kindness of our guard or the money you used to tip him, but because we told him to."

"On the day of the train attack, my husband was coming back from his farm when he saw a severely injured Nasreen lying unconscious in a ditch. He brought her home. It took months of care and treatment for her to heal."

"After she had recovered completely, we offered to help her safely cross the border so she could get back to her family in Pakistan, but she refused. We tried a few times, and each time her resolve was unwavering. Feeling that we wanted her out of here, she planned to leave us, but Babaji discovered her plan. We sat down with her to mollify her fears and told her she had become like a daughter to us. While we believe a woman's home is with her husband and children, but we would never force her to go. She could stay with us as long as she wanted. She told me she wanted a job to support herself and live the rest of her life here in obscurity as a nameless person. A life where no one would ever tell her what to do or where to go. Unable to convince her, Babaji made her the manager of the kitchen. She supervises everything superbly and sometimes helps with the cooking. She doesn't serve customers unless you are present."

"She is a kind, gentle woman who came up with the idea of distributing leftover food to the hungry and homeless who line up outside The Canteen each day. She makes sure no food is wasted. Nasreen is an angel."

"I had a daughter, our youngest child, my pride and joy, my most precious gem, the mother of my two grown grandchildren. She died of cholera last year." Humayun saw tears in her eyes.

"Having Nasreen in our lives has lessened the pain of losing our daughter."

She wiped the remnants of her tears. "We would be thrilled if she would return with you to her children. But know that we will not force her to leave or to let her be taken away by force, knowing how strongly she feels about going back after her experience in the train attack, and her fear of what she may face there."

She took a deep breath before continuing, "Nasreen told us all that you suffered for her, and we were deeply moved by your struggles. It shows the depth of your love for her. But there is a time to let go, to let go of your loved one so that she can be free, free of whatever it is that haunts her."

"Humayun Sahib, I am an uneducated person, so I don't feel competent to advise you, but I would suggest that you let her be for a little while. This has been a highly emotional period for her, seeing you and hearing about her children and the mountains you climbed to find her. She needs time to absorb all this. She will be as safe as any of my children. We will protect her from any harm. After you are home, you can write to her, but send them to Babaji to protect her privacy. She will get them unopened, I promise. A year or two down the line, she may change her mind and decide to go back with you to her children."

Rejection is painful, a lot more so coming from a person I love the most. It hurts a lot. I did whatever I could to find her and bring her back. I accept her wishes because I love her and because I promised her on our wedding night that no one will make her do something she didn't want to.

Insha-Allah, I will convince her the next time. I will be back.

He looked at Jind Kaur and spoke, "Dear sister, I cannot thank you and your husband enough for how you have taken care of my wife after her tragic nightmare of a journey. After listening to you so eloquently describe her situation, I have no reason to not accept what you so kindly offer me. It has been a harrowing year, and I cannot begin to describe how lucky I feel that you two were there for her."

"I need to examine what in our married life could have contributed to her feeling this way, and while I hope and pray that correcting it will change her mind, it will also help me be a better father to my children who have been so traumatized by the loss of their mother."

She smiled as she saw Nasreen entering the room from the back door.

"I will leave you two alone, now, *RabRakha*."[131]

Humayun took Nasreen in his arms. He had made a decision, a painful one to leave, to give her the space she wanted, something only she wanted, but he had to yield to keep his promise to her.

She was crying for letting her only love go, and with him, the hope of ever seeing her children again. But she was also crying with joy. For the first time in her life, she was successful in overcoming the pressures of society and her loved ones to do what she wanted.

She intended to keep it that way and would never return to her old life.

[131] God be with you.

GUNS FOR SALE

1953

Humayun was pacing the floor of the waiting room at the Lady Dufferin Hospital in Karachi. Saleem was reciting all the prayers he could remember. His wife, Firoza Fatima, was in the labor room delivering their first child. Gayti Ara was reading a copy of the Quran, praying for a successful surgery and safe delivery.

To break the tension in the air, Humayun asked Saleem if they have picked a name for their child.

"Seema! Malka Seema Nasreen, if it is a girl. We will let you pick a name if it is a boy." Saleem replied, then quickly added, "Although we will call him Raja at home."

That's a name I haven't heard for a very long time. I wish I knew more about him and his life.

A nurse ran into the waiting room and announced, "*Mubarak* to all of you. It's a girl."

Malka Seema Nasreen! May Allah bless you, my princess.
I know you will fill the gaping hole in my heart.
You will never do what another Nasreen I loved did to me.

***

While everyone believed Nasreen had died in the train attack, Humayun knew from Babaji's recent postcard that she was well, managing The Canteen kitchen, feeding the hungry every evening and teaching young children in the mornings. Before leaving Jandiala, he had given all the money he had with him to Nasreen, enough for her to buy a small house and to save some for a rainy day. She handed it all to Jind Kaur.

After leaving Nasreen, Humayun had gone to Amritsar. There, he booked a trunk call to Shershah to let him know he was fine. Shershah was furious at him.

"You are still here in India. I thought you would have escaped to Pakistan. I know all about your involvement in the Black Train hijacking, and so do the Special Police and everyone else in the Ministry."

"Hijacking? It was not a hijacking. I helped get the train to its lawful owners."

"It was so irresponsible of you. The Special Police has been looking for you for a month now. They have repossessed your car, your house and everything in it. They even raided my house early one morning and wanted to arrest me after not finding you there. Thank Goodness for General Shrigesh, who got my name cleared."

"Bhai, I am so sorry you had to—"

The operator interjected, "Sir, your three-minute call is over. Please hang up."

Shershah said, "Listen Humayun, turn yourself in to the police. That is the best path for you. General Shrigesh promised to keep you out of jail until the issue is cleared up. Call me when you—"

The operator cut off the call saying, "I am sorry Sir, the call is over."

Humayun had no choice but to quickly find his way to the nearest border and to safety in Pakistan.

In Pakistan, he was given a hero's welcome for the Black Train help and all his work for Pakistan.

Jinnah had passed away before he arrived. Prime Minister Liaquat Ali Khan received him at the PM house and decorated him with the highest civilian award for meritorious services to the nation. Shahid Hamid was with him at the ceremony. On the way back, he said to Humayun, "Bhaiya, the Black Train probably saved us from being overrun by a much bigger Indian Army. Knowing Pakistan had a huge trainload of state-of-the-art weapon systems, discouraged the Indians from opening up more fronts in the Kashmir war, and accepting a UN mediated ceasefire."

He was offered a position to lead the expansion of railway services in Pakistan. Although he was no longer interested in railway work, he accepted the position as a service to his new homeland.

Humayun wrote many letters to Nasreen, but never got a reply. Babaji knew she was not writing, so he made a habit of sending him a postcard every six months or so to let him know she was well.

He moved into a large, comfortable house in Karachi provided by the government. Saleem and Gayti Ara were admitted to the best schools in town. Everything was great, and he appreciated it all, but there was no joy in his heart as he reconciled with the reality of spending the rest of his life without Nasreen.

While on his first overseas trip to England to negotiate the procurement of electric locomotives, he called Richard to catch up. Richard was delighted to hear he was in town and invited him to come and stay with him for a weekend at his house outside London.

Richard owned a large arms business and had recently been elected to his father's parliament seat as an MP. He had invited several highly placed friends to dinner to introduce Humayun. He regaled them with stories of Sir Jonathon and Humayun and how they met.

The next day Richard took him on a pheasant hunt with a few friends, a novel experience for Humayun who had never fired a gun in his life. Richard gave him a lesson on the etiquettes and basics of shooting and safety precautions. Humayun, always a quick learner, was soon out-shooting most of the participants.

It must be a beginner's luck.

After dinner, they sat by the fireplace sipping coffee and chatting. The conversation turned to Richard's business. The arms trade had grown since the end of the World War. He was trying to open an office in Asia but had not found someone reliable to work with. To him, Humayun was a perfect candidate. He asked Humayun if he would be interested in helping him with his expansion in Asia. He would open an office in Karachi, and if Humayun were open to considering such a proposition, it would come with an equity partnership. Over the next few days, Humayun gave it a lot of thought and accepted the proposal. They completed the preliminary paperwork before he left London.

Back in Karachi, having successfully completed his mission to London, he got to work on wrapping up his work with the railways, and within a year he had left the Railways to start his arms business.

The business boomed. Pakistan, facing the threat of another war with India, was his first major customer. With Richard's help, he locked in his first multi-year arms contract, and his business took off from there.

BUSINESS AND PILGRIMAGE

1954

Humayun had learned early on that to be in the business of selling weapon systems to governments, he would have to make some hefty off-the-books payments to the buyers and intermediaries. He had strong reservations about paying under-the-table fees for making a sale, but Richard contended it was all part of doing business and not paying these fees would dry up orders rapidly. Being a newcomer to the world of arms sales, he went along with Richard's advice.

As his network of acquaintances in the arms trade arena grew, he started getting inquiries from unaffiliated independent operators looking for armaments. Upon further investigation of the inquiries, he learned that a bustling black market existed for weapons of all categories and that was where these weapons would end up. It was the place to buy weapons without drawing attention. This clandestine marketplace was where freedom fighters, mercenaries, and misfits bought their weapons of choice. It was shady business with high profit margins, but it also came with high risks of getting caught and blacklisted, or worse.

Richard was against dealing with buyers from the black market. Humayun argued that the needs of these buyers would be met, and if they didn't sell to them, someone else will. "We can make more money in one of these contracts than five selling to governments after making payments for all their fees and slush funds."

Richard, now an MP, preferred to limit his dealing with legitimate governments even if officials were fattening up their pocket while starving their own people. Humayun again went with Richard's experienced voice.

One such inquiry came from a German arms dealer known as Captain Morris. He came to Karachi to meet Humayun and told him he was helping the FLN,[132] an Algerian nationalist group fighting for independence from France, one of several decolonization struggles in mid-century Africa. The weapons would go to ALN,[133] the military wing of FLN. Humayun was all for helping freedom fighters, but did not want to deal with non-government entities. So he passed on that deal.

Besides, supplying arms to FLN would risk the wrath of France and its notorious external intelligence agency, SDECE, which was known for targeting anyone supporting its colonial enemies like the Viet Minh[134] and FLN.

***

Back at the hospital, holding the tiny Seema strengthened his resolve to bring back Nasreen, if for nothing else than for her to see her grandchild. Having been unsuccessful at trying to change her mind, he felt he needed some divine help and resolved to take his appeal to a higher authority.

***

Muslims from all over the world were gathered in Mecca for the annual pilgrimage of Haj. They came from all the countries of the world to fulfill one of the five duties of Islam prescribed for every Muslim of means. It was an invigorating sight for Humayun to see tens of thousands of men, women, and children moving from one location to the other and performing the steps of the Haj

---

132 Front de Libération Nationale.

133 Armée de Libération Nationale. Military wing of FLN.

134 Armed Group led by Ho Chi Minh, fighting the French in Vietnam.

in harmony and peace. He was immersed in the experience, humbled, and praying with a new hope of seeing his wife again.

It was a grueling week of prayers. He would have very few hours of sleep on hold-all beds, spread out on the rocky ground under the open sky, before waking up for prayers before daybreak, and then more rituals and prayers, until late at night.

At the end of the Haj, he checked into a hotel in Mecca for a few days of rest and to let his body recover. The hotel was conveniently located across the courtyard of the *Kaaba* for his five daily prayers.

On the first morning, just before sunrise, he was walking to the *Kaaba* for the *Fajr* prayers when he felt someone walking close behind him. He looked back and saw a tall, thin man also hurrying towards the *Kaaba* for prayers. The man smiled and gave him a greeting nod, and started walking with him. They exchanged pleasantries and small talk. The man introduced himself as Ahmed, a North African Arab. A large group of men gathered around Ahmed when they reached the vicinity of the *Kaaba*. Ahmed stopped to meet them and Humayun moved on.

The closer you get to the Kaaba, the closer you are to Allah and His blessings.

When he returned to the hotel from the prayer, he saw Ahmed sitting in the lounge area. He got up and approached Humayun.

"*As Salaam O Alaikum* brother, do you have a few minutes to speak with me? I am not asking for money or anything like that to embarrass you," Ahmed said with a strong French accent.

"Waleykum *Salaam*, Ahmed. I didn't think you would ask for money. May I know what this is regarding and how I can help?"

"Thank you, brother. It is a matter of great importance for us, and it would be preferable for me that we talk in private."

"Of course, let's proceed."

Ahmed took Humayun to his room, which was across the

hallway from Humayun's.

Is it a coincidence that our rooms are across from each other in this large hotel?

"Thanks again for your time, brother. My name is Ahmed Ben Bella. I am a member of the FLN in Algeria. I am sorry for bothering you in your time of prayers and reflection and will get to the point. Captain Morris visited you in Karachi with a proposal from us." He paused.

Humayun knew where this was leading, but played coy. "I am glad to meet you, Mr. Ben Bella. I am afraid I don't know much about FLN."

Ahmed smiled. "*Insha-Allah,* let me give you the background. We have started a *Jihad* against the French colonists, but we need small arms and ammunition to carry out this struggle to free Algeria. Pakistan lost hundreds of thousands of people during its independence movement, which thankfully did not involve an extended bloody war with the colonizers. The cunning English saw the changing winds and quickly quit India, as you were rightfully demanding. Unlike the British, the obtuse French are not paying heed to the winds of change sweeping my homeland. They think it is passing passion that can be dissipated by the application of force. They consider my land as an intrinsic part of France, a legacy of their forefathers, and as a result, they are brutally suppressing any voices for freedom. *Jihad* is the only way for us, and since we are much smaller, it will have to be a guerilla war. *Insha-Allah*, we will throw them out soon enough, but we need your help."

Humayun said nothing, so he continued, "You, my friend, are the only Muslim arms dealer in the world, and we hope you will help us achieve the second Islamic Republic in the world. You are a true *mujahid*.[135] Just think of it as another chance for you to help a second Muslim country get started with the supply of modern arms. Your company will be paid well, but your true reward will

[135] A person involved in a Jihad.

come in the afterlife when we will all stand before Allah on the day of judgement."

He said a second Muslim country. Was that a reference to the Black Train? How would he know I was involved?

Ben Bella described the atrocities being heaped on the Algerian people and how the living conditions of the common man had deteriorated to where they were ready to die rather than live under the draconian laws of the oppressive French.

Humayun had heard several special prayers being offered for the people of Algeria during the Haj. He had read articles about the inhumane treatment of the natives by European colonists, but hearing first-hand accounts of the torture moved him. He found Ben Bella to be a very charismatic individual, with a worthwhile cause, and resolved to support him with arms.

Helping Ahmed would come with its own perils. I would be in the crosshairs of the French. I will need a plan to keep my identity concealed while supplying arms to the Algerians.

He told Ben Bella that he required absolute secrecy. There were to be no middlemen involved in the deal. Payments to be made to a numbered Swiss account. Ben Bella was prepared to do anything to protect his supplier. He accepted every term Humayun put on the table. They agreed to meet in a few weeks in Karachi to give Humayun time to come up with a workable plan.

His plan involved having Ben Bella train and equip small groups of fighters as pirates to hijack cargo ships on the high seas. Humayun had some West African countries buying Soviet-sourced arms from him. The arms were loaded in Portugal onto smaller ships that traveled along the western coast of Africa to their destinations. He would provide Ben Bella with the names, dates, and route of travel of some of his ships.

Piracy had been prevalent near the shores of Africa for centuries. Unwritten rules for dealing with pirate takeover on the high seas recommend the crew to not resist and let the pirates take any of the ship's cargo.

Algerian fighters acting as pirates would follow the movement of the arms laden ships and board them under the cover of darkness. The crew, following the procedures for dealing with pirates, would not put their lives in jeopardy and stay out of their way. The pirates would then unload the materiel onto smaller speedboats and disappear into the night. There would be enough arms and ammunition on each ship to last Ben Bella's small guerilla force for a while.

The plan worked well for years, with Humayun keeping a very low profile while constantly adjusting the plan to stay a step ahead of the SDECE.

Georg Puchert, aka Captain Morris, who had approached Humayun in Karachi, was a second supplier to ALN. He was found and assassinated with a car bomb planted in his Mercedes in Frankfurt in 1959. Rumors were abound, linking it to La Main Rouge,[136] a branch of SDECE.

Humayun was quite shaken by this killing, but remained undeterred. At Ben Bella's insistence, he hired Abdur Rahman, a retired army Special Forces member, as his driver and bodyguard.

---

[136] La Main Rouge-the red hand, was rumored to have been created for the sole purpose of eliminating the supporters of Algerian independence and the leading members of the FLN and ALN.

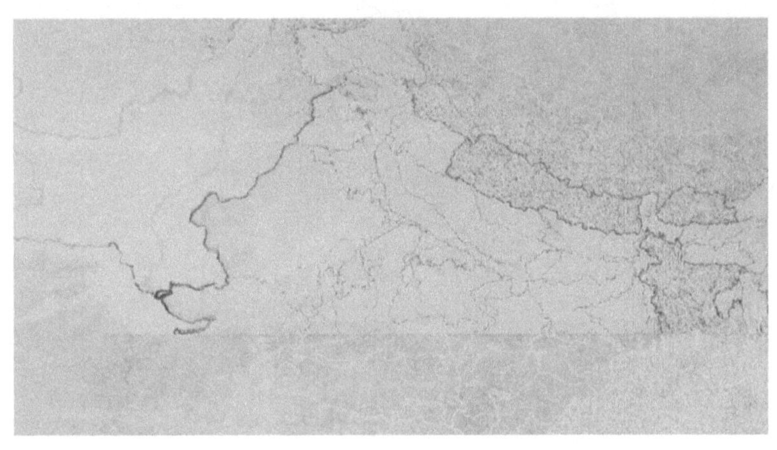

HUMAYUN & SEEMA

1965-2004

THE HOUSE WITH THE STONE EAGLE
1965

Humayun wished Seema, his extremely precocious granddaughter, whom he adored, didn't have such a shrill, nasally voice.

It drives me crazy. I get a migraine every time she starts with it.

Migraines headaches?

Maybe that's not a man's thing, but her ear-splitting voice makes me want to stuff my ears with those little foam earplugs only available to first-class passengers on Pan Am.

The thought of Pan Am first class calmed him.

Ahh, Pan Am, what service, what comfort- it's like being home at 25,000 feet above ground. Wish I was there right now, away from my little devil drilling a hole in my ears.

Jumping back to reality, suppressing his urge to get up and walk away, he leaned forward and hugged her.

"My dear little angel, what is it you want me to get for you?"

"*Dada*[137], I want nothing." She had just arrived, very upset at Firoza. "Mummy wants me to learn knitting. I don't want to learn to knit. I can always buy sweaters from Elphinstone Street."[138]

***

---

[137] Paternal grandfather

[138] Upscale shopping area in Karachi.

He was sitting enjoying a late breakfast on his lawn. He loved his house, which they all lovingly called The *Chowk*. It was a big, old house built by a Parsi trader, with a huge stone statue of an eagle crowning it. When a new bus service was started in the area, a bus stop was built across from the house. The bus stop had an official name no one remembered, but bus drivers, conductors, and passengers called it the *Cheel Wali Kothi*[139] bus stop.

When Humayun bought the property, it had been that way for years. The well-trimmed, fragrant flowering Frangipani bushes surrounding the lawn had seen him go from a railways administrator to the owner of the biggest arms trading company in Asia, which he had named CWK, the initials of his house name. He lived alone in the big house, with many household helpers. Saleem, an actuary, was living a few minutes away from him with Firoza and Seema in a small house. Gayti Ara lived in Peshawar with her husband and two sons.

"Seema, my little doll, you are the best granddaughter in the world. But you are again making those horrible sounds that you know give me a headache that lasts forever. You haven't touched your chicken corn soup or Tutti-Fruiti ice cream that I ordered for you." He whispered this in her ear, as was his way. Such specially delivered private messages would usually calm her down.

She was his favorite grandchild.

He had a feeling that this pre-teen was destined for something monumental. He saw himself in her, but felt that her achievements would be like a sun to the flashlight of his successes.

"Come, let's try some of this soup. I'll go first with my spoon to make sure it is not too hot for you, and after I have made sure it is at the right temperature, you can try it, like we always do."

As expected, after taking the first sip of the tasty soup, she calmed down. She began talking about school.

"You know my friend, Romaana? We both love history.

[139] The House with the Eagle.

We are always competing in history class to get first position."

"Can you get me some books on the history of independence movements?"

"I can take you to the Oxford University Press and you can buy as many books as you want. They have an impressive collection of history book."

"Thank you, Dada. So Romaana's mother always comes with her and a guard to drop and pick her up from the school. One day, I went to their car to say *Salaam*[140] to Auntie and noticed the guard in the front seat had a gun at his feet. Romaana says the driver also has a gun, and the car has special steel doors and bullet-proof windows because her father backed Fatima Jinnah in the presidential elections against General Ayub Khan. My friends Soody and Moody, and others, say that Romaana's father and his brothers are known as the Gold Kings of Karachi. They bring gold from the Gulf States, without paying duties, like what we had to pay when Abbu got Mummy that beautiful red ruby and diamond necklace for their tenth anniversary from Singapore. This way they can sell the gold at a cheap price and make a lot of money and throw big parties for their friends."

"Romaana's birthday party was so much fun. There were so many people there with their children, and clowns and magicians. They also have these exotic birds in a large outdoor aviary. They have so many friends. Maybe Miss Fatima Jinnah is helping them with the duty because he helped her in the elections against President Ayub Khan." She stopped to take another sip and continued, "I like President Ayub Khan because his election symbol was a rose. I love the roses in your garden. Mrs. Fatima Jinnah seems too stern to me. She chose a lantern as her symbol. Who needs a lantern these days, Dada? I know, I know. There are still poor people in Karachi, and they don't have enough money to get a light bulb in their homes. Our Karachi has so many lights. Karachi will soon be the center of the world and then there will be

---

140 Salutations.

no poor and needy left. Everyone will have light in their house and people will forget Mrs. Fatima Jinnah and her lantern."

She thought for a moment about something, then taking a bite of the bread she continued, "I've got an idea! How about we build some very high light towers all around Karachi and then shine the light towards poor people's homes so that they don't need to buy their own light bulbs. Come on Dada, let's do it. I am so excited about it! Let's do it! You have enough money in the bank to do this. Don't you? Maybe we can bring some gold like the Gold Kings without paying duty and make lots of money to make these towers. We can put the first giant light on the head of the giant *cheel* statue on top of our house. I love our *cheel*, her intense eyes, looking over the horizon. She is always looking out for us."

"Or is it a male *cheel*?"

He didn't want to interrupt her as he kept looking at the excitement build on her face as she talked about her plans.

Then, remembering something, she got up.

"Dada, I better go. Mummy would be worried about me. I will ask her to teach me knitting. It wouldn't be so bad. Maybe I will knit mufflers[141] for the children who don't have warm clothes. What do you think?"

"I think that is a great idea. Firoza will be thrilled to know that you have changed your mind."

"And you know another thing about learning to knit, Dada?"

"Yes, I know, you will be able to knit a muffler for me, too."

"Dada, you're a mind reader. But yes. The first muffler I knit will be for you."

She is always curious about everything around her and comes up with ideas about how to make this or that better. She is enamored with life, imagining the possibilities in human existence. Sadly, that is something that we lose as we grow older and our views get tempered by realities and experiences.

---

141 Woolen scarfs.

But here she is, innocent of the effects of age and experience that could taint her view of life and its possibilities.

Then just like that, she ran out calling out Abdur Rahman's name, to take her back home.

OF ANIMALS, WILD AND DOMESTICATED
1965

"Dada, were you a HumFewer?" Seema asked one day. Humayun had not heard this term for over 20 years. She never asked frivolous questions, and he knew that her queries always had a background and would always lead to other questions. He tried to be careful and somewhat vague in his initial responses.

"What do you know about the HumFewers and what brought about this question in this ever-active mind of yours?" he asked.

She looked up at him, disappointed and somewhat irritated, "Dada, why do you have to answer my question with one of your own? Why can't you give me a straight answer to my simple yes or no questions?" Then she turned her head away, pretending to look outside the window, her way of showing displeasure.

He waited until she had lost interest in whatever she was looking at outside and looked at him in anticipation of an answer.

He started, "First of all, I know you well enough to know that you never ask simple questions. There is almost always a follow-up waiting to sprout."

He counted to three in his mind. Now he had her full attention. "The first rule of a dialogue is to never start an answer to a question with a yes or no. You give up any advantage that you may hold over the outcome by locking yourself in a yes or no answer. By asking for more details of the question, it prepares you to think ahead and evaluate the outcomes of your two possible eventual answers."

After another pause to allow her young mind to absorb this, he continued, "Also, upon hearing a yes or no, the attention of the questioner gets diverted, and they miss most of the rest of your point. So, you want to hold their attention and describe your point of view before you commit to answering in the affirmative or negative. Do you understand?" he asked.

She gave him a thoughtful nod and continued, "Got it. I read about HumFewers was in a book Abbu was reading. It looks like an old book on the history of the British Raj in India, by two self-proclaimed HumFewers from the 1920s. I am always interested in history, so I started reading it too. They wrote about their privileged existence as a HumFewer in India. So, I was wondering if you were ever a HumFewer, or ever met or knew one."

Humayun had an answer, but he was still not going to answer it, which would have led to deeper questions about his family that he wanted to keep from her, at least while she was young. He started, "Well, as you would certainly have read in your book that over half of the ICS officers in India were members of the East and West India Club. In pre-partitioned India, I had dealing with some of those ICS fellows and so yes, I have met several of the people you referred to as the HumFewers."

"You want to hear a story about HumFewers?" He asked.

Her waning attention was sparked again. "Yes. I love interesting stories!"

"Okay, so the story goes like this. In the aftermath of the 1857 sepoy rebellion, a famous Member of Parliament had labeled all Indians as wild animals ready to kill any white British subject at the drop of a hat. Later in the Question & Answer session at the Parliament, he asked the Prime Minister whether there was a plan to make sure that these wild animals could never do what had happened in 1857 in Meerut and elsewhere in India. As was the custom in Parliament, the Prime Minister immediately rose and said, 'The Right Honorable gentleman must know we have been working on a plan for "domesticating" a part of the native Indian population by teaching them British ideals and training them. We will do so by creating institutions to guard against such a disaster ever happening again.' The East and West India Club was such an institution."

"For the longest time after this session of the Parliament, white ICS officers would privately call native Indian ICS officers, and some others, the domesticated set, like a cat or dog."

She shook her head like an adult and said, "What a sad story about humans. I wish we could all learn to respect and treat our fellow humans like we would like to be treated."

"Dada, you never went to England to study, so I think you were never a HumFewer. I know Shershah Dada studied at the Indian Institute at Oxford, and he later joined ICS, so he must have been a HumFewer. I would bet anything he was a HumFewer!"

"Seema, you know betting is haram in Islam, so no betting. Okay?"

"I know, I know. So wasn't he, Dada, wasn't he a HumFewer?" She exclaimed, her eyes wide in anticipation of an affirmative answer.

"Does it really matter now if he was or wasn't? He had a great ICS career serving his birthplace and helping build the careers of his children and some others. I never asked him, and he never told me whether he was or wasn't a HumFewer."

Detecting a dead end on the topic, she switched to another. "Dada, you never talk about growing up in Meerut. Abbu and *Phupi-jan*[142] know a little about that time, but not much.

---

142 Paternal aunt.

Roshan[143] *Dadi*[144] once told me that *Barey Dada* was a religious leader who was always helping people in need. She told me that Shershah Dada was very good at his studies and the government paid for him to go to Oxford University. But you were different from Shershah Dada and never wanted to leave India, and you did everything on your own. I am so proud of you, Dada."

Humayun smiled as a flood of memories came gushing in. He preferred only the good ones.

"After you have passed high school, I hope I can take you there and show you all those places in India."

"Dada, that will be so great. I wish I could pass high school tomorrow so we can go on that trip. Roshan Dadi said there were always relatives visiting with their children from out of town. They would stay for weeks. She remembers two enormous mango trees providing shade in hot summers in the backyard where she played with other kids. But you never mention Meerut. Why? What kind of place was it? What did you do all day with no radio to listen to in the evenings?"

"Did you all live in a big house like us? It must have been a happy home with all those kids there, picking and eating sweet mangoes off the trees in the backyard. I wish I could go back to that time and play with you and your friends in the cool shade of those enormous mango trees."

He said, "*Masha-Allah,* you have a great life with loving parents and siblings. A brilliant future lies ahead for you. Why would you want to go back to that time?" [145]

"I didn't mean it that way, Dada. I love my life, my parents, my family and above all, you. There is nothing that I want or would trade this life for. It would be so much fun using a time machine to visit your childhood and play with you and Roshan

---

143 Humayun's half-sister.

144 Meaning grandmother, also applied to siblings of grandparents.

145 Warding off the effects of 'evil eye' superstitions is practiced by Muslims by adding Masha-Allah when describing beauty, wins, etc.

Dadi under the mango trees. I would tell you I am your granddaughter from the future, and I have come from the future to play with you under your beautiful mango trees with the sweetest mangos in the world. Imagine how much fun that would be. This way I could find out everything about your childhood without bothering you with these questions, as I do now."

The thought of her showing up in his childhood brought a smile to his face. "I don't know how a time machine works. You probably know a lot more about it than I do," he said, smiling and nodding his head in deference to how quickly she had turned the situation around in her favor. "If you decide to stay in this time, you can be an eminent lawyer," he added.

She is such a natural with no pretense. I hope and pray that she will use all her knowledge and abilities for good and only good, but I worry about the hints of a darker side to her which I have noticed lately. She seems to be developing a fascination for things existing in the shadowy worlds.

"So Seema, here is the plan. I need to pick up something from my office. You can come with me and on the way back, I will drop you home.

SUNDAYS AT THE *CHOWK*
1965

As Abdur Rahman brought the car to a stop in front of Saleem's house, Seema didn't make any move to get out of the car. Humayun turned to her and said, "This is your stop, Madam."

The driver was already out of the car, holding the door open for her.

"Dada, why don't you come in? You haven't been in the house for years. The last time was for my birthday a few years back. Since then, all my birthdays have been at The *Chowk*. You are always so busy. We are there every Sunday for lunch and to spend the day. The *Chowk* is so big and nice. I love being there. Abbu says that visiting you every Sunday is our family tradition and he can never miss a Sunday at the *Chowk*. *Phupi-jan* and Mateen *Phupha*[146] were always there too until they moved to Peshawar. I miss Ahmed and Osman."

Sundays at The *Chowk* was a practice Humayun started, to keep up with his children after Saleem got married and moved to a newly constructed home that Humayun paid for. He looked at his watch.

It has been a long time since I visited Saleem's home. I can stop by, since I have nothing planned for the rest of the day.

"Come Dada, let's go."

---

[146] Aunt's husband.

Humayun smiled and got out of the car.

Holding his hand, Seema led him into the house shouting, "Abbu, Mummy, look who I brought with me!"

The elliptical lawn in front of the house was defined with low edging all around it. Bougainvillea bushes loaded with pink and orange flowers were perfectly placed on two sides of the lawn, against the boundary walls. Coconut and palm trees towered over the lawn, providing a shaded spot on the far side over a small pond where water lilies were peeking out of the water. A nicely trimmed Frangipani bush with its fragrant yellow and white blooms completed the picture at the far end of the pool. The path to the front door had low boxwood hedges growing vibrantly on its two sides, running all the way to the three steps leading up to a set of large hand-carved walnut double doors.

Humayun stopped to admire the garden, its balanced mix of grass, flowers, and water.

It HAS been a long time since I was here.

He remembered the front yard, covered with patchy grass and thin bougainvillea vines climbing over the walls.

Whoever designed this must know something about planning beautiful gardens. They have done such a marvelous job.

Turning to Seema, he said, "I didn't know you guys had such a pleasant garden. We should have one of our Sunday family days here."

"Yes, Dada, I told you it has been a long time. Don't you love it? Abbu tells everyone that a Japanese landscape designer has designed this garden."

Saleem, a smartly dressed 30-something with trimmed curly hair and thick eyeglasses, saw Humayun standing in the front yard. He came out and said, "Abba, how nice to see you here after such a long time. Is everything all right? I wasn't expecting you. I would have come if you had just called."

"Everything is fine. I was here to drop Seema off and she reminded me how long it has been since I stopped by. We meet every Sunday, so it didn't occur to me to visit your house. What a magnificent garden you have. I am impressed by your Japanese landscape designer. He converted the fairly plain lawn into such a well-designed oasis in the middle of the city. I am looking for a landscape designer. The side lawn at The *Chowk* needs work."

Saleem said nothing as they entered the house. Seema had gone upstairs to drop off her schoolwork. He led Humayun to the drawing room and waited while his father carefully examined the furnishings and fittings and the unique items in bookshelves and on the coffee table. The room was decorated in a French Provencal motif.

"Does your Japanese designer also do interior design?" Humayun asked, while examining a small replica of the Rosetta stone he had picked up from a bookshelf.

Saleem smiled, but still said nothing. He was happy to see his father appreciating the fruits of his labors. He always wanted his father to be proud of him, but those occasions were very few and very, very far in between.

Humayun put the replica back down and turned to him. "So...?"

"Sorry, Abba, I am so happy you like what I have done with this house. I am glad you had some time today to stop by and see all this. The idea for the drawing room came when we were in France for holidays."

"I thought so, and how about this Japanese designer that Seema was telling me about?" He wouldn't let go of the Japanese designer.

"Oh, that." he seemed a bit overwhelmed and replied timidly, "It's nothing, I just tell that to friends when they ask. Otherwise, they will want the person's name and on and on."

"Or you can just tell them the truth and tell them that the designer doesn't want to be bothered; that is, if he doesn't want to be disturbed."

"It's a she."

"Oh. Okay, so it's a she who doesn't want to be bothered" The two of them were alone in the big room.

"I can see it's not your wife we are speaking of. Who is she then? Or is it that you don't want to share your secret with your father, either?"

He forced a smile on his face, trying not to sound overbearing. He had failed.

"Abba, if you think I am having an affair with a landscape designer, you are way off. I love my wife and my child and would never think of doing anything like that to them."

"I would certainly hope not," Humayun said, but then pushed a little more. "But if you don't want to tell me the name of your designer, there are many others who would be happy to work on my garden redesign."

The rising tension in the room was ready to blow over when Firoza entered the room pushing a tea trolley piled high with fixings for an extravagant high tea. She had a pleasant face and was dressed in crisply ironed matching cotton *shalwar-kameez*[147] suit. Having gained a few extra pounds here and there, she looked older than her 33 years.

"*Aadaab*[148] Abba, so lovely of you to drop Seema yourself and stop in. We haven't had the pleasure of having you over for quite some time. I was in the kitchen helping prepare tea. Please, can you join us for some afternoon tea?"

Humayun had still not given up on the idea of discovering the secret of Saleem's landscape designer. "I would love to, Firoza. You are always such a good host, and your finger sandwiches are out of this world. The weather outside is perfect for a high tea in your colorful gardens. I love what your Japanese landscape designer has done to your front yard!"

"Thank you. Let me tell the servants to put out some chairs and table get this movable feast to the lawn." She said with a

---

147 Long shirt, tunic.
148 Salutations.

smile and bringing a smile to Humayun's face at her clever use of Hemingway's memoirs.

She had heard the tail-end of the conversation between the father and son. Not wanting to touch the subject, she left the room. Saleem mumbled something about washing his hands and joining them outside, also left.

Humayun picked up a book lying half-open on the coffee table and started reading the open page. The protagonist was preparing to travel in time.

He retraced his steps back to the garden, where rattan chairs and a table had already been set up for tea. Selecting the chair closest to the pond, he closed the book to look at its cover. It was H. G. Wells' "The Time Machine.". He started thinking about time travel a second time.

Hmm, so this is where Seema is getting her time travel ideas.

THE LANDSCAPE DESIGNER
1965

The day was pleasant, with a light breeze keeping the humidity low. Humayun sat in the oversized chair close to the pond, thumbing through *The Time Machine*. It seemed like an interesting book, and he made a mental note to add it to his reading list. He was watching a gasp of koi in the pond when he heard some movement behind him.

A maid was having trouble pushing a tea cart on the turf. Uncharacteristically, he got up to help her. She stopped in her tracks like she had seen a ghost, then she lowered her head and started pushing the cart harder. He grabbed the cart handle and pulled it next to the serving table. As she turned around to leave in a hurry, he addressed her, "Wait, what is your name?"

Without turning to look at him, she said, "Nadira."

"Are you new here? I haven't seen you here, or on Sundays, when Saleem brings his servants with him."

"How long have you worked here?"

"Many years, Sahib."

"You can go now."

She didn't look like any of the other female servants, and there was something about her. He had noticed the look on her face when she first saw him.

He called her back. "Listen, I am Saleem's father. Can you

get me a glass of water with two ice cubes?"

"Ji,[149] I know who you are." She left quickly. A few minutes later, another servant brought a glass of water with two ice cubes in it.

Seema came out, now also dressed in a traditional shalwar-kameez suit. "Dada, did you say something to Nadira? I just saw her; she looked a bit flustered."

"I just asked her how long she has worked here and to bring some water."

"Dadaaaa, you haven't been here for ages. She has worked here for as long as I can remember. She cared for me when Mummy was out working on the charity set up by the PM's wife. Nadira doesn't like to go out anywhere and stays in her room when she is not doing housework or helping Aleem prepare food for parties, etc."

"You know, she is Abbu's Japanese landscape designer. I am sorry I should have told you this before, avoiding the blowup between you and Abbu, mostly you, in the drawing room."

Ignoring the frontal assault on his role in the upheaval, he asked, "What blowup?"

"You were snooping on us?"

"Dada, this house is not as big as The *Chowk*. Everyone can hear everything. Maybe Nadira also heard your exchange with Abbu. The kitchen is right next to the drawing room, you know." She was looking straight at him, challenging him.

He leaned forward and hugged her as her parents joined them.

"What is all this love fest between Dada and *Poti*?"[150] Asked Firoza.

He picked up a cucumber finger sandwich offered by Firoza. "She is such a firecracker. She will chew up and spit out normal mortal saps. We'll have to find her a groom who can match

---

149 Affirmative reply.

150 Granddaughter.

and complement all the maneuvering in her little head."

"Dada, Nadira is reading this book you picked up in the drawing room. She told me about the time machine and how it can take you back to the past or forward to the future."

Humayun turned to Saleem and asked, "Your servants read English literature? You must pay them well. I am glad you can afford this class of help at home."

"Abba, you probably don't remember. This is the book you brought for me from England when I was in high school," Saleem said quietly. Humayun nodded absent-mindedly, still thinking about time travel.

Finishing up his tea quickly, Saleem asked to be excused to leave for a meeting. Humayun looked at him. "Go ahead, if the meeting is that important. You know you should find time to relax. You are constantly on the move."

"Abba, I get plenty of rest, but work is work. You know better than anyone about working. That is what I have seen all my life."

Humayun changed the subject, "Can you send Nadira to The *Chowk* tomorrow early afternoon, if you can spare her for an hour? I would like some ideas on redoing the open lawn area at the side of the house." Firoza gave Saleem a confused look, who nodded to Humayun, then looked at Seema for a couple of seconds, and left.

"Oops, I am in trouble," she said to her mother with a challenging smile.

A servant came outside and told Firoza there was a call for her. Firoza was telling the servant to take a message when Humayun told her to not worry about him and take the call since he was enjoying the garden and would stay awhile. She left to take the call.

Seema was still there, somewhat peevish, now worried about what was to come after Humayun leaves. She remembered something and said, "Dada, you know Nadira is quite smart. She meditates daily for about an hour. At her insistence, I tried it and I have been doing it for the last few weeks. At first, I didn't like it. My mind kept wandering to other things, so I couldn't focus as she had wanted me to, but she said to keep with it. Now I feel I have control over it and can keep my mind focused on it for the entire hour. It is very refreshing."

"Good for you, Seema. I have heard great things about meditation but have never had the time or inclination to try it. But if you like it so much, maybe I can find a good school and we can take a couple of lessons together."

"Dada, come on, we don't need to find a school to learn meditation. I can ask Nadira to teach us. It will be fun like we are taking a class together. What do you think, Dada? It won't take that much time, maybe twice a week for one hour."

"You know we need to maintain a distance with the servants, Seema. It's okay for you to learn from her since she is like an *Ayah* to you, but it would not look good for me to be taking lessons from a servant. What would the other servants say if they see me taking lessons from her?"

"She is much smarter than any of them. She carries herself with dignity, keeps to herself all the time, never mingles with other servants, and only speaks if something is asked of her. She is sad sometimes, but when I ask, she just smiles and changes the subject."

She continued, "Dada, you were the one who told me we should learn from wherever and whoever we can acquire knowledge from."

"Well, Dada, what do you think?"

"Okay, let me think about it. Anyway, she is coming to The *Chowk* tomorrow to give me some ideas on how to develop the side lawn. But no need to talk to anyone about this, at least not until I have decided, okay?"

"Dada, you know I won't! Why do you have to say that to me? Don't you think I know what to talk about and what subjects to stay away from?"

***

When Nadira arrived in Saleem's car the next day, Humayun took her directly to the garden behind his house. She was about his age, dressed in a clean white sari, the same as the last time. She looked more relaxed.

Her head and shoulders were covered with the last yard of her sari, like women from respectable families.

She must come from a family where she was taught how to properly carry herself around others.

Her face looked strangely familiar, but he couldn't place it. "I saw what you did with Saleem's garden. It is such a well-balanced garden. Did you get a formal training in landscape design?"

She shook her head but kept it lowered. "Sir, I was only taught basic reading, writing and the Holy Quran at home, the little I know about other things I learned by watching people."

"Where did you see people plan gardens?"

"I had been to some gardens in India before coming to Pakistan and would watch the gardeners there at work."

"You must have been a good learner. Seema seems to like you. She says you are helping her with many things. She is a very smart child. Do you have any children?"

She shook her lowered head. "Seema baby must have gotten it from her elders," she said, looking at his face directly for the first time and then quickly lowering her gaze.

"Hmm, so I would like to beautify this area into a formal garden and call it Seema *Bagh*,[151] Can you come up with some ideas about how this barren piece of land with overgrown bushes and banana trees can be turned into Seema Bagh?"

She nodded "Ji."

"I will tell my *maali*[152] to get the planting you think we will

---

151 Garden.

152 Gardner.

need. You will not have to do any physical labor. I am just looking for your ideas here. He will do all the work that will need to be done. If you are okay with this, I will speak with Firoza to see when she can free you up for the work."

She nodded again and another Ji. She started to leave.

"Wait, why did you seem to be shocked when you saw me yesterday? Even Seema said you looked flustered after that," he asked.

"I wasn't feeling well yesterday. Must've been something I ate at the numaish. Seema baby wanted me to go to the *numaish*[153] with her. She got something to eat from a kiosk and shared it with me. I am so glad that she didn't get sick."

He became alarmed. "She shouldn't be eating things from street vendors. You should have stopped her. I will have to tell her again, and you should also not let her eat from places like that. She can get anything made at home."

Another Ji and another nod followed by, "Can I go now?"

"One other thing, you look familiar, but I can't remember from where. Have you seen me before?"

"No, Sir, I don't think so."

"Okay, you can go now. Abdur Rahman will take you back."

She nodded, and she left.

He shook his head.

I may have seen her at some dinner party where she worked before she came to Saleem. But I am glad that I found someone to create that special space to name after Seema.

I hope Gayti Ara won't be jealous.

---

153 Fair/ Exhibition.

ENTER THE REVOLUTIONARY
1965

Humayun was upstairs getting ready for a trip to the airport, but this time he wasn't going there to fly out. A friend, Safdar Khattak, the Secretary of Defense for President Ayub Khan, had called him early in the morning and told him about a visitor staying at the KLM-Midway house hotel. Safdar had invited Humayun to accompany him to meet the visitor.

He rang the bell to the servants' quarters for Abdur Rahman, but also heard the doorbell. Looking out, he saw Saleem's car parked in the driveway. Hurrying downstairs, he saw a very upset Seema running in.

"*Aadab* Dada. Abbu and Mummy are still upset at me for telling you the landscape designer's identity. This time, they scolded me together when I returned from school. They said I am a chatterbox, and can't keep a secret, always talking to other people about things at home. Dada, I never do that, and you are not other people. You are the head of our family. Why can't I tell you something important without being labeled a tattletale?"

Being too careful of a person, he couldn't take sides. He hugged her. "My dear, it's a parent's duty to show their children the right path."

"But Dada, you teach me a lot of things every time we are together, but you never reproach me for anything, and I still remember every bit of your advice."

So, she thinks of my lessons as advice open to her acceptance.

"Dada, are you going somewhere? I want to come with you, as I don't want to stay by myself."

Seeing how upset she was, he didn't want to leave her alone there or send her back home.

"I am going to the Midway House to meet some people. You can come along. Abdur Rahman will take you to the snack bar there and you can have some ice cream while you wait. My meeting shouldn't last too long, so you should be fine there."

"Oh good. Can I have a club sandwich too? I ate nothing and left after they were done lecturing me."

"Sure, you can have whatever you want."

Her mood improved. "I am glad I came here. Moody insisted I come here, as you have a solution to all my problems."

The Secretary of Defense was waiting for him in the lobby, and they proceeded to the room where the visitor was staying. They knocked, and the door opened almost immediately.

Standing in his military garb with a half-chewed cigar in his mouth was Ernesto "Che" Guevara.

On the way up to the room, Safdar had told him the identity of the visitor. Che seemed to be a much bigger man than Humayun remembered him from his pictures.

Maybe because most of his pictures I saw were with Castro, who was a much taller man.

Seeing Che standing at the door, Safdar said, "Mr. Guevara, you didn't have to come to the door; we are honored. It is my pleasure to introduce my good friend, Mr. Humayun Babar. He is an honorable business executive in a world where honor is increasingly being replaced by an unrelenting drive for bigger and bigger profits. With a neighbor ruled by a reactionary establishment bent upon destroying us, Mr. Babar has helped protect our country. He can source, move and store all sorts of equipment, machines, and accessories needed for the defense of our country at a very nominal cost to our exchequer."

There were four other men in the room, one of them a Spanish interpreter. His wife, Aleida March, was also there.

After introductions, Che pointed to an empty sofa for Humayun to have a seat. He sat down next to him. The secretary took a comfortable chair next to the sofa.

So, the call was not what it sounded like this morning. It was all pre-planned. No wonder Che opened the door for us.

This should be interesting! A Secretary of Defense of a country aligned with (some would say a stooge of) the US, meeting a leader of an organization that overthrew a US-backed corrupt regime of Cuba.

I wonder what is of common interest between these two. I need to be careful.

Che opened up about a situation in Congo, a mineral-rich country burdened under the thumbs of western multinational corporations extracting the riches out of the lands, while keeping the people in utter poverty. The Congolese people had risen against their corrupt government, and their leaders had approached Che for help. They needed training for their fighters and military hardware to get rid of their puppet leadership. He was on his way to Africa from Beijing, where he met with Chairman Mao Zedong and Premier Zhou Enlai. They promised to support the Congolese people in their struggle, with weapons and other hardware, if he could arrange for covert transport of the weapons. China's name was to be kept out of this supply scheme. He needed facilities to re-label the armaments and then to ship them onwards.

"The Chinese are supplying the arms and ammunition as aid to the Congolese people for free and will also pay a generous fee for the re-labeling and transport."

Humayun had storage facilities in Keamari, near the Karachi Port area, for packing, unpacking, and storing imported machinery and equipment. He could easily add a re-labeling line at his facilities.

China had become an arms supplier to Pakistan for a few

years and Humayun had helped bring some urgently needed supplies to Pakistan from China during the Indo-Pakistan conflict earlier in the year. Since that war, he had become one of the major transporters of armaments from China to Pakistan. To keep his ship full on the way back to China, he started a business with Safdar Khattak for exporting Basmati rice to China.

He suggested to Che that they ask China to send the military hardware for Congo, with the other military weapon systems and hardware that Pakistan was buying from them, through their regular channels. Once the goods were in Pakistan, Chinese authorities would help separate the Congo-bound cargo from the shipment and hand them over to Humayun for re-labeling, storage, and shipment on to Congo.

Che loved his idea.

Being very familiar with moving arms, sometimes covertly, around the world, it was easy for Humayun to figure an estimate for his services. He then doubled his estimated cost to take care of the different "fees and charges for permits and fast-tracking the material through the different channels" according to the local trade and industry traditions. He then doubled the amount once again to arrive at his cost. Upon hearing the figure, Che looked at him with a surprised smile, then turned to Safdar and said, "All this news I hear of Pakistan still suffering from the Imperialist-Capitalist-British-infused corruption must not be true. Even my Communist brothers had quoted me a figure which was more than double what my friend, Huma-Yoon, will charge. I already like him."

Humayun replied, "It is my pleasure, Mr. Guevara, to be called a friend by you. We will do our best to help you help the Congolese people in any way we can."

Safdar Khattak, smiling broadly, probably thinking about his cut in the deal, said, "Humayun, Che had selected his room number 101, which can be read as 1 January, the date he overthrew the Batista[154] regime."

Che immediately corrected him. "I only helped Fidel overthrow Batista. He was the leader who made it all happen. I was only a minor cog in the Movement[155] that liberated the Cuban people."

He then turned to Humayun and asked, "Huma-yoon, my friend, any questions about this venture?"

Humayun was still curious to hear Che's opinion of Pakistan asked, "How do you like this capitalist-inspired hotel in our land of the poor?" A pun on the literal meaning of Pakistan, the land of the pure.

Che grabbed Humayun's hand with both hands. Shaking his head in a serious, sincere manner, he said, "*Demasiado distraídamente cómodo.*"[156]

Before his interpreter translated it, he pointed towards his wife and said in almost perfect English, "You can ask my wife. This bed is too comfortable for a warrior like me, so I slept on the floor." Aleida was nodding her head in agreement, which sparked guffaws around the room.

"Who is that little girl you came with, enjoying ice cream in the lobby? I have sent a man to bring her up. She must miss you by now." Che asked.

"She is my granddaughter, my son's daughter."

There was a knock on the door and as the door opened, Seema stood there, prim and proper. Abdur Rahman was behind her. His face was serious and eyes squinted, ready for action to protect her. Humayun motioned him to leave.

"Seema, I would like you to meet Mr. Ernesto Guevara."

"I know. I have seen his pictures with Mr. Castro in a book Abbu has."

---

154 Fulgencio Batista, US backed Cuban dictator overthrown by Fidel Castro and Che, on 1st January 1959 after a hard fought war that lasted over 5 years.
155 Castro's Cuban revolutionary organization that overthrew Bautista.
156 Too distractedly comfortable.

Turning to Che and shaking his hands with both her small hands, "Hello, Mr. Gurevara (sp.) I am glad to meet you."

Che Guevara, the revolutionary who had defeated forces much bigger and stronger than him, bent down to be at her face level and smiled. "It's G-u-e-v-a-r-a, Che Guevara. But you can call me Che, like all my friends."

"I am so glad my grandfather brought me here. I hope I can be as famous as you are."

"Señorita Seema, I know one day you will do much more, but remember one thing: it's never the enemy who beats you, it's you. Watch out, be strong." Then he continued, "Like you, I am so glad my friend Huma-yoon brought you along."

She asked him for an autograph, and while Humayun was searching his pockets for a piece of paper, Che pulled out a pamphlet from his oversized front pocket. The pamphlet had a picture of Patrice Lumumba, the murdered first president of Congo, and a brief history and information on the Congolese Independence movement. He signed his name on it with Humayun's pen and handed the autographed pamphlet to Seema. "He was a great man, my friend Patrice, murdered by reactionary forces aligned with the large American corporations trying to control us all. I am trying to help his people take back control of their land from the capitalists and their agents. This will remind you of our meeting this day."

As they all got up and shook hands, Seema's eyes never left Che's face as he stepped out of the room with his wife to bid them goodbye. He shook hands with Safdar and Humayun, then looked at Seema with a smile and did a friendly admonish-like gesture with his right index finger at her. Aleida, smiling broadly, gave her a hug and a kiss.

Seema was walking on Cloud nine and was not aware of what was being said on the way to the car.

Was it a dream or reality?

I want to be like him when I grow up.

The enemy can't beat me, only I can.

She heard Abdur Rahman say, "Baby, please." He was holding the door open for her. Humayun was already seated, deep in thought. She got into the car, clutching his autographed pamphlet like it was the most precious thing in the world. All she could think about during the ride was how much she loved meeting Che, and how she would dedicate her life to the people, like he did.

The next time I meet him, I will tell him all about the good work I would have done following in his footsteps.

Humayun heard her mumble, "I love him so much." and smiled.

Abdur Rahman brought the car to a halt at her home and opened her door. This time only she was getting off. Humayun hugged her and told her to be nice to her parents. She clung to him, repeating how happy and thankful she was for taking her to meet "Che Guevara, the best human on this earth."

Firoza came out of the front door. Seeing her, Seema flew out of the car and jumped into her mother's outstretched arms, "Mummy, Mummy, you will never believe who I met today!! Not in a million years."

NOT ALL ENDS WELL
1967

It was an unusually pleasant October morning in Karachi. The weather was mild after a long, hot Karachi summer that typically extends well into October. A cool Arabian Sea breeze was blowing in, neutralizing the effects of hot Sindh desert winds. Humayun was having his breakfast in Seema Bagh. The garden was blooming with tropical flowers. Their light fragrance hung all over. He was happy the way the garden was turning out and enjoyed spending time in this little island of tranquility in the middle of a loud, crowded city.

He noticed a rather thick envelope with Algerian stamps in the stack of unopened mail he had brought from work. It was an invitation from the Chairman of the Algerian Revolutionary council to visit Algiers as a guest of the committee on the sixth anniversary of its independence in July next year.

The invitation also included a letter informing him of his nomination to receive a national medal of honor for his "exceptionally vital help to the Algerian people in their hour of need." An honorary doctorate would also be conferred upon him by the University of Algiers.

He knew President Ben Bella had been removed from office through a coup d'état in 1965 and the country was ruled by a revolutionary council headed by Houari Boumédiène, another leader he had worked with during the struggle for Algerian Independence. He hadn't met Ben Bella or Boumédiène for many years, and wasn't sure if he would be allowed to meet Ben Bella there.

I appreciate what they are doing for me with this degree, but I wish I was educated and had earned this degree by actually taking classes and passing exams. I got nowhere with Saleem or Gayti Ara to convince them to study past their basic degrees. This honorary degree may help convince Seema to go for a higher degree.

He smiled at the thought and made a mental note of telling Seema when he saw her the next time.

He didn't have to wait long.

He had just started his breakfast when Seema burst in. "They killed him, Dada, they killed Che! Those terrible CIA people killed him." She was hysterical.

He was killed in a battle with the government forces, not the CIA, as reported in the papers. I am surprised that Dawn is now printing rumors, instead of confirmed news.

He had seen the news item about Che's death, in *Dawn*, the leading Pakistani newspaper. Che had been helping a movement of Bolivian revolutionaries fight a corrupt military junta.

The Bolivian government approached the US for help with fears of a Cuban-style revolution. Bolivia was the largest tin supplier to the US industry. Also, Che Guevara was one of the top enemies of the US.

Bolivian army units were soon being equipped and trained by the US. The Junta launched a propaganda campaign in the region about the presence of foreign communist fighters trying to enslave the Bolivian people. Large monetary awards were offered for any information on Che's location. Soon, a disgruntled farmer came forward with the information on his whereabouts. They were surrounded, and Che was killed in a battle with the Bolivian military.

To Seema, the stories from Bolivia, Cuba, Congo, and

elsewhere were evidence that the world was a place where power was everything, and the rights of the poor and downtrodden were nothing. They had to stand up and fight the tyrants to get their rights like in Cuba or die fighting like Che.

Dada told me that Mr. Jinnah believed India got its independence because Britain's power was on the decline, and it was afraid that a military uprising in India would be enough to send it packing.

Non-violence by itself wouldn't have succeeded in India.

I hope I can help the poor and the oppressed fight for their rights when I grow up.

She was sobbing in his arms. Humayun, having seen the iron hand of the English masters and the devastation that colonialism had brought to India, had a soft spot in his heart for people struggling all around the world.

After waiting for her to settle down, he started in his usual way, in a soft low voice, "My dear, I share your grief for your hero, the fallen warrior, an upstanding idealist who was overtaken by the reality of human greed,"

"To gain support of the general populace, the visible leaders and front-line soldiers must be local. Others, helping the struggle, need to stay in the background. Che, a great man, made a human mistake. He put his experienced, battle-hardened Cuban soldiers ahead of his Bolivians fighters, and sometimes even pushed his Bolivians aside to hasten the path to victory. The junta and its supporters used this information to divide the locals with a well-thought-out propaganda campaign against him and his Cuban forces. They declared him a Cuban agent and mercenary fighting for the control of the Bolivian natural resources and form a communist dictatorship in Bolivia, similar to Cuba. Their propaganda worked."

"Dada, what is a junta?"

"Sorry Seema, I am getting too technical with you. I keep forgetting you are still a 14-year-old. Junta is a term used for a military or a political group that rules a country after taking power by force. Like President Ayub Khan did in 1958."

"I now understand."

"So to finish my explanation, Che lost the battle for control of the narrative before he lost the battle on the field in Bolivia. His enemies had a stronger message. It relegated his status to that of a greedy mercenary in the eyes of those who were looking to him for salvation."

"Remember what he told you at the Midway house? 'Your enemy can never defeat you; it is always you.' It wasn't his enemies who defeated him, it was he, himself who lost the war."

Humayun concluded, "The battles for the hearts and minds of the people are won and lost on the airwaves, the local papers and in the media. If the media war is lost, nothing else can rescue a doomed struggle."

She was quiet and still looked shaken.

To get her mind off the news, he asked, "Well, are you ready for some good news after such terrible news?"

"Dada, yes, please. I have been so sad since I read about this and cried all morning."

"I am so sorry, dear."

"Okay, so the good news is that I have been invited to Algeria next July to receive a medal of honor by Houari Boumédiène. He is like the president of the country. You will be on summer vacations, so you can come along with me. I will ask your parents and Gayti Ara to come along too, if they don't have any plans."

Hearing this, the sadness disappeared from Seema's face. "Really? Wow, I would love to come with you to Algeria, Dada. Traveling with you is always so much fun flying in first class. Will we be meeting President Ben Bella there too?"

"Ahmed is the president no more. He is currently restricted from receiving guests or leaving his house. We will need permission from the revolutionary council. I will ask Houari. We'll see."

"Dada, I always wanted to meet him. He is like Che. I like fighters who win. I don't like those who lose. But Dada, why do all these leaders end up either being jailed or killed in the end?"

"I wouldn't say all of them end up like that, but many do. You see, fighting from the outside is different from governing from the inside. Running a country requires a different but unique set of skills. These great people may have been great at leading the struggle to overthrow tyrants, but while running the government, they sometimes make mistakes. Humans are fickle, and forget the work these people did for them, and turn on them at the smallest of missteps."

Seema was shaking her head up and down enthusiastically. "I get it. I will never forget."

With admiration in her eyes, she hugged him hard and said, "Dada, you are my hero and my teacher. I am your student and follower. I learn so much from you and follow in your footsteps. To me, you are like those who have defeated tyrants all around the world. You are the best. I love you so much."

"Seema, not everyone wins. Just because you lose doesn't mean you were a bad player. It is how you play the game, and how you get back up after a fall. So, you shouldn't dislike those who have lost. Maybe the odds were too great for them to overcome. They were humans, after all."

"Dada, I never lose. You have taught me to keep trying until I succeed. Even though Abbu doesn't have a son, but I will carry your legacy. I will be famous and they will all know I am your granddaughter, and you are my grandfather. I will change the world. You just wait and see."

THE TABLOID REPORTER
1972

At the end of her senior Cambridge coursework at Grammar School in Karachi, Humayun had given Seema a little envelope as her graduation present. It contained information for a college education account he had set up in England. Looking at the attached statement, she figured she could afford any four-year college or university in Europe without having to worry about tuition and living expenses. She spent her final A-level year researching and evaluating different college programs in England. She applied to three universities in the England, and at Saleem's insistence, a couple of American universities.

As one of the best students in her class, she had excellent reference letters from her Grammar School faculty, as well as a financial statement from a prestigious English investment house. Acceptance letters came pouring in. Saleem wanted her to go to the US, but she opted for the London School of Economics.

LSE, a premier educational institution, drew offspring of elites from around the world. Seema fit right in with her liberal ideas and thirst for knowledge. She also brought with her a healthy distrust of the West and their hunger for the control of the world's resources.

Living an independent life in London was exciting. It was all that Seema had imagined. Most of her school friends were now studying at British or American universities. She tried to keep in touch, but they were all busy at their schools. Soody and Moody were there, like always, providing clarity and opposing views about every question she faced, and every challenge she confronted.

***

Aadab Mummy,

I hope you are all well. I got your sixth letter, as well as all the ones before it. Sorry I haven't written. I suppose our monthly 3-minute trunk calls are not enough for a mother separated from her child by seven seas. This is the first of the letters I will write to you every week, *Insha-Allah*. Don't tire of them!

After this letter, I hope you will withdraw your threat of no more letters. I love your letters and wait for them. They are so detailed and well written; I feel like I am back home and never left. I keep your letters in a keepsakes tin and read them when I miss you and my home. Maybe we can do a book together, of your letters.

As far as your comment about me getting sick from all the work here, I can assure you, I am not that weak. I can handle it all. Have you ever heard of someone falling ill because of hard work?

I started taking evening classes to learn Arabic since I have to consult old records in Arabic from time to time for Islamic History, my second major. Some professors at LSE are Islamic History scholars and a joy to learn from. I have learnt so much from them about the cultural history and the rise of the Islamic civilization. Before this, I knew little about Muslim scholars and their contributions to medicine, science, mathematics, social sciences, and astronomy during the dark ages in Europe.

Islam freed the slaves, and gave women equality, a concept unheard of at the time. I believe Islam provides the foremost path of emancipation for the oppressed from western colonists and the corrupt puppet regimes installed by them to maintain control over the vast resources found in the under-developed areas.

I enjoy the vibrant environment at LSE, especially the different societies here. I joined the debating society two months ago, to further hone my communications skills and to grow my circle of friends and acquaintances.

I like to learn more about people from different regions, backgrounds, and cultures, and don't want to limit myself to Pakistani and Muslim friends, like all my friends now.

Recently, I joined a group of mostly European students who travel to Sudan during breaks for volunteer work there. My knowledge of Arabic will also help me develop a deeper understanding of the people there and perform better than others.

One piece of good news. The captain of the LSE debating team approached me last week. She invited me to join the team. I accepted on the spot. She told me I will be the first Asian woman on this team.

My bearable first year at LSE girls-only hostel is ending soon. The food here is surprisingly good. Living in the hostel has taught me a lot about English college culture.

Oh, a side story I am sure you would enjoy. Robert Frisk, a newcomer demonstrator for my Islamic History class, called me to his office. He thought I had cheated on my quiz. Imagine that, me cheating! What a nerve!

But he was cute, though!

Dada called me on a trunk call yesterday. He told me he will be coming to London soon. It would be nice if you can come with him.

Khuda Hafiz for now.

Well, that is all I can think of for now. Please give Abbu my *Aadab* and love.

Khuda Hafiz for now.

Your loving daughter,
Seema

***

Robert Frisk was a junior reporter, working for a conservative tabloid *Sunday Express* in London. Early in his career, he became interested in the history of the Middle East and its people.

To supplement his reporter's meager income, he had taken on a part-time demonstrator job at LSE with a professor teaching Islamic history. His first assignment was to grade a surprise pop quiz that the professor had given to his class. Grading the papers, he identified one submission superior to all the others in content, clarity, and specificity. It was so perfect that he thought the professor had included an answer sheet to help him grade the quiz. But an ID number at the top of the paper showed it to be a student test paper.

His next thought was that it was plagiarism. He couldn't tell who the author was, as students were prohibited from putting their names on any documents they submitted. He left a note on it for the student to see him in his office.

"You wanted to see me about my test?" came a nasally, somewhat shrill voice, in a tone of being inconvenienced. He looked up and saw a thin, average looking girl with glasses, in a long skirt, standing confidently in front of him.

"Yes. Thank you for stopping by. Please have a seat."

She kept standing. "You think I cheated on the quiz?"

Frisk found himself on the back foot, but quickly recovered. "To tell you the truth, yes, it crossed my mind."

"Or if you have taken this course for grade-bumping. Students are known to take an easy class to push up their overall GPA."

"I assure you, Mr. Frisk, that neither is true. Of all the courses I have ever taken, I have gotten one 2nd division marks, and that was in Home Economics, which my mother forced me to take. She believes girls need to know how to run their households frugally while their husbands are hard at work earning a livelihood." She paused for some reaction from Frisk.

He kept looking at her, "Actually, it is a course you English created, during the suffrage movement, to keep your women from becoming too heroic and wanting to stick their noses in finance, economics and other lofty affairs of the nation."

Frisk replied. "Please don't take it personally. This is something I have been instructed to watch out for. Your test performance was excellent and I will pass your test paper to your professor with my comments from this meeting and let him assign a grade to it."

He paused. "Any questions for me?"

"Please don't take it personally. But why do you work for a tabloid that uses half-truths and sensationalism to sell papers? You are a journalist. Your job should be to tell the people the truth, unadulterated truth." She was still standing, towering over his small desk.

He gestured her again to sit. This time, she took a chair across from him.

"I agree with you on the role of the journalist, and I would add that our role should be to challenge authority, all authority. Working for a tabloid, I am reminded daily that I am breaking my oath of providing truthful, unbiased information to people. I hope to jettison that job as soon as I am able to, hopefully soon."

The tension in the air had disappeared.

He continued, "I presume you are studying here on funding provided by your family, and I don't know what they had to do to finance your education. Most international students come from wealthy families who may not understand the hurdles poor and middle-class parents here have to overcome to educate their children who aspire to a university education. Had I come from the upper crust of English society, I would have had no problems paying for an education and securing employment at one of the premier newspapers. My middle-class Kentish parents took loans from friends and family for it. After getting my degree, with very good grades, I took the only job available to me to start paying back the loans. I had to look for a part-time job just to eat, since almost all of my *Sunday Express* salary went towards loan servicing and taxes. I was lucky to find this demonstrator's job."

I shouldn't have come in here ready for a fight. The poor guy was just doing what he has been told to.

She smiled to cover her embarrassment. "So I will get the graded paper in the class tomorrow?"

"Yes, but let me know if you don't."

"You know I have been stressed out with all the work trying-—"

He cut her off. "Don't worry about it. I don't take things personally." They talked for a few minutes more, then she left.

Over time, they became friends. She liked his guarded style of conversation and his liberal ideas about humanity. From time to time, she would invite him to her get-togethers with friends. He was interested in the different cultures, the problems of different societies, and even though he was a good seven years older than most of her friends, he soon became a regular in her group.

As she was starting her second year in college, he left *Sunday Express* for a real reporter's job at *The Times*. On his first major assignment, he was sent to Belfast to cover the ethno-nationalist conflict in Northern Ireland, commonly known as "The Troubles".

While on a visit to London, Seema invited Frisk to join her and her friends at an anti-Shah[157] rally at Trafalgar Square. Iranian students had organized it to protest the barbaric laws of the Monarchy in Iran.

When he got there, he saw a large gathering of people shouting anti-Shah slogans. They all had brown paper bags over their heads, revealing only their eyes. He saw her in the group. She was the only one without a paper bag. The demonstrators held up handmade banners deploring the Shah and his regime. They were banging drums and raising slogans for the Shah's removal and demanding introducing democracy in Iran.

Large crowds of curious Londoners had gathered to watch the paper bags covered demonstrators.

Seema was marching with the protestors. Frisk started walking with her. "They are all Iranian students studying in the Britain and Europe. Their faces are hidden, so as not to be

157 Shah Mohammad Reza Shah Pahlavi of Iran.

photographed by SAVAK[158] infiltrators. It can be a death sentence for family members back in Iran if their identity is uncovered."

He started taking notes on the event, and also using the occasion to interview some of the faceless students in the march.

A reporter covering the event for The Guardian approached Seema, the only one without a bag over their heads. "You are brave. Aren't you afraid of the SAVAK?" She asked Seema.

"No. I am a Pakistani, and I am not afraid of anyone."

***

A week later, Frisk was sent to his first overseas assignment in Portugal to cover the so-called carnation revolution where left leaning elements of the military had risen up against the authoritarian Estado Novo regime.

He had to give up his demonstrator's job and Seema didn't see him or hear from him after that.

158 Shah's secret police, domestic security and intelligence service.

DOWN WITH THE SHAH
1976

The family was in London for Seema's graduation. They were staying at Humayun's flat. He had bought the flat as an investment at Richard's suggestion. It was in Fitzrovia, a trendy area made famous by George Bernard Shaw and later by Virginia Woolf, who moved to his former house.

Roshan Ara and Hashim had flown in from Lahore for the graduation, and to spend time with Humayun. Hashim had been transferred to East Pakistan in 1955. He had recently retired from the army, after his release from a yearlong captivity in India. He was a Brigadier in the Pakistan Army's Eastern Command that had surrendered to India in the Bangladesh war of independence. Humayun had missed his sister terribly during the years she was living a thousand mile away in Dhaka.

Gayti Ara, Dr. Mateen, and their boys were there too.

They were all dressed up, sitting together near the stage. A young man was also sitting with them. Saleem introduced him to Humayun as Pervez Jaleesi, the son of one of his closest friends, and someone who Seema knew from her childhood. He was two years ahead of her at Grammar School and a recent Oxford graduate. He was attending a training program in London.

Saleem had invited him to the graduation.

Firoza had told Humayun that Pervez's parents had asked

her to let Pervez meet Seema to see if there was an interest. Saleem wanted to invite Pervez to the graduation.

Why didn't he ask me himself?

Humayun felt the graduation was a family affair and not suitable for inviting new people. However, seeing Firoza's strong desire to start the process, he relented and told her to make sure Seema was okay with it.

Seema had no issues with inviting Pervez.

The McDonalds were also there to cheer Seema on at her graduation. Richard had always been there for her during her college years in London.

After working in partnership with Richard for many years, Humayun had started his own arms trade business, but their friendship had grown over the years. They would still cooperate on large equipment and arms orders. Richard was now an influential member of British Parliament and a close friend of Margaret Thatcher, the new conservative party leader. He had handed the responsibilities of running his arms business to his two sons, keeping only his role as chairman of the board. Humayun's family had been invited to a celebration dinner later that evening, at his palatial estate outside of London.

The Graduation ceremony started like any other college graduation with pomp and ceremony, and welcome speeches. Dr. Abbas Ali Khalatbari, Foreign Minister of Iran, was to deliver the keynote address. As he started speaking, a large number of people showed up at the back of the hall with brown paper bags on their heads, like the demonstrators at the rally. They started shouting "Down with the Shah" in unison, followed by "People united, can never be defeated." Some graduating Middle Eastern students and their friends started clapping and raising their fists in support. Seema was one of them. She was standing in her seat, clapping along and raising her fists. School guards and some policemen came in and quickly removed the demonstrators from the hall, and the ceremony resumed.

After meeting Pervez at the graduation, Richard asked him to join them for dinner. He understood South Asian culture enough to know that wedding proposals usually started with the boy visiting the girl's family.

After dinner, Richard's sons invited everyone for a tour of their stables and the property. Everyone except Humayun went. He retired to the smoking room with Richard, who had a collection of some of the finest Cuban cigars in a large walk-in humidor. Humayun was not a smoker, but could not resist a good Cuban. They settled into comfortable leather chairs.

"Pervez seems to be quite a smart young man." Richard remarked. "Are you thinking of a match for Seema?"

Humayun replied, "If you ask me, Seema is too young to think about getting married, but Firoza thinks daughters need to be married off and settled in their new homes as soon as they are of marriageable age."

A waiter brought in coffee in a bone china coffee set on a silver tray. After he left, Richard said, "Humayun, we are not getting any younger. Saleem has stayed away from your business for reasons of his own, so I think a person like Pervez could be of help to CWK in the future. That can be the key to finding a match for Seema, don't you think? "

"Richard, I don't need anyone to help reduce the burden of my work. Seema has shown interest, and once we are back in Karachi, I will see how much she wants to get involved. But you know this is a tough business, no fit for women. But I think she has the germs to be successful in the arms business. She is mentally tough, very resilient, and never backs down. But if she is unwilling, I have other ideas."

"She is a caring young lady to her family and friends, but ready to walk over and crush anyone in her path. She is hard as nails. I am sure, with your guidance, she will be very successful in Pakistan and beyond."

They were quiet for a little while, enjoying the cigars and

coffee in bone china cups adorned with the McDonald family crest and Sir Jonathon's initials.

Humayun inspected the design on the cup while sipping the dark, bitter Colombian coffee.

"These cups are exquisite. I am glad to see how you have preserved your father's memory. I remember the night I met him in Behramgarh, like it was yesterday. He was a great man, and you have carried on his legacy with honor."

"Humayun, you know I try. Being a son is never easy. In my early life, I was constantly trying to come up to his standards and make him proud. My two-decade long stay in India after his return to England helped me overcome those feeling of inadequacy and become self-assured."

"Relationships are complicated and the father-son bond is the most complicated of them all. Especially when the father is a self-made man of high standing."

He took a sip of his coffee and continued, "Speaking of fathers, I have noticed Saleem struggle for your validation. He tries really hard to make you proud. I know what that is like, a constant state of mental torture. My friend, you are a tough man, like my father. He is your only son, and a very good one. Cut him some slack. You will be a happier man."

Humayun nodded, but kept quiet.

I don't think I act any differently than other fathers. In fact, a lot better than how my father treated me.

"Richard, thank you. It's good to have a friend who can shine a light on what we may not be seeing. But going back to Seema, I do think about what sort of man would be a good match for her. She is very independent, and I don't think she will marry the first man her parents throw at her. She was cool towards Pervez and showed nothing more than a courteous interest in him. Maybe she has met someone here who she likes."

Richard raised his eyebrows. Looking at Humayun intently, he said, "Over the years, I have met several of her friends at our annual summer picnics. They all appear to be the typical college types, you know. One of them who she seems to get along well with is Robert Frisk, a demonstrator at LSE. He is now working for *The Times*. She may have told you about him. I had a background check done on the man. You know you can never be too careful. He is from the Medway area, sorry, from Kent, of a middle-class background, smart, but a socialist and somewhat of a liberal hack. He is currently on assignment in Portugal. I don't agree with most of what he has written, but I suppose that is how the left operates. They try to show how bad we monarchists are, but thank God, the public doesn't believe everything they print. The report didn't find any entanglements with the fair sex. I hope you don't mind my being so forward about it, but I did this just to protect her."

"Richard, why would I mind? I am thankful to you for thinking about her like your own daughter. You are like a brother to me, a much kinder brother. Firoza and Saleem will be heartbroken if it turns out that Seema's interest in Frisk is more than just a college friendship."

Richard looked alarmed, and his face darkened. "Do you want me to make sure that doesn't happen? There are ways to stop this."

Now Humayun was alarmed.

Sir Richard is an extremely powerful politician with strong connections in the British civil and military services.

He quickly replied, "Let's see where this leads, if at all it does. From all my conversations about him, I gathered she thinks of him as a student of hers rather than a peer or teacher."

"I see, but do let me know if I can help. You know I will. I don't want Saleem to be heartbroken or disappointed. He is a quiet boy. These quiet types always keep everything locked up inside of them. I don't want him to suffer more than he already has."

Humayun noticed something else.

"Richard, I recognize that look on your face. There is more

to it. What's on your mind?"

"Is it that obvious? Or is it that our 45 year friendship makes us quite transparent to the other? Yes, there is another thing I wanted to speak with you about, but this is such a joyous occasion, and I was going to wait until the next time. It's nothing urgent."

"I am a grizzled old man who has seen and heard everything. Go on."

"Some of Seema's friends are not the right set that you or I would want our children to be associating with. You saw the demonstration today at the graduation."

"I did. Seemed a bit out of character for her."

"Seema organized this demonstration."

"Really? How do you know, Richard?"

"See, there is this group of extreme right-wing, mostly Egyptian students based in London called ELSA. They are connected with the *Akhwaan*.[159] They are no threat to us, so we have let them have their meetings, their prayer groups, and even their public demonstrations. Seema is not a member, but she is friends with the leadership and attends their meetings from time to time. She is also friends with some of the leadership of an Iranian students' group here that is a follower of a Paris-based cleric by the name of Ayatollah Khomeini. Even that was not a problem. However, a few months ago, I was reading a government report on ELSA's annual gathering. I was alarmed to learn Seema was one of the speakers. It seems she convinced the ELSA leadership to invite the Iranians to their annual gathering to look at areas of common interest."

"She conveyed the invitation to the Iranians for them. Being Shias, they were distrustful of the Sunni Arabs, but Seema convinced them to attend. They were present for her speech at the gathering. In it, she presented the idea of organizing protests at

---

[159] Akhwaan al Muslamoon – Islamic Brotherhood, an Egyptian fundamentalist group.

graduation ceremonies. Apparently, the demonstration today was the first implementation of her idea. We are expecting many more this graduation season."

"Is she in trouble with the government?" Humayun asked.

"Well, not at this time. I hope she stays out of trouble. I had the original report, and, as far as I know, no copies of it had been made. It was one of many reports for that day. I kit with me to read and never forwarded it to the records office for filing. I don't think anyone missed it."

Richard continued, "But please talk to her and tell her that both these groups are part of a large reactionary movement that is being watched carefully for future acts of terrorism, so she would be well advised to stay clear of them. She is a smart girl with a bright future; she will listen to logic. I am sure you can advise her without the mention of this conversation."

"I will ask her about the incident at the graduation to see if she comes clean with the information you've shared."

"Humayun you know how these types of activities could land one on the wrong side of the tracks."

Humayun shuddered at the thought.

"Richard, I can't think of anyone else who has done more for her. I thank you, and even though Saleem and Firoza will never know of this, they owe you a huge debt of gratitude."

"Please don't mention it. You would have done the same for my children. They are the future, and it is our duty to protect and guide them from straying."

BACK TO SEEMA BAGH
1976

Back in their Fitzrovia flat, they were talking about the ceremony, and how proud they all were of Seema's achievements.

Firoza asked, "What next?"

Seema replied, "I need to tie some loose ends in London and would return to Pakistan in a few weeks. London had been great, but I miss my home and you all. I will find some volunteer work in Karachi while I map my life plans and next steps."

"But please, don't ask me about getting married."

Humayun had tried to get Saleem to help run CWK, but he had other ideas and chose a different path that led him to become an actuary. He was happy and quite prosperous in his career, and kept his distance from his father's thriving arms venture, which he called the business of death and destruction.

Seema had shown interest in CWK, while in high school, even before she understood its true nature. She would ask Humayun detailed questions about running a business, dealing with customers, and marketing and sales. Humayun had high hopes for her.

Recognizing it as the right moment to strike, Humayun said, "Seema, I would like to offer you a management trainee position at CWK. Even with your journalism and mass communications background, I am confident that you will learn the business quickly."

Seema added, "Don't forget Islamic History, Dada."

To her, the offer was not unexpected; he had been hinting at it for years now. She let it hang in the air to see how her parents would react.

Everyone congratulated Seema on getting her first job offer. Roshan Ara took off her necklace and put it around Seema's neck. "Congratulations, my darling Seema, on your graduation and on Bhaiya's offer. I am so proud. Both of my children have sent graduation presents for you with me and love for *Mamoo*."[160]

Firoza spoke, "Thank you so much, *Phupi-jan*, you're so kind." Then, turning to Humayun, she said, "Abba, thank you for thinking so highly of Seema to offer her a position without your formal interview process. She is a lucky girl to have your confidence."

"She may be lucky, but it isn't luck or the fact that she is my granddaughter that has brought her the offer. I know what she is made of and what she can do. The interview process is for candidates I don't know. Asking her to go through a multi-interview hiring process would suggest that I have some doubt about her abilities. I don't!"

Saleem took Seema's hands in his. "I am so happy and proud of you, my dearest. I know you will succeed in whatever path you take in your life. But before you decide, take some time and think about Abba's kind offer."

Still holding her hands, he looked towards Humayun and said, "Abba, you made me a very similar offer when I graduated from college. I said no, and made a career in actuarial sciences, quite a different path from where life would have taken me had I accepted. While I am still happy about my career decision, what I regret is having said no to you. It was the most difficult decision of my life, but a life dealing in arms was not for me, as I was and still am a pacifist."

---

[160] Mother's brother.

Humayun stopped himself from saying something immediately, and instead, he went over to Saleem and put a hand affectionately on his shoulder.

"It hurt me at the time, but seeing where you are in your career and your life, I must say you have done very well for yourself. Besides, you have given me this fine granddaughter, and raised her very well."

He saw Saleem's eyes start to well up.

Richard, I remembered your advice.

I am giving credit where credit is due.

He continued, "Maybe it was all for the best that you didn't join what you once called my 'business of death and destruction'. You are successful in your profession, and happy, something a lot of very successful people lack. CWK never was and will never be, a business of death and destruction. It is an essential business that helps protect our country from its biggest enemies and brings valuable foreign exchange for it. I am also proud of the crucial role that CWK played in helping Algeria and other Muslim countries gain independence. Without it, Algeria would still be under the thumbs of the French."

Humayun saw a glint in Seema's eyes, but Saleem spoke, "Abba, I was so scared for you when Mateen Bhai told me our new driver was a Special Forces man hired to protect you from French assassins. I never told you, but I would have nightmares when you were gone, during the time of the Algerian independence war."

"I didn't know you had heard that rumors about the French trying to target me. Abdur Rahman's primary job was to protect my family while I was away."

Saleem added, "I wanted my family to never feel the way I did during those dark days. This was my primary motivation for seeking a different career path."

Seeing Mateen Shah with an embarrassed expression, Humayun moved on. "So Seema, take your time and think about it."

"Dada, I like to help people. The Palestinians, Kashmiris, and many others, Muslims and non-Muslims who yearn to breathe freely but don't have the resources or leadership. There are so many ways to help them."

Humayun nodded. "Yes, there are, Seema. The oppressors have adopted new methods and found new allies to suppress just struggles for freedom. We must find new avenues to help the exploited free themselves. I disagree with those who are in favor of the oppressed taking the war to the oppressors' backyards and attacking their homeland."

"Then what do you suggest they do?"

"Show the world and the citizens of the countries still active militarily in other countries what their armies are involved in. Bring the terror wrought upon people in other lands to the screens and airwaves of the occupiers."

"I don't get it."

"So Vietnam fought the Americans at home for years, but could only defeat them after some of the US networks started showing pictures and live footage of war to the American public. Battles of tomorrow will be won or lost on the airwaves. Television and radio broadcasts are going to be the bombs and rockets of today."

"I see what you mean."

"Seema, you have chosen journalism and mass communication as your career, so I can see you leading CWK's transition to an information and communication business. Information is a lot more powerful weapon than any arms or ammunition. Once our transition is completed, we will have stepped out of the shadows that we sometimes have to operate in. No one will ever be able to point at you and say that yours is an enterprise of death and destruction."

He had succinctly presented his vision of transitioning his business to his family. Even Saleem seemed impressed. "Abba, I didn't know you have given so much thought to converting CWK to something very different."

Humayun continued, "I have thought about it off and on for many years."

Saleem saw Seema's rising interest and excitement. He tried to calm it by pointing out that the transition would still take years to complete and that CWK would still be dealing in armaments for years to come.

Seema was quiet, so Saleem continued, "You will soon find a suitable match, get married and have children. I am sure your husband would be very uncomfortable with you involved in arms trade and its perils."

"Abbu, I have no interest in getting married anytime soon, so please let's not get into that right now. I agreed to invite Pervez to my graduation only because we were at the same school and he was always a very kind person - not to screen a prospective life partner." She smiled to cover the harshness of her response.

Firoza started to say something, but Saleem gave her a look and a nod that told her to save her thought for later.

Seema, noticing the non-verbal exchange between her parents, got up and hugged her father. "I love you so much. I don't want you to be sad or upset on my account. You have raised me to be an independent person and to express my opinion freely, so I did."

"After my graduation high dissipates, I will be thinking about this and everything in the months to come. You do not know how glad I will be to get back home."

Humayun shook his head at Seema's disarming style and her ability to take control of the situation

Was this emotional outpouring sincere or a ploy to buy time?

But I know that when all has been said and done, she would, like always, have had it all her way.

THE CAPRICIOUS YEARS
1979-82

Gayti Ara's husband, Dr. Mateen Shah Ghori, was the head of the department of surgery at the Khyber Medical Center. They had three children, all boys, Ahmed Shah, Osman Shah, and Omar Shah Ghori. The oldest one, Ahmed Shah, was the same age as Seema. Both Ahmad Shah and Osman Shah chose the medical profession to follow in their father's footsteps. Omar Shah, the baby of the family, was an 'unplanned gift from Allah', born 17 years after their second, Osman.

After the Soviet Union invaded Afghanistan on Christmas Eve, 1979, refugees started pouring into Pakistan through the Khyber Pass, a short drive from Peshawar. The Pakistani government set up refugee camps to provide shelter for the families flooding into Pakistan. More camps were organized by charitable and religious organizations along the border areas to accommodate these homeless, penniless refugees. At first, medical facilities for the refugees were nonexistent, but soon the larger camps started adding medical tents, managed and run by volunteers from Peshawar.

Dr. Mateen, with two of his students, would spend a day each week visiting the refugee camps, treating those needing medical help. On one of these trips, a patient was brought to him who was bleeding with no visible injury or having been in an accident. He was oozing blood from every pore of his body. To save his life, Dr. Mateen decided to operate on him in a hastily set up tent with minimal facilities, hoping to stabilize the patient before sending him to the nearest hospital, an hour away. The man died during the surgery.

He had never seen or heard of such a disease in his long service, so he decided to transport the body to his medical college for an autopsy. He got the body loaded up in his small van and drove to the hospital with his two students who had assisted him in the surgery.

It was a highly contagious disease and by the time they reached the hospital; they were all showing rashes on their arms with signs of bleeding. Dr. Mateen ordered isolation for himself and his two students, with no visitors allowed. Osman Shah, a final year medical student at Khyber, assisted the specialists examining his father. He called Humayun, who took the next flight to Peshawar with Saleem, Firoza and Seema.

Dr. Mateen and his two students died in the next two days. The medical experts were baffled by this disease and took the precaution of not letting the families anywhere near them before or at the burial.

Gayti Ara wanted to stay in Peshawar with Osman, who had a year left at Khyber, so Firoza stayed on with her after Humayun left.

After graduation, Osman followed his brother Ahmed to the US for further studies. At Humayun's insistence, and with no one left in Peshawar, Gayti Ara moved to Karachi with Omer, her fifth grader. Humayun had already gotten the upper story of The *Chowk* reconfigured to give her an independent living space.

Her older sons tried to convince her to move to the US to live with them, but she couldn't think of leaving her father by himself. They would visit her every winter, each time trying to convince her to move to the US, and each time getting the same answer. Her father was old and she believed that he needed her more than they did.

Omar Shah, Gayti Ara's youngest son was a quiet pre-teen. After the loss of his father at a very young age, all he cared about was his mother and being the best in his class. He kept to himself and would not engage much with his grandfather or others.

***

On the day after his seventy-fifth birthday, Humayun started working on a succession plan for CWK. He had some very good managers, but none he saw having the capabilities to run the large organization he had created. After a year's training, Humayun had given Seema a free hand to run projects and make decisions. She handled the responsibilities well above his expectations and, in his view, she was well on the way to a successful career.

His vision of transforming the business to an information and media business had not been realized, which he attributed to his declining health and loss of motivation, but didn't have any regrets over it, or anything else in his life.

Well, almost anything. His only regret was his failure to connect with Saleem. Even after Richard had called him out about it, things didn't improve.

Humayun, who always had a history of waking up in the middle of the night with bad dreams, had been having a nightmare where saw his own burial, with Nasreen, Shershah, Roshan Ara, and Gayti Ara looking on with sorrow. Saleem, Firoza, and Seema were not there. He would ask everyone where Saleem was, where Seema was, until he would wake up in a cold sweat. He was used to nightmares, so he paid no attention to it.

Common logic, science, and history prognoses sons to be at the father's burial, like they are supposed to.

Humayun learned the hard way that the projections of logic, history, and science don't always come to pass. One morning, he got a frantic call from Firoza, who was vacationing with Saleem and Seema in Singapore. Saleem had died of a massive heart attack in their hotel.

Humayun flew to Singapore and brought Saleem back home in a container. Firoza did not attend the burial. She believed women should not go to cemeteries[161] and Seema stayed with her. Everyone else was there. He thought he also saw Nasreen, Shershah, and even Hanafi Sarkar among the hundreds grieving with him. That was when it hit him. His nightmares weren't about his funeral. They were premonitions of Saleem's death.

My son was supposed to bury me, not the other way round.

This was the shock of his life. It would never be the same.

After Saleem's death, Humayun noticed a coldness in Seema's attitude towards him. She was still respectful, but something had changed. Firoza wanted nothing to do with him. She stayed at her home all the time. No more Sundays at The *Chowk*. It brought back painful memories of Saleem tortured by his inability to make his father warm up to him, to show real affection.

Humayun's regrets would spike at the worst times, and there was nothing he could do to change things in the past. He would wince at every thought of a missed opportunity that he let pass by when Saleem was still alive, to show him affection.

The passing of Saleem added to the agony of seeing Gayti Ara, his once happy, carefree daughter, grieve for years after the loss of her husband.

Gayti Ara's early widowing, Saleem's unexpected death, and my own health issues must be a punishment of sorts for me.

It must be Karma getting back at me for letting Saleem suffer a lifetime of an unrequited desire for acceptance.

His nightmares stopped after losing Saleem, but no amount of repentance would alleviate his suffering.

---

161 A school of thought in Islam proscribes women from going to cemeteries.

A NEW MORNING IN AMERICA
1983

America was throwing a big party for the opening of its newly rebuilt embassy in Islamabad, on the 4th of July, the 207th anniversary of the birth of the nation.

The Embassy building and grounds were gaily decorated with US Flags and red, white, and blue buntings saluting the founding fathers and their vision. A vision that had not only endured for over 200 years, but had gotten stronger by bringing the message of democracy, freedom, and human rights to people, some of whom were unfamiliar with these concepts.

The new American Embassy had been built like a fortress to withstand attacks of the kind that had destroyed the old building in November 1979 when an angry mob of thousands had attacked the embassy. They blamed America for being behind the seizure of the *Kaaba*[162] by a Yemeni fanatic and his followers.

It had been a tough decade since President Nixon had cut his losses in Vietnam and withdraw from an unwinnable war. A forgettable decade of civil unrest, rising unemployment, sky-high interest rates, and 52 of its top diplomats held hostage for a year. America was looking for someone to lead it out of the national doldrums and help put memories of that terrible period behind it.

---

[162] The holiest site in Islam. Haj pilgrimage starts and ends here.

An actor-turned cowboy-turned politician emerged, promising 'We can make America great again,'[163] and the race was on for the 1980 presidential elections. Ronald Reagan mesmerized the nation with promises of growth and prosperity. The nation elected him with the biggest margin in history, and he rolled up his sleeves to work on restoring America's standing in the world.

He brought back the hostages from Iran, slashed interest rates to kick-start the economy, and announced the so-called Star Wars missile defense system and even test fired some missiles to show that American technology still rules the roost. Outside political observers opined these actions to be a sign that America was back and ready to tango with the USSR in Afghanistan and elsewhere.

The Russians had been in Afghanistan for four years and were settling in, even allowing some soldiers to bring their families to Kabul. Many regional freedom fighter groups had popped up in Afghanistan since the Russian occupation. These fiercely independent ethnic or regional groups, with no operational coordination amongst them, were looked at by the Soviets as an inconvenience, but nothing that their newly arrived MI-24 gunship helicopters couldn't swat away like flies buzzing over a plate of *Plov.*[164]

President Zia of Pakistan and his ISI[165] had been waging a low-level proxy war for the CIA by providing small arms and training to a couple of these groups. Congressman Charlie Wilson of Texas had gotten Zia around $10 million from black appropriations fund[166] from the US congress to help these groups.

This 4th of July, Wilson was in Islamabad carrying a special message from President Reagan and a much bigger purse with promises of overt funding and support for the *Mujahidin*. Gen.

---

163 Presidential Candidate Reagan, Texas election speech on 19 July 1980.

164 A very popular dish of central Asian origins served at large gatherings.

165 Inter-services Intelligence, Pakistani Military Intelligences organization.

166 The Black Appropriations fund is a highly classified congressional fund allocated for secret projects or covert operations.

Herbert M. Wassom, special assistant to the US Army's Chief of Staff was accompanying Congressman Wilson to sketch out a greater role in training and equipping the fighters by the US Military.

A large Marine band was playing "America the Beautiful" on the lawns. Islamabad had never seen such fanfare at the American Embassy. Afghan *Mujahidin* leaders were special guests of the congressman. Zia's cabinet members, Military Generals, and other powerful men in Islamabad were all present.

Food and drinks of all varieties were being prepared and served from numerous stations, by smartly dressed bearers shuttling from one table to the other, keeping the guests well supplied.

Humayun was also present as an invited guest. He had brought Seema along to meet his contacts in the diplomatic and military circles. She had been helping Humayun with his business, but it was not something that excited her. Seema would go through the day taking calls from customers, filling orders, discussing the day's results with Humayun, and then repeat. She was antsy, wanting something where she could do more to help people - the exploited and the downtrodden.

She never wanted to be a traditional journalist running after people in power or men of wealth. She had strong convictions about current affairs and didn't agree with most of the narratives being offered. As she walked around with Humayun meeting people, they all seem to be the same to her.

These old graying men are here for free American whisky. They don't see that the world has changed. Still clinging to their outdated ideas of self-preservation, they're trying their best to maintain the status quo long enough to retire to their vast mansions by Margalla Hills.[167]

They try to show they are knowledgeable by dropping buzz words on the latest topic—Afghanistan. They loudly express their tired old ideas under the guise of experience and vision. These has-beens think America is here to

[167] Area of Islamabad where the rich and powerful live.

listen to them about this war, and how important they are for the Mujahidin to succeed. What they don't see is that America has thrown this party to let these bozos know it is now going to take control of the operation.

Drink my whisky but do what I say, otherwise get out of the way or be run over.

She turned to Humayun and asked, "Dada, why do you think the Americans have organized this big party?"

As usual, Humayun answered her question with one of his own, "You must have some idea on this, so why don't you tell me what you think and then we'll see if my thinking is up to date with that of the new hot-shot generation's."

"I think it is to let everyone here know that they will call the shots from now on in Afghanistan."

"Very astute, Seema. I agree, I think they are appraising the people, Pakistani and Afghans, who to bet on and who to jettison once they are running the show."

Thanks Goodness, Dada is still in the know and can see through all this razzmatazz, unlike all these walking caricatures from a time gone by.

"*Salaam* Bhaiya, I didn't expect you to be here? When did you get in?" It was Retired General Shahid Hamid.

Hearing Shahid's voice, Humayun jumped and embraced him. "*Waleykum As Salaam*. It has been so long since I saw you." Seema couldn't recall the last time Humayun looked so genuinely happy.

Shahid gave Seema a big hug. "Seema, weren't you in Grammar School when I last saw you?"

"*Aadab* Shahid Dada, what a wonderful surprise! Yes, I was. I remember all the stories Dada used to tell me about your adventures in the World War and the independence movement."

"I understand you joined your Dada's business after college. So, what do you do at CWK?"

"I am not a trader. Buying and selling is not my cup of tea, so I push papers for him and help bring the business into the computer age. It's all pretty boring work. Pushing paper is a mindless activity, but it frees the mind to contemplate deeper ideas and principles. We have ideas that will transform our business into something more suited for the 21st century."

"*Masha-Allah*! I am happy to hear that. I am sure you will. He has high hopes for you." Then turning to Humayun he said, "Bhaiya, why don't you and Seema have dinner with us at Shaigan tomorrow? My daughter Shama is here from London, with her children Mishal and Hyder. She will be happy to meet Seema and you."

"Shaigan? What is that, Hamid Dada?" Seema asked.

"It's the name Tahira gave to our first house in Rawalpindi. We still live there. Shaigan means precious or worthy in Persian. We'd love to have you there. I can show you a picture of the Black Train after it crossed over into Pakistan. Bhaiya is not in it. He had rightfully stayed back in India for his family."

"I would love to see it. What was the Black Train?"

"It was a project I did with Bhaiya long time ago. You should ask him about it."

An American Army captain walked up to them and whispered something in Shahid's ears. He shook his head, and the man left.

"I was waiting for Congressman Wilson. He just finished his meeting and is now ready for me. Bhaiya, why don't you two come and say hello to him? I'll introduce you to him. He is an interesting man."

"No, why don't you go ahead. You probably have important business to discuss with him."

"It will only take a minute. Come."

Congressman Wilson was waiting for them in a well-appointed office inside the embassy. He had a half-full glass of whisky on the coffee table in front of him.

He rose from his seat as soon as he saw Shahid entering the room. Smiling ear to ear, he said, "Hello, hello, General Shahid, so good to see you after an entire week."

"Good afternoon, Congressman. Seeing you a second time in a week is quite a treat. Let me introduce you to my brother, Mr. Humayun Babar. As I was telling you, he could be one of the best resources you will find in my country for the work you have undertaken."

"Glad to meet you, Mr. Babar.

"I am honored to have your acquaintance, Congressman Wilson. I have heard so much about you, Sir."

"I hope it's all good. I, too, have heard only good things about you. General Shahid had recommended we speak with you for some help with our interests across the border. We have your contact information and someone from the embassy will be in contact with you soon."

After some more pleasantries, Humayun and Seema left. Congressman Wilson sent one of his staffers with them to give them a tour of the new embassy. Shahid stayed behind with the congressman.

Humayun never heard from the Congressman or anyone else from the embassy again about their 'interests across the border'.

A FAMILIAR FACE
1983

The tour of the new embassy lifted Seema's spirits. There were framed testimonials of a great Pakistan-American friendship on walls all around. The visitors' room had pictures of Pakistani heads of state posing with American Presidents. At the end of the tour, the staffer brought them back to the lawn where the party was in full swing.

As they made their way through a large patio area full of people, she heard a familiar voice.

"Seema, is that you?"

It was Robert Frisk.

"Robert. What a surprise. I didn't know you were in Islamabad."

Frisk gave Seema a quick, culturally appropriate hug. He then shook hands with Humayun.

"Robert Frisk, Middle East correspondent for *The Times*. I presume you are Mr. Humayun Babar, Seema's esteemed grandfather."

"Pleasure meeting you, Mr. Frisk. I have heard so much about you from your student here."

"The pleasure is all mine, Sir. Somehow, we missed each other every time you were in London. Seema has told me so much about you, but I also happen to know about all the good work you have done over the years."

Seema was now walking purposefully. She had suddenly transformed from a bored teenager being dragged around by a parent to a very engaged adult attending an event organized for a noble cause.

"I hope I am not interrupting anything. Can I join you?"

"Please do. Seema here has gotten a little bored with all the old men I have been introducing her to. All very important people, but probably not interesting to her."

Frisk smiled and looked at Seema, who was looking back at him.

It has been a long time since we spoke. He looks good in his tan safari suit and his gold wire-rimmed eyeglasses.

I missed our long talks about anything and everything, and the depth and breadth of his knowledge of most topics.

Time to catch up to see what Mr. Frisk has been up to in all these years.

He looked around and said, "Looks like Mr. Reagan has America moving back into the limelight after a decade of licking Vietnam wounds. Everything looks shipshape here. You know, there are other events organized all around the world this Fourth of July. I was invited to one in Beirut too, but with the war in Afghanistan, I thought this would be more interesting. I also wanted to see the brand-new building with all its gadgetry."

Humayun nodded. "Yes, this new facade is quite intimidating compared to the old one." And asked, "So what do you think so far about your choice of coming here?"

"I think Islamabad was the right choice over Beirut. Freedom fighters from Afghanistan and most of the Pakistani brass helping them take the war to the Soviets are all here today. Looks like America is all locked and loaded for the USSR in this theater."

Humayun nodded his head in agreement, staying quiet.

"So, Robert, who all have you met here today?" Seema

asked.

"Well, let's see. I met President Zia's favorite freedom fighter- Gulbuddin Hikmatyar, who was boasting that thanks to his great leadership, the Soviets are on the run. He told me that with a little more help, in the form of ground-to-air missiles, he can push them back over the hills of central Asia in a matter of weeks."

"Did you believe him?"

"He has Zia's strong backing and so most of the aid is being channeled to him or through him. He has the Peshawar office in his control. Right now, he can do no wrong. Earlier this afternoon, he met with the Congressman and General Wassom, along with some Pakistani Generals."

"About getting ground-to-air missiles?"

"Yes. The newly arrived Russian helicopter gunships are causing devastation in the *Mujahidin* ranks. To counter this growing threat, ISI has asked the US for General Dynamics' Stinger missiles for them. These are lightweight, shoulder-fired ground-to-air missiles that could be very useful in this type of war. It is the state-of-the-art weapon against low-flying threats in their arsenal. Even the Israelis don't have these yet, so the Americans are hesitant about putting these into the hands of these ragtag *Mujahidin*."

They came up to an empty table with chairs. A smartly dressed bearer pulled the chair back and asked Humayun to have a seat. As they sat down, he asked if they would like some tea and refreshments.

After the bearer had left with their order, Frisk turned to Humayun. "Mr. Babar, can I ask you a question about the Afghan situation? It can be off the record without your name, if you wish."

"I am sure you'll get information of more substance from these giants walking the grounds here today."

Seema didn't like Humayun's answer. She said, "Dada, please. Robert has been my friend for a decade. He is an honorable journalist who never misquotes people for getting his stories published. You can trust him."

Then, turning to Frisk, she told him to ask his question. He still waited until Humayun nodded his assent.

"Thank you, Sir. Off the record. Given your record of being on the side of the oppressed everywhere, are you present in Afghanistan?"

"Every successful effort, regardless of its size, gets overblown, which was the case of my help to people struggling. I only got involved where they couldn't get help anywhere else." Humayun recited Urdu verses from poet Amir Minai[168] and said, "I am not like Amir Minai who said, 'All the pain and suffering of the world is encapsulated in my psyche.'"

"He never answers a question directly." Seema smiled and interjected before Humayun continued, "To answer your question, no one has asked us for help in Afghanistan. There is a high stake, high-value game being played out. The biggest US and Pakistani players are active. They don't need help from small-time businessmen."

Frisk smiled, "Where do you think they need help, well, other than this Stinger business?"

"We don't deal in such armaments, but they still need a lot of AK47s and light machine guns. We can supply those on short notice, but like I said, they haven't asked us. ISI is sending them its inventory of light arms, hoping to get upgraded weapons as replacement from America."

Humayun got up and said, "I need to go see what they have done with the bathrooms."

Frisk smiled and nodded as he left.

"Your grandpa doesn't let much out. I suppose, to be successful in his line of business, silence is an essential tool."

"He's not usually like this. It must be the environment here at the embassy that is keeping him quiet. You will like him outside of here."

"No, no. I like him already. Nothing to dislike about a man

---

168 Amir Minai - A notable Urdu poet of the 19th century.

who has helped so many, so much."

They talked about the elapsed years since LSE.

Frisk brought her up to date on his postings since Portugal. He shared eyewitness accounts of the days of the Sabira and Shatila camp massacres of hundreds of unarmed Palestinian women, children and men. She had heard about it, but hearing an eyewitness account was very different. Her ideas about the struggle between right and wrong, the oppressor and the oppressed, came surging back to her after hearing of the atrocities leveled on innocent Palestinian women and children at the two camps.

Seema lowered her voice to a whisper and asked him, "Robert, what about Yasir Arafat and his PLO? Have they lost their will to fight? Why aren't they fighting back and making life miserable for the citizens of their enemies too? Muslims should declare open war on the Zionists. I will give away all my money if it can help get freedom for the Palestinians."

He looked at her with a challenging smile and said, "…and what will your family have to say about that?"

Seema shot back, "You watch me."

THE TALL THIN SOLITARY MAN
1983

Robert Frisk was the first to recognize the ridiculousness and hazard of discussions. They were sitting in the embassy's compound, enjoying American hospitality, and talking openly of declaring war upon its closest political and military ally. He was a successful journalist and if anyone heard this conversation, he would find himself on a lot of *persona non grata* lists, the death knell for any journalist. It was time to move to a safer topic.

He pointed to a tall, thin, solitary young man with a wispy beard standing by a small table, nursing a glass of ice-cold water to hide his obvious uneasiness. "I would like to introduce you to someone really interesting. Be careful. I just met him earlier today. He is a very rich Arab turned Jihadi."

Switching to Arabic, he asked, "So, how is your Arabic?"

"Fluent." she replied in perfect Arabic.

They got up and walked towards the man. He was dressed in a somewhat-wrinkled white shirt - part of it untucked, and black pants that were a couple inches above his plain black shoes. This man in his mid-twenties could easily have been mistaken for a waiter or an usher waiting on the side to take orders.

"*As Salaam O Alaikum* Sheikh Osama, Robert Frisk again. I'd like to introduce my colleague from LSE, Ms. Seema Babar. She is trained in journalism, and is currently a managing director of

CWK Industries, the largest arms dealer in this part of the world."

"*Bismillah ir Rahman ar Rahim.*[169] Greetings to you, Mr. Frisk."

He looked at Seema with interest, expecting her to say something first. She gave him just a half-nod.

"Sheikh Osama is a son of a very successful Saudi businessman. He has been providing money and recruiting fighters for the Afghans. He is here at the invitation of the American government to discuss ways to improve the cooperation among the different groups fighting the Soviets."

"Brother Frisk, I don't need any invitations from anyone to get involved in the path of Allah. He is my one and only enabler. I do what He instructs me to. Right now, I see a battle between good and evil, a *Jihad*, and I intend to be part of it until this enemy of our Muslim brothers is defeated. I will do whatever it takes to win this battle, or lay down my life as a martyr of Islam."

Seema was struck by his solemnness. "How long have you been involved, directly or indirectly, in Afghanistan?"

"*Waleykum As Salaam* to you too, sister. May Allah show you and your family the righteous path. I recognized your father earlier sitting with you and Brother Frisk. Mr. Babar is a good Muslim, a businessman who has helped many Muslim brothers in their struggle against colonialism, and, recently, against tyranny."

"Thank you. He is my grandfather. So when did you get involved in Afghanistan?"

He kept looking down at his palms as if he were reading invisible notes on them.

"I heard the cries of help coming out of Afghanistan on the day the Soviet Union acted on their 200-year-old dream of reaching the warm waters of the Arabian Sea. My Afghan brothers, who were in their way, got overrun and faced the brunt of their brutal suppression, so I decided that day that I will do whatever it

---

[169] In the name of God, the Most Gracious, the Most Merciful. Common phrase recited by Muslims before starting a task.

takes to help them throw the invaders out. I came to Peshawar to assess the situation and saw the need for better armaments and more fighters. The first person I contacted was your grandfather, because I knew he was a friend of the oppressed Muslims. May Allah keep him. He refused to deal with us, saying he only collaborates with legitimate government representatives."

He let her note his complaint, then continued, "I said *Mae-Khalef*[170] and found other sources. We also launched a plea to Muslims all around the world, for volunteers to come help fight this *Jihad. Alhamdolillah,*[171] young men swarmed in not only from Muslim lands but also from America, Germany, France, Britain and Yugoslavia to help us fight the Soviets."

She was unimpressed but said, "Impressive, Sheikh Osama. May I ask you another question?"

Osama didn't reply, so she asked, "Kashmiri women and children have been calling out for help long before the Russians walked into Afghanistan. No disrespect to you, but why are you not affected by their cries for help?"

He raised his eyes for the first time to take a good look at this woman challenging him. There was no anger in his eyes. His expression remained constant as he looked away towards a sky where some clouds had started to gather. She thought she saw a hint of pain in his eyes when he replied, "Sister, an excellent question. You should ask your grandfather why his friends in the Pakistan Military are so afraid to do something about Kashmir. I have raised Kashmir with them, offering help in the form of money, men, and materiel. I have yet to hear their response."

Frisk asked, "Are there any Kashmiris fighting in Afghanistan?"

"Yes, *Alhamdolillah,* we have over 300 Kashmiri young men fighting the Soviet infidel."

Seema asked, "What will happen to all the *Mujahidin* after

---

170 No problem.

171 By the Grace of Allah.

you are successful in pushing out the Russians?"

Frisk was watching Seema and knew immediately where she was going with the question. Bin Laden either didn't pick up her point or ignored it and said, "Allah will find a path for each and every one of them, if not in this world, then in the next life."

Seema was getting irritated at not hearing answers to her questions, so she told him what she was thinking. "As you achieve victory in Afghanistan, you will need to keep your *Mujahidin* busy lest they turn in a direction that you may not approve of. Why not point them toward Kashmir, not far away, to answer the calls of the Kashmiri women and children? Once the battle-hardened victorious *Mujahidin* start pouring into Kashmir, the Pakistan military will not have a choice but to join them."

Frisk seemed impressed with Seema's thinking. Regardless of whether Osama bin Laden agreed with her plan, she had raised an important point of what to do with thousands of battle-hardened, fully equipped private warriors at the end of a war.

Bin Laden didn't yield to Seema's prodding and brushed it off. "*Insha-Allah*, He will deliver our Kashmiri brothers from their misery soon."

She wouldn't let it go. "In my Western attire, it may not be obvious to you that deep down in my heart, I am a Muslim who feels the pain of my suffering brethren. I would like to help free the Afghani and the Kashmiri people."

His eyes moved from searching his palms to his watch, an old golden Rolex worn with its face on the inside of the wrist. "Only gift from my dear departed father; it reminds me every day that there is a time for everything. *Insha-Allah*, your time will come."

Then, without letting her reply, he added, "It will be *Maghrib* soon. I should find a place to say my prayers." He walked away slowly towards the main building, a solitary figure trying to find his way to a *Jai-Namaz*, his door to redemption.

With him out of their earshot, Frisk said, "He may seem to

be uneasy here, but he is a force to be reckoned with, out on the front lines. He is a real fighter."

"Is this the first time you've met him?"

"I heard his name a few months back in Beirut. He has been donating a lot of his money and raising a lot more from within Saudi Arabia. He has a small army of foreign fighters who are paid from his funds, but all the *Mujahidin* respect him for his help and bravery in battlefields, and yes, this is the first I've met him in person."

"Looks like he doesn't trust anyone here, so why is he here, then?"

"They need some real warriors like him to take the battle to the Soviets. Hikmatyar is a lot of talk, very little action. They must have heard of him and his band of warriors, so now they are trying to recruit him into their circle of fighters. I think he is here to see if they can be of any help to him. I got the definite impression that he doesn't trust the Americans, and considers them as big, if not a bigger enemy of the Muslims."

"You seem to have done your homework on Afghanistan before dropping by here."

"There is another warrior they would like in their camp. His name is Ahmad Shah Massoud, a Tajik fighter from northern Afghanistan, a brilliant commander of men and, from what I gather, an excellent administrator. If the Afghans are ever successful in throwing out the Russians, he could be a very capable peacetime leader. He is in Islamabad too, but being a careful fellow, he doesn't want to be seen rubbing shoulders with the representatives of '*the Great Satan*'[172] and jeopardizing his relations with Iran, his first financier."

She added, "Smart man!"

He changed the subject again. "I have been the one doing all the talking, telling you about my life since LSE. What about you? Are you happy? Did you ever get married?"

---

[172] A term of rancor for America, coined by Ayatollah Khomeini.

"I am okay. Mummy invited Pervez Jaleesi, the son of one of their close friends, to my graduation. After that, she tried constantly to convince me that he was an excellent match for me. She believes that girls' lives are not complete until they are married and have children. I think women needing to have a man to be complete is complete hogwash. He is a banker, and would be invited to our house every so often, even though I had not shown any interest in him. Over time, I found him to be a decent man, well-read and quite knowledgeable about events, people, and ideas. We became pretty good friends. One thing that always bothered me about him was that, no matter what, he would agree with me on everything."

"Hmm, so a very compliant fellow."

"Yes. Abbu never pushed me towards him. He was a man of few words who had a torturous relationship with Dada, something about fathers and sons I don't understand. One day, while Mummy was visiting her sister in Lahore, Abbu was talking about missing mummy when she was away and then he started talking about life and the role of life partners. Anyway, he told me how important it was for him to feel that I have a life partner to lean on after he was gone. I didn't pay it much attention thinking it to be a father worries about his unmarried daughter. I loved my father very much, everyone does, but I now feel that being around Dada all the time, I never really got to know him. He died while we were vacationing in Singapore."

"Seema, I am so sorry. I didn't know."

"Thank you. It was the toughest time of my life. His death was such a shock and the only thing I remembered was the long talk he had with me. I resolved to make his wish come true. Pervez was at my father's funeral. By this time, he had gotten engaged to some girl from his class. I would have gone to the funeral, but mummy didn't go, since she believes women shouldn't go to cemeteries, so I stayed with her at home. Pervez came to visit us after the funeral to express his condolences. Seeing him, I lost all self-control and cried on his shoulder for what seems like hours. The more I cried, the more I felt the need for a life partner, Abbu's last wish. He called me the next day and asked me if I meant what I said. Seems like I may have expressed my unconditional love for him while crying. I didn't say no. He broke his engagement, and we got married a few months later."

"Oh, so you married him."

"The marriage lasted less than two years and that was because he tried so hard. He really loved me. I found marriage to be too constrictive. He was heartbroken and moved to Dubai. I moved to London to help Dada run his business from there. We never divorced, still good friends. Abbu is not happy with me wherever he is."

She looked at him with sadness.

Frisk didn't know what to say, except, "I am sorry to hear that. I suppose you don't find out these things until you are married. Maybe these are the fears that prevent me from marrying."

SWAN SONG
1992

After losing Saleem, and with Seema living in England, Firoza lived alone in her home. Over the years, she lost her will to keep a grudge against Humayun, who always treated her like his own daughter. At Gayti Ara's insistence, she finally decided to sell her house and move into the vacant apartment that Humayun had built for her upstairs at The *Chowk* after Saleem passed.

Nadira had been living with her, keeping her company and taking care of most of the household affairs for her, while also working at a hospital for the elderly. She didn't relish the idea of moving to The *Chowk*. Firoza was sad to see her go but helped her buy a small flat across town near her work.

By the summer of '92, Firoza and Gayti Ara were both living at The *Chowk*. Humayun was in London, his favorite destination in the world. He enjoyed visiting the many museums full of what he called "stolen goods and chattel from all around the world," but he admired the British for preserving those artifacts for posterity.

He had been planning a trip to London for late summer, but his old friend Ben Bella had sent him a letter telling him he would be in London for a few days and wanted to meet him, if possible. Not wanting to miss seeing Ben Bella, Humayun changed his plans.

Ben Bella had been released from his house arrest after Boumédiène passed away. Having retired from politics, he spent the 80s living in exile in Geneva, but like a lion in his old age, he kept one eye open even when sleeping, lest a good prospect comes strolling by. Then one day, an opportunity came knocking.

For years, a military dictatorship had ruled Algeria with an iron fist. Algerians were getting restless and wanted a return to democracy last seen three decades earlier when Ben Bella was president. The people also wanted him back. Ben Bella heeded their calls and returned to Algeria. His wily leadership and the use of street power helped force the Military to call general elections. His party won big. He was in London for meetings with his old contacts and friends, some of them exiles in Britain and Europe, to help form his new government.

Seema didn't know about this visit until he called her before heading to the airport. He told her that being in his methuselah years; he was cutting down on all his travel. This was going to be his swan song trip to London to meet old friends, the ones still alive, while he could still travel.

Gayti Ara was with him. She would not let her 85-year-old father travel alone since complications from a bypass surgery had sidelined him for an extended period. During those months, Seema ran CWK from its London office.

Over the years, she hired more managers to run the day-to-day business as she focused more of her attentions on her own passion, charity projects. She would tell Humayun about the charities she was helping and how they were bringing change. Happy that she was balancing work with her personal interests, he felt it was not something she would be able to continue much longer. Running CWK required a full-time CEO. Rather than letting the business fail, he was contemplating selling it, but needed Seema's assent before doing anything.

Humayun's old friend, Safdar Khattak, had become a very wealthy man exporting the world's finest Basmati rice after his retirement. He had expressed an interest in buying CWK a few months earlier.

Selling the business would free up significant capital. Humayun had resolved to divide the proceeds of the sale equally between Saleem's and Gayti Ara's families after putting aside a quarter of everything for welfare and charitable causes. Technically, this was going against Islamic Sharia law, which required a son's share to be twice that of a daughter's, but he wanted to reward Seema for having helped him run CWK for almost two decades. She would get an extra share along with her own share of his estate. The inheritance would be enough for her to pursue her interests and still provide for a very comfortable life for everyone in his lineage.

In the heydays of CWK, almost all of its transactions were done in American dollars or British pound sterling. The State Bank of Pakistan rules for foreign exchange controls were a hindrance in making quick payments. To expedite these transactions, CWK had to make under the table payments through expediters.

Tired of the changing demands of the expediters, Humayun set up accounts in Singapore, and the Cayman Islands, to make it easier to process foreign exchange payments. Recently, he had noticed some large payments going out from CWK's Cayman Islands accounts. Seema had not discussed these payments with him, and he was curious to see where Seema was investing all this money. This was the other purpose of his visit.

Humayun asked Seema about the general state of affairs of CWK, but she only wanted to talk about her charities.

"Have you invested in these charities?"

"A little here and there. I mostly work to get them money from large donors."

"I noticed some of the large outflows from the Cayman and Singapore accounts. I am curious to know what you have been investing in."

Seema looked at him and flashed an unkind smile. "Dada,

is that why you are here? Checking up on my expenditures?"

"No, I completely trust you to do the right thing, and it has nothing to do with checking up on you."

"As the president of this company, do I not have the authority to decide where I invest?"

"Yes, of course. But I was wondering why you used the money from the offshore accounts instead of the ones right here in London."

She was getting irritated. "So, now I have to explain the rationale for all my decisions."

"Seema, you know that is not the case. All I am asking is why you are using the money from the offshore accounts when you have enough money available here in London. Are you trying to hide the payments from the government?"

"Look, if you want me to run this business, let me run it my way."

"Okay, I won't ask, but be careful. The laws have gotten very strict on offshore account activities. Right now, as you know, those accounts are not included in our registration filings here in London, but legal under British laws-"

"Anything else you want to know about?" She cut him off.

"No, but I wanted to let you know the reason for my visit to London. I am seeing Ahmed tomorrow morning. Are you are free to come along?"

"Mr. Ben Bella?"

"Yes, I am here to meet him."

"I would make time to me him. He is such a remarkable man."

Thinking of something, she got up and hugged Humayun. "Sorry Dada, I didn't mean to be that way. I have no excuse. I hope you can forgive my rudeness." But she still didn't reveal where the overseas account money was being invested.

***

Ben Bella was thrilled to see them. He had aged and gained

some weight, but was still mentally acute and very alert, with no visible signs of his tough life. He showed Seema a Pakistani passport Humayun had gotten for him to travel freely under an assumed identity during the Algerian war.

After discussions of the Algerian elections results, and stories of the old times had run out, the topic turned to current affairs. Ben Bella told them about the Bosnian War of Independence and the suffering of the Bosnian people.

"There are so many similarities in this struggle to the Algerian Independence movement, but one characteristic that makes it very different is the treatment of the civilian women and children in this war. Don't get me wrong, the French sometimes acted like vicious animals towards us, but the Serbs are worse in their treatment of the Bosniaks. They want to erase the Bosnian people from the Balkans. They kill the men and children, and rape the women and girls to put a terror in their hearts. Bosnia needs help to fight back and break the Serbian military stronghold on them."

Seema said, "You are helping the Bosnians?"

"Yes, I have been helping the Bosnians get ready for an all-out war against Serbia. Dr. Alija Izetbegović,[173] the President, is an old friend of mine, a true humanist and one of the most decent heads of state I have met. He is facing some real hurdles from the West in acquiring arms to protect his people and Bosnian territory against the vile Serbs. The United Nations hasn't helped; they have put on a ban on supplying arms to Bosnia. The Saudis have provided money to buy arms. They asked Pakistan to help bring arms to Bosnia and ISI defied the UN ban by delivering the much needed arms and anti-tank missiles. *Alhamdolillah*, the missiles are proving very effective against the Serb heavy armor."

Humayun spoke for the first time. "I know of the ISI's involvement in the supply of arms to Bosnia. I thought ISI was giving its weapons to the Bosnians, but it sounds like they are

---

173 Head of the Presidency of Bosnia and Herzegovina 1990-2000

getting paid by the Saudis for the arms."

Ben Bella smiled and looked at Seema and said, "Saudis and CWK. Thank you. But don't worry, according to your instructions, CWK's name will not show up anywhere. Izetbegović is an honorable man. He also asked me to meet you in person to deliver his thanks. I was hoping you would bring along Seema, as you did."

Humayun understood where the offshore payments had ended up. He looked at Seema, who had a knowing smile on her face.

Turning to Ben Bella, she asked, "Uncle Ahmed, is there a way for me to visit Sarajevo?"

"It is a very dangerous place, my dear. The Serbs have surrounded the city and they shell it day and night, targeting civilians and military alike. I can call Izetbegović to arrange a visit for you, but brother Humayun needs to tell me before I send his granddaughter into hell on earth. I hope my two daughters, Nouria and Mehdia, can be as brave and confident as you. Are you sure you want to do that?"

Humayun didn't think it was a good idea, but before he could say anything, Seema responded, "Yes, I would like to. Dada and I will speak about this, and I may inconvenience you again if he agrees to let me go there."

"Ahmed, have you been there?" Humayun asked.

"Yes, I was there a month ago to see Izetbegović. We walked the last few miles to get to Sarajevo, mostly through heavily wooded areas with almost no defined paths. He had sent a guide and two soldiers to escort me to town. I could hear the shelling and small gun fire off and on, not too far from us."

"Would Izetbegović provide the same for Seema?"

"I will call him and tell him that besides being a financier of his weapons, she is also my daughter. I am sure he will do everything to keep her out of harm's way."

"Uncle Ahmed, I will be so grateful if you can arrange this

for me. I plan on doing an article on the plight of the people in Sarajevo based on my trip."

"I will call him tonight and let you know tomorrow."

***

As they got into a taxi to return to the flat, Humayun asked, "Did you think I wouldn't agree to help the Bosnians?"

She was in deep thought, looking at all the missed calls on her Motorola phone that she always carried with her.

I wish it would let me send messages, besides just making calls. Now that would be great. I will never have to call anyone.

She would have to wait a few more years before her wish became a reality.

"I understand you a lot more than you give me credit for, Dada. I was sure you would be supportive and proud of me, otherwise I would have never given away your money to them. It was just that I didn't want to bother you with it."

"It is not my money. It belongs to all of us. The way I see it, you will be the single biggest shareholder."

"Actually, that was another reason for my trip to London. I wanted to see what you feel about selling the arms business portion of CWK. You remember my friend Safdar Khattak, the one who introduced us to Che? He wants to buy our arms business, and if you agree, it can be done quickly upon my return next month. It will be a clean break from the arms business. The sale will free us to do what we have been working on. We can then look at acquiring a media company, a newspaper, or even an advertising agency with the cash."

"I am all for it. Let's close out the transaction as soon as we can. Another war is looming in Europe and you can get a very good price for CWK. But let's not sell our brand, CWK."

He nodded. "I wasn't going to."

"Maybe then Abbu will have some peace up there." She said, glancing up at the sky.

"And your mother will too, down here." He added.

A FEW DAYS IN HELL
1992

"Robert, how would you like to go to Sarajevo with me?" He was asleep when Seema called. It was early morning. She had received word that President Izetbegović had arranged a visit to Sarajevo for her and a companion, if she so chose. She had been planning to go there by herself, but the message made her think it sensible to bring someone along.

She called the first person she thought of.

"What time is it?"

"Time to get up. I have been invited by President Izetbegović to visit Sarajevo. I will be there for four or five days. You will find enough stories there to fill your column at *The Independent* for weeks."

"Okay, let me think about it. How about security? How about guides to get into the city? Sarajevo is surrounded by Serb guns pounding it for hours, daily. I heard they are planning an all-out assault to take the city. It could be dangerous."

"Are you coming, or should I find someone else?"

"Can I bring my cameraman? I just started work on a documentary for Channel 4 and the American Discovery channel. It is about Muslims and the West. This developing war in Bosnia could provide a lot of material for it, but I will need my cameraman."

"You can't handle a camera? I can bring only one person, and I don't want to go back and ask for another favor from Prime Minister Ben Bella."

"You got Ben Bella to help you get an invitation from Izetbegović?"

"Are you coming or not?"

"I can't not say yes to a visit anywhere with you."

"You're welcome, Mr. Double Negative." She was in a cheerful mood from the news from President Izetbegović.

"Thank you. Let me get my gear ready. You need anything from me?"

"No, just your inquisitive self will suffice. Don't worry, I will be there to protect you if the Serbs attack."

"Hilarious, Seema. Humor becomes you. Try to call on it more often."

"Humor has its place, but a majority of humanity lives under some form of terror. They don't recognize drollery."

"Okay, okay. Now let me sleep. It is my first full day off in a fortnight."

Having lived in England for over a decade, she had a British passport. Frisk was able to convince his editor at *The Independent* that Seema would be invaluable in getting the local Muslim women from Sarajevo to talk. They may be hesitant about speaking freely with a man. No western journalists had made it into Sarajevo since the start of the war. The editor, excited at the thought of exclusive stories from a war zone, was more than happy to not only let Frisk go but also, at his suggestion, temporarily place Seema on his payroll as a journalist. The journalist credentials made her eligible for all protections afforded to them in war zones per International Conventions.

Frisk had done all this without informing her. He couldn't do anything about the falling bombs, but with her journalist credentials, the chances of her being harmed or mistreated by the Serbs would be reduced.

Seema was surprised when Frisk took her to his editor to receive the papers. She was thankful, but ambivalent about this.

I want to experience war in the raw in my first foray into a combat zone, how a warrior feels on a battlefield. Like the outnumbered Afghan fighters in pitched battles with the Soviets.

Humayun was relieved to hear that she would not be going alone. She asked him to not tell Firoza.

***

They found passage on a small cargo ship running goods from Ancona, Italy to Split, Croatia. Two British journalists traveling to Croatia to cover the Bosnian war and its effect on Croatian population. They arrived in Split after an uneventful, 12-hour journey across the Adriatic Sea. After clearing immigration, they took a cab to an address in town provided in their instructions. There, they found the guide who would take them to Sarajevo. From Split, they traveled in a truck to a small village on the Croatian/Bosnian border, where they checked into a small boarding house. Just after midnight, there was a knock on the door. A new guide was there to take them on the next part of their journey. They walked a few miles through a dense jungle to cross into Bosnia. A small truck, loaded with small arms, was waiting for them. Two gruff-looking men with automatic weapons gave up their seats next to the driver to them.

They reached the outskirts of Sarajevo very early in the morning. From there, the guide led them on foot, accompanied by the two men, through some dense jungles until they arrived at what looked like an entry to a cave on a mountainside. They could see Sarajevo not too far away. Seema heard heavy cannon fire for the first time in her life, and it mesmerized her.

The guide showed them in, and after walking for a few minutes, they arrived in a cavernous open area inside the cave. There were doors leading to different rooms from the open area. They were led to an empty sitting room on one side. It could have been a family room in a house, with some chairs and a table. The place had electric lights supplied by generators. There were bookcases along the walls full of books and folders. A map was spread out on a large campaign table.

The guide said, "President Izetbegović sends you his greetings and will send someone to meet you later. So, we wait here. Please rest here until the afternoon when the guns go quiet. I will bring some refreshments for you."

Frisk was taking meticulous notes, talking to people on board and taking some pictures after they boarded the ship at Ancona. He had tried to talk with the two armed men from the arms truck, but they just grunted. The guide and the driver were more cooperative. They told him about the war, how everything changed after the death of Marshal Tito in 1980, and that everything since then had pointed to the coming of this war. The resentment that the Orthodox Christian Serbs carried for the Muslim Ottomans, from the time when the Ottoman ruled the Balkans, had not diminished. In fact, one of their main nationalist anthems was a song called "Remove Kebab." It was played on very powerful loudspeakers from hilltops surrounding Sarajevo by the Serbs before the shelling started.

The guns went quiet at noon.

Six heavily armed soldiers came into the room. All their credentials were checked and re-checked. A female soldier did a body search on Seema while the others checked Frisk and his photographic equipment. As soon as she sent an all-clear message on a handy walkie-talkie, another group of people walked in, among them President Izetbegović, whom she recognized from pictures.

"Welcome, I am Alija Izetbegović." He shook hands with them and pointed them to chairs nearby. As they all sat down, he said, "Welcome to Bosnia, Miss Seema Babar. I wish you had visited us in better times in 1984, when we hosted the 14th Winter Olympics here in Sarajevo in 1984. It was a great showcase event for us to show Sarajevo, our beautiful city, to the world. We were recognized as the best host of the Winter Olympics ever. But it is what it is, and I am glad you have made it safely to Sarajevo."

"Dear Mr. President, Sir, I am thankful to you for the opportunity to come see for myself the situation here. I could have never made it this far without the security umbrella provided by your men and women. Mr. Frisk, a colleague from my school days at LSE, now a very busy journalist at *The Independent*, has accompanied me to see and record the events of this war that has engulfed Bosnia."

"Welcome, Mr. Frisk. I am glad to have your acquaintance. We are honored you have taken time from busy schedule to visit us in this difficult time. We would like you to take our message back to the world for everyone to see. I hope we will provide you an unbiased view, difficult as that may be, of the events here and their causes."

"Thank you, Mr. President." Frisk replied, "It is my great pleasure to meet you. I look forward to visiting the sites and speaking directly with people to learn as much as possible about the causes and effects of this war. I hope to provide the world an accurate picture of what I observe."

Izetbegović nodded and turned to Seema. "Ms. Seema, I would like to thank you on behalf of the Bosnian people for the monetary help you have provided us. It has been a godsend for defending our people from the marauding Serb gangsters, who would like nothing better than to kill us all and take our lands for themselves."

Frisk was taken completely by surprise. He had no inkling of the level of Seema's support for the Bosnian cause.

Izetbegović pointed to the female soldier and continued, "Let me introduce Captain Mersida Mesetovic. She is one of our best minds for strategy planning. To make your stay as safe as possible, I have asked her to be your liaison during your stay here. She is responsible for your safety for the duration of your stay. You are welcome to stay in Bosnia for as long as you wish. Captain

Mersida already has a list of locations for you to visit and people for you to meet. If you would like to add to the lists, she will arrange for those as well. Just let her know. She will go through all the plans, the security precautions, your schedules, etc., later. But before that, I would like to invite you to a simple lunch her team has prepared for us, something that more than half of Sarajevo's population does not have ready access to."

Captain Mersida led them all into another large hall with tables set up to accommodate up to eight people each. At the end of the hall, there was a much larger table.

As they were getting ready to sit down, a group of eight Arabs entered the hall from the other end, all carrying AK47 rifles. Captain Mersida quickly approached them and said something in a hushed tone. They placed their weapons on a nearby table and came over to join the President's party. Seema recognized their leader.

It was Osama bin Laden.

Izetbegović walked over and shook hands with Bin Laden and the others.

He introduced the Arabs as friends from Saudi Arabia who were there helping the Bosnian people in their struggle.

Seema stood near her chair, while Frisk went around the table to shake hands with Bin Laden, "*As Salaam O Alaikum*, Sheikh Osama. Robert Frisk, Journalist from *The Independent.* We met at the American Embassy a few years back."

"I remember you very well, Mr. Robert Frisk. I read your articles. I hope you are writing what is in your heart, honestly, and not to get money from rich Arabs."

Frisk smiled wryly, "Sheikh Osama, I write what I believe to be the truth and have suffered from it. Writing the truth these days can land you in a lot of trouble, but there are still some of us left, who seem to be gluttons for punishment. I am here to report on the plight of Bosnian people affected by this war."

Bin Laden glanced at Seema. She could see a sign of

distaste on his face.

I don't like the way he is looking at me.

He thinks I am Robert's bitch or something.

I have to fix that.

But before she could say anything, Izetbegović spoke, "Ms. Seema Babar is the chief executive of CWK, the largest arms dealer in the Muslim world. She is the single largest individual donor to our cause. Her company has helped many Muslims in their struggle against oppression. My great friend Ahmed Ben Bella asked me to arrange a visit for her. He didn't have to. She could have called us directly and we would have been more than happy to arrange all this for her. But the fact that he did, says a lot about CWK's importance to struggling Muslims all over the world."

Bin Laden gave her another glance, accompanied by a short nod, his face a blank slate now.

Thank you, Mr. President. I am glad you were here to correct his preconceived presumptions about Robert's presence here. If it weren't for you, I would have done it myself.

"Thank you, Mr. President, for your kind words. CWK is a business like any other. We happen to be in the arms trade. The one principle that separates us from other such businesses is that we only serve those who we feel are working to improve the lives of their people. I am proud to be a Muslim and very proud of the work my grandfather has done over the years helping our brothers in Islam. I have followed in his footsteps and *Insha-Allah* will not miss a chance to jump in with everything we have, to help in righteous struggles."

She paused and then added, "Bosnia is just the start. After helping our Bosnian brothers remove the Serb instruments of terror, we will move to free Kashmir, Palestine, and all those living in subhuman conditions under tyranny."

***

After lunch, the Arabs left, followed by the President and his men. Captain Mersida and two of her men stayed behind to go over plans for the next two days with Seema and Frisk. When Frisk enquired about the location they were sheltered in, she told them that the cave house was part of a large network of natural caverns deep under the mountains encircling Sarajevo. A 13th century graveyard, full of historical Stećak[174] of all shapes and forms in the caverns, was a very popular tourism site. When the war started, some areas adjoining the graveyard were repurposed by the government to an underground command-and-control center of sorts that also provided shelter and storage facilities. From time to time, it also served as the president's office.

---

174 Medieval tombstones found at hundreds of graveyard sites across Bosnia and rest of the Balkans.

THEY CALL IT RADICALIZATION
1992

Their tour was a whirlwind. Captain Mersida took her on tours of bombed-out schools, homes, hospitals, office buildings, and homes and introduced her to families, many of them refugees from surrounding areas that had fallen into Serb hands. They had lost their fathers, brothers, and everything they held dear. She patiently listened to countless women tell stories of rape, murder, and pillage. There were too many at each stop.

This is a side of humanity I have only read about.

Man is capable of such cruelty.

The Serbs probably blame the Ottomans for starting all this, centuries ago, and carrying the grudge to this day. They seem to have an unquenchable loathing of Islam, its language, and its customs. Bosnians are scapegoats facing the full brunt of the Serbs' displaced aggression.

The indiscriminate shelling would start without notice and they would stay in place as long as it continued. They would run from one shelter to the other during lulls, never sure when it would start again. It was an experience like no other for Seema, her mind remembering every little detail of people she met and places she visited. She felt energized, not knowing if the next shell would be the last one she would hear going off. The constant threat of death was an elixir for her. She wanted more. Danger was turning out to be the best stimulant she had experienced. The high she was experiencing was a sensation she had never felt before.

She loved the look of hope she saw in the eyes of the sobbing women and crying children crowded together in small, cramped rooms in hospitals and shelters. She told them she has put her own life in danger by coming here to help deliver them from the terror that lurks in their hearts wrought upon them by yesterday's friends and neighbors.

By the third day of seeing huddled women and children, looking up at her like she was a messiah, she had become enthralled with a vision of single-handedly freeing them from their pain and sufferings.

Yes, I am here to rid you of your fear and misery, and I will stop at nothing to end your suffering. I will be your Ben Bella. Your Che Guevara, your Mao Zedong. I will be your Messiah. You are my people and I will not lose.

I will be your Sultan Salahuddin Ayubi.[175]

Seema was in a zone and started taking unnecessary risks by walking out on the street even during the shelling.

Seeing her behavior, Captain Mersida ended the tour for the day. "Let's go back. I have been summoned to headquarters. We will start bright and early tomorrow."

They returned to their underground refuge.

After an early dinner, Frisk was working on his daily report in the sitting room. Seema was reading a book that she had picked up from a bookshelf. They could hear bombs going off in the distance.

It was getting late when Bin Laden returned with his men. One of them had a large bandage on his shoulder. Frisk got up and enquired about the injury. He found they had been at an advanced base and came under fire. The bandaged man's shoulder was scraped by a bullet.

Bin Laden came over and sat down across from her.

---

[175] The revered 12th century Muslim Sultan of Egypt and Syria, who defeated the crusaders and liberated Jerusalem.

"*As Salaam O Alaikum* sister."

"*Waleykum As Salaam*, Sheikh Osama. Did you have a successful day visiting the advanced positions of the Bosnian *Mujahidin*?"

"*Alhamdolillah*, we were fortunate to return unharmed, except for my son over there. A bullet grazed his shoulder, but *Insha-Allah*, he will be fine."

"That is your son? I hope he didn't damage any muscles in his arm."

"No, *Alhamdolillah*, one of my warriors is a doctor. He examined Abdallah's wound thoroughly. No damage. Plus, this kind of thing will make him a better fighter."

"He can't be over 16. No doubt a very brave Muslim boy. So how many men will you be bringing here to fight?"

"They have enough brave *Mujahidin* here, but they need more weapon and ammunition urgently. This war differs from the Afghan War, where they needed fighting men. Here they need good armaments. The Serbs are much better equipped."

"You have a good understanding of war."

"*Alhamdolillah*, I have studied wars for many years and fought in many battles. Allah gives us all knowledge."

"So, how are you going to help the Bosnian people?"

"I will raise more money for them. They need a variety of armaments. I have to find sources for them."

"What are they looking for? We can source most types of light arms, RPGs, short range anti-tank missile launchers, etc."

"I will have a brother from Egypt contact you. His name is Ahmed Al Halim. He will send you the list."

"Have him send your requirements to my company. I will have someone contact him."

"Why not you?"

"I only deal with the top people, but you can reach me at this number, but it's not to be given out."

She wrote a phone number on a generic CWK card handed

it to him.

"*Insha-Allah.*"

"I am glad you are helping the Bosnians, but you still have done nothing for our enduring Kashmiri brothers and sisters."

"*Insha-Allah*, their time will come, too. I am one man. Why haven't you helped them?"

"I need someone to take the leadership and I will be there to help. Sheikh, I will, if you do something."

"*Insha-Allah*, let me think about this."

He got up and was going to leave when Seema said, "You haven't given me your phone contact."

"Sister Seema, my phone numbers changes as often as sand dunes on a windy day. But hold on."

He motioned to one of his men, who wrote something on a piece of paper and handed it to her.

"Here is a number for a satellite phone. You keep it to yourself. If you call this number, ask to speak with Abu Abdallah and they will find me."

I should get one of these satellite phones, too. May come in handy someday.

***

On the way back home, Frisk and Seema were watching the port of Split slowly disappearing from sight, as their ship moved west towards Italy. It was early evening. They were both euphoric for their own reasons, but the sense of relief was common to both, for escaping unscathed from the gates of hell.

They were the only passengers on the cargo ship. The crew had gone below deck at the first dinner bell. The deck was empty. They were leaning on the rails, watching the coastline. Frisk turned to her and said, "I have something I have to ask you."

"Go ahead. I hope you got your story, but you have to keep me out of it. I can't afford to be seen or heard. This has become my war."

"I noticed that." He said and then added, "Thanks to you,

I got the greatest story, a real scoop that no one will top, at least not for a few weeks. I know, being the CEO of CWK, you need to stay out of the limelight. So, I have written the story from the perspective of a war correspondent who is working with a woman translator. Would that be okay?"

"People can still put two and two together pretty quickly. Can you do a correspondent only story, please?"

"You have arranged this entire trip for me, so that is the least I can do."

"Okay, so before you ask your question, I have a request for you from Sheikh Osama."

"Yes?"

"Can you keep his name out of it? You can say you met a group of Saudis there without mentioning names."

"Hmmm, that's a difficult one. I will have to think about it."

"He promised to give you a one-on-one interview at a time of your choosing, with access to any of his men who you would like to speak with."

"I thought he likes the publicity. Seems out of character for him, but okay. Now, back to my original question."

He paused until she turned to look at him. He was kneeling down on one knee. Looking up at Seema, he spoke, "Seema, there was something about the way you walked into my office ready for battle for what you felt right, and we became good friends. You stood up to protest against what you believed was wrong with the Shah and it showed me how similar our philosophies of life are."

"The time we met at the embassy, I realized how much I had missed you over the years. I was ready to ask you to marry me and come with me to Beirut. But you told me you were married, so I walked away. The last two years with both of us living in London have been great, even though I didn't see you as much as I wanted. This trip to Bosnia has made me appreciate the fragility of life. I have lost count of the people there who told me they lost their loved ones and now regret not having said something they wanted to tell them. I have never been surer of my love for you and I don't want to let you go this time."

He took a deep breath, "So, Malka Seema, will you marry me?"

THE RELUCTANT TERRORIST
1993

Seema made a second trip into Sarajevo a year after the first. This time she brought along Aslam Khattak, the new CEO of CWK and the son of Safdar Khattak, who now owned CWK. She wanted him to see for himself what things were like on the ground. During his visit, Aslam heard about the difficulties in locating weapons for the fighters mostly because of a ban imposed by the United Nations on the sale of war materiel to Bosnia that prohibited arms manufacturers and traders from selling weapons to them.

Upon hearing about the plight of Muslims in Bosnia, Safdar Khattak agreed to sell them the weapons, but she will have to figure out how to get it through the almost impregnable siege of Sarajevo.

The war raged on as more and more civilians perished in non-stop shelling. The unrelenting punitive siege continued unchecked, making medical supplies scarce and causing pervasive food shortages. People who survived the bombing were dying of malnutrition and simple treatable ailments.

Seema had previously organized some airdrops of medicines, food, and clothing into Sarajevo with the help of several European NGOs during the initial days of the siege. She switched to night airdrops of guns and ammunition, all closely coordinated with the Bosnian ground command, and soon the Bosnian warriors were repelling Serb incursions.

***

It had been a few months since she had told Frisk that she was still married to Pervez and she can't be married to two people at the same time. She knew it was an obvious cop-out; and so did he.

He was heartbroken, but knowing Seema, he knew her mind was made up. He had to let it go.

It was a very difficult decision for her, because she loved Robert like no other man, and in another world, he would have been her ideal life partner. Her reasons were many, including the realization that she was a loner, craving complete isolation from time to time. It was something she had learned after getting married.

Seeing the treatment of Muslims, by their centuries-old Christian friends and neighbors, she had little confidence in cross-religion marriages surviving the stresses of social, ethnic, and religious pressures. She believed that even though they were the best of friends, her *Farangi-Desi* marriage would not work.

***

On February 26, 1993, a truck bomb exploded in a parking garage of the World Trade Center in New York City. On the day after the bombing, Osama Bin Laden was in Sudan watching new recruits train with live ammunition. His satellite phone rang.

"Was that you?" Bin Laden heard as he strained to hear the woman over the noise of weapons going off. It was the only woman who had this number.

"*Salaam O Alaikum*, sister. No, it wasn't us. We don't believe in killing civilians."

"Regardless of who they were, they didn't know what they were doing. If you want this done properly, let me know."

Bin Laden had known men to make big claims. If it was a man disparaging the *Mujahidin* who had taken on America, he would have hung up on him. But this was new to him. He was interested in hearing what she had to say.

"Sister, I know you are a smart woman, but as you can see, some very brave men have failed to bring it down. What makes you think you can be successful?"

"Sheikh Osama, I didn't say it would be easy. It will take careful planning, large amounts of cash and five or six very dedicated *Mujahidin* who are ready to lay down their lives for their principles. Unlike those who just tried and failed, these men will not come out of it alive. I know I will succeed where your *Mujahidin* failed."

"They are *Mujahidin*, but not my *Mujahidin*."

"What is your fax number? I'll fax you something."

Without questioning her, he gave her a fax number.

"And now that I have your interest, I will put a workable plan together."

Bin Laden raised his voice for the first time. "Absolutely not. I am not interested in hurting the naïve, but innocent, civilians whose only fault is believing the propaganda fed to them by their rulers. And why shouldn't they believe in their government? It provides them ample cheap food, shelter, and clothing while they are young, and free health care in their old age."

He took a pause. "No, those are not who we want to target. We want to kill their soldiers and the agents of the state. We aspire to walk in the shoes of the *Shuhada*[176] who slew 241 American soldiers in Beirut—"

She cut in, "You are naïve, Sheikh Osama."

He didn't respond, so she continued, "The general populace is not as innocent as you believe them to be. Historically, they have given large shares of their income to bring war and death to people everywhere else."

He kept quiet. "They call their armies volunteer forces. Your so-called naïve and innocent people line up to volunteer to be part of the largest killing machine in the history of the human

---

176 Plural of Shaheed - Martyrs.

race. President Eisenhower said that a camouflaged military-industrial complex runs the from behind the curtains of democracy, which they call the longest-surviving democracy in the world. If they had any compassion, they would have found their leader's actions reprehensible and voted them out of office."[177]

"No, Sheikh Osama, the American people are equal collaborators in the crimes against humanity. I will —"

This time Bin Laden cut her off. "Sister, it's time for *Maghrib* prayers. Allah help and protect you in your *Jihad.*"

Seema was done anyway. "Sheikh. It is just a matter of time before you will change your mind. I am certain of it. You have my number. Call me when you are ready to shake the foundations of Capitalism and Zionism. I'll fax you a list of my conditions to work with you."

Before hanging up she said, "I will expect your call soon. *FeeAmanillah.*"[178]

---

[177] The two paragraphs are from a transcript of an actual conversation recorded by a western intelligence service from a call to Osama Bin Laden by an unnamed supporter.

[178] Goodbye.

AMAL AND AMIR

1995

After leaving LSE, Seema had kept close contact with faculty members and staff there, hoping to be accepted for a PhD program. A year after she moved back to London, she was accepted into a PhD program on Islamic History. Her dissertation would be on the role of *Jihad* for the emancipation of the *Umma*.[179]

Periodically, she would help a professor teach courses and give talks on her research topic. She visited the campus as needed to meet with her committee members to discuss the progress of her research and discuss related issues. Seema was in no hurry to finish her degree. The PhD program was a tool for her to grow her visibility in the Umma. She had made some large donations to the school to keep the LSE powers-that-be happy and letting her continue her PhD at her pace.

Coming out of a meeting with her adviser one day, she noticed a well-dressed, petite Middle Eastern girl sitting a couple of doors down from the admissions office. She had on a stylish hijab and was dressed in what Seema considered proper attire for a Muslim woman in public places, although Seema herself did not cover her head. The girl kept fidgeting, touching her face, and nervously looking around. The place was busy. There were students running to their classes, professors walking leisurely from

---

179 The community of Muslims bound by a common religion.

one class to another, and even some visitors walking through the high vaulted hallways. The girl would look expectantly at everyone who seemed to move towards her, and then her hopes would be dashed as they passed her and moved on.

If I had a daughter, she would have been about the same age.

Seema introduced herself and asked if she needed any help. Her name was Amal. She was from Syria. She had been offered admission to the Town Planning degree program and had arrived at the appointed hour to meet her adviser at the admissions office. The door to the admissions office was closed, and no one had come out to meet her, so she waited. Seema took her inside to find help for her. Soon, Amal was filling out admissions paperwork and registering for her first class. Seema had no appointments for the rest of the morning, so she stayed with Amal until all the paperwork was completed. Amal was relieved and kept thanking her. She invited Amal to have lunch with her in the Dining Room for faculty and PhD students. Amal went with her but wanted to pay for lunch. Seema wouldn't hear of it.

"I belong to a group of Palestinian refugees from Jerusalem. My family had lived there for many generations, but after the 1967 fall of Jerusalem, my parents were forced to migrate to Jordan. I was born there. A few years later, the Jordanians kicked us out, and we moved to Syria. My father, a surgeon, provided us with a comfortable life in Aleppo where I did most of my schooling. I got a diploma in town planning and took on a job at Aleppo City Planning Bureau. While working, I came across a UN-sponsored scholarship for women. I always wanted to complete my degree, but never had enough money. This unexpected opportunity was Allah's gift, so I applied for it, and by *His* grace, I was selected. I chose LSE and here I am."

After lunch, Seema took her to the housing office and helped her get a room in one of the college halls of residence. Amal was overwhelmed by Seema's kindness, but didn't know how to repay her.

She seems like how I was when I entered LSE, but a lot more observant than I was then, or now.

They became good friends despite their age and religiosity differences. Amal liked Seema's pragmatic approach to life and became a regular at Seema's flat, coming and going as she pleased. She started calling Seema *Ukhti*.[180] Seema soon became Amal's 'London-Mum' to her friends.

***

One evening, while they were having Pakistani food that Seema had ordered from Khan's, a popular Pakistani restaurant in the Knightsbridge, when Amal's cell phone rang. She answered the call and stepped into the other room. When she returned, she told Seema an acquaintance from Aleppo, Mohamed Amir, was in town and wanted to meet. Seema was a bit surprised, as the only males Amal had spoken of previously were her brothers and her father.

"Tell me about this, Amir."

"He doesn't live there anymore. I met him when I was working at the Aleppo City Planning Bureau. He came to work with us as a town planning trainee. He had just completed a degree in architecture from Cairo. His work involved updating project drawings with changes and additions to buildings owned by the city."

She continued, "I was responsible for the file-room, which contained drawings of projects. Each morning, he would to come to my desk to pick up material that he would work on. He was very careful to always return all the material to me, even unfinished work, at the end of the day. The other engineers typically kept the material with them until their work was completed. The office secretary, Iman, would tease me that Amir likes me and that is why he turns in everything before leaving, so he can come to see me the next morning."

Seema smiled, but said nothing.

"He was religiously conservative and socially aware, very

---

180 Sister or older sister.

respectful, and would never raise his voice. He mostly kept to himself and did his prayers by his desk. I never saw him frivolously chatting with others in the office."

"On a trip to visit his parents, he brought back two boxes of Egyptian sweets for me. He told me to give the smaller one to Iman, to keep her happy. This was the first time I saw him smiling."

Seema nodded and asked, "What happened then?"

"At the end of his training, he enrolled in a Master's degree program in Town Planning and left for Germany."

"So, sounds like you liked him. Did he keep in touch?"

"This is the first I have heard from him since he left Aleppo."

Seema asked, "Did he say anything about why he wants to see you now?"

"I remember, one day while picking up some drawing, he said that he likes the Aleppo area wants to settle down there after he gets his Master's degree from Germany or the US. I didn't know if he was telling me something or just making a random statement. Iman was sure that he was telling me to wait for him."

"So you waited. Now that he has reappeared, what is the plan?"

"Well, he wants to meet me somewhere."

"So?"

"You know, I can't go out alone with someone who is not a *mahram*."[181]

"I know. So why don't you invite him here? I can be your chaperone?"

Amal's face lit up at the suggestion. "*Ukhti,* that would be great. Thank you. You are always solving my problems. I don't know what I would do without you."

Seema asked Amal to invite him to dinner and ordered a mix of Arab and Pakistani foods. She brought along some

[181] Close family males like Father, Brother, son etc.

homemade traditional Arab desserts.

Employed part-time by an international design firm in Germany, Amir was still working on his master's degree. Over dinner, he talked about growing up in Egypt. Even though he came from an upper middle class family, he hated the wide income gap that existed there between the rich and the poor in Egypt and the rest of the Muslim world. He explained how the corrupt leaders help the rich get richer and more powerful, in return for their support in maintaining the status quo. They continue their corrupt practices to stay in power and lining their pockets with national wealth.

Seema learned that while studying in Cairo, he had become a member of the student's wing of the *Akhwaan*. They were fighting to have Egypt and other Arab leaders institute the laws of *Sharia*,[182] and he strongly supported their message. As he spoke about it all, Seema could see his facial expressions harden as he spoke of the greed and corruption of contemporary Muslim leadership. She couldn't help but agree with almost everything he was saying.

He also told them he spent a couple of years in Bosnia helping the Mujahidin after leaving Aleppo, where people thought he had gone to Germany to study.

Masha-Allah, you are the prototype of the mujahid we need to help deliver the Umma from the clutches of the western puppets and Zionists.

Their discussions covered a lot of serious topics, and while Seema was enjoying listening to Amir's thoughts, she knew he wasn't there to discuss his socio-political views. He was there to reacquaint himself with Amal.

"You wanted to meet Amal, so can I ask about your interest in wanting to meet her?" Seema abruptly asked Amir.

The sudden change of topic found Amir stumbling a bit, searching for words. His face softened, and he thought for a

182 Laws formulated by Prophet Mohammad during the formative years of the Islamic civilization.

minute before he said, "*Ukhti*, I am indebted to you for giving me this opportunity to come visit Ms. Amal here under your kind supervision."

Seema leaned forward, impatiently waiting for an actual answer.

You are buying time to tailor your response. I like people who think. But get to your point.

He continued, "I met Ms. Amal two years ago in Aleppo and was very impressed by her. I found her to be a model Muslim girl who was not influenced by western propaganda and culture. While working in an all-male office, she carried herself with dignity and the brothers at work respected her for her dignified behavior towards them. She was always kind to everyone, but never giving one a chance to misunderstand her words or actions."

Seema nodded, as he continued, "My reason for wanting to meet with Ms. Amal was to reconnect with her, to find more things that are common between us. I am so thankful to you for providing me with that chance in a safe environment for her to meet me."

As planned, Seema excused herself and left the room to let them speak freely. Amal and Amir talked for some time. Seema was reading a book when Amal knocked on the door. He was ready to leave.

After saying goodbye to Amir, Amal said to Seema, "I don't know, *Ukhti*. I am not sure about him. He seemed too radicalized to me. I will have to think about it."

I don't have to think about it. I am happy that Amal was not interested in him. It would mean less pain for her in the future.

IT ALL TURNS REAL

1996

It was late fall in England. The days were getting shorter, and nights longer, heralding another long, wet, gloomy winter. Seema was looking through her mail, which she had brought home to read in her spare time. There was a piece of mail from the President of Bosnia's office. It was an invitation to attend an event in Sarajevo where she would be recognized for her services to the country. Reading the invitation carefully, she was reminded of the time she had gone to Algiers with Humayun where he was recognized for his work for the Algerian independence. She was feeling warm all over when her phone rang. The call was coming from a private number. She answered. It was Osama Bin Laden at the other end. He told her he was declaring war on America. He wanted her to join him in the *Jihad.*

"I am guessing you are now ready to cooperate with me, but unfortunately I will have to say no this time. *Khuda Hafiz.*"

She hung up.

Not that she was hanging up on him, she just didn't want the call to be tracked. She searched into her desk drawers and found her seldom-used satellite phone. She next retrieved his phone number and her plan papers. After charging up the phone battery, she called him back.

"I am glad you reconsidered, sister."

"Sheikh Osama, I hung up on you to keep any prying ears off track. This is the number you will use going forward. I have the plan sketched out, along with what I will need for it to succeed. I will send you the details soon. But there are certain other things that I would like you to agree to before we can proceed. I don't know if you still have the list I faxed to you after our last call, but let me read it out to you."

"I am listening."

She took out a list from the papers and started reading the items one by one.

"One: You will take full responsibility for it after the plan is executed. No need to give me credit."

"Two: I will donate half the amount required for the operation and you will raise the other half of the budget."

"Three: I need six very dedicated young men who know they will die in this operation."

"Four: I will not deal with anyone other than you. I don't want my name, background, or gender to show up anywhere."

"Five: The men you provide will not know my identity either. You will tell them I will contact them to give them instructions. I will take it from there. You will be free to contact them and discuss their work, but you will not discuss their work with anyone else."

"Six: I will choose the day and time of operation and will not be pressured into starting it earlier, no matter what."

"Seven: I will provide you with updates as we progress through the steps. You can contact me anytime to get an update on the status of the project. You will not ask the men for status updates."

"Is this all acceptable to you, Sheikh?"

"I have your fax here. I wouldn't have called you if the terms were not acceptable to me. But there is something I would like you to add."

"I am listening, Sheikh. Go ahead."

"How many buildings are in your plan?"

"The World Trade Center."

"Only one building?"

"No, it's actually two separate buildings, two operations."

"I need a plan to target four buildings."

"Are the other two buildings in DC?"

"*Masha-Allah*, you understand. Yes, besides the New York towers, we should also destroy the Pentagon and the Capitol buildings."

"Sheikh Osama, I like how you think, but it will double the budget and the number of people required to get it all done in one fell swoop, but I am sure you knew that before you called."

"*Insha-Allah,* He is our provider and helper. When will you be ready to discuss your plan?"

"I have been invited by President Izetbegović to the celebrations of the lifting of the Sarajevo siege and the ceasefire under the Dayton Agreement brokered by President Clinton. I can meet you there to go over the plan."

"He invited me, too. I think he gave away too much to the Serbs under American pressure, but since you will be there with the plans, I will go."

A few weeks later, Seema was in Sarajevo, her third trip. This time, she didn't bring anyone with her. She was honored in a small, closed ceremony by President Izetbegović. She wanted to keep her name out of the commemoration events, but at the insistence of the President, she agreed to have her name placed in a one-hundred-year time capsule to commemorate the city's deliverance. The capsule would be buried deep under a memorial to celebrate the fighting spirit of the city during the war years under a siege. Seema's name would be near the top of the list of the names of volunteers in it.

An unaccompanied Bin Laden met her there.

She started, "We will hijack four large passenger airplanes to fly into each of the four buildings within minutes of each other." She then went over the plan in minute details. He was distracted and didn't really seem interested in the details. He just wanted the work done, but he let her finish.

She ended her presentation saying, "One last thing, Sheikh. I will pilot the first plane into the North tower of the World Trade Center."

Bin Laden came out of his stupor at this revelation, but stayed calm. "Sister, I have discussed the requirements with our leadership and they agree to your conditions, but I object to you leading the attack."

"Why?"

"We would like men to pilot all the aircrafts."

"They will, all except one. There would be four men on board my plane who will commandeer the plane before I take over as pilot."

She paused. Bin Laden was looking at the palm of his right hand. "Sheikh Osama, it is imperative that I fly the first plane. My participation in this operation depends on my leading the first attack."

"We will get back to that, but let's discuss another point. I would like my close advisors to be part of the planning stages. They are in town and I would like to bring them to our meeting tomorrow."

"Sheikh, it seems to me that you are not interested in my participation, just my plans. You want to take it and do everything your way."

They had reached a deadlock. She had not shared any papers of the plan. Seeing such strong conviction, Bin Laden relented on her piloting the first plane, but still wanted to bring in his advisors into the planning phase. After some more back and forth, she yielded to allowing him to share her plan with three of his closest advisors. Her personal information still needed to be kept out of any discussions.

The second meeting with Bin Laden was held the next day.

He told her that his advisors wanted the plan to be broken up into two parts: she run the World Trade Center operation and his advisors manage the rest of the campaign. She accepted the suggestion to split the work, but only with the condition that the date of the operation be the same, and Bin Laden remains her single point of contact since he was the one who had agreed to her leading the attack. His advisors still didn't approve of the idea of a woman flying one of the planes. She needed him to deal with them.

***

There are hundreds of small flight training schools found in almost every town with an airstrip throughout the US. She selected a school in Florida for her flight training. Two other would be hijacker joined her school.

During the flight certification training, Atta made an offhand comment to her about how he doesn't like the Aviation School owners' wife, always leading her husband in instructions and in classes, even though she was a woman.

The way he said this struck Seema hard. She got worried that her leading this operation was a distraction in his mind. Someone she thought she knew much better than the others participants.

The others must have similar doubts.

A fundamentalist can never be open-minded enough to accept a woman as his leader and there isn't enough time to change his mentality.

I need them to be completely focused on the mission, without distractions or doubts.

This was very different from having disagreements with Bin Laden's advisors.

She called Bin Laden that evening and told him she was giving the lead role in the attack to Atta. Bin Laden sounded relieved to hear this, as he had continually heard the same objection from his advisers. Praising her decision as mature, he accepted it.

To provide the team further motivation, she suggested, and they agreed on a symbolic date for the operation: 23rd *Jumada al-Thani* of the *Hijri* calendar. The day of the elevation of Salahuddin to the throne of Egypt and Syria. He had gone on to liberate Jerusalem from the Crusaders.

23rd *Jumada al-Thani* that year would fall on Tuesday September 11, 2001.

THE SEARCH FOR SEEMA

2001

Humayun's nightmares returned one night. He was transported back to the time of his very first rail journey. The train was chugging along with happy passengers all around him, all going to some place new. He was happy as he could be, enjoying his maiden train journey. Suddenly there was a deafening sound and a crash and he flew across the train bogie towards its front wall and everything went dark after that.

He woke up shivering. His mind was numb.

Allah have mercy. I am too weak to bear another tragedy.

I hope Seema is okay.

Her last call, a short one to Firoza, was three months ago. Seema was very busy helping train volunteers for a humanitarian relief operation to be conducted in South Sudan. She told her mother how excited she was that after years of fundraising, planning, gathering the right set of people, the world would soon see the results of her work. Cairo will be her base for a few months, where she was flying to after the training. She would be very busy, so not to expect many calls.

Humayun was healthy for his advanced age. His eyesight had worsened, but his mind was still sharp. The most frustrating things was not being able to read as he did before. Abdur Rahman was still his driver, even though he hardly ever went anywhere and certainly didn't need a bodyguard anymore. Aleem was still the cook and his wife took care of cleaning and general housekeeping.

He had used up all his resources trying to trace Seema's whereabouts. Her home phone was never answered, calls to her cell phones resulted in a message informing the caller that the person was out of the area, or the phone was turned off.

Which one is it?

He had located Frisk, now married, but he couldn't help Humayun as he had not heard from her for a year.

Firoza, living upstairs, had tried all of Seema's friends she knew, to no avail. Pervez, Seema's estranged husband, was also at his wit's end in trying to locate her. He had reached out to all their common friends and acquaintances in London but had gotten no leads.

No one had any clues to her whereabouts. It was as if Seema had disappeared from the face of the earth.

One day, after finding Firoza crying alone in a corner of the Seema Bagh, Humayun decided to take things in his tired and weak 94-year-old hands. They would all go to London and search for Seema from there.

A week before leaving, he emailed Seema, letting her know of their plans.

It was a long but comfortable flight. Heathrow, as usual, was very busy. Humayun, Firoza, and Gayti Ara were in the long immigration line along with other weary travelers when a well-dressed young man of Eastern European origins stepped forward and introduced himself as Nejdet Dikilitaş. He gave Humayun his business card, saying how glad he was to finally meet Seema's family. His travel company helped passengers through immigration and customs. Along with the business card, he also gave him a typewritten note from Seema.

"*Aadab* Dada, so sorry I couldn't come to the airport. I am out of town. Please stay awhile and don't worry. I will see you soon. If you need anything, please let Nejdet know. The cleaning service comes at 10 am every Wednesday. You don't have to be in the apartment, as they have the keys. Love S."

Since when have you started calling a flat, apartment like the Americans?

Humayun had already adjusted the time on his wristwatch to London time, an old habit of his. He adjusted his watch every time his flight landed in a different time zone, even during transit stops.

Soon, they were out of the airport and into Nejdet's limousine for the drive to his Fitzrovia flat, where Seema had lived since moving to London. On the way, Nejdet told them he was a Bosnian raised in England. He had known Seema for many years, and sometimes worked with her.

A travel agent? I can't imagine her in the travel business, even though she has been traveling a lot recently.

Peter, the aging door attendant at the building, saw Humayun getting out of the limousine and came running out to help them unload. He accompanied them to the flat and unlocked the door while Humayun searched for the spare key in his briefcase. Nejdet left them after bringing their luggage up. Humayun noticed him give a smile and a nod to Peter before he left.

A regular visitor?

The flat looked unused. Everything was neatly in its place. A few pictures of family members hung on the walls, along with a large framed print. It was the autographed pamphlet that Che Guevara had given Seema.

Humayun picked up the phone; there was a dial-tone.

The phone is still connected.

Peter told them that Seema had not been back for months and continued, "This has been her usual pattern of living here. She would stay for a few weeks before leaving for months, and so on. I remember seeing four people, three gentlemen and a lady visit her, not all at the same time, though. Other than the cleaning service, no one else visited her for at least a year or more."

Quite an observant fellow, this man.

Peter continued, "You have already met Nejdet. He visits Seema often and seems to be a good friend, always very respectful and pleasant to talk with. The others were also younger than her. I don't remember, but I will get their names from the visitor's book. As you know, visitors are required to register at the front desk before proceeding to their host's flat."

"I really appreciate your help, Peter." Then, pointing towards his companions, he continued, "You know Firoza and Gayti Ara."

"Glad to see you again, Ms. Firoza and Ms. Gayti Ara. Welcome back. It's been a very long time. Let me know if there is anything I can do to make your visit pleasant."

"Thank you, Peter." Firoza said.

"Miss Seema has been extremely busy and will certainly welcome a healthy, home-cooked meal when she comes. Please call me if you need anything. I am here to serve you."

As they settled in at the flat, Humayun started examining the books and other printed material on the shelves for any clues to her whereabouts. A lot of the printed material was from charities helping the poor. There was nothing on a Sudanese or Egyptian charity.

He found a handheld device about the size of a small book with the words "GPS" printed on it. Its battery was dead.

A GPS device to help find location and direction out in the middle of jungles and deserts.

But why did you leave it at home if you were going there?

Are you still in town?

Humayun was still looking around the flat when Peter returned with more information. He had the names of the three other visitors. The girl's name was Amal El-Dib, and the two men were Waleed Shehri and Mohamed Atta. Humayun didn't recognize any of the names.

"When were they here the last time?"

"Ms. Amal was here about a year ago. Mr. Atta and Mr. Waleed together visited Ms. Seema when she was here two months ago."

"Mr. Waleed told me once that he lives in America."

THE FLIGHT SCHOOL
2001

It was the middle of the night when Humayun woke up with a start, in a cold sweat. It was the same nightmare.

Allah rahem karey.[183]

Where are you? You haven't called in a long time. We just want to hear your voice and know you are in a safe place of your own volition. Nejdet must have informed you of our arrival here, but for some reason, you are avoiding direct contact with us.

Why are you avoiding us? I know you are out there somewhere. I don't think you are in any trouble, but I worry. You are too smart to get into the troubles of common men and women.

It's something else, isn't it? You are doing something that you don't want your family to know. Why? What could it be?

If you were in any kind of trouble, I know you would tell me about it and ask for my opinion.

Something illegal? But it couldn't be anything run-of-the-mill illegal.

You have been telling us about your charitable work with different organizations, but never get into details. Is it something to do with your charity work?

What could be illegal work in charity? Moving migrants across borders? No!

Uniting families of illegal migrant workers in Europe and the US by

---

183 Allah have mercy.

helping them cross borders in the darkness of the night? This could be something, but you have never brought up illegal immigration in our conversations.

There aren't many colonies left in the world, so if this is what you are involved in, it must be to overthrow some dictator. There are so many of those in the Muslim countries.

This sounds promising. So, I can mark that as one area to investigate. Is it something to do with Kashmir or Palestine?

Now that could be something up your alley.

I should start with the boxes I found in the storage room with some old test books and class notes, and the suitcase with old clothing.

His body was exhausted, but he got up and moved a chair to the storage room. He started carefully examining the contents of each box. The first box had some papers, the font was small, almost unreadable under the dim light in the storage room. He got up and brought in a table lamp from the living area and plugged it into an outlet near the floor. The lamp would not turn on. He toggled the switch several times, but the lamp didn't turn on. It was a standard outlet, with a switch next to it, on a six by eight panel.

Hmm, the panel size is an overkill for a single outlet.

He started to get up to look for an extension cord but his legs gave way, and while struggling to get up in the small area, his hand landed on the panel and it came loose.

There was no wiring behind the panel cover plate.

The outlet and its switch were real, but not connected to anything. Carefully removing the panel from the junction box, he saw a rolled-up plastic bag sitting in the cavity behind it. He found her unexpired British and Pakistani passports in the bag. There was a sheet of paper with some names, addresses, and phone numbers, as well as a for-sale listing brochure for a house in Anaheim, California. A faxed copy of a handwritten note from Jill, a realtor, was attached to the listing.

Priced to sell by a motivated seller in the heart of Little Arabia. A really good price. Let me know if you want me to move on it. It won't stay on the market long.

One address on the list he found earlier was the same as that of the for-sale house from the brochure.

Deeper into the wall cavity, he found a large cellphone and a pilot's training logbook for someone named Asma Khalid. A passport photograph of Seema was affixed to the logbook. It showed Asma Khalid had completed over half of the hours required for a commercial pilot license. All the training flight entries were crammed into a period of less than six months.

Just the discovery of this hidden chamber behind the electric outlet with its contents would have been enough to convince him that Seema had secrets she was not sharing with him, but the pilot's logbook had made the hair on the nape of his neck stand up. It had been a long time since that had happened. The rest of his old body was expressing something else. It wanted rest and sleep and couldn't take it anymore. He put everything back in its place and went to bed.

You are learning to fly commercial jets at the Huffman Aviation School in Venice, Florida, under the pseudonym of Asma Khalid. If you wanted to learn to fly a plane, why couldn't you have done it under your name?

But that's not it. It's something else, something you are hiding from us and most of everyone else. Isn't it?

You have left your passports here, so you must be traveling as Asma Khalid. Something really bizarre is going on, something illegal.

Something dangerous!

The next morning, Humayun was at a cellphone shop near his flat. The owner took one look at the large cellphone and said, "This is not a cellphone, Sir. It is an Iridium satellite phone from Motorola, a product well ahead of its time for areas with no cellular phone service, like the top of Mount Everest, in the middle of the Atlantic Ocean and places like that. You can even make a call with it from an airplane flying high above the clouds. They discontinued making these two years back. But the good news is that you can still buy service on these. Would you like me to test it to see if it works?"

"Yes, please."

He went to look for a charger and a new battery pack.

After he put on the fully charged battery pack, the Iridium phone turned on. "Let's move outside to get service. These satellite phones need open skies to work."

Once outside, he extended the antenna, the phone beeped and then made some more beeps before it went quiet.

"It's working now. Says here it's ready to make a call, but the account balance is zero. It shows the phone was last turned on a couple of months ago."

After playing with some buttons on it, he smiled and said, "There are some unread text messages here. Whoever sent them must have lost all hope of getting a reply by now."

"Can you help me add money to it, so I can use it when I fly next time?"

"Yes, Sir, the number is on a pre-paid account, so you can add money to re-activate it. How much do you want to add? The service is expensive on these phones, about five quid per minute for any call anywhere and fifty pence for text messages. You will be charged for outgoing and incoming calls and texts."

On the way home, Humayun stopped at a public call office and rang Huffman Aviation School in Florida, the school listed on the pilot training logs. The call went to voicemail, where a recording instructed him to leave a message or call after 10 am local time.

Back in the flat, Gayti Ara and Firoza had been worried about him. He told them he had gone for a long walk and showed them the satellite phone. He said he bought it from a guy selling old gadgets at a store, and that the next time they fly, they will be able to make calls while in the air.

He kept the rest to himself. Gayti Ara had fixed him a breakfast of eggs, sautéed potatoes, toast and jam. After breakfast, he started reading the messages on the phone. They were from the same three numbers, but there were no names of the senders in the messages. The last outgoing message caught his attention.

Before you guys leave, please throw out all your leftover stuff in the garbage and tidy the place up. But don't throw away any of my things which I have kept in the walk-in closet. I will stay there for a little while once it's all said and done.

It confirmed his fears.

I need to visit this place. I am bound to find something there. Gayti Ara won't let me travel alone; she would come with me.

He didn't have any time to waste. He could have called Nejdet to arrange the tickets, but he didn't want Seema to learn of his plans.

Back at the call office later that afternoon, he called the Aviation School again. A receptionist, who later turned out to be the wife of the owner, answered.

Must be a small operation.

Humayun told her that his daughter, Asma Khalid, had dropped out of the program and he wanted to know why she did not complete her training. The friendly woman remembered Asma very well. She was her first female trainee from the Middle East. She had enrolled in their expedited training program and had quickly achieved her private pilot's license, but quit after running out of money six months into the commercial pilot's program.

He threw in a trump card. "Thank you. I will pay for her to finish the program."

Hearing this, the sales lady opened up to him. "You know she was quite outgoing and an excellent student. She can probably finish the training in a much shorter period than others."

"Did her boyfriend accompany her?" Humayun took a shot in the dark.

"A few months into the program, she introduced us to this man who also wanted to get a commercial pilot's license. But I don't think he was her boyfriend. He was very different from her, much younger. The guy was very serious, talked little, always quiet, very smart though. He completed his certification a few months ago. My husband once congratulated him with an Atta boy, which he didn't like since his name was Atta."

So you were training to be a commercial pilot but dropped out in the middle. It couldn't be because you ran out of money.

What is your connection to this Atta, and who is he?

His next call was to the realtor, Jill.

Jill picked up the phone after quite a few rings. She sounded bored. It was still early in the morning in California. As soon as she learned Humayun was calling from England, she perked up. She remembered the house; it was bought by an overseas investor, in a land trust. A real estate lawyer, who she never met in person, had handled the closing.

"Are you are the owner of the property?"

"No, I just wanted some information on it and whether someone is living there now."

"It was rented to some Arab students from Fullerton College. I don't know who is living there now, but I can find out for you. I have other properties, even better than this one, better location, great prices and motivated sellers ready to meet your price range. It's a safe and vibrant community here, a neighborhood of all ethnicities living together in harmony."

"Thanks. Were these male or female students?"

"Sir, they were all boys. The Arab people don't send their daughters to live on their own. A great custom, I must say. We used to be that way too, but the women's lib movement of the 70s has destroyed our family values. It's all about the individual now. Me, me, me."

"Thank you. I can call you tomorrow to see if you got any more information for me?"

"I will see what I can find out and call you back this afternoon. We are here to serve."

"I am calling from a payphone in England, so you won't be

able to reach me. I can call you back."

"Absolutely, or after 4 my time today, up to you. I hope everything is all right."

"Yes, yes, everything is all right. Thank you."

He then walked to a travel agent's office right across from his flat to reserve two seats on the earliest available flight to Los Angeles with hotel accommodations in Anaheim, California, the site of Little Arabia and the house where he hoped to find Seema

CALIFORNIA, HERE WE COME
2001

Humayun and Gayti Ara arrived at Heathrow for their 5 am flight. It was not a direct flight. The travel agent had suggested he take this one since the first available direct flight was a week later. Waiting longer was not an option for him.

After he was handed the tickets, the agent had cheerfully added that as a special service for their first-class clients, an airline staff member would escort them through immigration to their connecting flight in Boston.

There are still some perks still left for those flying first class.

Even with all the glad tidings from the sunny travel agent, Humayun had resigned himself to missing the LA flight because of a very short transit time. He was okay with waiting for a few extra hours and catching the next available flight to Los Angeles.

Couple hours in the first-class lounge wouldn't be that bad. Maybe I will take a quick shower there.

He was wrong. The transfer worked like clockwork, and they made the connection with some time to spare. Humayun was feeling drowsy as the American Airlines Flight 11 to Los Angeles took off from runway 4R. As the plane banked right on its westward journey, sitting in a window seat, he could see the shipyard and Boston harbor coming to life. The sun was shining on Beantown, waking up to a beautiful autumn day.

He eased his seat back. Gayti Ara grabbed his hand and kissed it. She had tried to convince him to stay in London and wait there for any leads on Seema. It was a lost argument from the get-go. She didn't want him going alone, so she was with him.

She half-smiled at him, perhaps in the realization that this journey would soon be over and maybe then he would be able to relax.

"I am so proud of you, Abba. What will you not do for your loved ones? Look at you. Most men half your age would have thrown up their hands and just waited in Karachi for their Seema to show up. I mean, she is a middle-aged woman, she should be allowed her freedom without the grandfather worrying about her every step. And here you are, a 94-year-old, crossing seven seas to locate her because she hasn't called you in a little while. Promise me that once we are in LA, you will stay there and relax for a few days."

Humayun smiled at her, "I will try, my dear, I will. But after checking in at our hotel, let's take a taxi to that address in the Little Arabia area in Anaheim."

Maybe we will find her there, safe and sound.

"No, seriously Abba, promise me that."

"Should I give you a false promise that I will do as you ask, even though my heart and mind will be restless until we locate her? You are my daughter. I won't lie to you. You know I can't let it go for someone so dear to me. I can't let them be at peril if I can help it."

He sighed and continued, "After Nasreen's abduction, I had pledged to never let my loved ones face adversity, or risky situations, without me leading the way for them."

Her eyes welled up at the thought of her mother. Humayun put an arm around her to comfort her. "It's okay, I am fine. Everything resolves itself in the end. This will too."

Gayti Ara was sitting in the aisle seat next to him. Across the aisle from her, Humayun saw two young Middle Eastern men looking curiously at her. Upon getting his attention, they quickly turned their heads forward.

Earlier, when following Gayti Ara into the first-class cabin, Humayun had noticed the two men in their seats. They both seemed nervously preoccupied and brooding. The man in the window seat had seen him, but had quickly lowered his gaze. A cheerful stewardess, Karen, stepped forward to help them place their hand luggage into the overhead bin. She saw the tense young men and asked if they would like coffee or water before takeoff. Without looking at her, they shook their heads in unison.

Fear of flying? Claustrophobia?

The airplane was still climbing to its cruising altitude when a man in a blue jacket rushed past their seats to the front of the plane, where Karen was setting up to prepare breakfast for the first-class passengers. She let out an agonized cry and fell to the ground. Humayun craned his neck to look over the seat in front of him and saw her on the floor writhing in pain while the man in the blue jacket banged on the cockpit door. She had been stabbed. The man sitting across the aisle from Gayti Ara got up and held up a knife to protect the first man, who was now throwing his body at the cockpit door to break it open.

What is going on? Who are these people?

Oh Allah, we are being hijacked!

Suddenly, a tall, well-built man seated behind Gayti Ara got up and landed a hard blow on the second man's head, with what looked like a baton. The man fell back and dropped his knife. Seeing the knife drop, the tall man, possibly an air-marshal, picked it up and slashed him. As the blue jacketed man turned, the air marshal moved forward and hit the blue jacketed man's knife hand with his baton. The blow knocked out his knife.

The air marshal then pushed him hard into the closed cockpit door and held him there with his knife at his neck. It looked like it was all over.

Thank God for the tall man.

It was not to be, as another hijacker rushed in from the back and stabbed the air marshal with a box cutter.

The man in the blue jacket picked up his knife and started pounding on the cockpit door again. The door opened and the first officer appeared with his hands raised.

There were now three hijackers standing in the aisle, while Karen and a fourth hijacker lay on the floor, both bleeding profusely.

The men gave a shout of *Allah O Akbar* as the blue jacketed man cut open the first officer's stomach with a powerful thrust of his knife. Raising his hand with the first officer's blood dripping off it, he announced, "My name is Mohamed Atta. Everyone stay calm; you'll all be okay."

Mohamed Atta? Seema's visitor?

He entered the cockpit where the Captain had just radioed this as a hijacking. Soon the plane was in the control of Mohamed Atta, who sent the captain out of the cockpit to be stabbed by one of the other hijackers.

It was now clear to Humayun what Seema had been involved in. He looked towards the back of the plane to see if there was a woman among the hijackers, or Seema. He saw one other man standing in the aisle with a knife in his hand, telling everyone to calm down.

An announcement started in all the cabins: "Nobody move. Everything will be okay. If you try to make any moves, you'll endanger yourself and the airplane. Just stay quiet."[184]

With this announcement, the plane banked hard to the left.

The passengers in first class were told to move to the economy section of the airplane. Gayti Ara was trembling with fear and didn't move. Humayun helped her up and held her tightly as they moved to the back. The hijackers in the first-class cabin pulled the curtain that separated the two classes from each other.

---

[184] Actual announcement received from American flight 11, recorded by ground control. 9/11 Commission Report.

In the economy cabin, Humayun's eyes scanned the faces of the passengers and hijackers for Seema. She wasn't among them. He saw two vacant seats on the left side of the plane and took them.

Trying to calm his daughter, he said, "It will be okay. They are returning the plane to the airport. They probably want money or some captives released."

Gayti Ara, not hearing any of this, was hysterical and crying loudly and reciting all the verses of the Quran that she could think of. Other passengers were in similar or worse state, some crying, some praying, some completely stunned with mannequin-like expressionless faces. Humayun seemed to be the only one with his wits about him.

Hijackers wanting money or freeing imprisoned colleagues wouldn't murder three helpless crew members in cold blood. Something bad is going to happen. Allah have mercy!

Then someone yelled "Look."

Humayun looked past Gayti Ara, out the window. He was shocked to see the plane was passing within a few hundred yards of the Empire State Building. He could see people on the observation deck intently looking in astonishment at the giant plane flying so close to the building.

And then the same person screamed, "Oh my God! They are going to crash it into the World Trade Center!"

There was commotion all around as people started yelling and crying. The hijackers had all gone into the cockpit and locked the door. Some passengers were banging against it, trying to break it down, others clinging to their loved ones. Some trying to call their loved ones on cell phones, almost all praying for deliverance from this imminent calamity.

A thought of calling Seema on his satellite phone flashed in his mind, but it was in his briefcase, still in the overhead cabin over his original seat.

Humayun felt fortunate at the knowledge that his life

would end quickly, without a protracted suffering period. He thanked God for all he had in his life. A feeling of serenity engulfed him, a calmness that he had never felt in his life.

His arms were around his now quietly sobbing daughter. Wishing he hadn't brought her along, he kissed Gayti Ara's head and held her tightly while reciting the *Shahaada.*[185]

He could hear nothing around him as he peeked at his wristwatch, which he had not forgotten to adjust in Boston.

It was showing 8:46 am Eastern Standard Time.

They never made it to California.

---

[185] A Muslim prayer asserting the basic tenets of Islam, recited in a calamity or when facing death.

A DATE THAT WILL LIVE IN INFAMY

11 September 2001

The fateful day began very early in the morning for Seema. It was still dark when her alarm went off. Seema was already sitting up in the bed of a palatial Waldorf Astoria suite. She called room service to order some tea and toast with jam.

It's going to be a big day. I better take a shower and get ready.

The phone rang.

It was Nejdet. He had stopped by her flat to check if her family needed something. Only Firoza was there, and she told him they had left for the US to see Gayti Ara's children.

Using his IATA credentials, he was able to find Humayun's itinerary. He told Seema that Humayun and Gayti Ara were on a flight to Boston on their way to LA. Hearing the flight details, Seema couldn't believe it and asked Nejdet to double check the flight information.

I have to save them. I can't let Dada and Phupi-jan become collateral damage in my war against tyranny. I need to call off Atta's part of the operation.

She called Atta. No answer. She figured he must be asleep in his hotel room. The call went to his voicemail. She left him a message to call as soon as possible.

Waiting for Atta to return her call, she thought of another plan to save them without disturbing Atta.

People arriving in the US from overseas and connecting to local flights still need to clear immigration and customs at the first port of arrival. After customs, they are required to re-check their bags for the local flight. She would have someone waiting to meet Humayun and Gayti Ara as they come out of customs in Boston, and have them call her.

She looked through her contact list and found the phone number of her limo driver in Boston.

He will do what I tell him to, without asking why.

Atta's plans would remain unaffected.

This would be perfect.

She took a deep breath and went over the details of her plan once more before calling her limo driver when her phone rang.

It was Atta calling her back. She asked if he was ready. He was and went over the plan specifics. She told him that the plan was a go, and Allah would bless him for his bravery. As she was ending the call, she sensed Atta was hesitant about hanging up.

"Anything else you wanted to tell me, brother?"

He was silent for a moment. "*Ukhti*, can you do something for me?"

"Yes, what is it?"

"Can you buy the biggest gold coin you can from my September salary and give it to Amal?" He paused. "Please take care of her and tell her I was sorry it didn't work out for us, but I always loved her."

The reality of what was going to happen hit her for the first time. Up until then, it was all a plan on paper involving names and places and times. Adrenalin had kept her going without ever thinking about the human impact on Atta and the other hijackers destined to perish under her plans.

Atta's words had shaken her. It was a dead man talking, expressing his last wishes to his executioner. She felt a shiver go down her spine.

"*Insha-Allah*, I will do that and pass on your message to her. I will also make sure to offer any help she may need."

Satisfied, he hung up the phone.

She got a glass of water to calm herself and to think some more before making the call to the limo driver.

The more she thought, the more she realized the new plan would expose her identity to the scrutinizing eyes that would fall on everyone and every action that took place at Boston Logan airport before the LA flight departed. The authorities would find the two passengers missed the flight and the limo driver. He would tell them the reason for him contacting the two passengers and their connection to her. She had been very careful not to leave any tracks of her work. Bin Laden was not worried about hiding his identity. She thought he secretly relished the notoriety these events brought him. Everyone would point to him as the mastermind of this operation, which was fine with her. But with the driver's help, they would easily pinpoint her as his co-conspirator.

I am not afraid of getting caught or dying, but it will leave a lot of unfinished work. I still have a lot of work to do. The world is full of oppressed, tortured humanity, which can only breathe freely after tyrants, despots, and oppressors are eradicated from the face of planet earth.

There is still so much more to be done.

She expected a worldwide manhunt for those behind the unprecedented attack on America, on its own soil.

The structures of protection that she had carefully built over the years around her identity, her network of contacts, and the channels of payments for funding her clandestine activities would all come crashing down like a house of cards.

To succeed in the future, I need to keep my structures intact and my identity uncompromised.

If fate has written for Dada and Phupi-jan to die on this flight, there is nothing anyone can do to save them. It is all in His hands now.

Her faith had trumped her concerns for her family.

A peace returned to her.

She would not make the call to Boston.

***

It was still early in the morning when Seema walked out of the hotel. Her cab was waiting.

"World Trade Center North Tower."

A guard at the ground floor entrance welcomed her and asked her to sign in electronically. She entered her name, Malka Seema Ara Babar, CEO, CWK Industries, London, arrival time 7:30 am, purpose 8:00 am meeting with Marsh Insurance, 96th floor, into a terminal provided for entering such information.

"Thank you, Miss Babar. Marsh has a pleasant reception area up there. You can wait there, or you can get a coffee in the Windows on the World restaurant up on the 106thth floor."

"Thank you. I'll wait in their reception area."

She took the elevator to the 96th floor. There were already some employees working in the offices past the reception area. A young man walking behind glass walls smiled and waved to her.

Must be a friendly man. Too bad.

The receptionist hadn't arrived yet. She saw the washroom next to the reception area and quickly walked in.

Coming out after a few minutes, she made her way down to the mezzanine level and came out of the building by a side entrance to avoid the guard at the front desk.

The cab was waiting for her. "Empire State Building." She said as she looked at her watch.

Almost 8 am. Plenty of time.

***

Seema stood atop the Empire State Building, having taken multiple elevators to get there. She dialed the number for her flat in London.

Firoza picked up the phone. She was very livid.

"Where are you? Why haven't you responded to all our messages? What's wrong with you, ignoring us like that?"

"Mummy, I lost my phone. I just got a new one. You are

my first call on it. I am in New York. I've been busy like never before."

Hearing the flimsy excuse, Firoza almost hung up on her, but continued to vent. Seema let her, while continuously apologizing for her carelessness, and complaining about her work and how bad it had gotten.

Firoza told her about Humayun and Gayti Ara flying to LA in search of her.

"Mummy, I am in a hurry for an appointment in a few minutes with our business insurance people. After that, I will be free to talk. I have reserved a flight to LA this afternoon. I know where they will be staying. Nejdet sent me a copy of their travel arrangements. I will bring them back to London with me. If you hear from them in the meantime, tell them I will see them at their hotel. Once we are back in London, you can do whatever to me, but please don't stay upset at me. I love you so much."

Hearing these words, Firoza calmed down. "Okay, and promise to call me after you are done."

"I will Mummy. You know I will. I promise."

"By the way, I am on the 96th floor of the World Trade Center, waiting for the meeting. It's an amazing view from here, just like when we came here with Abbu."

"Why didn't you call? We didn't know what to do, where to look."

"Sorry, I will explain everything later. I have to run now. I love you, more than anyone else, including Dada."

"I love you too, Seema, but don't make me go through this again."

"I never intend for you to suffer like this, Mummy."

"Be careful, New York has very bad traffic and lot of muggings."

"I will, love you. Can't wait to see you. *Khuda Hafiz.*"

She hung up, sadness on her face.

THE BEST SEATS IN THE HOUSE

11 September 2001

It was past 8:30 am. She kept looking north, searching for something in the sky. Her surprisingly young unpainted face that looked more like that of a young 30-something than her 48 years reflected deep angst.

A few more minutes passed before she spotted a small speck on the horizon. It grew to become a plane flying in from the North-Northwest. It was coming straight at her like her late pet golden retriever, Kishi, used to when he saw her from a distance.

Come to me, baby, I have a treat for you up the road.

The airplane grew bigger and bigger.

Slow down my baby, let me absorb every detail of the fine dagger that is ready to plunge into the heart of a monster, who thinks of itself as invincible as God Himself.

The plane adjusted its path just so slightly southwards. Onlookers gasped as it passed in front of them, just a few hundred yards from the observation deck where they stood. They didn't know they were about to see a once-in-a-millennium event unfold right before their eyes. Watching proudly, like a mother seeing her child take their first steps, she could almost see people looking out from the tiny windows.

The passengers must all be repenting for their sins by now.

What would they be thinking? Do they even know why they are being punished? I hope Atta announced that they are all guilty by association for the crimes against humanity.

The aircraft headed straight south over the morning traffic clogging Manhattan streets below.

No one saw the satisfied smile on her face as the plane struck the North Tower. She didn't even flinch at the loud noise that arrived a second after the impact and the big fireball. She kept looking at the sight without blinking.

I want to imprint this picture, in my mind, of my payback to America, the only pole left in this new unipolar world.

The first step of this glorious victory has been taken perfectly. It is time for the world to sit back and watch the climax, the unfolding of a new chapter in the world's history.

Seema looked at the burning building with her black eyes, her soul blacker than her eyes.

A tremor from the collision travelled from the World Trade Center to the Empire State Building and up to the observation deck, where she stood triumphantly absorbing the details of it all. The quiver rose up her legs, to the pit of her stomach, to the sides of her body, to her neck, up to the head, bringing with it a strange warmth that could only be described as deeply sensuous, an arousal only experienced in the first steps of the procreative process. Her eyes closed as after a deeply spiritual experience. It was a state of euphoria she had never experienced. If she were to climb over the protective railing and let herself go, she felt she could fly unaided on the strength of this high.

"Ma'am, do you hear me? I said I need you to move. The observation deck is now closed, and you need to leave now!" A big African-American policewoman was looking at her, probably wondering whether she was intoxicated or paralyzed from shock.

Seema nodded and moved towards the bank of elevators, still looking back at the burning tower. She saw another enormous ball of fire come from around the second tower. A second plane had struck the South Tower.

She could not resist smiling and quickly lowered her head and covered her mouth.

Bravo Marwan. Having laid down your life for a high purpose, you are now among the Shuhada in Heaven,

Inna lillah wa Inna alaihey rajaoon[186].

Two more to go.

There was pandemonium on the deck as people frantically ran towards the elevator banks. Everyone around her was in a state of shock, some crying at the sight of the burning towers. A few tourists were still hanging back, trying to take more photos. They didn't want to miss anything.

Seema fought her way into the next elevator.

A heavyset Caucasian man stood in front of her. She had noticed him earlier holding a pair of high-powered binoculars, gazing around and searching for something on the horizon before the first plane struck the North Tower.

As they exited the elevators on the ground floor, he turned to look at her and said, "I wonder what it would feel like to find out someone dear was on one of the planes."

Before Seema could respond, he disappeared into the throngs of people heading south towards the twin towers.

Who was that man? What did he mean?

Did he see me smile?

He must know something. Are there others?

I need to get out of here, fast.

She crossed the Street and spotted her Yellow Cab parked in a no-parking zone, its emergency lights blinking. The young Middle Eastern driver in a green skull cap must have just fallen into a peaceful sleep while America woke up to what would be the defining event of the young century.

"Penn Station and watch for a tail," she said as she settled into the partly ripped seat.

---

[186] Verily we belong to Allah and verily to Him shall we return. A prayer recited upon hearing of someone passing away.

All traffic was at a standstill. People were pouring out from buildings, and from stopped cars and buses. A mass of humanity filled up every square inch of open space, some dazed, others crying, still others confused about what had just happened. They were all looking up towards the burning towers.

As the cab started to move, she couldn't help but think of her father.

Dada would be so proud of Abbu's daughter, a recognition Abbu couldn't ever get from him.

Abbu, I have what you chased all your life. So, you can rest now, Abbu, wherever you are. Dada must have joined you by now. You can gloat to him about what your daughter achieved, striking a blow for all the downtrodden of the world.

Please don't be so meek. Speak up for once and tell him how you feel. Dada was a mortal like you.

Deep in these thoughts, but she was looking out, searching for something, until she saw the signs for the Lincoln Tunnel.

"Listen, on second thought, take the Lincoln Tunnel and then stay on Route 3 to get to Essex county Airport."

The driver followed her instructions and soon they were traveling through the dimly lit tunnel. When they emerged on the New Jersey side, the car radio came back on. There was news of another plane crash.

The driver screamed, "Now a plane has crashed into the Pentagon! What is going on? Allah help us."

Seema nodded but kept quiet.

All those fat generals must be burning in a sea of aircraft fuel.

One last strike on that terror factory on the hill and this phase will be complete, but our war on their terror shall continue, bigger and deadlier.

***

Halfway around the world, Roshan Ara was home alone, watching a TV drama serial. She had moved to Karachi to be near Humayun after her husband passed away.

She loved her brother dearly, but ignored his regular

lectures about living alone and resisted his pressure to move into a third apartment upstairs at The *Chowk*, which he had built for her after Hashim's death. He had been on her mind since he hadn't called after flying to London.

The broadcaster cut away to a special announcement of the New York attacks. She was aghast, wondering who could have committed this dastardly act.

"May Allah punish that Osama Bin Laden for this." She mumbled as she got up to answer her phone which had been ringing.

***

Seema walked into the county airport terminal. It was empty, except for a few people huddled around a TV at the far end of the small terminal building. She rushed through the terminal to the aircraft parking area. A Piper Saratoga was parked there, fueled up and ready to go, as she had requested.

She started the engine. As the plane was taxiing to the runway, a man ran out of the terminal, gesturing wildly and shouting. Seema looked back, shook her head with a smirk and gunned the engine as the plane turned on to the runway.

She flew the Piper an east-northeast route over Long Island Sound, a path she had flown several times in practice runs, the same route that John Kennedy Jr. had taken to his accidental death in July 1999.

Seeing the Point Judith Lighthouse on the Rhode Island coast, Seema turned the aircraft sharply right heading straight east towards Martha's Vineyard.

EPILOGUE
2004

AFTERMATH

2004

The US Government 9/11 Commission was established on November 27, 2002 to investigate the causes of, and the events leading up to, the September 11, 2001 terrorist attacks.

A final 585-page report was issued on July 22, 2004. Buried in the middle of the report were five brief paragraphs titled "Civilian Aircraft crash on 9/11 near Martha's Vineyard."

A small aircraft was reported missing off the coast of Martha's Vineyard on the evening of 11 Sept 2001. During a search for the missing plane, the same evening, a United States Coast Guard vessel picked up some floating debris, later identified as a piece of the right wing of the missing aircraft. Its fuselage was located deep on the ocean bed, in an area only reachable with highly specialized equipment. Efforts to reach the wreckage with standard onboard cranes and retrieval gear were abandoned because of high winds and rough currents on the day.

No request was received by the USCG for the fuselage retrieval, so no further action was taken for its recovery.

No passengers were reported to be on board the Piper Saratoga, which had taken off from the Essex County Airport. A formal flight plan had been filed a day earlier. The pilot's name on the flight plan was Asma Khalid, a British citizen, single, holding a private pilot license with over 400 hours of flying experience. She was declared missing, presumed dead in the crash.

The National Transportation Safety Board declared that the probable cause of the crash was "the pilot's failure to maintain control of the airplane".

The 9/11 commission conducted its own investigations and found that the pilot, Asma Khalid, had taken flight lessons at the same school where two of the other 9/11 hijackers, Mohamed El-Sayed Atta and Waleed Shehri, had learnt to fly.

After the examination of all the evidence and relevant data, the pilot was deemed not to have been complicit in the attacks.

The End.

APPENDIX

HUMAYUN FAMILY TREE

		Taimur Babar - Raja b 1820-			
		Zaheer Babar - Pir Sahab b 1853-			
Wafa Begum (Wife 1) b 1876- m 1894-1897		Rajjan Bibi (Wife 2) b 1881- m 1898-1914		Abida Khatoon (Wife 3) b 1895- m 1914-	
Shershah Babar b 1897- Sakina Begum b 1903- m 1923-		**Humayun Babar** b 1907- Nasreen Fatima b 1897- m 1926-		Malka Roshan Ara b 1915- Syed Hashim Pasha b 1911 m 1935-	Ayaz Babar b 1915-
	Malka Gayti Ara b 1932- Mateen Shah Ghori m 1951-		Saleem Babar b 1932- Firoza Fatima m 1952-		
Ahmed Shah Ghori b 1953-	Osman Shah Ghori b 1955-	Omar Shah Ghori b 1972-	Malka Seema Nasreen b 1953 - Pervez Jaleesi m 1979-		

VALUED CONTRIBUTORS

My sincere thanks also goes to (in alphabetical order) Aysha Sharih, Imran Sharih, Katie Shea, Lucius Peterson, Molly McNett, Najmul Azam, Randy Caspersen, Sally Hewitt, Sehrish Alikhan, and Zuviya Alikhan for their comments, suggestions, corrections and criticisms of the manuscript before it was released. Some of the above were beta readers of the full document, while the others provided commentary on the selected sections presented to them.

Last, but not the least, this book is dedicated to my grandson Idrees, who found a copy of the unfinished last chapter lying around and started trying to read it by enunciating the sound of each letter into words as he went along. He got through the first two paragraphs before his mother stopped him from what was to come next. He is a precocious little 5 year old.

www.ingramcontent.com/pod-product-compliance
Lightning Source LLC
Chambersburg PA
CBHW020248030826
48979CB00030B/2662/J

* 9 7 9 8 9 8 6 9 0 1 3 8 1 *